The Great

For nearly forty years the Great War has raged across the continents. There are few left who remember a time before, and what historians will write cannot be known, for the fragile pendulum of victory has been wildly swinging all these years.

The free nations have joined together to form the Union under the keen leadership of President Thomas Edison. For years, only their tenacity and strong will have kept them from being overwhelmed. But the tide turned when a mysterious ship crash-landed in Roswell, New Mexico. The technology gleaned from the remnants has given the Union hope…

The lands of the European Reich lie under a cloud of darkness. The liche Kaiser rules with an iron fist, sending his Obscura Korps to the ends of the earth to seek out and harness the dark energies that will unite the Kaiser's power to that of the U-Worlds. Demons have been seen in the form of man and beast…

The mighty Matriarchy, thanks to the mystical technology of Nikolai Tesla, has ushered in a new age of gods. The old Slavic deities that once demanded worship from their people now march alongside the *soldati* of the Matriarchy, enslaved with in constructed suits of armor. Their forces have been divided, however, with the emergence of the New Guard…

In Japan, Emperor Meiji attempted to overthrow the Shogun and remove the Samurai class. This started a civil war that raged on for decades. Through some sort of currently unknown science, the Emperor was able to consolidate his power by re-instituting the Shōgunate under Shōgun Hatamoto (an unknown). Under their joint rule, Japan has united once more, and now marches into the mainland, joining the war at last…

Balance will never be found while the war still rages, for there can be only one victor. That victory will determine the fate of man.

This is the world of Tannhäuser.

A

TANNHÄUSER™

Novel

Rising Sun, Falling Shadows

By Robert Jeschonek

Fantasy Flight Publishing, Inc.

To Wendy, for sharing my dream.

© 2012 by Fantasy Flight Publishing, Inc.
All rights reserved.
Paperback edition published in 2012.
Printed in the United States of America.

Cover illustration by Anthony Palumbo.

ISBN: 978-1-61661-180-4

Fantasy Flight Publishing, Inc.
1975 West County Road B2
Roseville, MN 55113
USA

Find out more about Fantasy Flight Games
and our many exciting worlds at

www.FantasyFlightGames.com

Rising Sun,
Falling Shadows

CHAPTER I

*G*eisha women weren't known for punching soldiers in the face, but the one accompanying Takeshi "Taki" Takata did just that. In a most un-geisha-like gesture, she hauled back her arm and plowed a fist smack into the kisser of the Japanese soldier who'd made a grab for her, his brown cap flying off from the force of the blow.

The soldier was shocked, to say the least. So was his buddy…but not Taki. The woman in the geisha getup was as headstrong as they came. She'd been a thorn in his side since minute one of this covert mission.

Now there was nothing left to do but follow her lead, wrap this up fast, and hope their cover wasn't blown to kingdom come.

They might still have a chance at that, if they were lucky—the brawl had broken out in a shadowy alley on a dark night. Passersby on the street outside might not be so quick to gravitate toward the sounds of a scuffle in the shadows.

7

Taki undid the button on his tuxedo jacket, freeing himself for action. The other soldier, the one who hadn't been punched in the face, dropped a hand to the gun holster on his belt. Before he could get his fingers on the grip, Taki lashed out with a swift kick to his chest, stunning him.

Sparing a quick glance in the geisha's direction, he saw her pump another punch at the first soldier. This one caught him in the throat.

The geisha could take care of herself. No surprise there, considering who she was under the *kimono*, black wig, and all that heavy white makeup. Taki had heard she was as tough as any man, and he believed it.

The fact that she was a member of the 42nd Marine Special Forces said it all.

Turning back to his own opponent, Taki saw the man wrench his gun from its holster. How long would it take for him to swing it up and fire? Mere heartbeats.

It wasn't enough time for Taki to deploy the weapons secreted on his person, but it was still more than enough time to take other measures. In a flicker of motion, Taki lunged toward the geisha, snatching one of the long pins from her wig. Whirling, he swept it around and let it fly, point first, like a dart out of a blowgun.

He knew he wouldn't miss. He was a master of Okinawan *kobudō* with a special talent for turning everyday objects into deadly weapons. His aim was instantaneous and precise, whether he was hurling a *shuriken* throwing star or a hairpin.

But he took no joy in the sight of the long pin piercing the soldier's left eye. He and Taki shared the same heritage. Did it matter that the soldier lived in Tokyo, and Taki had grown up in San Francisco, California? They both had Japanese blood, didn't they?

Not that Taki would let that stop him from completing his mission. When the soldier fell screaming to his knees, he moved in fast to silence him. Wrapping him in a choke hold, he squeezed hard, cutting off the man's air until he went limp. Then he laid him gently on the dirty bricks. There was no need to bang him up any worse, now that the threat had been silenced.

Or had it? The geisha's foe also flopped to the bricks, unconscious, but before she and Taki could make another move, new voices barked from the alley entrance.

Taki looked up to see two more soldiers in brown uniforms and caps glaring at him with pistols raised. "*Teiryuu!*" There were soldiers everywhere these days, now that Japan was at war. An invasion force had struck China weeks ago; with the conquered northeastern city of Tianjin as a base, Japanese forces were making great strides in spite of heavy Chinese resistance.

"*Teiryuu!*" repeated the soldiers. "*Teiryuu!*" The word meant "halt," but of course Taki meant to do no such thing.

Taki's mind raced. What could he say to these men? The evidence of what had happened was laid out around him—signs of a struggle plus two unconscious soldiers, one with a hairpin stuck in his eye. No amount of fast-talking was going to get him out of this mess.

It was time for another fight, and he knew it. He was sure the geisha knew it, too.

Could he get to the hairpinned soldier's gun fast enough? Or should he go for the makeshift shield first—the garbage can lid propped against the wall three feet away?

Just as Taki was making up his mind, one of the soldiers at the mouth of the alley yelled and doubled over. Suddenly, his head twisted sharply left and his neck snapped.

As the other soldier gaped and backed away, the soldier with the broken neck crumpled to the street...but his pistol remained aloft, floating in midair. The barrel swung toward the second soldier, seemingly of its own volition, and took aim at his head.

Before it could fire, the soldier shrieked and turned to run, but not quickly enough. His own pistol fell as he followed it to the ground in a heap.

The airborne gun turned toward Taki and the geisha. It bobbed down the alley, pointing at one and then the other, drifting toward them inexorably.

Neither Taki nor the geisha flinched. If anything, they relaxed a little.

Because the unseen hand that held the gun belonged to a friend and ally.

"You morons," a woman's high-pitched voice chimed from thin air in the vicinity of the gun. "Can't you do *anything* right?"

Maybe "friend" was too strong of a word, thought Taki.

"*We're* the morons?" The geisha planted her fists on her hips. Her eyes were wide, her throaty voice cracking with rage. "Weren't you supposed to cover us? Take down anyone who got *curious*?"

"That's exactly what I *did*." The invisible woman waved the gun back and forth. "Not that I'd have to if you dopes were better at not attracting attention!"

"It's not easy, dressed up in this clown suit." The geisha spread her arms wide. "I'd like to see *you* try it."

The gun bounced and landed over a subway grate. "I'd be happy to." There was a humming sound, and a shimmering silhouette appeared in the air in front of the geisha. Silver light arced and flowed around the edges, and then a female figure flashed into view. Her hand was on a control knob on the buckle of her belt. Her jumpsuit, the source of her invisibility, was made from black metallic material that shone with rainbow highlights when she moved. "At least I have the *looks* to pull off that outfit!"

Taki clenched his teeth. The two women had been butting heads since the start of the mission twelve hours ago. And when they weren't butting heads with each other, they were butting heads with *him*.

Taki was new to the 42nd Marine Special Forces. He couldn't understand why Command had put two such strong-willed women together on the same covert operation. He'd heard something about their teamwork and effectiveness in the field, but frankly, he hadn't seen much proof of it yet.

At the rate they were going, he doubted that the vanishing woman—Second Lieutenant Caitlin "Hoax" Lamsbury—and the fake geisha—Corporal Tala Aponi—would make it home alive, let alone complete their assignment.

"Looks? You?" Tala laughed. "You're not even in my *league*, honey."

Hoax sneered. "I look better than you when I'm *invisible*." She combed the fingers of one hand through her bangs, which she'd rebelliously streaked pink. The rest of her hair, which was cut in a short shag all around, was naturally black. "I heard they almost gave you the Joshua Suit just so they wouldn't have to *look* at you anymore."

Tala's long raven hair was wrapped up under her geisha wig, but she flicked her head as if she were tossing it anyway. "Well *I* heard they're getting a trained monkey to do your job."

Hoax lunged forward. She was shorter than Tala by a few inches, so she had to glare up at her. "That's it!" Hoax lashed back a fist, ready to throw a punch.

And Taki caught it before she could swing. "That's enough! Both of you!" He knew he was on shaky ground as the rookie member of the team, but the clock was ticking. The longer they bickered in the alley, the more the mission was jeopardized. "If we don't get moving, we'll miss the rendezvous!"

Hoax and Tala glared at each other for a long moment. Taki thought they might still go at it after all, with him caught in the middle.

Then, both women visibly relaxed. They didn't break eye contact, but they did lean back from each other.

Taki felt safe in letting go of Hoax's arm, though he didn't move out from between the two women just yet. "We're in enemy territory here, remember? Can we save the in-fighting for when we're back on the sub?"

Hoax and Tala turned their gazes to lock on him instead of each other. Both women looked thoroughly disgusted.

"Who died and put *you* in charge of this mission?" asked Tala.

"No one, that's who." Hoax snorted. "He must be feeling superior since he's back home on Japanese soil."

Taki shook his head in disgust. He'd stopped them from fighting with each other only to have them turn their irritation on *him*. "I'm from San Francisco." He chopped his hand through the air definitively. "I've only ever *visited* Japan."

"Whatever, Taki. We don't have time to discuss it right now." Hoax let her angry stare linger on him a moment longer, then reached for the knob on her belt. "Let's get rolling, you two. We need to make that rendezvous."

Taki gaped at her. A few moments ago, he'd had to stop her from punching the geisha Sabotage Specialist; now, all of a sudden, she was barking out orders again as if her command style had never wavered.

Was that one of their strengths as a team? That they kept their fighting edge sharp by constantly sparring with each other, then snapped into well-oiled action the second they caught a whiff of combat?

Frankly, Taki thought tea and meditation worked just as well. But his was not to reason why, not with the Japanese military on the move. Not when a secret agent with the key to their battle plan was out there in the night, waiting to hand it over. Not when this could be the Union's only chance to gain insight into the ruling Shōgunate, whose mysterious machinations had until recently been confined to Japan's home islands.

"Bring their weapons." Hoax nodded at the unconscious soldiers. "Any I.D. papers they're carrying, too."

She didn't have to say it. Tala was already gathering guns and papers from the first pair of soldiers. Taki avoided the soldier with the hairpin in his eye and salvaged weapons and documents from the pair near the mouth of the alley.

"Let's go, people." Hoax snapped her fingers impatiently. "Shake a leg already."

This time, it was Taki and Tala's turn to do the glaring.

"Got a problem with that?" Hoax turned the dial on her belt and a silvery nimbus rippled to life around her. "Tell it to the thin air." With that, she flickered out of sight, disappearing into the shadows of the Japanese night.

* * *

Tala was dying to kick off her wooden clogs, whip off the wig, and free herself from the binding geisha kimono once and for all. She was sick of hobbling around after Taki Takata like some subservient little concubine, staying several paces behind him at all times as the culture dictated. It was only an act, a temporary disguise, but it ran against her grain so much that she could hardly stand it.

She couldn't imagine living like a geisha, or even a more ordinary, but still submissive, Japanese woman. The thought of it made her feel sick to her stomach. For a Navajo like her, being trapped in such a role—living like a slave under the oppressive Meiji Civil Code— woule be worse than death itself.

As she followed Taki down the boulevard, she passed an actual geisha, shuffling behind her escort with head bowed. The woman glanced up and their eyes met...but Tala saw no spark of life in them. The spirit had been crushed out of her.

That poor woman would never know how it felt to be a Navajo, riding bareback on a charging horse in the Arizona desert heat, wearing nothing but a doeskin bodice and leggings. She would never know what it was like to light the fuse of a bomb and hurl it, the roar of the blast mingling with her war cry in the blistering wind.

Poor woman. And now the Japanese wanted to make more of her, claiming new foreign lands in which to oppress the female soul. That made the bastards Tala's special enemies, and this mission deserving better than the lousy attitude she'd dumped into it so far.

As the other geisha moved on, Tala straightened. She was going to get through this, even if it meant getting along with Hoax and Taki.

The invisible woman's voice came to her just then, from somewhere off to her left. "Almost there, guys. The rendezvous point is in that little park up the block on the right."

Tala forced herself not to say something nasty in reply. The truth was, Hoax had a way of grating on her like no one else—and that was really saying something, because *a lot* of people grated on Tala. It probably had a lot to do with the intense level of competition between the two hard-edged women. It might also have been a factor of Hoax being five years younger but still outranking Tala. On this particular mission, there was also the matter of Hoax beating Tala in a bar fight a week ago.

So Tala had good reason for butting heads with Hoax…but she resolved not to let it affect the mission from this point forward. It was far more important to stop the Japanese from spreading their influence.

Anyway, if there was one thing she was sure of, it was that she could depend on Hoax in a fight. Could she say the same about Taki?

"This is it." Taki straightened the jacket of his tux and turned right off the boulevard, following a cobblestone path into the parklet.

Tala wobbled after him with some difficulty. The wooden clogs didn't agree with the cobblestones, not a bit. She hoped no one was watching who might blow her cover.

As she followed Taki down the path, her way was lit by paper lanterns hanging from the cherry tree branches on either side. The lanterns rocked softly in the breeze wafting in from the sea; nearby wind chimes played a tinkling melody.

Bouquets of pale blossoms enrobed every branch, freshly opened to mark the arrival of spring. The air was thick with the blossoms' scent, a sweet perfume like blooming roses.

Tala inhaled deeply, and a sense of peace flowed through her. The blossoms reminded her of home…of one of her homes, anyway: Washington, D.C. She'd known some happy times there, even with all the craziness and trouble.

It was such a pretty little park, she thought. How could the Japanese create something so lovely, yet be capable of such brutality? How could such a monstrous war machine arise from a land that could also give birth to something so peaceful?

Up ahead, Taki paused at an intersection of paths and looked both ways. As Tala approached him, she heard Hoax's voice amid the ringing of the wind chimes, the sound of a woman where no woman could be seen.

"Go left," said Hoax. "Our contact's at a fountain, alone. I scouted the area and couldn't find anyone else hanging around."

Taki nodded and turned left. Tala fell in step behind him, wobbly on the cobblestones and keeping her distance as always.

Not far ahead, they emerged into an open circle that seemed to be the heart of the park. As promised, there was a fountain, and a man standing in front of it.

He had close-cropped silver hair and wore a black robe with white trim. As he gazed into the fountain, streams of water trickled from the triple mouths of the three-headed cement fish perched in the middle of it.

When Taki drew up alongside the robed man, he turned and bowed without smiling. Taki bowed in return and cleared his throat. "The cherry blossoms are lovely this time of year." He said it in English. It was the prearranged signal for the meeting.

The man in the black robe stared at him with narrowed eyes and clenched jaws. For a moment, Tala thought they might have the wrong man, that he might not give the correct countersign.

But then he did. "I cannot enjoy them because of this cold I have." He spoke with a Japanese accent, but his English was flawless. He'd gone to school in the U.S., Tala knew that much; she guessed that was why he was sympathetic to the Union cause.

Taki looked at Tala and nodded. She moved closer so she could catch the whole exchange.

The man in the robe bowed for her benefit. "I am Dr. Kichida. I have something with me that you might find of interest." He wasted no time pulling a folded and sealed manila envelope from the sleeve of his black robe. He handed it to Taki without a word of explanation.

Taki slipped it into an inside pocket of his tux jacket. "Do you think it will be a stormy spring, my friend?"

Dr. Kichida fixed his gaze on Taki. His dark eyes glittered in the flickering light of the paper lamps. "I have no doubt of it," he said. "It could well be the stormiest on record."

Taki turned to Tala and they shared a look. They both knew what "storm" he was talking about. This confirmed it: the Japanese Shōgunate had big plans, and they were happening soon.

"A wise man should hurry in out of the rain," said Kichida. "He should take his umbrella and try his best to beat the storm."

The implications of what he said were not lost on Tala. He'd handed over information concerning Japan's battle plans; now it was up to the Union's covert team to get those secrets into the hands of those who could put them to use.

It was all up to Tala, Taki, and Hoax.

"Thank you for the kind advice, Doctor." Taki bowed. "I promise your insight will not be in vain."

"I will hold you to it," said Kichida. "I love this *Nippon*, this land of the rising sun, with all my heart. I cannot bear the thought of her future falling permanently under the influence of shadows."

Just as he said those words, Tala heard the twang of a bowstring. Even amid the splashing of the fountain and the tinkling of the wind chimes, she heard it. The sound was unmistakable to a Navajo woman like her, who'd been attuned to it for as long as she could remember.

A second later, before she could make a move to defend against it, an arrow leapt from the trees and plunged into Dr. Kichida's chest.

He gasped and clutched at the shaft, eyes wide with shock and horror. It looked to Tala like the point had sunk into his heart, or at least damn close.

As Taki grabbed him, Tala spun and looked in the direction from which the arrow had flown. She saw the shadowy figure of a man standing stiffly in the darkness under the cherry blossoms, bow raised. The man drew a fresh arrow from a quiver at his hip and swung it up to nock it into place.

Tala knew she had only seconds before the bowstring twanged again. Shoving a hand through the folds of her kimono, she took hold of one of the little surprises she'd hidden in there for just such a moment: an M15 white phosphor smoke grenade.

As she pulled the pin and rolled her arm back for the throw, she rode a wave of mixed emotions. On the one hand, she was furious at what had happened to Dr. Kichida. On the other hand, she couldn't help feeling secretly glad—not for his misfortune, but for the opportunity to do what she loved best.

As she hurled the grenade toward the archer, and clouds of white smoke billowed out to obscure his shot, Tala felt like herself for the first time all evening. The hell with pretending to be a submissive little geisha hobbling through the streets of Tokyo.

She was the kind of girl who liked to blow things up and hurt people—the ones who deserved it, of course.

She was only too happy to kick off her wooden clogs, pitch the wig, and rip off the bottom three feet of the kimono, leaving her legs bare from the knees down. As she shook out her long black hair and reached for another smoke grenade, she smiled ruefully.

Whoever had done this, she was about to make them pay.

CHAPTER 2

Theater District
Tokyo, Japan
12 April 1952
2417 Hours

For the most part, Hoax didn't disagree with Tala's strategy. The smoke from the grenade obscured the archer's next shot and spoiled the view for whoever else was about to attack. There was just one little problem.

The smoke showed the outline of people who were invisible. It revealed *Hoax's* outline, in other words.

So much for stealth mode.

But maybe she and the others could get away before it became an issue. From the sound of their movements, they weren't more than ten yards away. Hoax ran toward them, hoping to whisk them quickly to safety in the smoke and confusion.

But a speedy escape was not in her future. She sprinted through the grey billows, heading for her teammates...and then, suddenly, she ran into someone. It was a woman; she could tell by the curves.

At first, she thought it was Tala. But then a black-gloved fist lashed out of the smoke at her. Hoax caught a glimpse of a spiked knuckle weapon as she ducked back, the spikes still nicking her left cheek.

The sounds of hand-to-hand combat raged around her, but Hoax stayed focused on her opponent. She didn't really have a choice in the matter; whoever the woman was, she moved like the wind.

And she stayed well hidden. After the first strike, she disappeared into the smoke. Hoax turned in a slow circle, watching for signs of movement—and barely spotted the short blade slashing toward her in time.

She felt the blade whipping past as she twisted aside, just dodging it by the smallest of margins. Gritting her teeth, she sprang forward in the weapon's wake, making a grab for its handler.

But all she got for her trouble was a handful of smoke.

Hoax spun, watching for the next attack. It was as if she were fighting a shadow woman, an invisible foe…as if she were fighting herself. The enemy was free to strike at her from thin air at any time, from any direction, and all Hoax could do was react. Now she knew how people felt when they went up against her in the Joshua Suit.

Hoax heard the blade swooping toward her from behind and she lunged forward. She felt the tip of it rush through her hair, barely missing the back of her neck.

She was off balance, though, now, and her foe took advantage. Before Hoax could regain a firm footing, she felt a foot crash into the small of her back, throwing her forward.

She gasped when she hit the cobblestones. The second she touched down, she rolled over and scrambled up to her knees, getting ready to launch herself to her feet.

Just then, the points of two blades pierced the smoke, sliding under her chin and pressing against her throat.

The smoke was starting to clear, drifting off on the rippling breeze. Hoax's wide eyes stared along the length of the blades into the thinning haze, searching for the face of her enemy.

At first, all she saw was a dark figure, a woman's silhouette. Then, little by little, she made out more details: a black hood and mask concealing most of the face; Japanese eyes peering out of the eyeholes, devoid of emotion; a long silver braid twisted over one shoulder; a lithe figure, small and slender, clad in a black singlet, arm-length gloves, and thigh-high boots. She held identical Japanese weapons in each hand: short blades seated between curved double prongs, almost tridents. Hoax remembered the name—*sai*—from the briefings before the mission.

She remembered the eyes, too…the same cold eyes she'd seen earlier on the street. They were the eyes of the geisha whom the team had passed on their way to the park.

She'd been stalking them in disguise, as invisible in her own way as Hoax. She had no need for a Joshua Suit; she was a true mistress of concealment, a warrior of the shadows.

There was a name for people like that. Hoax remembered it from the briefings. *Ninja*.

The woman was definitely a ninja, and the point of one of her sai was the tiniest flick away from cutting Hoax's throat.

* * *

When the smoke grenades first blew, Taki gently laid the body of Dr. Kichida down on the cobblestones by the fountain. A little of the water splashed onto the dead man's face, a soft spray that Taki liked to think Kichida might have appreciated. After all, it was the water of his beloved homeland, his precious *Nippon*.

Rising, Taki reached down into his pants pockets, which he'd torn out earlier to give him easy access to the weapons strapped to his thighs. There was a wooden club tied to each leg, and he pulled them free in a single smooth motion.

The clubs were his personal favorite weapons: Okinawan *tonfa* clubs carved of hard red oak. The polished wood was warm from his body heat; it was fitting, since he thought of them as being alive, as extensions of his body. He certainly knew how to make them come to life in battle.

Taki wrapped his fingers around the handles of the tonfa. He braced the clubs against his forearms, spanning the length of his arms from his wrists to his elbows.

Then, mentally reciting a passage from the Buddha's Diamond Sutra to prepare himself, he stepped into the smoke.

Shadows coiled and uncoiled in the corners of his eyes like snakes in the mist. Things whispered and rustled around him. Focusing, he felt the presence of hidden men, cold and malevolent, equally focused on his own presence. The fact that they moved with such near-perfect silence meant they had to be ninja—agents of the fearsome Shin organization, most likely.

The Diamond Sutra tingled in Taki's brain like electricity, like snowflakes, like birdsong. He took a breath, as he had been trained, and then he went to work on the enemy. Fearsome they might be, but he resolved to be fear*less* in defense of his teammates and mission.

> *All conditioned phenomena*
> *Are like a dream…*

As the Diamond Sutra flowed through him, Taki slipped left. Lashing out his arm, he cracked a tonfa across the head of a lurking foe. Then he brought the club back down for a second blow, harder than the first. The man fell at his feet, blood soaking his black hood and cloak.

> *…an illusion, a bubble, a shadow,*
> *Like the dew…*

Taki spun and lunged back, driving the short end of a tonfa into the gut of another ninja. As the ninja folded with the blow, he slashed a sword across Taki's chest, gashing his tux jacket without cutting into his flesh. Taki caught the man's sword arm with a tonfa, keeping it from slashing back down, then blasted the other tonfa across his face.

Another ninja body crumpled to the cobblestones.

> *…or like lightning.*
> *You should discern them like this.*

Striding forward, Taki spun both tonfa and gripped them tight with the long ends protruding. He heard the soft hiss of movement approaching from his left, and he ducked down suddenly, just as a *kama* sickle cleaved the smoke where his head had just been.

Darting toward the sickle's wielder, he spread his arms wide, then brought the tonfa together hard on either side of the man's head. At the hint of another faint hiss, he threw himself down and somersaulted out of the path of whatever was coming. When he finished the roll and sprang to his feet, he saw four shuriken stars stuck in the ninja's chest and throat.

The smoke was thinning enough for Taki to catch a glimpse of the star thrower's dark, sprinting form. Zeroing in, Taki spun and whipped his clubs where he thought the man was about to be.

His mastery of objects and trajectories did not let him down. The flying tonfa clocked the ninja in the side of the skull, and he dropped.

Taki felt the breeze picking up. The wind was carrying off the smoke, clearing the view so he could assess the full situation.

On the cobblestones around him lay a ring of four unconscious ninjas, the ones he'd battled in the smoke. But beyond them, his teammates were in trouble.

Off to one side, twenty yards away, a female ninja with a long silver braid stood poised with her sai dipped low, their points pressed against Hoax's barely visible, misty form. According to what little Taki had heard of the Shin, there could be only one woman ninja with twin sai and a silver braid: Mizu Kage, the legendary dark mistress of the Iga clan. Mizu had a reputation as an unbeatable, death-dealing fury. People claimed that no one who fought her lived to tell of it.

Ten yards farther and closer to the trees, Tala was being held captive by another ninja, her right arm wrapped in a chain. She was struggling to break free, but the ninja gripped the chain tightly and stayed out of reach of her punches and kicks.

Clearly, Hoax and Tala needed help. Taki took a deep breath and prepared to run to their assistance…at least, until he heard a telltale sound from the trees.

It was the twang of a bowstring, released by the archer ninja who'd murdered Dr. Kichida. The smoke had cleared enough to give him a clean shot again.

The arrow raced toward Taki, its black point gleaming in the light of the paper lanterns.

* * *

Tala was sick and tired of being chained up by the ninja. He'd kept her under control so far, wrenching her around with the chain every time she tried to get sound footing and mount an attack, but enough was enough. It was time to use the bastard's own weapon against him.

Letting loose a battle cry like the roar of a lioness, Tala grabbed hold of the chain with her free hand and yanked it toward her. The ninja came with it.

Throwing herself backward, she took him down with her, then pitched him off over her head. That was when he finally let go of the chain.

Tala rolled off her back fast and came up out of the roll in a crouch. She saw the ninja was on his feet, too, whipping a bundle out of a pack on his back. He unfolded it lightning fast, revealing a kind of black weighted net.

He held it with both hands as he started toward her, ready to use it against her. Whatever Tala did next, she would have to do it quickly.

* * *

"I said *give* it to me!" The ninja woman with the blades at Hoax's throat pressed the points a little deeper. "Last time: give me the charm or device that renders you *invisible*."

Hoax was afraid to swallow, lest that slight movement puncture her throat. She was afraid to move at all…and that made her angrier with each passing second.

The ninja's eyes narrowed. "I am a ghost woman feared even by the ghosts themselves." She leaned closer, continuing to speak in a low, accented English. "And I will make a *true* ghost of you if you don't hand over your secret."

The threat made Hoax's hackles rise. She was a brawler at heart, a take-no-crap-from-anyone kind of woman. Hell, she'd once punched a molar out of the head of Sergeant Barry Daniel Brown of the 42nd Marines, who was as tough as they came; she still wore that tooth on a chain around her neck as a reminder.

It wasn't in her to let this ninja cow get the better of her. The time had come to make a move.

The breeze was clearing away the last remaining wisps of smoke that had given away her outline and location. She was back to full invisibility now; once she got away from the points of those sai, she'd have an advantage over the ghost woman.

All she needed was some kind of distraction.

* * *

As the black-tipped arrow streaked toward Taki, its telltale whisper alerted him just in time. He dropped down out of its path at the last possible microsecond, letting it cruise past overhead and shunt into the fountain behind him.

With mere heartbeats to go before the next arrow took flight, he looked around when he went down, casting a net for the nearest object he could use. His tonfa lay nearby, but he wasn't sure they could do the job this time. Closer at hand, he saw a loose cobblestone.

Driving his fingers into the gaps around the cobblestone, he yanked it free. But the twang of the bowstring told him he hadn't been quick enough for an immediate throw.

Taki flung himself down on his side and rolled out from under the passing arrow. Then, he leaped up, aimed, and flung the cobblestone in one smooth blur of motion.

He heard the sound of the stone cracking against bone, and the head of the archer snapped back from the blow. As she fell, her last shot sprang out of the bow but flew wild, curving off into the trees.

* * *

As the ninja with the net advanced toward Tala, she plunged a hand into a fold of her tattered kimono and came out with a weapon of her own: a customized grenade. But *this* grenade wasn't of the smoke bomb variety.

She'd been holding back on deploying explosives because the covert team's orders had emphasized stealth. But the time had come for stronger measures. If she didn't bring out the firepower, the vital intel Dr. Kichida had died to provide might never make it back to Command.

Tala turned and sprinted away from the net man. She yanked the pin on the run, watching the ninja over her shoulder as he gave chase, and then she chucked the grenade. As the explosive went off behind her, she flung up her arms to shield her head.

Debris rained down around her. She didn't look back to see what was left of the ninja at ground zero.

* * *

The grenade explosion gave Hoax the distraction she needed. When the blast hit, the ghost woman looked away, and the pressure of the points of the sai let up the slightest bit.

Hoax flung herself backward, away from the tips of the blades, then rolled hard right. Fully invisible now that the smoke had cleared, she had a fifty-fifty chance of avoiding the next stroke of the ninja woman's weapon. As long as it came down on her left, she'd be fine. It all depended on just how keen the ninja's senses were, if she could tell which way Hoax had moved without seeing her.

At first, it seemed she couldn't. She swept both sai left, missing Hoax by a wide margin.

But then, just as Hoax prepared to lash out and take her down, the ghost woman snapped right. The move to the left had been a feint, just a setup for the strike that came next.

Before Hoax could duck out of the way, the ghost woman's sai flashed toward her. The blade plunged deep into her left side, driving the twin prongs in after it and crushing the hilt hard against her flesh.

Suddenly, Hoax's body flooded with agonizing pain. She couldn't stop herself from screaming at the top of her lungs. And that was before...

Before the ghost woman tore the blade back out of her.

* * *

When the sirens started, Taki was watching Hoax reappear. In the back of his mind, he knew the sirens meant trouble, that the authorities were on their way to the park. But his teammate's condition was a much more immediate concern.

Her body became visible as she fell on the cobblestones, and he could see why. Blood was gushing out of a hole in her left side; clearly, the Joshua Suit had been damaged by Mizu Kage's last strike.

Now another strike was about to happen. Mizu was bent over Hoax, drawing back both sai; in a heartbeat, they would pierce Hoax's flesh as if it were a pincushion...and that would surely seal her fate. Maybe she could heal from one severe stab wound, but three would end her right there on the cobblestones. Her life depended on whatever Taki did next.

Instinctively, he grabbed his tonfa off the ground, leaped into a throwing stance, and hurled a tonfa toward Mizu. It blasted into one of the sai, knocking it out of her grasp.

Mizu looked up, her cold eyes staring in his direction. Without a word, she straightened, twirling her remaining sai, and stepped over Hoax's body. She was coming for him.

Taki stood, raising the single tonfa he had left. He spun it around, changing hands, switching grips, preparing for all-out weapon-to-weapon combat. Then he settled into a pose that he thought would serve him well, a posture that would allow him to unleash any number of surprises.

Any average weapons fighter might have hesitated in the face of his obvious skill…but not Mizu. She continued to stride toward him, eyes impassive, hips and shoulders swaying with easy grace.

Taki's heart pounded. If the legends were true, if no one who fought Mizu Kage lived to tell about it, he was a dead man.

Was this how the mission would end? After Taki and his teammates had come so far and fought so hard, would Dr. Kichida's secrets never make it to Command? For that matter, would Taki not live to see another sunrise?

He braced himself for the epic struggle to come. Mizu was twenty feet away. She took another graceful step, giving her sai a twirl.

And then a grenade rolled up next to her and hit her foot. Even from a distance, Taki could tell the pin had been pulled.

Instead of trying to kick it, Mizu dove away from it…but her escape attempt was too late. The grenade exploded, hurling her across the parklet, sending her sprawling into the triple-fish fountain.

As for Taki, he started running the second he saw the thing roll up to Mizu. The blast still caught him, knocking him down to the cobblestones, but he stayed conscious and relatively unhurt.

That was more than he could say for Mizu. She lay face up in the fountain, unmoving, apparently out cold.

As Taki got to his feet, he saw Tala get up from her hiding place behind the fountain. She ran right past him and made a beeline for Hoax.

Meanwhile, the sirens were still keening, getting louder with each passing moment. Now came the hard part: escape. The team had a very brief window in which to get away.

And one of them was injured and unconscious.

"Taki!" Tala's voice was urgent as she crouched beside Hoax. "She's in pretty bad shape!"

Taki retrieved the tonfa he'd thrown at Mizu and ran to Hoax's side. Stuffing the clubs in his jacket pockets, he squatted down and shoved his hands under Hoax's prone body. Grunting, he lifted her in his arms, then pushed himself up to his feet.

"Should we be moving her?" It was the first time he'd heard Tala sound worried. "There's so much blood…"

"No choice." Taki adjusted Hoax's weight in his arms and started walking toward the park's rear exit. "We have to get her out of here." His new mission was to get the three of them past the Shōgunate authorities and make it to the extraction point. At least he was the right person for the job: he knew Tokyo from childhood visits and had studied mission maps so hard he'd started dreaming about them.

Tala thought for a moment, then nodded. "All right then."

Taki picked up his pace. He hoped the police wouldn't think to block the back access route; the sirens were practically on top of them now.

The race to the extraction point was on. It could get tough as word spread and the authorities locked down the city, but he had no intention of failing. The envelope of secrets in his jacket pocket had already cost Kichida's life, and now it might cost Hoax's, too.

It was up to Taki and Tala to get the envelope into the hands of the man who could use it to make a difference in days to come. It was up to them to deliver it to the officer who'd launched this mission in the first place and was waiting offshore to receive the results.

That man was Major John MacNeal.

CHAPTER 3

Imperial Palace
Tokyo, Japan
12 April 1952
2448 Hours

When Hiruko Orochi first heard the sirens, he was standing with dozens of other soldiers in the courtyard of the Imperial Palace, listening to a speech by Shōgun Hatamoto Omokaze.

The soldiers were about to ship out; their duffel bags lay on the ground at their feet, stuffed with clothing and gear. They were on the verge of a great new adventure on behalf of the Shōgunate, and they cheered with growing excitement at the Shōgun's stirring words. Their voices roared in the grassy courtyard, and their fists pumped under the blaze of electric lights that made the night as bright as day.

The Shōgun stood before them behind a podium on a stage, speaking into a microphone. Behind him hung enormous white curtains with a red disk at the center—the Rising Sun, symbol of great *Nippon*. As always, his personal magnetism radiated like a blazing beacon, flowing out over the crowd. It was impossible not to bask in it, not to share in his inspirational vision.

So why did Hiruko feel a strange tug in his heart? Why, even as he got caught up in the Shōgun's words, even as he joined the other soldiers' cheers, did a shadow linger in a distant corner of his soul?

"As you go forth on this grand mission, know that my heart is with you." The Shōgun nodded and smiled. As he turned his head, his good left eye drifted over the men; so did his blind right eye, milky white under a diagonal scar. "I think of you all as my sons. I want only the best for you and our homeland. Which is why I ask you to undertake this noble task, to the glory of Nippon!"

The men roared and clapped, Hiruko among them. Like everyone, he was fiercely loyal to the Shōgun. His greatest desire was to serve the Shōgunate and the land of his birth, beautiful *Nippon*. He was a *jōtōhei*, a superior private in the royal guard, and he was proud of his station. He was a linguistics specialist, and he was deeply honored to use his language skills as part of the Shōgunate's expansionist destiny.

So why did he still feel that tug in his heart? It made no sense to him. His devotion to *Nippon* and her leaders was unshakeable, his dedication to his duty complete. Why then did he feel this dull ache, this unease?

"You will never forget this night!" The Shōgun spread his arms wide, as if to embrace all the soldiers at once. "Someday, you will look back, and you will say, 'I was there when everything changed. I was there when *Nippon* took the next leap forward. I was there. I helped make it happen.'"

This time, Hiruko led the cheers. He pumped both arms in the air, and so did all the other men. He did it to reaffirm his faith, to banish all thoughts of unease from his mind. The last thing he wanted on the outset of this critically important mission, this culmination of everything he'd worked for and dreamed of, was the slightest seed of doubt to hinder his efforts.

He cheered again, louder this time, and the others chimed in as before.

The roar of the crowd was like the crash of a wave on the shore. Hiruko got chills up his spine as he stood on the crest of the tide of adulation.

The Shōgun let the roar continue a few moments longer, then leaned close to the microphone. "I have spoken to our beloved Emperor Meiji." His voice, as it boomed over the loudspeakers, cut through the adoring roar, and the men quieted. "He gives you all his divine blessing, and offers one solemn promise." The Shōgun cleared his throat, pausing as if the mere thought of the Emperor's words had deeply affected him. "He pledges that if you bring back the heavenly prize, he will use it to forge an even more glorious destiny for our precious *Nippon*."

The cheering and clapping was louder than ever. The Shōgun waited, beaming at the audience. Then, reaching down to the scabbard at his waist, he drew out his sword and raised it overhead.

"My sons! The Emperor himself has given his blessing! Go forth secure in the knowledge that your mission, divinely inspired as it is, can have but one result!" The Shōgun waved the sword as he chanted into the microphone. "Success! Success! Success!"

"*Seikouri! Seikouri! Seikouri!*" The ranks of soldiers chanted along with him in perfectly synchronized cadence. However, just as the chanting reached a fever pitch, sirens went off in the distance. And it was then, for a brief moment, that Hiruko saw the curtain fall away…literally.

At first, there were just a few sirens, wailing in some far district of the city. The crowd and Shōgun kept chanting, ignoring the sound. Perhaps there was just a fire somewhere, or a vehicle accident.

But then the sirens spread and grew louder. Voices in the crowd dropped out, and the Shōgun stopped waving his sword. Soon, it sounded like the whole city all around them was filled with shrill wailing.

By then, no one in the courtyard was chanting anymore. The troops looked around, looked at each other, looked to the Shōgun for guidance.

And the Shōgun turned his back on them.

Confused and agitated, the troops broke ranks. They fell into groups, talking about what could possibly be happening and what they should do next.

As for Hiruko, he stayed at attention and remained silent. He never took his eyes off the Shōgun.

When the Shōgun turned away, he took three steps to the back of the stage and threw open one flap of the white-and-red Rising Sun curtain. It was then that Hiruko saw someone was back there, looking out at the Shōgun...*two* someones.

Hiruko's blood froze when he got a look at them. One was a corpse of a man, withered and cadaverous. He wore a flowing black overcoat with red lapels, and a black leather military cap. At his throat hung the emblem of a foreign power—an iron cross, symbol of the Reich.

Looming beside him was an even more monstrous man, bald and thickly muscled, with eyes that glowed like twin fires. His face and bare arms were etched with scars that seemed to be burning, the swirls and whorls radiating an unearthly, shifting light. He wore a uniform, black as pitch, with the sleeves torn off. Instead of an iron cross, he wore an enormous iron eagle on a chain around his neck. That, too, was a symbol of the Reich.

Just seeing those two was enough to make Hiruko shudder. It was enough to make him want to look away.

But he didn't. Even when the hulking, scarred brute seemed to look right back at him.

Because he knew it wasn't right. Those men did not belong there. The Shōgun was supposed to stand beyond the influence of foreign powers; he might have treaties or accords with them, but they were not supposed to consort clandestinely on *Nippon* soil.

The Shōgun walked through the curtain and let it fall into place behind him. Hiruko's view of the strangers had lasted only an instant.

But it had been more than enough time for him to know that something wasn't right with the Shōgun; it had been enough time for him to wonder if the sense of unease he'd felt had happened for a reason. Perhaps the shadow on his soul had been the result of very definite malevolent presences.

And perhaps those presences were casting a dark pall over the mission on which he was about to embark.

After the Shōgun had been gone a moment, the curtains parted again, and another figure strode out, clad in crimson armor. His purposeful steps carried him quickly to the microphone, and he bent to speak into it without hesitation.

"Attention!" His voice snapped commandingly over the loud-speakers, overpowering the keening sirens. "All of you, return to formation *immediately!*"

Every man on the field fell silent at once and scrambled back into the ranks they'd occupied during the Shōgun's speech. The voice they'd heard inspired instantaneous respect and compliance from all of them.

It was the voice of Iroh Minamoto, "the *Daimyō*"—widely regarded as the single greatest warrior in the Shōgunate. No one would speak or step out of line when he was addressing the troops.

The Daimyō cleared his throat and glared at the men arrayed before him. "Those sirens are not your concern," he declared, jabbing a finger at the crowd.

The men on the field stood stiffly and listened like children to the words of a stern parent. The Daimyō had complete control over every one of them.

"Pick up your belongings and prepare for transport," said the Daimyō. "We leave immediately to fulfill our divine mission in the land of our birthright."

A few of the men applauded, but it didn't last. They respected the Daimyō, practically worshipped him…and with that respect and worship came fear.

As ordered, Hiruko picked up his duffel bag. He slung the strap over his shoulder and fell into formation with the others, lining up at the gates leading out of the Imperial Palace courtyard.

He was as afraid as the rest of the soldiers, but for a different reason. He couldn't get the sight of those two men behind the curtain out of his mind. He couldn't escape the feeling that their presence boded ill for what until now had seemed like a divinely blessed quest.

Hiruko had hoped the Shōgun's rally would lift up his heart and erase all his doubts. But now, as he marched out of the courtyard, the tug on his heart was stronger than ever.

CHAPTER 4

UNS Pershing
Off the coast of Tokyo, Japan
13 April 1952
0502 Hours

It's them!" The young ensign manning the periscope on the submarine's shadowy bridge shouted with excitement. "Holy cow, it's them!"

He had good reason for it: the *Pershing* had just been about to dive. The crew of the sub had waited as long as they could for the covert team.

And now, there they were. "They're signaling!" said the ensign. "Morse code on a flashlight!" He white-knuckled the periscope handles and pressed his face tight against the hood of the eyepiece. "Those are their call letters. It's definitely them!"

Suddenly, a muscular figure burst from the shadows and clamped a hand on the ensign's shoulder. The ensign yelped and looked up with evident fear and surprise.

"Mind if I have a look?" The man who'd grabbed the ensign's shoulder had a deep, soft voice. But even someone who knew nothing about him would know from the start that he wasn't a soft man.

His eyes burned with a fierce intensity. His craggy features were battered and scarred, his cheeks rough, his nose lumpy and crooked. He was middle-aged, in his forties perhaps, his thick brown hair streaked with grey along the temples. And there was a tightness to his movements, a sense of barely restrained power. He looked like the kind of man who could erupt into violent action at any moment if provoked.

Because he *was* that kind of man. The kind whose reputation preceded him wherever he went, be it within the borders of the Union or on any foreign battlefield anywhere in the world. His name was known far and wide as the name of someone to be reckoned with.

He was Major John MacNeal of the 42nd Marine Special Forces.

The ensign locked the periscope in place and stepped away without hesitating. "Yes, sir, Major MacNeal. I mean, *no*, sir, I don't mind if you have a look."

MacNeal nodded and helped himself to the scope. Pressing his forehead against the hood, he peered into the dark view of the surface above the sub.

Sure enough, dead in the middle of the crosshairs, he saw a blinking light. As it bobbed on the rippling waves, the flashes spelled out letters in Morse code. It was their call sign, all right.

"Thank God." He muttered the words to himself, then pushed away from the scope. "Bring 'em in, Admiral! Bring 'em in!"

"Better do it fast!" another ensign spoke up from the radar station. His eyes were glued to the blinking blips of green light on the round screen in front of him. "They've got multiple bogeys in hot pursuit!"

"Battle stations." The sub's commanding officer, a hard-bitten Mexican Admiral named Gustavo Suerte, shot out of the command chair as the lights went red. "How many bogeys?"

"Three, sir." The ensign never looked up from the screen. "And they're moving fast. Some kind of gunboats, I'd say, sir."

"How close?" asked Admiral Suerte.

"Mile and a half and closing, sir," said the radar ensign.

Suerte didn't miss a beat. "Surface, gentlemen! Ready fore torpedoes! I want a firing solution on those gunboats."

As the klaxon rang, MacNeal didn't wait around to watch events unfold on the radar and periscope. His people were in danger, the fate of the Union was at risk, and his place was no longer on the bridge.

Pushing into the corridor, he headed for his quarters. Several times, he had to squeeze against the wall as sailors hurried past in the midst of their duties.

When he reached the door to his room, he spun the wheel to unlatch it, threw it open, and lunged inside. Scooping his Mk I flashgun off his bed, he slung the strap over his shoulder and barged back into the hall, nearly knocking down a sailor on the way.

MacNeal made one more stop, hammering on the door next to his. "Boomer! Topside, now!" He shouted the words and kept on going, leaning forward with dark intensity.

Seconds later, the wheel on the door spun, the door shot open, and a mountain of a man burst forth. Dark skin glistening over rippling slabs of muscle, he hurtled down the corridor on MacNeal's heels. Belts of ammo were draped over his chest and shoulders, feeding into the massive weapon he toted: an A6a flash machine gun. The plentiful hash marks scored on the brass casing of the gun's accumulator power pack represented kills he'd made in the line of duty.

He was Sergeant Barry Daniel Brown of the 42nd Marines, Heavy Weaponry Specialist and right-hand man of Major MacNeal. He was also one of the meanest son-of-a-guns to come anywhere near the secret ops battlegrounds of the Great War.

MacNeal's heart pounded as he and Brown stormed through the vessel. He was determined to bring in his team at all costs. The information they'd retrieved was irreplaceable; so were their lives.

Armed sailors were already waiting at the base of the conning tower when MacNeal and Brown arrived. After the klaxon stopped, signaling they'd reached the surface, one man turned the valve wheel and pulled open the hatch. Rifle slung over his back, the sailor moved to start up the ladder...but then MacNeal grabbed his arm and pulled him aside.

Everyone stepped back at the same time. MacNeal didn't need to say a word.

He was going up first.

As he scrambled up the ladder, he heard the telltale double *whoosh* of torpedoes being launched. He heard a distant explosion when he reached the outer hatch and spun the wheel; he hoped to God his people weren't the ones being blown up.

MacNeal pitched open the hatch, letting it clang against the hull. As he clambered out onto the conning tower, he saw the sky had brightened considerably, which was a good thing. The light of dawn would make a big difference in sighting the incoming escapees and their pursuers.

MacNeal swung up his flash-gun and ran to the railing, ready for action. Brown wasn't far behind; in an instant, he appeared at the rail alongside MacNeal, flash machine gun aimed out at sea.

MacNeal felt a flicker of relief when he looked down at the water alongside the sub. The covert team was already heading toward the sub in a motor launch, no more than thirty yards distant.

But MacNeal's relief was short-lived. Taki was at the wheel, Tala was turned around, firing a Japanese rifle she must've snagged during the escape…and Hoax was sprawled on the deck between them, covered in blood.

At the sight of her, MacNeal's heart jackhammered in his chest. He always felt responsible for Hoax's well-being, ever since her father, General of the 3rd Division of the Army of the Potomac, had made him swear to look out for her. Not to mention, he'd come to think of her as he might think of his own daughter…a rebellious, pain in the ass daughter, but a daughter nonetheless. Seeing her like that turned his blood to boiling lava.

It was more critical than ever that the launch reach the *Pershing* as soon as possible. Unfortunately, the Japanese gunboats weren't far behind. There were two of them left, plus a smoking hunk of wreckage that must have been the third. They were thirty yards away and gaining as Taki cut the launch's engine to draw up to the sub.

The Japanese guns chattered. MacNeal and Brown answered by lighting up their flash weapons, unleashing a storm of blistering high-velocity rounds.

The armed seamen from inside the sub followed their lead, pouring up out of the hatch and opening fire on the gunboats. Others raced along the spine of the sub and down the ladder to help bring the covert team aboard.

As the Japanese closed in, their bullets clattered and zinged off the launch and the skin of the sub. They came toward the broadside, which was smart: the sub's torpedo tubes were mounted at the fore end.

Japanese rounds traced a path up the conning tower, climbing toward MacNeal and Brown. They responded by tracing their own swath along the length of the enemy gunboat from stem to stern. Their high-velocity rounds nipped at the boat's armor and chewed up the crew with fierce efficiency, cutting down the pilot and gunners and chipping open the fuel tank at the rear.

The gunboat suddenly veered to one side and exploded, sending an orange fireball rolling up into the sky.

The other gunboat kept coming, focusing its assault on the covert team and the sailors on the fin trying to help them aboard. One sailor took a hit as he reached for the rope to tie off the launch; he cried out and dropped face down into the water. The other sailor, halfway down the ladder, caught a slug in his shoulder and dropped, then crawled to the high side of the fin and lay there panting.

The remaining gunboat continued to hurtle closer, guns blazing. MacNeal and Brown kept pouring high-velocity rounds into it, blasting away at the armored cowling around the pilot. The armor buckled and broke under the relentless barrage, and a fury of rounds punched through into the cockpit.

MacNeal heard the pilot scream. The boat's motor cut out, and it drifted to a stop against the hull of the sub. The two surviving gunners kept shooting, but they were sitting ducks to MacNeal and Brown on the high ground above them. Within seconds, no one was left alive in the drifting gunboat.

As soon as the danger was over, MacNeal ran to the top of the ladder and raced down to the water. Standing on the sub's sloping fin, he stretched as far as he could, reaching for the rope held out by Taki. Seizing the end of it, he clenched his teeth and hauled the boat closer.

By then more seamen had climbed down to join him. Two moved in behind him and grabbed hold of the rope; together, they pulled the launch up onto the fin.

Gingerly, Taki and Tala lifted Hoax from the deck and handed her over to MacNeal. The first thing he did was lower his ear to her lips, checking for breath, dreading the absence of it.

For an instant, there was nothing, and his blood froze. But then he felt it, faint and soft: an exhalation. Thank God, she was still alive.

Sailors lowered a gurney basket from above, and MacNeal loaded her in. As they smoothly raised the basket back topside, he turned to the rest of the team.

Tala sloshed through the water on the fin, looking miserable. Her hair and torn-up geisha clothes were soaked; she had cuts and bruises everywhere…but no visible bullet holes.

Instead of a salute, she tossed off a half-hearted wave in MacNeal's direction. "Whiskey. Now." Those were the only words she said as she limped past.

Taki splashed over next, looking the least battered of the group. "Major MacNeal, sir." His tuxedo was soaked, but somehow still looked smart on him. He snapped off a salute, plunged his hand into an inside pocket of the jacket, and came out with a folded manila envelope. "The package, sir. As requested."

MacNeal nodded and took the envelope. It seemed like such a small thing, to be so important. It hardly seemed possible that the tides of war could turn on the simple sheets of paper tucked inside.

But according to the Union's best source within the Shōgunate, they could. "I trust you thanked Dr. Kichida properly for his efforts, Corporal Takata?"

Taki slumped. "I did, but…he's dead, sir. A Shin task force attacked us at the rendezvous point." He narrowed his eyes. "They must have suspected Kichida was an informer."

MacNeal shook his head slowly. "Damn. He was a good man." Then, as the implications settled in, he looked at the envelope. "So how accurate is this information, I wonder?"

Taki shrugged. "It depends on when they started suspecting him, I guess. Maybe they only caught on to him *after* he secured the information."

"We can only hope." MacNeal stowed the envelope in his hip pocket, then watched the flurry of action around them at the base of the ladder. A medical corpsman was treating the sailor who'd been shot and fallen off the ladder. Other sailors, clad in wetsuits, were heading down to retrieve the body of the shipmate who'd been killed by the Japanese guns.

Taki started after them. "I should help. He died saving us."

MacNeal grabbed his arm. "Leave them to it. You've done enough for one day."

Taki tried to pull away. "But they need to recover him fast. The Japanese navy and air force will be all over us soon."

"And *you* need to be fully debriefed, Corporal. That package might not be the only valuable information you've brought us." MacNeal steered him toward the ladder. "Now get inside, Corporal. That's an order."

Taki resisted a moment more, then gave in and went along with MacNeal. "Yes, sir." He was a good soldier, a rule follower prone to accepting the wisdom and virtue of Command.

MacNeal wondered how long that would last, now that he was working with the 42nd Marines. How long would it take for the bad influences to rub off on him?

Based on past experience, he didn't suppose it would take long at all. Not that that was necessarily a *bad* thing. The tougher and more unpredictable the 42nd got, the more decisively excellent the results of its missions seemed to be.

And truth be told, MacNeal preferred working with those hard case types, no matter how difficult they tended to make his life. So as much as he appreciated Taki's good work and current good manners, he looked forward to seeing the rebellious son-of-a-gun he was sure to become once the rest of the unit got done with him.

No matter how much trouble that future pain in the ass was destined to cause him.

CHAPTER 5

*K*amchatka?" Admiral Suerte gaped at the pages from the envelope as if they'd suddenly burst into flames. "Why in God's name would the Japanese invade *Kamchatka*?"

Major MacNeal sat across from him at a small, square table in the Admiral's cramped quarters, arms folded on a jumble of maps. Now that the *Pershing* had dived and moved out to a safer distance from the Shōgunate, the two men had time to discuss Dr. Kichida's message and plan their next move.

"Kamchatka." Suerte shook his head. "It doesn't make *sense*. They've made major gains in China. Korea's wide open, not to mention the Philippines. They've got a real shot at controlling all of Southeast Asia."

"So why deploy forces to an isolated Russian peninsula north of the 49th parallel?" MacNeal nodded. "That's a damned good question."

"If they *wanted* a piece of Russia, why not extend their existing supply lines north from China?" Suerte smacked his hand on the table. "Why not go after the Siberian oil fields?"

"Actually, there've been rumors they might do just that," said MacNeal.

"*See*? Who'd want *Kamchatka*? It's sparsely populated. It's seismically unstable, on the intersection of several major fault lines." Suerte ticked off the points on his fingers. "It's riddled with active volcanoes. It has no strategic significance—"

"That we know of."

"—that we know of," continued Suerte. "*And* staging *any* kind of landing there is sure to draw the attention of the Russian Matriarchy."

"Maybe not right away, though," said MacNeal. "It's the boondocks, that's for sure. Are there even any significant defense forces based there?"

"I have no idea." Suerte got up and started pacing. In the tiny cabin, that meant walking three steps one way and three steps back. "And we're on radio silence, so we can't contact Matriarchy Command to ask them about it."

MacNeal shrugged. He wasn't sure how much the Russian Matriarchy would tell them even if they could be reached. They'd been allies since earlier that year, when they'd signed the Union and Matriarchy Treaty of Mutual Assistance (UMTOMA), but the alliance was an uneasy one. It had primarily been a response to the Nippon Accords, a neutrality pact between Japan and the Reich; it had not done away with the friction and mistrust between the Union and the Matriarchy. The Russian leadership, headed by Tsarina and Grand Matriarch Anastasia Romanov and her husband, the notorious Grigori Rasputin, was especially tricky and troublesome. In MacNeal's experience, in spite of UMTOMA, the odds of the Matriarchy *hurting* Union interests in a given situation were about the same as the odds of them *helping*.

"Radio silence." MacNeal rubbed the rough stubble on his chin. "That means we can't warn the Russians, either."

"Our own allies." Suerte shook his head. "I wouldn't like it if they didn't warn us of an impending invasion."

"Maybe it's for the best," said MacNeal. "Depending on what the Shōgunate's after. What if the Matriarchy doesn't even know about it? Whatever it is, maybe it's better off in our hands than in the hands of the Japanese or the Russians…"

Suerte nodded thoughtfully. "So you're suggesting we steal it out from under them?"

"Assuming there's anything to steal." MacNeal leaned forward and picked up Dr. Kichida's papers. "Also assuming this information is accurate, even though Kichida got made."

"That's a pretty big assumption, if you ask me." Suerte stopped pacing and leaned against the door. "Wouldn't Shōgunate intelligence be able to guess what he passed along based on information he had access to?"

"Depends on how many pies Kichida had his fingers in, I suppose." MacNeal shook the pages in his hand. "If he knew a lot about a lot of things, maybe they can't narrow it down. Or maybe they don't care what intel he passed us. Maybe they're too committed to shift gears. Maybe they're just too cocky to worry about us."

"They have reason to be, if the rumors are true." Suerte raised an eyebrow. "If they've conquered death itself."

MacNeal waved off the comment. "Death and I are old friends, Admiral. And let me tell you, that SOB will not be conquered."

"So what do we do?" Suerte spread his arms wide. "What would President Edison want us to do next?"

"We know where they're going. We know their landing coordinates, the size of their force, and their estimated time of arrival." MacNeal stared into space, sorting the facts as he said them aloud. "We don't know *what* they want, but we can assume they want it *badly*."

"*If* the information's accurate," said Suerte. "If it isn't a diversion meant to draw us away from the real operation."

MacNeal thought for a moment, flicking Kichida's pages against the map of Kamchatka on the table in front of him. How many times had he been in situations like this, forced to make a judgment call in the field without knowing all the facts? How often had he agonized over difficult decisions on which life and death and the future itself hinged?

This time, the options were twofold: trust Kichida and head to Kamchatka, or assume his information was unreliable and go somewhere else. Maybe, if they decided against Kamchatka, they could observe fleet movements and try to determine the Shōgunate's next big move.

But what if Kamchatka *was* that move? What if whatever was hidden there turned out to be the key to the whole damned war? The Union, Reich, and Matriarchy had been fighting that war since 1914; after so many years, they were running on empty. It might not take much to tip the balance in favor of a fresh new player like the Shōgunate. A secret weapon from Kamchatka might just do the trick.

Would President Edison want him to leave such a potential ace in the hole on the table for someone else to scoop up?

Negative. "All right." MacNeal dropped Kichida's papers and clapped his hand down on top of them. "Time to set a course, Admiral." With that, he got up from his chair and headed for the door.

Suerte stepped aside. "Where to, Major?"

"Kamchatka." MacNeal clapped him on the shoulder on his way past. "Where the hell else did you think?"

* * *

Sailors squeezed past in a hurry as Tala shuffled down the corridor with her whiskey bottle. Men shouted, lights flashed, and the hull rumbled—but she just kept walking, her bloodshot eyes droopy and unfocused.

When she reached the infirmary, she paused outside the door, not wanting to go in…afraid what she might find. What if Hoax had taken a turn for the worse? What if she'd already died from her injuries?

In spite of the feud between them, Tala didn't want to think about Hoax dying. She hated that it made her feel guilty, as if she were somehow to blame.

She knew she wasn't. It wasn't her fault, plain and simple. She'd had her own battle to fight back in Tokyo; she couldn't have been expected to fight for Hoax, too.

But still, a voice inside kept telling her otherwise.

Tala took a deep breath, turned the wheel on the door, and pulled it open. When she looked in, she saw an empty bed. Her heart pounded and her breath caught in her throat.

Then, she pushed the door wider, and saw the bed on the other side of the room. Hoax lay there, eyes closed, with Taki at her side. Her face was stitched and bandaged; a blood-soaked dressing covered the wound in her left side, where her hospital gown was laid open.

She looked like she was in terrible shape, like she'd gone six rounds with a gorilla…but her chest rose and fell with the motion of her breathing. She wasn't dead yet.

Tala let loose a sigh of relief. "How is she?"

"Fighting." Taki looked down at Hoax and nodded. "That's what she does best, isn't it?"

Tala closed the door, turned the wheel to latch it, and positioned herself on the side of the bed opposite Taki. It didn't occur to her that he might have been complimenting Hoax, not insulting her. "Maybe you could *learn* something from her."

Taki stared at her blankly. "The doc says she'll be touch and go for a while." Apparently, he wasn't going to take the bait.

That was too bad, because a good dust-up was exactly what Tala needed. And Taki was the perfect target. He'd been annoying her from the get-go. Plus, he was relatively unhurt, while Hoax was hovering between life and death. Not to mention, he was the rookie member of the team, well below Tala in the pecking order. As much of a pain in the ass as Hoax was, she still had seniority over Tala since she served as MacNeal's XO in the 42nd. Tala never let that stop her from bucking Hoax's authority, but she knew it bordered on insubordination. Taki, on the other hand, could be put in his place with impunity.

"We've got a policy in the 42nd Marines." She raised the whiskey bottle and had a swig. "Guess what it *isn't*? 'Every man for himself.' That's the opposite of our policy."

Taki looked like he was about to say something. But instead, he just clamped his mouth shut and nodded. His hazel eyes narrowed in an expression of what might have been deep understanding.

Or, as Tala saw it, deep contempt. "Bastard." She glared and shook her bottle at him. "For all we know, you're some kind of double agent working for the Shōgunate. Maybe *you're* the one who tipped off the Shin!"

Suddenly Taki erupted in a flurry of motion, seizing the metal bedpan from the nightstand and lashing it back over his shoulder. He froze in that position, perfectly poised, with the bedpan aimed at Tala, ready to throw.

Her eyes got big. She hadn't expected him to make a move like that.

"I was hand-picked by Major John MacNeal," he said in a calm, even voice. "I've got commendations you haven't even *heard* of. I don't have to prove myself to you or anyone." He reeled the bedpan back a little farther, its gleaming metal catching the overhead light. "So *watch* your *mouth*."

At that very instant, the wheel on the door spun, the door flew open, and Major MacNeal marched into the room.

Immediately Taki relaxed and lowered the bedpan. MacNeal just stared at him for a moment, then shook his head. "That didn't take long," he said under his breath.

Taki frowned. "What didn't take long?"

"Nothing." MacNeal took the bedpan out of his hand and dropped it on the nightstand. "Welcome to the family."

Tala snorted and threw back another swig of whiskey. It turned out to be her last tug on that bottle. MacNeal lunged over and snatched it from her hand, then stomped to the sink and dumped it down. "Enough of this. You're back on duty, both of you."

Tala glared at him. She'd had plans for the rest of that whiskey. "What *kind* of duty, exactly?"

MacNeal tossed the empty bottle in a garbage bucket and jabbed a finger at her. "The kind that requires you to follow orders, Corporal. And remain *sober*."

Though Tala's first instinct was to lay into him with everything she had, she held herself back. She had a gift for bouncing back from career suicide—she'd made a *career* out of it—but something in his voice told her this might not be her lucky day.

"Operation Shadow Rise." MacNeal clasped his hands behind his back and stood stiffly at the foot of Hoax's bed. "We are following up on the information obtained from Dr. Kichida."

Taki nodded approvingly. Tala folded her arms over her chest and leaned back against the bulkhead, looking bored.

But in reality, she was glad for the chance at a new mission, for something to take her mind off what had happened to Hoax. In all the ways that mattered, action in the field was the only thing that gave her life meaning. It was the only thing that never let her down.

"The *Pershing* will shadow the Shōgunate task force dispatched to the Kamchatka peninsula," said MacNeal. "The 42nd Marines will surveil task force operations ashore."

"Kamchatka?" Tala scowled. "*That* isn't in China."

"Correct. It's part of Russia." MacNeal smirked. "Give yourself a gold star, Corporal."

Tala shrugged. "They're already kicking China's ass. Why the sudden fascination with the Matriarchy?"

MacNeal focused in on Taki. "I was hoping you might provide some insight, Taki. Can you think of any reason the Shōgunate might have for targeting Kamchatka?"

"Nothing comes to mind, sir." Taki shook his head. "It's a pretty remote area. I can't think of any strategic value. If anything, it seems like the exact *opposite* of what the Shōgunate would be interested in."

"Are we even sure Kichida's information is still accurate?" asked Tala. "They knew he was a traitor. They sent assassins to *kill* him. I'm pretty sure they'd change any plans they thought he had access to."

"Good point." MacNeal nodded curtly. "But we've decided to proceed as if the intelligence is sound. We can't afford to overlook a possible high-value asset hidden in Kamchatka, if indeed there is one."

Taki looked relieved. "Dr. Kichida would be pleased to know he didn't die in vain."

"What about Hoax?" Tala gazed at the body of her teammate on the bed. "Think *she'll* appreciate dying for a good cause, too? Or is there a Navy hospital en route that I don't know about?"

MacNeal shot her a look that said she'd pushed him too far. Often he seemed to appreciate that she kept him on his toes…but she did have a habit of going overboard.

"My gut says we need to go to Kamchatka. Now." MacNeal left the foot of the bed and walked over to push his face close to Tala's. "It also says I need to shoot you out a torpedo tube for that last crack. But I'm not listening." He leaned forward, smiling grimly. "*This* time."

Tala didn't back down, she never did…but she did hold her tongue. She had a pretty good idea of when not to push back, and now was one of those times.

MacNeal locked her in his gaze a moment more, then turned his eyes to Hoax. "Decision's been made. We're already underway."

Reaching down, he softly touched Hoax's shoulder, one of the few parts of her that hadn't been cut, bruised, or broken. Then he cleared his throat and stepped back. "Grab some rack time. Both of you." He looked at Tala, then Taki. "You're going to need it."

Without another word, MacNeal opened the door and marched out of the room, leaving Tala and Taki with Hoax.

"Well, ain't that a kick in the head?" asked Tala once the door had closed and latched.

Taki shook his head at her. "I kept hoping I was wrong about you. But no such luck."

Tala squared her shoulders and tipped her head back. "Why don't you finish what you started, Taki? Go on and let me have it with that bedpan. See what happens next."

"I won't waste my energy," said Taki, and then he headed for the door.

Tala thought about blocking his way but didn't do it. She let him go, and then she was alone with Hoax.

Only then did she reach into her pocket and pull out a single turquoise bead—a Navajo prayer bead—from her medicine pouch. Drawing on her knowledge as a shaman, she whispered a blessing, urging the spirits to heal her sister-in-arms quickly.

Leaning down, Tala pressed the turquoise bead under a corner of the bedding at the head of the bed. As she tucked in the corner, she told Hoax to get better soon, because she needed her to help keep the boys in line.

Also because Tala owed her an ass-kicking for getting her in trouble with MacNeal, even if she *was* unconscious the whole time.

* * *

Early the next morning, MacNeal rushed onto the bridge behind the seaman who'd just woken him from a sound sleep. He didn't know the reason for the summons; just that it was urgent.

As soon as he walked in, Brown called out from the radar station. "Over here, Major. Looks like your gut was right."

MacNeal rubbed his eyes hard. Whatever stage of sleep he'd been in when the seaman had pounded on his door, it had been deeper than deep. He was well used to springing from out-cold to a state of total alertness in the field, but still, he was having trouble making everything work right.

When he got to the radar station, he didn't need Brown to point out the three blinking blips on the screen, but Brown jabbed them with his thick fingers anyway. "There's that task force you were expecting. I guess Kichida set us straight after all."

"Doc delivered, God rest his soul." MacNeal smacked Brown between his shoulder blades. "What's the profile on these contacts?"

"Too big to be fishing boats," said the ensign manning the radar console.

"I'd bet my commission they're not decoys." Admiral Suerte walked over with two steaming tin cups. "We're just about to confirm. Thought you might want to see the show." He handed one of the cups to MacNeal.

Coffee. The bitter smell made MacNeal feel perkier just by sifting it into his nose. "Thanks, Gustavo." The first sip was hot enough to burn his tongue, but it didn't matter. After two gulps, his head started to clear. "When did they show up?"

"Ten minutes ago," said the radar ensign. "We verified they were hard targets before we called you."

"Helm," barked Suerte. "Maintain course and speed. Take us up to periscope depth."

"Aye, sir." The helmsman eased down a lever on his board. His eyes remained fixed on the gauges and dials in front of him. "Releasing ballast."

As the helmsman called out depths, each closer to the surface than the last, Brown leaned in close to MacNeal and met his gaze. "About Hoax." He kept his voice low, for MacNeal's ears only. "She hasn't turned the corner yet."

MacNeal narrowed his eyes. "But she's not losing ground, either?"

Brown shook his head. "That woman's a prizefighter." He smirked and pointed at his cheek. "And I've got the hole in my jaw to prove it."

"Periscope depth, Admiral," said the helmsman.

Suerte gulped the rest of his coffee and set the empty cup down on the arm of the command chair. "Up periscope."

"Up periscope, sir." Another ensign pulled down the mechanized column of the periscope and unfolded the handles that were tucked against the sides. Gripping the handles, he pressed his forehead to the hood over the eyepiece.

For a moment, the pinging of the radar was the only sound on the bridge. All eyes were on the ensign as he slowly turned the column, scanning the view above the water's surface.

There wasn't much doubt about what was up there. The *Pershing* was on a heading for Kamchatka, which was supposedly the target of a Shōgunate task force. Three large, hard target contacts on the radar were heading the same way. MacNeal knew it wasn't a stretch to think the radar blips were Shōgunate vessels.

Still, he was nervous as he waited for the verdict. If the ships were Japanese, the *Pershing* and the 42nd were committed to Operation Shadow Rise. And the fact of the matter was, MacNeal never shied away from a fight or failed in a mission…but the Japanese were an enigma. Men like Taki had opened a window on their closed-off society, but opened it just a crack. And there were rumors that the Shōgunate had some astounding capabilities, including a secret weapon that could shift the balance of the Great War forever.

A possibility had occurred to MacNeal, one he hadn't shared with Suerte or Brown or anyone else. It was one of the factors that had helped him decide to head for Kamchatka, whatever the veracity of Kichida's information.

What if the Japanese were going to the desolate Russian peninsula not to find some secret weapon, but to *test* one? What if this whole task force operation of theirs was just a field test of an asset that could win the war?

If true, it would be an opportunity to take the weapon away from them…or at least destroy it. Perhaps, if the 42nd could ensure that the test was a failure, they could buy the Union precious time for a preemptive strike on the Shōgunate. Such a strike could head off the weapon's deployment and stave off a terrible fate for the free and not-so-free world…a fate MacNeal and his team had been fighting for years to prevent.

Out of all the worries the Union had about the Japanese, perhaps the biggest were related to their dark allies. To many in the Union's upper echelons, the doomsday clock had started counting down on the day when the Shōgunate had signed a neutrality pact with an-other power half a world away.

That power, the Reich, was perhaps the greatest threat the world had ever known.

"Three ships, sir," said the ensign at the periscope. "Looks like a troop transport and two destroyer escorts."

"Markings?" asked Suerte.

The ensign took a moment more, adjusting the scope's magnification and peering into the eyepiece. Then he stomped his foot excitedly. "Shōgunate, Admiral. They're flying the rising sun."

"And they don't care who knows it, huh?" Brown sneered. "Cocky bastards, aren't they?"

"That confirms it." Suerte clapped his hands together. "You made the right call, MacNeal."

"Always does." Brown clamped a hand on MacNeal's shoulder and squeezed till it hurt.

"Care for a look, Major?" The ensign at the periscope moved aside and offered his spot.

MacNeal nodded and stepped up to the scope. There they were, as soon as the view came into focus: three ships, all flying the flag of the Shōgunate. They cruised in a tight formation under bright blue morning skies, leaving foamy white wakes on the sapphire sea.

And they were heading for Kamchatka, as Kichida had promised.

"What if we just blow 'em all to hell right now?" asked Brown. "Save ourselves the headaches?"

"Then we'd never know what they're after." MacNeal drew back from the scope and rubbed his tired eyes. "And we'd never know if it's something *we* might want."

"All right, people," said Suerte. "We will remain at condition yellow until further notice." Pushing past MacNeal, he had a look through the scope for himself. "Now let's take her down to cruising depth. Dive."

"How long will it take to reach Kamchatka?" asked Brown.

"That's up to the Japanese," replied Suerte.

"Actually…" The helmsman scribbled fast on a notepad. "Assuming they maintain their current course and speed, I'd say about two and a half days."

MacNeal nodded, then was overcome by a yawn. It was as if, now that the initial excitement was over, his body was remembering how tired it was. "Plenty of time for a nap, then." He socked Brown in the bicep and turned toward the door. "What say we meet at 0900 and talk strategy, Admiral? We've got mission parameters to map out here."

"Are you sure you wouldn't rather make it 1000?" asked Suerte. "I can wait."

"O-nine-hundred's fine." MacNeal shot him a wink. "Don't want to let the Japanese out of my sight for too long, Gustavo."

"Don't lose too much sleep over them yet, John." Suerte chuckled. "There'll be time enough for that when you get to Kamchatka."

CHAPTER 6

Southern Kamchatka
17 April 1952
0430 Hours

The sky was still dark when the first landing craft threw down its ramp on the shore of Kamchatka. Two dozen Japanese soldiers ran out, feet splashing in the ankle-deep water.

Jōtōhei Hiruko Orochi was one of the first to hit the beach. Rifle at the ready, he scanned the tree line beyond the sand, expecting to see the muzzle flashes of Russian fighters defending their soil.

But there were no flashes. The expected retorts of enemy gunfire never came. If there was a single soul anywhere in the vicinity, they did not seem to notice the invasion in progress.

On the orders of Daimyō Minamoto, Hiruko and the other men fanned out and took up positions along the beach, weapons aimed at the shaggy evergreens lining the coast. The mission of the moment was to defend the other landing crafts rushing in from the three Shōgunate ships anchored in the bay.

Beyond that, Hiruko had little knowledge of what the operation entailed. According to the Shōgun, the Emperor had spoken of a "heavenly prize" that he would use "to forge an even more glorious destiny for our precious *Nippon*." What exactly that heavenly prize was and how they would obtain it was unknown…at least to the ranks of the royal guard.

Hiruko trusted the Shōgun, Emperor, and Daimyō with all his heart, but he still wished he had the status for that level of information. It was the root of a daydream he had often, a fantasy about being someone important, someone in power with the knowledge of all secrets in the Shōgunate. Sometimes his daydreams were so clear, they seemed as real as memories to him.

A second landing craft slid up to the shore, and its ramp splashed down. More soldiers hurried through the surf, gear bundled on their backs, rifles cradled in their arms.

The third transport to make landfall was an amphibious craft. At the water's edge, the tank treads mounted on its lower hull caught purchase on the sand and rolled it forward.

Hiruko tried to look inside as he moved out of the way to let the vehicle through, but the few windows were small and tinted. The interior of the craft was hidden from him. It was the special transport, the one that he and the other soldiers had been assigned to protect at all costs. The only thing he knew about its contents was that they were top secret, and had something to do with the one scientist traveling along with the unit—Dr. Hideki Kondo, a highly regarded physicist.

As the special transport passed, he thought back to the men of the Reich he'd glimpsed behind the curtain at the rally—the walking cadaver in the black overcoat and the brute with the glowing eyes and scars. He wondered if they might be inside that vehicle, rolling through the darkness on their shadowy errands. If so, what did the Shōgunate have to do with them? What was their connection to the "heavenly prize" desired by the Emperor?

As the amphibious craft rumbled toward the trees, Hiruko heard another transport slide ashore. When he turned and saw that the latest craft had a single occupant, his breath caught in his chest. The Reich agents weren't the only intimidating-looking beings in the expedition.

Even before the ramp slammed open, Hiruko could see the pale horns gleaming in the starlight, jutting up from the hood of a black cloak. Only one being in the Shōgunate—in all the world as far as Hiruko knew—had horns like those.

His name was Itami.

When the ramp dropped, he towered at the top of it, shrouded in his cloak. He was six feet five inches tall, a giant compared to the average Japanese soldier. The cloak couldn't hide the mountains of bulging muscle on his arms, chest, and shoulders…and it couldn't conceal the monstrous *kenabō* club he carried over one shoulder, a knobbed cylinder as thick as his arm and nearly as long as he was tall.

Even cloaked, even by starlight, he was an intimidating figure. The mere sight of him was enough to strike fear in men's hearts… Hiruko's included. In the three days' journey from Tokyo to Kamchatka, Hiruko had managed to cross paths with him only once aboard ship. Now, it seemed, he would have no choice but to endure his presence.

It wouldn't be easy. The sight of Itami wasn't the only aspect that brought on fear. He gave off something—a chemical? a force?—that seemed to give birth to terror. The closer Hiruko, or anyone, got to Itami, the more scared they became.

Itami's appearance only amplified the effect. His great size suggested vast reserves of pure physical power. As for the horns and the rest of his elaborate costume—it could only be a costume, though no one knew the costume-maker who'd designed it—they made him seem like an *oni* out of myth. What could be more terrifying?

As Itami swept forward in the wake of the amphibious craft, Hiruko did his best to stand his ground. He pushed back his fear as best he could, desperate not to show weakness. After all, Itami was the Daimyō's chief enforcer; though he held no rank, he also took orders directly from the Shōgun himself.

Hiruko shivered as Itami approached. Even knowing they were both on the same side of the mission, he had to fight the urge to flee.

Itami marched closer, ever closer. His massive body swung from side to side like a great bull under the cloak. His power, even at rest, was undeniable.

Hiruko turned to fix his gaze upon the trees. Perhaps, if he was lucky, Itami would pass him by this time.

Sweat trickled down Hiruko's sides. He heard Itami's heavy footfalls in the sand, one after another, getting closer.

Then, another landing craft splashed ashore, and there was shouting. He recognized the Daimyō's voice, shouting orders at the water's edge. But Itami's footsteps were drowned out by the commotion.

Hiruko stole a glance right, then left, but saw no trace of the horned man. Heart thundering, he thought of looking behind him, but didn't do it.

He didn't need to. A gust of hot breath washed over the back of his neck.

Itami was there.

Hiruko clenched his jaws and forced himself not to react. Every nerve in his body felt electrified, snapping like downed power lines on pavement...but he kept himself perfectly still.

He felt Itami's hand close around his shoulder. The hot breath moved from his neck to his right ear.

And then he heard the voice, deep as the bottom of the ocean. The words slid into his ear on the stream of hot breath, like bubbles on a flow of cherry red lava.

"Hello, little brother," said Itami.

Hiruko's blood froze. "Hello, sir."

"You are doing a most excellent job of securing this beachhead," said Itami. "I commend you."

"Th-thank you, sir." Hiruko hated himself for stuttering, but he simply couldn't help it. As well-formed and complimentary as Itami's words were, the thing behind them was terrifying.

"Do you have every confidence in the impending glorious success of this enterprise?" Itami sounded like he was sneering when he said it. "Do you pledge to do whatever is necessary to serve the Shōgun and Emperor, whatever the cost to your own body and soul?"

Hiruko nodded five times fast. "Yes, sir."

Suddenly, Itami pressed closer. Hiruko could feel his lips against his ear. "*Promises, promises.*" The words were a hiss, like the flame of a candle blowing out.

Hiruko looked over just far enough to see Itami's fingers on his shoulder, blue as ice, with ebon nails. They squeezed tighter, digging in deeper.

And then, suddenly, they released him.

Itami whisked past in his billowing dark cloak without another word or a look back. He disappeared into the trees like a ghost, leaving Hiruko struggling to regain his composure.

* * *

Taki paddled for all he was worth, helping push the inflatable raft toward the shore. Four men paddled alongside him, as did the occupants of the other rafts.

There were three rafts altogether, coming in without motors from the UNS Pershing. The team was landing a full five miles northeast along the curving coastline from the Shōgunate beachhead, but they still didn't want to take any chances. The success of their mission depended on stealth.

Behind them, the *Pershing* had already submerged and moved off. The landing party was on its own—thirteen men and one woman sent to stalk a much larger Shōgunate force. They wouldn't even have radio contact with the *Pershing* until the end of the mission because the sub had to stay submerged, out of sight of the Shōgunate vessels. It was up to the landing party alone to keep the secret of Kamchatka out of the hands of the power-mad Shōgun of Japan.

Looking back over his shoulder, Taki saw the sky on the far horizon was starting to brighten. Soon he wouldn't need the HB-5 night vision goggles that MacNeal had handed out back on-board the *Pershing*. A new day was dawning; he wondered what it would bring. The 42nd had a reputation for success…but also a reputation for recklessness. He had faith in MacNeal, but Sergeant Brown remained a question mark. As for Tala, she had a chip on her shoulder the size of California. Her dislike of Taki actually seemed to be getting stronger; he wasn't sure she wouldn't try to trip him up on purpose, let alone watch his back in a firefight.

In other words, as Taki's raft rode the breakers toward shore, he felt like he was heading for shaky ground in more ways than one. Not only was he approaching unknown terrain, stalking an enemy with mysterious capabilities and motives, but his own unit's loyalties were unpredictable.

Still, all he could do was move forward. When his raft brushed the bottom, he dropped his paddle and leaped out. So did the other men, three of the ten Alpha Commandos assigned to the mission. Together they dragged the raft the rest of the way through the surf and up onto the beach.

When they reached the tree line, they organized their gear. Taki switched off and removed his HB-5 goggles, stowed them in his pack, then hoisted the pack onto his back. He slung his Mk I flash-gun on his left shoulder, then checked the snaps and straps of his bulletproof BG-42 Ilirium vest. Everyone in the landing party had one, thanks to MacNeal, who'd "requisitioned" them from the Applied Science Division before the mission. The fact that he'd been able to get his hands on them was a mark of his influence and the mission's critical importance.

Once Taki was satisfied that the vest was secure, he patted the sleeves and legs of his camouflage fatigues, checking for his personal weapons. They were all present and accounted for: a tonfa club strapped over his pants on each thigh, a *jitte* in a scabbard on the left side of his belt, and a *nunchaku* in a sheath on the right. Though his kobudō training had prepared him to use any common object at hand, he still felt better in battle with those key pieces at the ready.

Taki and the commandos stowed the raft in the brush along the tree line, covering it with branches and debris. Then they marched across the sand to join the teams from the other two rafts, who'd done the same.

Once the groups came together, MacNeal did a quick head count, then nodded. "Everyone's here." He looked around, taking in the woods and the brightening sunrise. "Time to head out. It's getting late. Boomer?"

Sergeant Brown stepped forward. "Silent running, people, don't forget." He waved his walkie-talkie overhead. "Radios are for scheduled check-ins and emergency use only. The Ilirium in them extends their range and shields the signals, but don't assume they can't be intercepted."

"As you all know by now," said MacNeal, "we're running a long tail surveillance pattern. We'll have a two-person far-forward vanguard followed by a formation of fireteams. At the first sign of trouble, we collapse the formation and concentrate firepower."

"Who's our first vanguard?" asked Brown.

MacNeal slid his HB-4 night vision eyepiece up from his left eye. "Aponi and Takata."

An expression of pure disgust crawled over Tala's face. She didn't even bother looking over at Taki. "I respectfully decline, sir, on the grounds that stealth is critical to a far-forward scout, and I am prone to blowing things up."

"Your declining is declined," snapped MacNeal. "You're our best tracker, Tala. And Taki, your physical appearance could allow you to infiltrate enemy units as needed."

Taki nodded. "Sir, yes, sir." He wasn't thrilled at the prospect of working with a woman who seemed to hate him, but he wasn't about to make an issue of it.

Tala, on the other hand, scowled like she'd just spotted a cockroach in her coffee. "But, sir…"

MacNeal slashed his hand through the air, cutting her off. "Corporal Aponi, get your bearings and move out. That is an order."

Tala glared at him, then puffed out her breath and looked skyward. Turning in a slow circle, she gazed at the stars above for a long moment.

Taki looked at them, too, watching their fading light in the spreading glow of dawn. He knew enough to perform basic navigation by the North Star and certain constellations, but what little he could make out in the brightening sky was no help. At least to him.

Tala was a different story. "I have it." She looked down and nodded. "I know where we are."

"And you know the estimated course and speed of the Japanese land convoy." MacNeal pointed toward the trees. "I want you to check in as needed, at least twice a day. Now what the hell are you still standing around for?"

Without another word and without bothering to salute, Tala darted into the tall pine forest. Taki didn't dare linger another second among the rest of the team; if he had any hope of catching up, he had to run after her.

Even at that, he nearly lost her in the woods. Her lithe form sprinted through the shadows like a doe, like an untamed and untouchable creature of the wilderness.

As graceful as Taki was in martial combat, melding body and weapons in a single flexing force, he felt like the most ungainly elephant as he stumbled along in her sinuous wake.

* * *

Now this was more like it. Tala felt much more at home running through the forest of Kamchatka than she had wobbling through the streets of Tokyo, dressed up like a geisha. It was also much better than being cooped up on a sub or stuck in a smelly sickbay watching Hoax cling to life.

The cool spring air scented with pine instantly cleared her mind. She had a well-defined mission, her shaman's medicine pouch on a cord around her neck, and a backpack full of explosives. It was more like her idea of vacation than work, to be honest.

Except for the dead weight straggling along behind her. Except for Taki, in other words.

She seriously thought about losing him in the woods. She bet she could do it; he wasn't bad in a fight, but she doubted he was a seasoned tracker. So what if her orders were to work with him as the vanguard of the surveillance team? So what if she got in trouble with MacNeal for ditching her assigned partner? Would anyone really care as long as she got the results they wanted?

She could hear him back there, stomping on twigs, crackling through pine needles, making enough noise to be heard a mile away. Did she have time to train him on stealth techniques in a forest setting? No, but that was clearly what he needed.

Suddenly, another solution occurred to her. Maybe there was another way to deal with this liability before she got too close to the targets.

At the base of a little hill, Tala came to a stop and waited for Taki to catch up. While she waited, she pulled the canteen from around her neck and shoulder, unscrewed the cap, and had a drink. The water inside was warm but at least it was wet.

Taki watched without raising his own canteen. To his credit, Tala noticed he was hardly sweating. Not bad, considering the pace she'd set and the weight of the gear on his back.

It was time to play her hand, she decided. "Okay, Corporal." She looked around as if sizing up the site, then nodded firmly. "I'll meet you back here at 1200."

Taki frowned. "You want me to stay behind?"

"You're my lifeline. If I don't return by 1200, you bring the cavalry." She screwed on the cap of her canteen and offered it to him.

He didn't take it. "I don't remember Major MacNeal saying anything about this."

"We have a certain amount of discretion in the field," said Tala.

"Improvisation and flexibility are essential in any surveillance operation."

"I'll keep that in mind as we continue to follow our orders." Taki bowed his head a little. "Thank you for sharing your philosophy. This is turning out to be quite a learning experience."

Tala trained her coldest stare at him. Didn't the guy know how to take a hint? "What's your problem, Taki? Are you *trying* to scuttle this mission?"

"I might ask the same of you." Taki narrowed his eyes. "Taking out your frustrations on your teammates is one thing, but jeopardizing mission-critical surveillance because of some personal grudge is quite another."

"Grudge?" Tala snorted. "You're not even important enough to *rate* one, Taki."

"You know, I think we might have something in common after all, Corporal." Taki slashed his hand through the air. "Neither of us wants to work with the other."

"Is that so?"

"Look what happened to your other teammate. You think I want to end up like *Hoax*?"

Tala glared. She had the urge to light him up with a short-fused quarter stick of dynamite. "Then stay here like I told you. Problem solved."

"Not on your life." Taki adjusted the pack on his back and took a step toward her. "I'm in this whether you like it or not. Whether *I* like it or not."

Tala stared at him for a long moment. He wasn't backing down. She couldn't ditch him *that* easily.

Maybe there'd be a better opportunity later. "Suit yourself." She'd just have to minimize the damage he caused and wait for her chance. "Just do me a favor and try not to crack *every* branch in the woods when you sneak up on the target."

Taki shrugged. "I didn't know we were close enough that it mattered."

"It *always* matters," said Tala. "What if the target has a scout surveilling *us*?"

"Point taken." Taki smiled and gestured for her to proceed. "Henceforth, I shall be quiet as a winter leaf settling onto a bank of new-fallen snow."

"Whatever you say." Tala rolled her eyes and started walking, resuming her former course. At first, she heard a few of his footfalls behind her, crunching on the carpet of pine needles.

But then, somehow, he did fall silent. She actually couldn't hear him at all and had to look back to be sure he was still there. He gave her a wave and a grin that just went right through her, in a bad way.

Though he was quiet now, she wanted more than ever to cut him loose.

* * *

The Navajo woman had been right about one thing, though she didn't seem to know it. As she and the Japanese-American continued on their way, someone else was indeed conducting surveillance on them.

The figure of a man hovered in the shadow of a great spruce tree, his eyes trained on them through the lenses of compact binoculars. He had needed no device to hear their last argument; their voices had carried exceedingly well through the forest.

He'd listened to every word, and he wasn't impressed. The Navajo, Tala, had shown considerable talent as a spy and warrior in past encounters, but she seemed to be distracted and off her game. As for Taki, the new addition, he was hiding something—secret loyalties or unknown motives, it was impossible to tell.

But if these were the best the 42nd Marines had to offer, perhaps the outcome of the coming struggle would not fall in the Union's favor after all.

Smiling to himself, the man slipped the binoculars into a pouch on his belt. He'd worked alongside the 42nd Marines in the past—also against them—and one thing was certain: they always managed to surprise. He wondered how they would surprise him this time; in fact, he looked forward to it. For someone like him, who'd been just about everywhere and done just about everything, surprises in life could be few and far between.

Like the predator for whom he'd been nicknamed, Wolf thrived on challenges. He lived for the hunt. And he believed that the greater the challenge, the greater the reward.

Pushing out of the shadow of the great spruce, he resumed following Tala and Taki. For now, his work was relatively easy, no challenge at all. But he knew it was about to become more difficult. The bickering scouts from the 42nd had no idea how much danger they were in; they had no idea what monstrous opponents awaited to test their resolve. Wolf knew, because he'd already been to see them and back again.

As for Tala and Taki, they would find out very soon. And that was when Wolf would find out what they were *really* made of.

CHAPTER 7

Southern Kamchatka
17 April 1952
0603 Hours

Taki was starting to wonder if Tala had super-human abilities. She never seemed to tire in her run through the forest; she never broke a sweat, even after she'd been running for miles. Plus, she didn't slow or hesitate in her course, though there was a notable lack of landmarks as far as Taki could see.

But after a while, without explanation, she *did* slow her pace and began to move with greater stealth. Taki peered into the woods up ahead and listened carefully for whatever had tipped her off, but he didn't see or hear anything unusual. Just more of the same sights and sounds he'd noticed for miles: birds singing, bugs buzzing, wind whooshing, and trees creaking.

Tala crouched and crept forward, unsnapping the holster of her double-action Smith and Wesson revolver. Taki followed close behind, scanning his surroundings with every sense for any trace of their quarry.

Just as he was starting to wonder if she was setting him up, getting ready to leave him behind, he heard a distant rumble. He stopped and listened intently, wondering if it might be one of the many active volcanoes on the peninsula, but after a moment, he could tell it wasn't seismic in nature. It was mobile, in fact; the source of the sound was on the move.

And it was getting closer. Once Taki caught up with Tala and stopped to listen again, he could hear the source approaching from the south, the direction of the Shōgunate beachhead. He and Tala were moving due east, the rumbling was headed due north…and they were both about to cross paths.

Tala led him a little farther, then stopped and held up a hand. She stood for a moment with her eyes closed, listening. Then, she opened her eyes and pointed left, in the direction of the rumbling.

At the same instant Taki glimpsed movement, Tala darted behind a tree. He quickly did the same, throwing himself against the trunk of a nearby spruce.

As the rumbling grew louder, Taki leaned out for a look. He saw a column of Japanese soldiers some fifty yards away, moving through a gap between trees—a road, perhaps? There were ten men in brown Shōgunate military uniforms, all marching rigidly, eyes scanning back and forth. When one looked his way, he ducked back behind the tree, heart pounding.

Glancing at Tala, ten feet away, he saw she was also staying out of sight. Her eyes met his, but they were not as cold as always; perhaps, in the danger of the moment, she'd forgotten to put her icy, loathing glare in place. Whatever the reason, she looked at him without hate, without a defiant glint that suggested she was trying to prove something. In that moment, he caught a glimpse of something under the surface, perhaps a different person altogether than he'd guessed existed there.

Or maybe it was a mirage, because he blinked, and it was gone. The same old ice slid back into place, and she looked away. Bracing herself against the tree, she slowly tipped her head out, gazing toward the approaching force.

Taki took a deep breath and followed her example. By now, the column of soldiers was almost past, and he could see the source of the rumbling noise.

A boxy transport with treads like a tank and a sloped prow like a boat was rolling along the dirt track through the woods—an amphibious vehicle. Its armor was painted with a splotchy green, brown, and grey camouflage pattern. There was a cockpit in front with small, tinted windows. Helmeted Japanese gunners manned heavy artillery topside—two long-barreled wide-bore machine guns, plus some kind of launcher that looked capable of discharging armor-piercing shells.

More soldiers marched beside and behind the amphibious vehicle, armed and alert, looking everywhere. Again a soldier gazed in Taki's direction, and again Taki ducked back behind his tree.

The rumbling rose and fell as the vehicle trundled past…but then there was more of the same noise. When Taki looked out, he saw more soldiers, followed by another amphibious craft. There were still more soldiers after that, and then a third identical vehicle. Another group of soldiers brought up the rear.

Taki frowned as he ducked behind the tree again. The task force wasn't a big one; it certainly wasn't big enough to qualify as an invasion. Clearly, the Shōgunate's objective in Kamchatka was something other than conquest.

Assuming, of course, this wasn't just one element of a larger expedition. Also assuming the Shōgunate didn't have any surprises in store.

When the last soldier had passed, and Taki was sure the coast was clear, he left his hiding place. Tala did the same and marched over to meet him.

"Impressions?" Tala gestured in the direction of the convoy. "Observations?" She said it like she didn't expect him to offer either one.

Taki rubbed his chin. "They're moving with purpose. They definitely know where they're going."

"Heading for a precise location. A specific objective." Tala nodded. "Anything else?"

"One thing does bother me, actually." Taki spread his arms wide. "Where the hell are all the *Russians*?"

"Good question." She scowled as she scanned the surrounding forest. "Kamchatka's remote, but I didn't think it was *deserted*. There ought to be a defense force of some kind at least."

"Maybe they're massing farther north? Waiting for the supply line to stretch thin, then striking back with everything they've got?"

Tala's bangs fluttered as she blew out her breath. "I guess we'll find out soon enough. Ready to roll?" She gave him a nasty look out of the corner of her eye.

Taki smirked. "I say full speed ahead."

"Whatever you want, Taki." A cloud of ambivalence settled over her face, as if she didn't even care enough about him to be annoyed. "Just try to keep up. And in case you're wondering, the answer is yes, we still need to stay quiet."

"Thanks for the reminder." Taki didn't bother trying to keep the sarcasm out of his voice. He made a little bow and gestured in the direction of the convoy. "After you, Aponi."

Tala shrugged and moved off through the trees, raven tresses bouncing against her back. Taki watched her for a moment, then forcefully shook his head when he realized what he was doing. All he needed was for her to catch him admiring the curves of her body, which were visible even through her fatigues. A woman like that, with the personality of a rattlesnake, wasn't likely to cut him any slack.

It would be best, he decided, as he ran to catch up with her, if he never thought of this moment again.

* * *

When the convoy emerged from the forest, Hiruko, at the head of the line, was the first to march out into the meadow.

That wasn't a bad thing at all. As he stood there, surrounded by wildflowers, he was able to forget, if only briefly, that he was part of a military operation. He was able to empty his mind of the mysterious unease that had been troubling him. He could just look around at the bobbing heads of flowers flashing in the bright morning light, painted in shades of yellow, red, and blue. Their fragrance washed over him, bathing him in sweet perfume; he couldn't help breathing deep and smiling.

A serpentine stream of crystal clear water trickled through the meadow's heart. On the far side, a mile or so distant, scattered fir, pine, and spruce trees marked the foothills of a mountain range. The forest thickened as the hills turned to mountains, but the mountains fell bare as they ascended like pyramids into the sapphire sky.

The snow-capped peaks reminded Hiruko of Mount Fuji back

home. At the same time, he felt almost overwhelmed by the vastness stretching out before him. *Nippon* was a land of mountains, but few expanses. Here was a place of enormity, where nature was unconstrained.

The scenery stirred his heart. He felt the beginnings of a poem come upon him, like the memory of a dream.

> *The falcon's wing brushes sun-dappled petals,*
> *Catches the twisting breeze with rippling feathers,*
> *And rises, intending never again to touch ground*
> *In this lifetime or the next, no matter how perfect*
> *The mountain peak, meadow, or lover.*

Suddenly, his reverie was shattered by a ruckus behind him. He turned in time to see the hatch slam open on the side of one of the amphibious vehicles. Then the Daimyō burst out, crushing patches of wildflowers with his booted feet.

Hiruko shivered when he saw who emerged from the vehicle next. It was the man he'd glimpsed behind the curtain at the Shōgun's rally, the Reich agent in the black overcoat. He must've been hidden away or on another ship on the trip out; Hiruko hadn't seen him and hadn't expected him to be part of the expedition.

Now, not only was the Reich officer along for the mission, but he and the Daimyō were approaching Hiruko. They marched toward him with hands clasped behind their backs, engaged in conversation.

Hiruko spun and straightened, standing at attention. His mind raced as he wondered what the Daimyō and the Reich officer could possibly want with him. Had he done something wrong? Had he done something right?

Their footsteps and voices grew closer…and then they passed him. They walked ten yards farther into the meadow, leaving Hiruko to feel a wave of relief, followed by a tide of curiosity. He watched and listened to the two men as they stood and gazed out at the meadow and mountains. The wind carried their conversation back to him; they both spoke German—not that it mattered, given Hiruko's linguistic training.

"We have run out of dirt road," said the Daimyō. "Tell me, where do we go next, *Marquis Generalleutnant* Von Heïzinger?"

"Can't you feel it, Minamoto?" Von Heïzinger's voice was a raspy croak, like the voice Hiruko imagined a dead man might possess. "Out there, across the miles, humming and pulsating like Satan's own fevered brain?"

"No," said the Daimyō. "I do not feel it."

"Of course you don't, because you don't have *this*." He held up his left hand and pulled off his black leather glove, revealing a hand as pale and rubbery-looking as tofu. On his index finger, he wore a gold ring with a glittering crimson crystal. "The *Orbis Christus*. It grows warmer as our prize grows closer." Von Heïzinger stuffed his glove in a pocket of his overcoat. "Already it is much warmer than it was aboard ship." He lovingly twisted the ring from side to side on his gnarled finger.

"Incredible." The Daimyō did not sound impressed. "Now does this 'feeling' tell you which specific route we should follow?" He stroked his pencil-thin mustache as he turned from right to left, scanning the landscape. "Or might a *map* help us navigate this foreign terrain?"

Reaching into the folds of his overcoat, Von Heïzinger drew out a black velvet pouch over a foot in length. Holding it next to the Daimyō, he loosened the drawstring and pulled down the neck of the pouch.

He uncovered something gleaming white and roughly cylindrical, almost as thick around as Hiruko's arm. Hiruko glimpsed some kind of dark etchings cut into the surface, a web of intricate line work, before the Daimyō leaned in closer and blocked his view.

"We are here," said Von Heïzinger as he and the Daimyō huddled over the white object. "At the base of the mountains. We will follow this pass, here, which will lead us to the Valley of Geysers."

"What kind of map *is* this?" The Daimyō sounded puzzled. "It looks like a scrimshaw carving."

"It is the first map, carved by the hand of the very man who discovered Kamchatka." Von Heïzinger raised the object to eye level and turned it slowly like a precious gem. "Vitus Bering himself."

The Daimyō scowled, but he did not tear his eyes from the object. Free of the black velvet pouch, it was nearly two feet long. It was shaped like a giant tooth, broad at one end and coming to a sharp point at the other. "Is that so?"

Von Heïzinger nodded. "The man who discovered Kamchatka and the Bering Strait carved this map before his death. It was only recently uncovered, and then acquired by agents of the Reich."

"You are certain of its provenance?" The Daimyō rubbed the patch of beard under his lower lip and leaned closer. "Its origins and accuracy are beyond question?"

"A horde of experts have sworn it. And *this* confirms it." When he held his ring near the object, the jewel in the setting glowed with a glittering crimson light.

Hiruko gazed at it, mesmerized. He wondered what properties the ring and object must have to react the way they did—or if the cause was some kind of magic trick.

The Daimyō had concerns of his own about the map's nature. "You never did answer my question, Marquis Generalleutnant. This map…is it some kind of scrimshaw?"

"I should think it obvious."

"But the ivory on which it's carved…" The Daimyō reached up to touch the object. "…it doesn't look like a fossil…but I've never seen a tooth that large from a *non-extinct* species of beast."

"Then perhaps there are species you haven't met yet." He carefully slipped the map back into its black velvet pouch. "Perhaps the world is more *interesting* than you know."

"I doubt it." The Daimyō shook his head and stared into the distance. "So it's through the pass then? That's where we're headed?"

"I will lead us to our objective." Von Heïzinger pulled his black leather glove from his overcoat pocket and tugged it onto his pasty hand. "On one condition."

The Daimyō planted his fists on his hips and glared at the generalleutnant. "What condition is that?"

"I need a warm body." Von Heïzinger turned and fixed his icy gaze on Hiruko. "That one will do."

Hiruko's eyes flashed wide. His blood froze in his veins as Von Heïzinger and the Daimyō focused their undivided attention upon him.

* * *

Tala slipped between the trees with great care, easing up to the edge of the forest. Taki, to her surprise, was moving equally quietly not far behind her; perhaps she'd underestimated his stealth capabilities.

Breathing slowly and evenly, Tala glided between branches and twigs, staying in complete control at all times. As she drew closer to the forest's edge, she heard the voices of men speaking Japanese. She heard engines idling, the occasional miss of a piston, doors slamming open and shut—the sounds of the three amphibious vehicles that had rolled out of the woods and parked in the meadow beyond.

Why had the convoy stopped? Was there a problem? A weakness that could be exploited? Any change in pattern could be important enough to observe.

So Tala got as close as she could to the tree line and the convoy while staying far enough off to the side that she was clear of the soldiers straggling into the woods to relieve themselves. She found a good vantage point in the brush and got ready to hunker down for the duration.

That was when she got the biggest shock she'd had all day. That was when she saw *him*.

She gasped in surprise. Nowhere in any briefing had she been warned that *he* might appear. But maybe she should have known; he had a way of turning up.

"What's going on?" Taki scooted up and crouched beside her, taking in the convoy at rest in the meadow. He kept his voice to a barely audible whisper. "What do you see?"

"Bad news." Tala didn't need binoculars to recognize the distant figure, but she pulled them out anyway. She zeroed in and focused, verifying beyond a doubt that what she thought she saw was true. "The Japanese brought along a guest." She handed the binoculars to Taki. "A non-Shōgunate guest."

Taki had a look and blew out his breath in a faint almost-whistle. "Is that who I think it is?"

"If you think it's Marquis Generalleutnant Hermann Von Heïzinger, one of the wickedest SOBs to ever walk the face of the Earth…" Tala glared from her hiding place, wishing she had her hands around the Reich monster's throat. "…then give yourself a kewpie doll."

* * *

"What is your name?" The generalleutnant strolled toward Hiruko, gazing appraisingly from the shadows of his cap's black leather brim.

When Hiruko didn't speak right away, the Daimyō answered for him. "Jōtōhei Hiruko Orochi of the Emperor's Royal Guard."

A bright glint flickered in Von Heïzinger's left eye. "Orochi, is it?" He continued to speak German as he addressed Hiruko. Had he been briefed about Hiruko's training as a linguist? "Your services are required, Orochi." His hand flashed out and grabbed Hiruko's wrist. "Here is what you must do: stand right here until you see them."

Hiruko swallowed hard. Words came to his lips, though he feared they could be his last. "Th-them who, sir?"

"My associate, Karl Zermann." Von Heïzinger's lips pulled back from his grey teeth and purple gums as he attempted a smile. His breath was as putrid as rotting flesh. "He and his blue-skinned 'friend,' Itami, are out hunting. They will come here when they are finished."

"Itami's with Zermann?" The Daimyō sounded surprised. "But I sent him to reconnoiter alone."

"A change of plan, Minamoto." Von Heïzinger sounded amused, as if there were an inside joke that only he understood. "The two of them have much in common. They are drawn to each other."

Hiruko shivered. Something in Von Heïzinger's voice made his skin crawl. Hearing him up close was much more unnerving than hearing him from a distance; up close, he sounded as much like a cadaver as he looked. There was a gurgle at the low end of his raspy croak, as if something were loose—decaying, perhaps—in his throat. Hiruko heard a soft rattle, too, every time he took a breath, like air wheezing through holes in a punctured windpipe or lung.

"Understood, Orochi?" asked Von Heïzinger. "You will wait here for Zermann and Itami. They don't know our chosen route, and they don't have radios. It will be up to you to point them in the right direction."

Hiruko nodded. "Yes, sir."

Von Heïzinger let go of Hiruko's wrist and turned away. He started to take a step, then stopped. "Ah. There's just one more thing."

With speed that didn't seem possible for such an old man, Von Heïzinger reached inside his coat and yanked a dagger from a sheath on his belt. The silver blade gleamed in his grip as he swung it around. Then Von Heïzinger suddenly grabbed Hiruko's wrist again and slashed the blade across the palm of his hand before he could tear it away. Hiruko cried out in pain and surprise. He lashed out with his free arm to block the next stroke.

But it never came. Von Heïzinger let go of him as quickly as he'd grabbed and cut him.

As Hiruko quickly backed away, Von Heïzinger wiped the knife on his overcoat. "Now I can be certain Zermann will find you. That dog can catch the scent of blood from miles away like a shark."

Hiruko clutched his wrist, watching the blood ooze out of the gash. He didn't dare utter a word of complaint, not with both the Daimyō and Von Heïzinger staring him in the face.

Von Heïzinger clapped his gloved hands together. "Enough of this. Let's get moving."

As Von Heïzinger marched off toward the convoy, the Daimyō came to Hiruko's side. "You will be all right." He nodded. "As you wait, consider the glory you are helping to bring to the Shōgunate by this small sacrifice." His voice had a sarcastic edge. Hiruko could tell he didn't mean what he said.

"Yes, *Rikugan Chūjō*." The words meant "Lieutenant General." Hiruko used them to show respect to the Daimyō, though in truth, he wasn't feeling very respectful at that moment. He knew the Daimyō must have had his reasons for not stopping Von Heïzinger from cutting him, but still. Hiruko had never thought he'd see the day when a Shōgunate officer would stand by and let a foreigner attack one of his men.

The Daimyō shook his head and cast a sour look in Von Heïzinger direction. "We will see you soon, Orochi." He pointed toward the mountain pass in the distance. "That way, yes?"

"*Hai.*" Hiruko's nod was short and sharp. He would do his duty, as always, for the Shōgunate he loved…not that he would *like* it.

The Daimyō smiled faintly, then he spun on his heel and marched off to the convoy.

Once everyone was back in formation—everyone but Hiruko—the convoy set off across the meadow. The soldiers and amphibious vehicles moved past, the men staring with obvious relief as they left Hiruko standing there. After all, it was better him than them, wasn't it?

Though from the looks on some of their faces, perhaps they'd arrived at the next logical possibility: that one of them could be the man left behind next time.

* * *

Taki adjusted his binoculars, changing focus from the convoy to the man called Hiruko. "They're just leaving him there," he whispered. From his hiding place lying flat in the brush at the edge of the woods, he watched Hiruko gazing at the convoy pulling away. "Poor guy."

Tala grunted and pushed herself up on her knees beside him. "Von Heïzinger was right about Zermann. Eventually, he'll sniff out that blood and come running. But who's this 'Itami'?"

Taki had been translating the conversation between Von Heïzinger and Iroh Minamoto—as much as he could catch from reading lips—but he hadn't gotten everything. "Someone like Zermann, I guess. Von Heïzinger called him Zermann's 'blue-skinned friend.' At least I think that's what he said."

"Someone like Zermann. Just what we need." Tala shook her head disgustedly. "We need to call this in."

"Absolutely." Taki got up on his knees and slid the binoculars into his shirt pocket. Then he pulled the walkie-talkie from his belt and switched it on. Pressing a button to open the channel, he spoke into the microphone set into the faceplate. "Victor Tango to Whiskey Foxtrot, over."

There was a slight pause and then, "Go ahead, Victor Tango." The voice from the speaker was MacNeal's.

"Von Heïzinger and Zermann are in-country," said Taki. "The Reich has joined the party."

There was a pause. "Please confirm, Victor Tango. Did you say Von Heïzinger and Zermann?"

"Roger that," said Taki. "Also someone called 'Itami.' Someone with, uh…blue skin."

"Did you say 'blue skin'?" asked MacNeal. "Are you sure about that?"

"Maybe I got that part wrong." He shrugged, though MacNeal couldn't see it. "Could be a Zermann-level threat, though."

"Damn." Another pause. "Roger that, Victor Tango."

"We are in pursuit," said Taki. "Victor Tango out."

"Whiskey Foxtrot out," said MacNeal, and then his voice was replaced with static.

Taki switched off the radio and put it away. "We'd better get moving if we want to catch up with the convoy."

"This wide open space presents a problem." Tala gestured at the meadow. "We'll have to stick to the tree line and circle around to stay out of sight. At least until we reach the foothills."

Taki nodded grimly. "We'll need to double time it."

"All right then." Tala rose. "Try and keep up."

CHAPTER 8

Southern Kamchatka
17 April 1952
0833 Hours

After Taki's last check-in by radio, Major MacNeal kept Fireteam Bravo moving at a brisk pace through the forest. There were four men in the fireteam arranged in a wedge formation—one ahead, three spread out behind. The other two fireteams—Alpha, commanded by Brown, and Charlie—flanked Bravo from ten yards out on either side.

For the moment, things were quiet. MacNeal could have been walking through a pine forest back home; all he could hear were chirping birds, chattering squirrels, sighing wind, and the soft footsteps of his team.

As he and the three Alpha Commandos of Fireteam Bravo marched along, he let himself imagine, just for a moment, that he was back home in Maine. It did him some good to take a brief mental vacation, to let himself drift to a simpler, safer place. He deserved it; he might not make it back to Portland for a long time…if ever. At least he could daydream that the branches of those pines and firs and spruce, which looked just like the ones back home, were those very same branches, thousands of miles from Kamchatka. At least he could pretend he was having lobster rolls and blueberry pie for dinner, served by a beautiful New England girl with a special smile just for him.

Naturally, it couldn't last. The sound of gunfire snapped him back to reality. It was the sound of Brown's flash machine gun, blasting away at three o'clock—the direction of Fireteam Alpha.

MacNeal's hand shot up, and his commandos froze. He started to give the signal to form on Fireteam Alpha.

But before he could finish the signal, he heard more gunfire from a different direction. This time, it was coming from nine o'clock, from the vicinity of Fireteam Charlie.

MacNeal, who only moments ago had imagined he was taking a nature hike in Maine, switched smoothly into warrior mode. Two teams in the formation were under attack, and he had to make a decision: should he help one, help the other, or split his team and send half in either direction?

The sound of a man's anguished scream from the direction of Fireteam Charlie rang out amid the gunfire. He kept screaming, as if something was tearing him to pieces.

"Hamilton, Beaudreau—reinforce Alpha Team." The two men were off and running before he finished his sentence. "Shankar, you're with me."

The screaming continued as MacNeal and Shankar bolted toward Fireteam Charlie. There was no need for stealth anymore; speed and brute force were the only requirements.

Adrenaline pumping, MacNeal burst through the brush and got his first clear look at what was happening. He was a hardened combat veteran—more than that, he was special ops, accustomed to bizarre missions tinged with the occult, though he still had a hard time believing it—but what he saw was enough to startle even him.

Two Alpha Commandos stood with their backs to him, firing flash-guns at a massive figure looming twenty feet away. The figure looked like some kind of monster, with pale horns jutting from his forehead. Apparently, Taki's intel about Zermann's "blue-skinned friend" hadn't been so crazy after all, because there it was, plain as day: the creature had bright blue skin.

He was at least six and a half feet tall, not counting the horns. He wore brown pants and black boots and the shredded remnants of what looked like had once been a hooded black cloak. Vast tracts of bulging muscle rippled as he lifted a monstrous club—nearly as long as he was tall—and brought it down so hard the ground shook.

He brought it down with crushing force onto an Alpha Commando, the one who'd been screaming. At which point, the screaming stopped.

The blue beast grunted as he lifted the club, which was as big around as a utility pole. It was dripping with blood from the commando's mashed body.

MacNeal, Shankar, and the surviving commandos of Fireteam Charlie fired round after round at the creature. Several caught him square in the chest, and he staggered back. Sapphire blood bubbled from the wounds.

But instead of collapsing, the blue-skinned monstrosity swung the club like a baseball bat, howling a single word so loud it drowned out the gunshots. "*Uchitoru!*"

MacNeal recognized the word from his briefings before the mission. It meant "kill" in Japanese.

Not that it mattered when he charged headlong toward the two commandos. They never quit firing; neither did MacNeal and Shankar.

And then the blue-skinned monster was upon them. With one swing of his mighty club, he knocked the flash-guns out of the commandos' hands, sending them flying. His next swings bashed their heads in and sent them sprawling at his feet. He did it all with what looked like hardly any effort. The tough-as-nails, armed-to-the-teeth Alpha Commandos of the 42nd Marines might as well have been rag dolls to him.

Gritting his teeth, MacNeal poured more rounds at the blue beast. The horn-headed mountain of muscle howled as bullets sank into his flesh, drawing more of the sapphire blood. Then, he spun and glared at MacNeal.

MacNeal stood there and kept shooting. When the creature began to stomp toward him, he reached for a grenade.

MacNeal bit down on the pin and jerked it free with his teeth. Still firing his flash-gun, he hauled the grenade back and pitched it at the monster.

The grenade blew when it hit the ground at the great beast's feet. The blast blew him backward; he stayed on his feet but went reeling over the commandos' corpses.

MacNeal grinned a death's head grin and reached for another grenade. Maybe he had a chance after all.

The creature howled with rage and pain. He staggered to a stop and stood wobbling in place, shaking his head hard as if to clear the fog. Before he could marshal his resources, MacNeal lobbed a second grenade at him.

Like the first grenade, this one didn't blow the beast to pieces, but it did stun him. He stumbled and howled and wagged his head, fighting to shake off the shock.

MacNeal reached for a third grenade from his belt, planning to press the advantage. Before he could pull the pin, though, the monster stopped reeling and swung up a hand. He aimed it in MacNeal's direction with fingers spread wide, black nails glistening like obsidian.

Suddenly, waves of blistering pain ripped through MacNeal. The grenade dropped from his grip, pin intact, and so did the flash-gun. Then MacNeal himself dropped, slumping to the ground. Shankar did exactly the same beside him.

MacNeal writhed in agony, biting back screams. He felt like he was being clawed open from the inside out; he truly thought he was being gutted like a fish, literally torn to shreds. From the sound of Shankar's howling, he felt the same way.

MacNeal's mind flared into a white-hot blank, focused only on the pain inside him…even as the creature stalked toward him, leering cruelly.

It took everything MacNeal had to keep from screaming. The pain grew stronger with every passing second. The closer the blue beast got, the more the pain intensified.

The creature shouted something in Japanese, and then laughed.

MacNeal was still oblivious, thrashing in the dirt and pine needles, clutching his head. All he wanted was for the pain to end, whatever it took.

The creature seemed prepared to make that happen. His giant club dragged on the ground, leaving a blood-streaked trail.

The pain doubled. MacNeal seized up, his body arching off the ground.

In a sudden flash of movement, the creature swung up the club and brought it down hard, bashing in Shankar's head. Then, he shuffled closer to MacNeal and raised the club again.

Suddenly, there was a loud crackling noise from somewhere nearby. The beast paused with the club overhead and looked right, in the direction of the sound.

At that instant, a sizzling bolt of bright blue energy blasted into him, like horizontal lightning coursing through the woods. The bolt slammed him aside, kicking the club from his hands and hurling him off his feet and away from MacNeal.

As soon as the blast struck, the pain in MacNeal's body switched off. He slumped, panting and soaked with sweat, reeling from the assault he'd just endured.

Another bolt of energy sizzled past overhead. MacNeal followed its path to the blue-skinned monster, ten yards away. The beast stood his ground for an instant, roaring like a lion, letting the blazing spike of lightning splash off his chest…and then he tumbled backward. He crashed into a patch of brush, smoking from the attack.

MacNeal heard footsteps approaching from the other direction. He turned his head to see a beautiful woman sprinting toward him carrying a long scepter topped with a circular tube that was sparking with pale blue energy. Blond and slim, the woman was clad in shades of brown and a ruddy red: brown helmet, wine-red uniform jacket, brown pants, crimson leggings. The red was so dark and dirty she was hard to see in the shades of the forest. On her left arm she wore a metal-plated gauntlet studded with glass power packs the size of votive candles, glowing with the same blue energy seething through the scepter's circular tube.

As she hurried up to MacNeal, she kept the scepter aimed in the creature's direction. Her eyes kept flicking that way, too, watching for renewed danger.

The first words out of her mouth were Russian. MacNeal knew the language; he'd studied it some and learned more in the field out of necessity, though he didn't speak it as fluently as he would have liked.

When he frowned and shook his head, she got the idea and switched to English. "I said are you all right?" MacNeal nodded, and she looked away. "Stay here!" Then she braced herself and fired another scepter blast toward the creature.

As MacNeal watched, she gestured with the gauntlet, flickering her fingers as if she were playing an invisible piano. Immediately, a three-foot-tall mechanical pod skittered past on three legs, humming and clicking, heading for the creature. The woman flickered her fingers again, and another pod skittered past, making the same sounds. Both pods emitted the same blue glow as the woman's scepter and gauntlet.

As MacNeal pushed himself to a sitting position, he remembered what the pods were called: *voïvodes*. He knew them well from past experience—deadly robotic constructs that served the Russian Matriarchy's Zor'ka. No one else had been known to command them... at least until now. Somehow, the woman's gauntlet gave her power over them.

And she knew how to put it to good use. When the voïvodes moved in on the blue-skinned creature, one pod zapped him with blasts of crackling energy; the other shot out a gleaming, electrified blade and spun around at high speed, slashing at the creature's calf muscles.

As the voïvodes hammered the creature with synchronized strikes, the woman marched over to join them. She unleashed blast after blast from her scepter, pumping fresh bolts of bright blue power at the horned monstrosity.

The creature tried in vain to swat away the searing blasts. Roaring, he kicked at the knife-wielding voïvode, but the automaton whizzed just out of reach. He tried to lunge at the other voïvode, but its concentrated energy beam kept him at a distance.

Finally, with one last howl of rage, the creature whirled, grabbed his massive club from the ground, and loped off into the forest, his hide smoking, his calf bleeding sapphire.

The woman got off a final shot, then wiggled the fingers of the gauntlet. Her voïvodes responded by skittering after the fleeing beast on their segmented triple legs.

Just as the mechanisms gave chase, MacNeal heard crackling sounds from the woods around him. Suddenly, a squad of soldiers emerged from the trees, clad in fur hats, black gas masks, and flowing ruddy red overcoats. MacNeal counted ten in all, each armed with a carbine rifle or flamethrower.

The soldiers converged on him quickly, weapons at the ready.

MacNeal wasn't sure what to expect; technically, the Union and Matriarchy were allies, but treaties like UMTOMA seldom meant much in back country places like Kamchatka.

Tensing, he thought of moves he could make to fight back. He was still in a daze, but he'd been in worse shape in tighter spots and lived to tell about it. Carefully sizing up the closest red-coated soldier, he got his knees under him, then pushed himself up into a crouch.

That was when the woman with the scepter came back around. "*Privyet.*" It was Russian for "hello." She held the scepter with her gauntleted left hand and reached out to him with her right. "My name is Oksana Gusarenko."

MacNeal nodded. "*Spaceba.*" *Thank you.* He took her hand. "I'm Major John MacNeal of the 42nd Marine Special Forces."

She helped him to his feet. Meanwhile, the red-coated soldiers formed a ring around them, watching the woods for signs of trouble from behind the smoked lenses of their gas masks.

MacNeal didn't have time to stand around. "I need to get to my other team." Heart racing, he pushed through the ring of Russian soldiers and found his flash-gun where he'd dropped it on the ground. Scooping up the gun, he ran off into the woods, not wanting to waste another moment with lives at stake.

CHAPTER 9

Southern Kamchatka
17 April 1952
0905 Hours

Hiruko stood and waited in the meadow, as ordered, for Itami and Zermann. His hand oozed blood, but he was afraid to dress the wound; he wasn't sure if it might interfere with Zermann's ability to home in on the scent.

As he gazed out over the wildflowers, they didn't seem as beautiful as they had before. The sun was just as bright, the colors just as vivid…but he couldn't appreciate them. Everything seemed darker to him now.

He was standing alone and bleeding, serving as bait for a pair of monsters. They could do just about anything to him and get away with it. If they returned to the convoy without him and claimed they'd never found him, who would complain?

Hiruko understood the excesses of wartime, the lengths men would go to in pursuit of victory. Further, he knew and accepted his station in life; he understood that he was expendable in defense of the Shōgunate's interests.

But this duty cast a long shadow on his soul. The casual way Von Heïzinger had slashed his hand and left him in the meadow like an animal carcass…it felt twisted and cruel. It felt inhumane.

Back in Tokyo, at the Shōgun's speech, he had felt a tug on his heart, a sense of unease. When he'd first glimpsed Von Heïzinger and Zermann behind the curtain, conferring with the Shōgun, that tug had intensified. Now, it was stronger than ever.

Hiruko's feet grew tired, and he settled down to sit cross-legged among the wildflowers. He took off his cap and stuffed it in his jacket pocket, then combed his fingers through his jet black hair.

He frowned up at the bright blue sky, wondering how long the monsters would take to find him…wondering, when they finally did, if they might slaughter him for sport…

And he wondered, if he did die at their hands, if his sacrifice would make any difference at all to the Shōgunate to which he was dedicated and the *Nippon* he so loved.

* * *

MacNeal made a beeline for the last known position of Fireteam Alpha.

He prepared himself for the worst. More than that, he prepared to accept it and move on to complete the mission, whatever it took. He would sacrifice more if need be, sacrifice everyone dear to him and even himself. All that mattered was stopping the Japanese from seizing their objective, whatever it was, and unleashing it on the world.

When he reached the spot where Fireteam Alpha should've been, he stopped. Oksana, who'd been following him, stopped beside him and pointed right. "There." She indicated a mass of grey stone through the feathery hemlock branches. Without a word, MacNeal broke into a dead run.

It was then that he heard voices calling out—all of them speaking Russian. No gunfire, though, and no screams. Whatever action had happened here, it was over.

MacNeal charged through the hemlocks with Oksana at his heels. As branches parted around him, he saw the stone was part of a for-mation, a ridge of upthrust granite pushing six feet at its highest point. It must have seemed like a perfect natural shield, a defensible position…but had it been enough to save any lives?

Heart hammering like a boxer's fist against his ribs, he bolted toward the stone outcropping. Men walked out from behind it, looking his way—but every one of them was a Russian soldier. There wasn't a Union Marine in sight.

Oksana yelled something, and a tall, bald soldier with a black mustache and goatee shouted back. Unlike the other men, he didn't wear a fur hat or gas mask; his voice was firm, his bearing authoritative.

Holding out a hand, he moved to intercept MacNeal. Though MacNeal had him pegged as an officer, he wasn't about to submit. He plowed right past, knocking the man's hand away like a swinging door at an Old West saloon.

The bald officer hollered behind him, but MacNeal kept going. He had to know, one way or the other, what had happened to his men. He had to see for himself and make peace with the outcome.

As he hurtled around the formation, he held his breath. What had happened to Fireteam Alpha? What about the two men he'd dispatched from his own Fireteam Bravo? Had he sent them to their deaths?

The answer surprised him. He'd been expecting the worst. Yet there they were, all six of his people, milling around behind the stone ridge.

A huge grin spread over his face. He couldn't stop it. Neither could Sergeant Brown, the first to see him coming. "Major!" Brown waved the barrel of his flash machine gun. "Good to see you, sir!"

MacNeal's grin faded as he marched over to the group. "What's the debrief, Boomer?"

"It was Zermann, sir. Our old scar-faced buddy." Brown shook his head ruefully. "Bastard gave us a hell of a fight. We'd all be dead right now if not for the cover." He nodded at the rocky outcropping. "Plus the fact that that crazy Luger of his seemed to be on the fritz."

"The one he calls 'Doom'?" asked MacNeal.

Brown nodded. "It almost never misses, right? Except this time, those weird glowing bullets went every which way. A couple of near-hits was the best he could manage."

MacNeal narrowed his eyes. "That's hard to believe."

"Lucky for us, though," said Brown. "Between Doom misfiring

and the good cover, we hung in long enough for the reinforcements to get here." He looked back over his shoulder at a cluster of Russian soldiers standing nearby, then returned his gaze to MacNeal. "What about Fireteam Charlie, sir?"

MacNeal set his jaw. "No survivors."

Beaudreau, one of the men he'd sent from Fireteam Bravo to reinforce Brown's group, cleared his throat. "Not even Shankar?"

"Just me." MacNeal felt sick in the pit of his stomach as he said it.

Beaudreau's face fell. "Okay." The lanky Cajun sharpshooter had been Shankar's best friend.

Brown let out a low whistle. "What kind of monster are we talking about here?"

"It looks like a blue-skinned devil. Nothing but muscle and horns." He stuck out a finger like a horn from his right temple. "High tolerance for bullets. Took a lot of rounds and walked away."

"No kidding." Brown was a no-nonsense kind of guy, but he'd been with the 42nd long enough to see his share of unbelievable things. And of course, MacNeal had earned his trust a hundred times over, so he knew he'd never lie to him. "How'd you and the Russians take it down?"

"We didn't," said MacNeal. "They drove him off with some kind of energy rod, but he's still at large."

Brown frowned and spat on the ground. The other men looked around nervously, hands tightening on their guns. "So how do we take it out? You think the Matriarchy folks will provide backup?" He nodded toward the Russian soldiers.

Just then, Oksana rounded the corner of the formation. "First of all, don't call us 'Matriarchy.'" She stopped beside MacNeal and squared her shoulders, sticking her chin out. "Second of all, we are not here to be your 'backup.'" She shrugged. "But we might still be interested in making you a proposition."

* * *

The sun drifted behind a cloud. The wind picked up, then died down. Hiruko thought he heard Itami and Zermann approaching.

He stayed sitting among the wildflowers, watching the woods. Part of him didn't want to be found; he was afraid of what would happen when he and the creatures were alone together in the meadow.

His worry was so distracting, he hadn't made any progress on the poem he'd started, though he'd had plenty of time to himself in that scenic setting. He'd dug and reached for feelings and words, straining to find the next lines, to no avail. He'd finally given up when he heard the sounds of sticks cracking and branches rustling in the woods.

Moments later, a dark figure emerged from the tree line. His heart raced as he watched it amble from the shadows into the sunlight.

Only then did he realize it was neither Itami nor Zermann... not that his heart slowed down any at the realization. Because the truth was, the danger was no less great; if anything, it might have been greater.

The figure approaching from the forest was a huge bear with dark brown fur. It wasn't the kind of bear you might find in a circus, either; this one was massive, with muscles like giant pistons pumping under its fur coat. Hiruko knew the type from books he'd read, and he knew further how deadly it could be.

It was a Kamchatka brown bear, and it was coming straight for him.

It was probably attracted by the smell of the blood from the gash in his hand. It was a possibility Von Heïzinger hadn't mentioned: the same bait put out for Itami and Zermann could attract other predators, as well.

So now what? Hiruko's rifle lay in his lap, loaded and ready. He knew he could get off a shot, but would it be enough? What if the bear was fast and fearless enough to charge him before he could crank off the next round?

But if he waited till the bear was so close his first shot couldn't miss, Hiruko would have zero chance at a second shot if he needed it. Neither choice was perfect.

Slowly, he raised the rifle from his lap and eased the stock against his shoulder. He swung the barrel left until he caught the animal in the gunsight. Then, holding his breath, he slid his finger around the trigger.

The bear kept lumbering toward him. The power in its massive body, magnified by the gunsight's lens, was clearly immense. Hiruko had no doubt the animal could tear him to shreds with little trouble.

Cool sweat trickled down his back and sides as he waited for the perfect shot. The bear lumbered closer…closer…its spade of a skull fixed in the heart of the gunsight.

Hiruko took another breath and pulled the trigger. And nothing happened.

His heart skipped a beat, and he squeezed the trigger again. Still, the gun did not fire. The mechanism was jammed.

And the bear was still coming. It didn't slow its pace at all; if anything, it moved a little faster.

Hiruko pulled the trigger again, with the same result as before. Then, swallowing hard, he gently placed the rifle across his lap and tried to force himself to relax. It was too late to leap up and run; he could never get away from that fur-covered freight train. His only hope now might be to appear as neither rival nor prey, to achieve perfect stillness and present a harmonious profile to the approaching beast.

In spite of his hammering heart and fluttering nerves, he had to attain a state of calm…all while making peace with the idea that he might very well become food for the beast in a matter of moments.

* * *

"All right." MacNeal slung his flash-gun over his shoulder and crossed his arms over his chest. "What's this proposition of yours?"

Oksana removed her padded helmet. "Your manpower has been…depleted. We, in turn, lack information related to the Japanese incursion." Her pale blond hair was mostly matted down, but the tips flittered in the breeze. "Both our forces could benefit from a conditional alliance."

MacNeal was struck by her delicate features and fair complexion; she looked fragile as a china doll, in sharp contrast to the way she'd handled herself on the battlefield. "Conditional in what way?"

"Conditional in that it does not imply a permanent arrangement." Oksana raised an eyebrow. "We are not yet certain we wish to tie our future to the Union's fortunes."

Brown chose that moment to interject. "Isn't that like closing the barn door *after* the horses ran out? Or are you so cut off out here, you didn't know we already have a treaty with Russia?"

Oksana tapped her chin with a fingertip. "Tell me. Was the *New Guard* included among the signatories of UMTOMA?"

Brown frowned. "'New Guard'? Doesn't ring a bell. Who are they?"

"*We* are." Oksana spread her arms. The bald, goateed officer who'd tried to stop MacNeal marched around the outcropping, and she gestured at him, too. "All of us. We seek change in the Motherland. We stand against the excesses and failures of the current regime."

MacNeal nodded. "Which is how you ended up out here in the wilderness."

"Just so." Oksana smiled grimly. "But this exile might yet backfire on the powers behind the throne. And perhaps the Union as well as the New Guard may benefit from what we find here."

MacNeal didn't need to think about it. He'd just lost five men, and the blue creature might well take the rest of them if they crossed paths again. He couldn't see a way for his team to complete their mission without the New Guard's manpower and weaponry.

But he knew better than to let them think he couldn't do without them. "My men and I need to discuss this." He drew Brown aside, and the others followed. "We'll let you know."

Oksana, to her credit, did not press him. "The New Guard awaits your decision." With that, she strode to intercept her officer, who was scowling up a storm. He kept pointing at MacNeal's group, but Oksana just patted his shoulder and led him away, back around the outcropping.

MacNeal proceeded to talk to his men as if he hadn't already made up his mind. They discussed the possible alliance, bringing up pros and cons, considering the alternatives. They even argued.

And after a while, they came to the same decision he'd already made.

* * *

The bear slowed its pace as it closed in on Hiruko. It stopped ten feet away and stood up straight on its hind legs, roaring at the sky.

But Hiruko did not flinch. He sat cross-legged among the wildflowers, keeping his mind empty and his body perfectly still. His heart pounded—how could it not?—but he managed to keep from jerking or jolting at the terrifying sight of nine feet of brown bear towering over him.

The bear roared again, baring its white teeth and bright pink tongue and throat. Again, Hiruko remained perfectly still. He imagined he was somewhere else, far away, and the bear could not hurt him. The trick helped, mostly…though a big part of him still cowered in sheer mortal terror.

With one last roar, the bear dropped back down on all fours. It sniffed at the air and cocked its head sideways as if puzzled.

Hiruko sniffed, too, and immediately wished he hadn't. Now that the bear was so close, its smell was overwhelming—so rank, it made his eyes water. Whatever musk it gave off was like a cloud of noxious gas on the battlefield, wafting over the trenches.

Still sniffing, the beast nosed closer, its glossy black eyes fixed on Hiruko's face. Its odor grew steadily worse, and Hiruko realized that smell alone might be his undoing. He could feel his gag reflex twitching; he thought he might throw up before much longer.

The bear pushed closer still. Its head, with those monstrous teeth, was only four feet away…then three…then two.

It took every bit of willpower Hiruko could muster not to choke on the beast's stench. It took all his strength not to try to scramble away and run for his life.

Burrowing deeper into himself, he used one technique after another to try to calm his mind. He thought of his body as sunlight and air, impervious to swipes of the great beast's black claws. He imagined his body as solid stone, able to shatter the beast's teeth like shards of glass.

Each technique did its part to help him stay calm, but the effects didn't last. All of them fell aside as the bear's snout pressed closer, drifting from two feet away to one…from one foot to six inches… then closer still.

Soon, all the world was boiled down to just the two of them, bear and man, nose to nose. Life and death circled them like lazy bees on a looping, random course; where they landed would be as arbitrary as choosing which flower in a meadow to pollinate.

The bear's wet, black nose touched Hiruko's, those powerful jaws so close to rending his flesh. The creature nuzzled his cheek, then dropped its snout to sniff his fragile neck.

Hiruko felt himself slipping. He closed his eyes, fighting to retain control. It was like he was sliding down a steep hill, grabbing at anything to try to stop his fall.

Then, suddenly, he caught hold of something. It was the very thing he'd been struggling with earlier, while waiting for Itami and

Zermann…and now there it was, strong and steady, supporting his weight.

His *poetry.*

* * *

After MacNeal and his men came to a decision, he rounded the outcropping and found Oksana. "We accept your offer of a conditional alliance," he said. Then, just as he was about to reach for a handshake, he decided to put a little curve on the ball. "However, we do have one condition of our own."

Oksana looked amused. "And what would that be?"

"Equal rights to the objective," said MacNeal. "Whatever the Japanese are after, we want a fifty-fifty split…or the equivalent, if it can't be cut in half. We won't help you get it if we can't share it."

"Fair enough." She raised an eyebrow and extended a hand. "I would insist on the same condition if our roles were reversed."

"All right then." MacNeal smiled and returned her handshake. "It's a deal." As he said it, he gazed into her sparkling blue eyes, looking for a tell—any sign that she was untrustworthy. He couldn't find one, but of course he knew he could only trust her so far; he knew their alliance was far more conditional than either of them could say. As soon as their individual interests were jeopardized, the deal would be off. The alliance was beneficial to both sides for now, but all was fair in love and war. He just had to prepare as best he could for the inevitable moment when the team-up went sour.

"We will drink to this later." Oksana released his hand and nodded. "I have some excellent vodka secured in our provisions."

"I look forward to it," said MacNeal.

Just then, there was a commotion in the woods. Immediately Oksana spun and ran toward it, gripping her scepter with both hands. MacNeal followed.

Her bald officer was already in the thick of things. He looked up and gestured for her to come closer. "Our friends have returned."

At first, MacNeal thought he meant the blue-skinned devil and Zermann, and he tightened his grip on his flash-gun. But when the cluster of Russian soldiers parted, he saw enough to make him relax.

The returned "friends" were voïvodes, the two mechanical pods that had battled the creatures. They squatted on their segmented tripod legs, steam rising from the bronze metal skin of their grenade-shaped bodies.

Oksana strode right up and crouched before them. Instead of the humming sounds they'd made before, they hissed softly and occasionally ticked, like a car's radiator cooling off. "Lucifer recalled them fifteen minutes ago. Their quarry moved too fast for them to keep up. See? They have overheated." She reached out but didn't touch the shell of the nearest voïvode, which was still steaming.

MacNeal frowned. "Lucifer?"

"Don't worry about it, American," snapped the bald officer.

"*Pervyja Lejtenant Svyatogor!*" Oksana glared up at him. "*Ivan!* He is our ally. Answer his question."

Ivan scowled. "Lucifer is what she calls the glove." His voice was almost a snarl. "It is the control interface for the voïvodes."

"I see." MacNeal kept his expression neutral. He didn't think it would take much to tip hothead Ivan over the edge.

"It is more than that." Oksana raised her left hand and wiggled the gauntlet's fingers. "It *connects* me to them. It provides a limited awareness of their status and whereabouts."

"Right." MacNeal nodded like it didn't surprise him, but it did. Union intelligence knew about the voïvodes, but the link between automaton and human operator was uncharted territory.

"They are undamaged." Oksana leaned close and frowned intently at the closest voïvode, then scooted over to examine the other one. "But this overheating concerns me. It should not be this extreme, even with all the running and blasting they have done."

"Perhaps the enemy did something to them?" asked Ivan.

"I don't know." Oksana's frown deepened as she flicked the gauntlet's fingers above the voïvode's surface. "The Tesla coil is behaving erratically. The charge is fluctuating unnaturally."

"Could this pose a threat?" asked MacNeal.

"It could." Oksana continued to study the steaming voïvode. "It could also be a sign of things to come."

"The effect of an enemy weapon?" asked Ivan.

"Or the endgame of this entire expedition." Oksana leaned back from the voïvode. "Perhaps the ancient legends are true."

"What ancient legends?" asked MacNeal.

"We will discuss them later." Oksana got to her feet. "For now, we need to make ready to move out again. The voïvodes will be cooled down shortly and ready to travel. The burial detail should be back by then."

MacNeal narrowed his eyes. "Burial detail?"

Oksana stepped toward him and met his gaze. "I took the liberty of sending a detail to bury your five men."

"Without asking me?" MacNeal frowned. "While I was still only *considering* an alliance?"

"Just so." Oksana shrugged. "It seemed wise. I knew once you had made your decision we would need to leave as soon as possible to pick up the invaders' trail. And I thought it was unlikely that you would move out until your men were buried."

MacNeal was irritated, but he knew she was right. Though he wanted to argue the matter on principle, he couldn't deny that she'd done him a favor.

He stewed for a moment, glaring at her. "All right then." He nodded curtly. "Thank you. As long as your men mark the graves and note the coordinates, their help is appreciated."

"Of course." She bowed stiffly. "The New Guard is well-versed in tending the dead. We have *had* to be." Oksana returned her attention to the voïvodes. "Perhaps you should prepare your own men for the journey ahead. We will leave within the hour, I am certain of it."

"I'll do that." MacNeal turned and headed back to Brown and the others. He'd committed them all to a new course of action; their destinies were bound to those of the New Guard.

He only hoped they could manage to work together long enough to get what they needed before the alliance fell apart.

* * *

Hiruko's poem, which had been so slow in coming when he wasn't in danger, flowed freely through his mind as the bear nuzzled his neck.

The sigh of death caresses your throat
Infused with a thousand elegant whispers.
Words in unknowable languages,
Songs in impossible keys
Awaken the forgotten instrument in your chest.

Every muscle in Hiruko's body was taut as a bowstring, every nerve quivering like wires being struck in a piano. His throat was as dry as dust, so ready for a cough he could hardly stand it. He had to urinate so badly, he could barely hold it.

One stray, unexpected move could kill him, he knew. But as long as the lines of the poem kept flowing, he managed to control himself.

Immersed in rays of light, you dissolve like fog,
Spreading out through the cool valley air,
Each wisp and tendril vibrating with those mystic tones,
Raising a shimmering aria that overlays death's sigh
And melts into the falcon's kingly cry.

When the bear's nose left Hiruko's neck, he opened his eyes, daring to hope that the creature had finally gone. But the bear's head had only dropped to his wounded hand.

Pagodas glimmer amid the shivering cherry blossoms,
Stamping the sapphire sky with their

The bear's tongue rolled out of its maw and licked the wound on Hiruko's palm. The creature sniffed it, then licked it again.

Stamping the sapphire sky with their pale afterimage,
Dancing reds and whites bathed in the same golden rays,
The same

Teeth. Hiruko saw the bear's front teeth hovering at the edge of the wound.

The same sweet fog that encompasses all the lay of priestly Heaven
And every farmer's field and ship's rocking mast and

Tears flowed down his cheeks as he felt himself drift toward the ledge of finality. Once he fell, he knew, there would be no coming back.

And every farmer's field and ship's rocking mast and
Every pealing bell in every tower at that singular hour
In which everything

Then, suddenly, his terror was gone. The bear was still looming over him, but Hiruko

In which everything changes forever.

Hiruko in some way he could not then define,
Hiruko among the wildflowers,
Hiruko lover of all things *Nippon*,
Hiruko of the great devouring beast,
ceased
to
fear.

Slowly, he pulled his hand away from the bear's snout. The bear raised its head and stared at him...but there did not seem to be bloodlust in its obsidian eyes.

Hiruko gazed back at it, this time in wonder. He marveled at the immensity of its body...the texture of its rippling fur coat... the perfect pale sharpness of its teeth. He could almost feel its mind ticking along inside its skull, thinking its own unknowable thoughts about Hiruko.

The creature was beautiful. A sublime work of art. He wished he had noticed it sooner. He thought about trying to touch it. He lifted his uninjured hand from his lap...

But before Hiruko could make contact, Itami's enormous kenabō club swung down from behind and crashed into the animal's head. In that one horrific moment, something beautiful died.

All it took was one moment.

As the bear toppled forward, someone grabbed Hiruko under his arms from behind and hauled him backward. The next thing Hiruko knew, he was being swung around and tossed through the air. He landed ten feet away, tumbling through the wildflowers until he finally came to rest. It was then he saw who'd grabbed and pitched him—Zermann of the glowing scars and eyes that flared like twin fires.

Hiruko, sprawled in the wildflowers, had to look away. His eyes blurred and burned with tears; a lump caught in his throat. He knew he could have died at the hands of that great beast, but he didn't think it deserved to be killed by Itami.

"Well, then." Itami turned his attention to Hiruko. "You again." He slung his club over his shoulder. "Little brother."

As Itami ambled toward him, Hiruko got to his feet. His heart was pounding, his stomach churning. He wondered if he was going to be the next to die in that meadow.

"Do you remember the question I asked you on the beach?" Itami grinned behind his upthrust tusks. "'Do you pledge to do whatever is necessary to serve the Shōgun and Emperor, whatever the cost to your own body and soul?' Do you remember that question?"

"Yes, sir." Sweat trickled down Hiruko's back and sides. "I do."

Itami closed the gap between them and leaned down to leer in his face. "Does that include dying for my amusement?"

Hiruko stood stiffly. He knew what the answer had to be, but he hesitated to say it.

"What was that?" Itami cupped a black-clawed hand behind his ear. "You will have to speak up."

"I said yes, Itami, sir."

Itami pushed his face closer, ever closer. "Good." He only stopped when his tusks pricked Hiruko's cheeks, just below his eyes. "Then here is what I want you to do."

Hiruko held his breath.

Itami's voice dropped to a whisper. "Lead us to the convoy." He grinned. "That is why they left you here, is it not?"

"Yes, sir."

"We have important information for the Daimyō," said Itami. "It seems the Union and Matriarchy have sent hounds to dog our trail."

Hiruko slumped as Itami swept away from him. For a moment, he had truly believed he was going to die. And the fear he'd conquered while similarly facing the bear had come back to him. His newfound courage had ebbed in the presence of that blue-skinned giant, the way it always did when he was near. Hiruko had felt helpless and terrified, reduced to an echo of his stronger self. The change that had come over him with the bear had felt so revolutionary, so complete...but Itami had banished it just like that.

Hiruko wondered why the fear had returned. He wondered how to get rid of it again, for good.

It was something he was going to have to work on.

CHAPTER 10

Southern Kamchatka
17 April 1952
1213 Hours

Taki shrugged off his pack and threw himself down, stretching out on his back behind a grassy knob. Tala landed beside him, but she sat instead of lying in the grass. As always, she seemed to have something to prove.

As Taki lay there, he shut his eyes and caught his breath. The two of them had been double-timing it for a while, working their way around the edge of the big meadow. They'd managed to stay out of sight of the poor lone sentry left behind, but they'd had to cover a lot more ground. And they'd had to do it at a fast clip in order to catch up with the moving convoy.

They still weren't caught up all the way, but they were past the meadow and well into the foothills, close enough to take a break. Judging from the vehicle noise up ahead, the convoy wasn't more than a mile distant.

"How long until Zermann and Itami catch up, I wonder?" Taki opened his eyes and and gazed up at the pale blue sky. "And the man left behind by the convoy?"

"Not nearly as long as it took us." As usual, Tala didn't even sound winded. "They'll get to take the shortcut across the meadow instead of having to circle all the way around."

Taki rolled his head over and turned his gaze to her face. She didn't seem to notice. She just stared off into space, hair fluttering in the breeze. At a moment like that, he could easily forget her difficult personality.

Taki felt the need to say something. He knew he probably shouldn't, but he couldn't help himself. "You know something? I really don't have a problem with you."

Tala frowned and bobbed her head back, looking dumbfounded. "What is *that* supposed to mean?"

"Just what I said." Taki sat up and reached for his canteen. "Take it for what it's worth."

"All right." She gave him a brief side look. Shrugging her pack off her shoulders, she swung it around and unbuckled the side pouch flap. Reaching in, she pulled out a map and started unfolding it.

Taki opened the canteen and had a drink. Leaning toward her, he fixed his gaze on the map. "So where are we headed, do you think?"

Tala spread the map across her lap and stared at it intently. She tapped her finger on the beach where they'd arrived, then slowly ran it up through the wooded south and stopped in the foothills of the mountains. "This is where we are now, more or less." She moved her fingertip forward from there, inching northeast in a line through a V-shaped gap between mountain ranges. "It would make sense to follow this valley...which would lead us right here." She forcefully circled an area on the map with her finger.

The area was dotted with peaks, each with a Russian name followed by the abbreviation "Vol." "Volcanoes." Taki raised an eyebrow. "What could they want with volcanoes?"

Tala reached up and pulled her hair back behind her ears. "Be sure to let me know if anything comes to mind, Taki."

Just then, a gust of wind suddenly picked up the map and pitched it in her face.

Taki tried to hold back, but he couldn't. As Tala wrestled with the big sheet of paper, peeling it away from her face, he laughed out loud.

There'd been so much tension between them, it felt great to just open up and laugh. He knew it might make her angry, but he didn't care.

At least that was what he thought until he got a look at her expression—eyes wide, jaws clenched, nose crinkled. He thought at first she looked mad enough to start swinging.

But then the oddest thing happened. The look on her face changed the slightest bit. The corners of her mouth turned up just enough to suggest she might be smiling.

And that was when she threw the map, letting the latest gust plaster it over Taki's head and shoulders.

As he wrestled the wrinkled sheet off his face, he heard something he'd never heard before: the sound of Tala laughing.

Tala pointed at him as she rocked back. "You should've seen your face!" She laughed so hard, she was squinting.

Taki clowned a little, balling up the map and tossing it aside. "That'll teach it," he said as he dusted off his hands.

Tala laughed some more, then pulled her walkie-talkie from her belt. "We'd better check in. We need to let MacNeal know what's going on."

"What's going on with this, you mean?" Taki pointed at the balled-up map.

Tala grinned and shook her head. "With Itami and Zermann."

"The fewer surprises, the better, right?"

"The fewer *bad* surprises," said Tala as she switched on the radio and signaled MacNeal.

* * *

The man called Wolf had stopped following Tala and Taki a while ago. He'd been much more interested in watching another old acquaintance: Major John MacNeal.

A brave man, MacNeal. Wolf had fought against him, and alongside him, many times. He respected him, which wasn't something Wolf could say about too many people.

Wolf just hoped MacNeal wasn't setting himself up for a fall by forging an alliance with the Russian New Guard. There was more going on with them than met the eye, he was sure of it. They represented an x-factor that could interfere with the struggle to come.

As they marched past his hiding place, the 42nd Marines and

New Guard alike, Wolf considered the new dynamic and rethought his strategy. In order to accomplish his mission, he would have to change his plans.

Possibilities flashed through his chess-player's mind, narrowing down to a series of moves most likely to win the board. Unfortunately, as too often happened in such a high stakes contest, the price to the pawns would be steep.

As he watched them stomp off down the trail, blissfully unaware of the true dangers lurking just under the surface, Wolf almost felt sorry for them.

* * *

MacNeal and Oksana marched side by side at the head of the mixed column of Marines, Russians, and voïvodes. Tala had checked in by radio just moments ago. MacNeal had updated her about the Marines who'd been killed in action, and the budding alliance with the New Guard. Tala, in turn, had identified the blue-skinned warrior as Itami, and provided general coordinates of the enemy forces. Thanks to her, MacNeal knew just where to take his unit and what lay ahead.

What lay behind was another matter. Cocking an ear to listen, he noticed it was pretty quiet toward the rear of the column—just the sound of combat boots tromping in the dirt. The Union and New Guard forces had yet to integrate, which didn't bode well for the inevitable moment when they found themselves in battle together.

The language barrier was part of the problem, but he doubted it was all of it. If Oksana and Ivan spoke decent English, there had to be other English speakers among them. Unfamiliarity and suspicion were more likely to blame for the division.

Maybe it would help if MacNeal set an example. He turned to Oksana, noting the delicate lines of her features once more. "How long has the New Guard been in exile here?"

"Two months," she said. "Too long away from home…but not long enough to truly know this vast place."

"Where have you stayed? Is there a settlement?"

"There are…communities." Oksana lifted an eyebrow. "But they are not very welcoming. My men and I have camped and lived off the land."

MacNeal frowned. "So where are these communities? We haven't seen any locals since we got here."

"Oh, they are around." Her voice was full of cryptic meaning. "A number of native tribes live here, mostly *Koryaks*. They are all very... bashful."

"But you've met them?" asked MacNeal. "You've spent time with them?"

"A little. One of our people got to know them quite well, actually. She has a magic touch, you might say."

MacNeal nodded and shifted the weight of the flash-gun strap on his shoulder. "Did she find out anything interesting?"

Oksana smiled. "You can ask her yourself soon enough. We are heading for a rendezvous with her as we speak."

Now it was MacNeal's turn to raise an eyebrow. He wondered why she hadn't mentioned this other person until now. "You sent her to scout ahead?"

"You might say that." Oksana chuckled. "If Tatiana ever listened to a single order I ever gave, that is. She has her own mind, MacNeal."

He grinned ruefully. "I know the type."

"But she has skills like you have never seen before," said Oksana. "You will be very impressed."

"I look forward to meeting her, then," said MacNeal.

* * *

Oksana led the combined Union and New Guard unit on a winding route through the forest. They marched for miles among old-growth pines and firs, across streams, around rock formations. Finally, for no apparent reason, she stopped the march. The column drew up behind her, each man looking around with wide eyes and hands locked firmly on weapons. The two voïvodes looked around, too, skittering on their triple legs and scanning the surroundings with the red electric eyes mounted on their podlike bodies.

From what MacNeal could see, they were standing in a dense patch of woods like any other. He examined the area, but saw nothing to suggest why Oksana had decided to stop there. Frowning, he opened his mouth to ask for an explanation.

That was when the flame-haired woman literally dropped down

from above and landed in front of him.

She plunged down from the trees and landed in a crouch, glaring up at him. As she slowly straightened, it became clear she wasn't wearing any clothes. Her body was caked with dark mud, covered with leaves and grass and twigs...but she was otherwise naked.

And apparently not the slightest bit embarrassed. Standing before MacNeal, meeting his gaze with eyes that seemed all the whiter because of the mud smeared around them, she held a challenging posture: chin thrust forward, shoulders squared, hands planted on her hips. She was like some wild creature raised by wolves or bears, completely unselfconscious and animalistic.

At least until she opened her mouth and spoke. Her Russian came fast and fluently in the manner of a civilized woman. There was nothing bestial in the quick-fire stream of conversation between her and Oksana.

And when, after several exchanges, she switched smoothly to perfect English without a trace of a Russian accent, the illusion of a savage forest-child had all but melted away. She was by no means a feral creature of the wilderness, though she did seem to have mastered the skills and adopted the dress code of one.

"So you are Major MacNeal." The naked woman tipped her head to one side and stared at him. "Oksana tells me we're allies."

"If she says so, it must be true," said MacNeal.

The woman shrugged. "I suppose."

Oksana touched MacNeal's arm. "Major John MacNeal, meet *Vtorogo Lejtenant* Tatiana Zakharova."

MacNeal nodded once. "I've heard a lot about you."

Tatiana spread her arms wide. "Do I live up to what you have heard?"

Just then, Ivan stormed over with a brown blanket. He flung it over her shoulders and drew in her arms, wrapping it around her. "Here. You must be cold."

Tatiana's gaze stayed glued to MacNeal. "The heart of the goddess Baba Yaga never fails to warm me."

MacNeal wasn't sure if she was staring right through him or just trying to make him nervous. Either way, he did feel uncomfortable. It didn't help that he'd gotten a good look at the curves of her body before Ivan had covered it.

Fortunately, Oksana stepped between them and broke her penetrating gaze. "What do you have to report, Tatiana?"

Tatiana tossed her head, shaking bits of debris from her red hair. "The convoy has entered the mountains northeast of here. The blue-skinned monster and the Reich's tattooed dog are in pursuit. A Japanese man and a woman with long, dark hair are also following. Unionists from the looks of them."

"Those are my people," MacNeal verified with a nod.

"What about the Koryaks?" asked Oksana.

"I do not know." Tatiana shook her head. "Nobody is home. It is like they have all disappeared."

"That is strange." Oksana frowned. "Do you think they are massing to repel the Shōgunate and Reich?"

"Or maybe they have just gone into hiding," offered Ivan. "*Deeper* hiding, that is."

"Who knows?" Tatiana shrugged. "All I can tell you is, I looked in the usual places, and I concealed myself perfectly. No foreign objects or scents on my person. I cloaked myself with local mud and herbs and used an incantation from the Baba Yaga order to become one with the forest. The Koryaks could not have detected me. Whatever they are up to, they are nowhere nearby."

"That is too bad." Oksana sighed and shook her head. "I was hoping for an alliance with them."

"It would not have happened anyway," said Tatiana. "But I will go back out and keep looking, if you like." She opened the brown blanket, but Ivan jumped in and closed it again.

"Not yet." Oksana waved her scepter toward a creek running twenty yards away. "Clean up, get dressed, and fall in. You can lead us to the convoy."

"Or I could just wait and let the rain wash it off." Tatiana looked up at the sky.

"What rain?" Oksana looked up, too. "The sky is blue."

"It is coming." Tatiana dropped her gaze and craned her neck to see around Oksana and Ivan. "Just you wait." She shot a wink at MacNeal.

Ivan saw it and shot MacNeal a look of his own—wide-eyed and fiercely jealous. At that moment, MacNeal knew he was going to be a problem.

Oksana spotted the dirty looks and cleared her throat. "Ivan? Do you have her uniform and gear?"

Ivan made a show of slowly tearing his angry gaze from MacNeal. "Of course I do, *Kapetan*."

"Then get it," snapped Oksana. "Let us get a move on. We have got a long way to go to catch that convoy, yes?" She raised an eyebrow at Tatiana.

Tatiana nodded. "I can reach them faster on my own. Perhaps I should go on ahead?"

"I have already told you what I want you to do." Oksana's voice was cold. "If you still consider yourself part of this unit, you will do it."

Tatiana, smiling grimly, locked eyes with her. "Whatever I do," she said, "it is not because *anyone* wants me to do it."

With that, she threw off the blanket and marched off toward the creek. Ivan darted after her.

Oksana blew out her breath and shook her head. "That one is a handful. We cannot afford to lose her, and she knows it."

"I don't have a problem with that." MacNeal grinned as he watched Tatiana march away naked. "I've got a whole unit of handfuls.

CHAPTER 11

Southern Kamchatka
17 April 1952
1727 Hours

When Itami and Zermann got within a mile or so of the convoy, they took off, leaving Hiruko to make his solitary way along the trail.

By that time, Hiruko felt on the verge of collapse. He slowed to a trudging shuffle, though he dared not slow down too much; he doubted the creatures would ever stop the convoy or send someone back to get him.

As he struggled along, he was soaked with sweat. He'd taken off his uniform shirt and covered his head to keep off the worst of the sun, but he was still drenched. The sheer effort of running all those miles—he'd lost count of how many—had exhausted him.

What a day it had been. He was tempted to stop and drop right there and leave the convoy to its own devices. He could become a resident of the bear's stomping grounds, roaming the forest and living off the land, keeping his distance from creatures like Itami and Zermann for the rest of his life.

Of course, then he'd never know the exact cause of the tug on his heart…or what the Shōgunate was seeking in Kamchatka…or if it was too late to stop the monsters of the Reich from corrupting his beloved *Nippon*.

So Hiruko stopped just long enough for a sip of water from his canteen, and then he kept moving. He even managed to pick up the pace again, breaking into a modest jog.

To his surprise, when he ran around a bend at the base of a mountain, he saw that the convoy had stopped up ahead after all. He was almost disappointed.

Especially when he saw who was waiting for him at the rear of the column. His heart sank, and his stomach twisted like a rope in a hangman's knot.

Von Heïzinger stood like a dark obelisk, a human shadow waiting to devour him. The Daimyō stood beside him, hands clasped behind his back, looking stern.

Hiruko jogged up and stopped ten feet away from them. He bowed but felt light-headed and had to lean his hands on his knees.

"Jōtōhei Orochi," snapped the Daimyō. "Is there a problem?"

Hiruko gathered in a deep breath and straightened, snapping off a salute. "No, sir." He still felt light-headed, and he thought he might be weaving in place, but he was determined to stay at attention. "No problem, sir."

"Zermann and Itami have already told us of their encounter with the Union and Matriarchy." He spoke German again, though only the Daimyō and Hiruko would understand him among the Shōgunate troops. "It took you so long to catch up with us, we thought perhaps the Union and Matriarchy had captured you."

"That's not true." The Daimyō marched toward Hiruko with an irritated look on his face.

"Of course it isn't," said Von Heïzinger. "Minamoto here refuses to recognize what a *threat* the Union and Matriarchy forces represent. He won't concede that they must be *dealt with* immediately… especially if MacNeal is among them." Von Heïzinger glared from the dark depths of his leather cap. "And based on Itami's descriptions, he *is* among them."

The Daimyō ignored him, grabbed Hiruko's right hand, and turned it palm up. He shook his head disgustedly as he gazed at the diagonal gash. "This man needs treatment." He let the hand fall and looked back at Von Heïzinger.

"Treatment later." Von Heïzinger's eyes glittered. "First, I have another job for this man."

"What kind of job?" asked the Daimyō.

"Personal assistant." Von Heïzinger turned, gesturing for Hiruko to follow, and led him to the second of the three amphibious vehicles in the convoy. "Your charge is within. I will introduce you to her." Without taking his eyes off Hiruko, he rapped his gloved knuckles on the hatch on the side of the vehicle.

Her? Hiruko frowned. He hadn't been aware of any women in the convoy. What was Von Heïzinger playing at?

The hatch swung open and black-gloved hands pushed out a ramp. Then someone emerged—a nightmarish soldier clad head to toe in black. His blocky body was shrouded in a long black overcoat. He wore black gloves, black boots, and a black helmet. The metal plate that covered his face was black, too, and forged in the shape of a death's head skull. Not an inch of bare skin was exposed. He looked more like some kind of automaton than a human being.

Instinctively, Hiruko took a step back, then another. The soldier towered over him, brandishing an assault rifle in his gloved hands.

"Nadia?" Von Heïzinger peered into the cabin of the amphibious vehicle.

For a moment, no one emerged. Hiruko took another step back, fearing what might come charging out at him—another monster, perhaps, craving a meal of human flesh. A sister to Zermann, maybe, with his same mechanical devotion to destruction?

Finally, Hiruko heard sounds of movement in the vehicle—shuffling footsteps that could have belonged to some shambling ghoul, approaching with darkest intent.

He backed up a little more when the footsteps reached the hatchway. From his viewpoint off to the side, he couldn't see who or what might be coming.

Suddenly, a cane of twisted black wood pushed through the hatch and landed with a thump on the ramp. As soon as it hit, a second cane thumped down on the opposite side of the ramp; this one had been carved from some kind of bright blond wood.

An old woman shuffled out of the hatch, leaning heavily on the two canes. She was tall and spindly, but stooped with age. Her long, black dress had frilly cuffs at her wrists and throat; the hem hung down below the ankles of her black leather boots.

Her face, when she looked in Hiruko's direction, was deeply ingrained with a mesh of fine wrinkles. She looked out with bright blue eyes like twin natural gas flames flickering in the deep wells of their sockets.

But Hiruko's first thought when he saw her was not one of terror. She did not appear to be the monster he'd feared.

"Nadia." Von Heïzinger left Hiruko and strode to the woman's side. Standing at the base of the ramp, he took her elbow and guided her down. "The wilderness suits you."

Nadia stopped at the bottom and smiled at him. "It always has."

A second mechanical-looking soldier lumbered out after her and took up position alongside the first, rifle gripped rigidly in his gloved hands. The two black-clad figures towered over the old woman like obelisks, eyes and expressions completely concealed by dark goggles and death's head faceplates.

"Give us some room, *mein Schocktruppen*." Von Heïzinger waved at the soldiers, and they both stepped back. "Nadia, allow me to introduce your new personal assistant." He swept his arm out dramatically, extending a hand toward Hiruko. "His name is Hiruko Orochi."

Nadia's floral print babushka head scarf—the only splash of color in her dark outfit—fluttered in the breeze as she nodded. "Pleased to meet you, Mr. Orochi." The scarf was bright red with flowers of gold, pink, purple, and white. "Yet I don't recall *asking* for a personal assistant."

Von Heïzinger gestured at Nadia. "Orochi, meet Nadia Valkova, an old friend."

"*Very* old," said Nadia. "As old as the hills and twice as crusty."

Hiruko bowed. "I am honored."

"Now, Orochi." Von Heïzinger fixed him in his burning gaze. "I expect you to follow her orders in all things."

"*Hai*." Hiruko nodded. "As you say, sir."

"However," said Von Heïzinger. "I advise you to beware this old witch. She is a priestess of *Baba Yaga*." His attempt at a smile looked as much like a death's head rictus as the Schocktruppen's helmets.

"She might give you *chicken legs*, just as Baba Yaga is said to have given to her legendary house."

Nadia shook her head. "If I had such powers of transformation, don't you think I would've changed myself into a young woman by now?"

"Then it's settled." Von Heïzinger clapped his hands. "We shall meet for dinner to celebrate." He bowed, then turned and jabbed a finger at the Daimyō, who was standing nearby. "Minamoto! What are you standing around for? We need to march another hour before we make camp."

The Daimyō's eyes flared. For a moment, Hiruko thought he might stand up to Von Heïzinger…but then he nodded instead. "As you wish, Generalleutnant." With that, he marched off, barking orders to the men to prepare to move out.

Von Heïzinger pointed at the towering Schocktruppen soldiers. "You will remain outside the vehicle to make room for Nadia's assistant. Take the beast with you." He stuck two fingers in his mouth and let out a shrill whistle. Immediately, Hiruko heard the sound of thumping and thrashing from inside the amphibious vehicle.

Suddenly, a bald man leaped from the hatch and landed in a crouch in the dirt. He squatted there a moment, snarling and snuffling behind a muzzle-like mask of grey metal. His glowing yellow eyes zeroed in on Hiruko, lancing him with a penetrating gaze.

"*Mein Stosstruppen*, go with the Schocktruppen." He pointed at the Schocktruppen.

The Stosstruppen slashed his clawed hands at Hiruko and howled behind his muzzle. Then, with a gait that was more like a loping ape than a man, he bounded over to the black-clad Schocktruppen.

Von Heïzinger returned his attention to Nadia. "Until dinner."

"Until dinner." Nadia smiled as he walked away. Her gaze remained fixed on him until he was out of sight at the front of the column. Then, she turned to Hiruko. "Mr. Orochi? Can you arrange for me to return to the Ukraine immediately?"

Hiruko shook his head. "I cannot."

Nadia's face tightened with a businesslike severity he hadn't guessed she was capable of. "I thought he told you to follow my orders."

"Yes." Hiruko nodded. "But what you ask is beyond my power."

"Authority, you mean. Power and authority are very different things." Suddenly, she stood up straight; the canes were loose in her grip, as if she didn't need them to support her weight. "You can have all the power of a goddess and still not have the authority you need to go home."

Hiruko stared at her, stunned. From her full height, she stared back at him, radiating serene, intimidating confidence…then slowly bent down again, resuming her stooped old lady's posture.

"Well, if you can't do the one simple thing I've asked, you might as well come with me." Leaning heavily on the canes once more, she trudged back up the ramp. "Perhaps I'll find a use for you yet."

* * *

As the 42nd Marines and their New Guard allies crossed the meadow, MacNeal realized Tatiana had been right about the rain. He could smell the increasing moisture in the air and he could feel the rising pressure in his sinuses the way he always did when a storm was coming.

Then there were the clouds. The sky, which had been clear blue for most of the day, was carpeted with them. They were darker in the distance; farthest away to the west, they were blurred with the grey haze that could only be caused by falling showers.

Yes, the rain was coming. Somehow, hours ago, before MacNeal had noticed any sign, Tatiana had correctly predicted it. She was a true wild child, attuned to the environment around her…or maybe her goddess Baba Yaga had conferred certain gifts upon her. After years of strange encounters, MacNeal knew better than to rule out anything.

Either way, he was impressed. Looking back, he saw Tatiana meandering alongside the column, fully clothed in a brown uniform with black fur trim and twin sawed-off shotguns holstered on her hips. She twirled a lock of her flaming red hair around her finger and had a dreamy look on her face, as if her mind were drifting somewhere far away. What new prediction or mystery was she pondering this time, he wondered.

He didn't get to watch and wonder much longer, as Ivan stormed up beside Tatiana and into his line of sight, glaring. His long nose was wrinkled in a hateful scowl, leaving no doubt as to his jealous disgust.

Before MacNeal could react, Oksana rushed up beside him. "I would not poke a stick at that hive of bees if I were you."

He took one last look at Ivan and Tatiana and turned away with a snort. "We should make camp. I wouldn't mind beating the storm, would you?"

"That is exactly what I came to discuss," said Oksana. "I think we need to put some room between us and that stream."

MacNeal eyed the stream meandering through the meadow and nodded. If the storm was big enough, the stream could overflow its banks. "Agreed. How about fifty yards closer to the foothills? That would keep us clear of the stream."

Oksana nodded. "But not so close to the mountains that runoff would be a problem. Good plan, MacNeal."

"It's about time we stopped, anyway. Not long till sundown now." He gazed at the darkening sky. The storm clouds and lowering sun were in a race to see who could turn out the lights first.

"It will be our first night together as allies," said Oksana. "Hopefully, it will not be the last."

"It shouldn't be." MacNeal looked over his shoulder at the mixed unit of Union and New Guard troops. "The alliance seems to be holding up fine."

"No, I mean because of the *danger*. This wild land is filled with terrible secrets. We must never let our guard down for even an instant."

"You and your men have survived," said MacNeal, "and you've been here for months."

Oksana's face hardened. "What makes you think *all* of us have survived, MacNeal?"

With that, she stalked away from him, pushing on ahead with Vesper in her right hand and the Lucifer gauntlet on the left.

* * *

The last rays of the sun were sinking slowly behind the mountains. Wolf watched through binoculars as MacNeal and Oksana's combined forces set up camp for the night.

A rush of nervous energy flashed through him as he thought about what would come next. Very soon, he would have to take action. He would have to make his first move.

And when he did, the game would change. That, in turn, would lead to other changes, all directed by his guiding hand.

Some of what happened would seem cruel, but it would all contribute to the greater good. Those on the board might not see it, but Wolf never lost sight of the big picture. He never allowed the concerns of pawns to temper his hand when the time came for decisive action.

His former ally MacNeal should relax now, he thought. MacNeal should enjoy whatever moments of peace and pleasure he could find.

Because Wolf knew all hell was about to break loose, and MacNeal would be in the middle of it, as always.

CHAPTER 12

**Kamchatka
17 April 1952
1940 Hours**

As sunset turned to twilight, Taki and Tala chose a spot to bed down: a recess scooped out of the slope of a mountain, sixty feet above the floor of the pass winding around it.

The recess was an ideal shelter from the rain blasting down from above; it would make the night a lot less miserable for the two of them. Tumbled boulders blocked most of the entrance from view, and the gaps between the boulders provided perfect vantage points for spying on the Shōgunate and Reich forces camped out below.

They checked in with the main unit by radio, trading updates with MacNeal. They filled him in about the mysterious old woman traveling with the Shōgunate convoy, and MacNeal told him how the 42nd and New Guard were making camp in the meadow near the foothills.

After closing the channel, Taki and Tala sat against the dirt wall at the back of the recess, dug canned rations out of their packs, and ate dinner together. The rain poured down in a torrent outside the opening, sluicing off the lip of the entrance just inches away from their booted feet.

"I've got beef stew," said Taki as he peeled off the lid of his main course. "What about you?"

"The label says 'herring.'" She raised her open can and had a sniff that made her nose crinkle. "Smells a little too fishy for me."

Taki offered up his can. "I'll trade you."

"Do you like fish?"

"Can't stand it." Taki chuckled. "I know, I know. Japanese supposedly eat a lot of seafood. Not me, though."

Tala smiled. "You're too much of a red-blooded American."

"Well, I am, but that's not why I hate seafood." He shrugged. "It all goes back to an experience I had at a fish hatchery. I was five years old."

"What kind of experience?"

"I fell in." Taki shuddered. "The trout just kind of *mobbed* me. They swarmed all over me. My dad had to dive in and get me out."

"Sounds pretty scary for a five-year-old." Tala looked at him out of the corner of her eye. "Yet you would still eat herring for me?"

"We're teammates, aren't we?" Taki pushed the can of stew toward her.

He expected her to make some kind of smart aleck quip, but she didn't. She didn't take the stew, either. "I won't ask you to eat something you hate." She pulled a fork out of her pack and stuck it in the grey mass of herring.

Taki pulled back the stew can. "Well, thanks." He pulled out his own fork and scooped out some cold stew. "I owe you one. That smells pretty…"

Before he could finish his sentence, Tala put down the herring and grabbed the stew from his hand. "On second thought, sharing is good."

Taki grinned as she dug out a forkful of stew and shoved it into her mouth.

They both sat and laughed, passing the can back and forth, each eating their share as the rain rushed down outside the recess.

* * *

MacNeal and Brown ducked inside the Russians' tent and

shrugged out of their sopping wet rain gear. Now that camp was set up and the men were situated, they'd been summoned for a meeting with the New Guard leaders.

"Welcome." Oksana was sipping something from a tin cup. She and Ivan sat on folding camp stools across from each other. "Make yourselves at home." She gestured at two empty stools.

"Thank you." MacNeal took a seat. He admired the tent, which was big enough to sleep four men, and the tidy arrangement of gear. There was even room in the corners for the two voïvodes, which seemed to be deactivated, their Tesla coil power supplies dark. The other Russians were sheltered in pup tents, as were MacNeal's men, but the larger tent served as a mobile HQ.

"Ma'am." Brown tipped his cap to Oksana, then nodded at Ivan before sitting down beside MacNeal.

Oksana had another sip from her cup. "We have a long day ahead of us tomorrow. Fortunately, Tatiana assures me the rain will end by morning."

"That's good news," said MacNeal. "Not that we'd let a little rain slow us down."

Brown smirked. "Neither rain nor sleet nor driving snow nor plagues of locusts will stop the 42nd from kicking ass."

Ivan snorted. "The same goes for us. We are Russians. Bad weather only inspires us."

"So tell me." MacNeal leaned forward, resting his elbows on his knees and clasping his hands between them. "You've been here two months. You must know this place by now. So what's ahead of us?"

Oksana put down the cup and picked up a folded map from the ground beside her. "Incredibly beautiful land, MacNeal. Sights you will not see anywhere else on Earth."

"Also incredibly *deadly*," said Ivan.

Oksana raised the map, which was hand-drawn in pencil, and jabbed a finger at the base of a rough *V* formed by two mountain ranges. "We are here, more or less. The Shōgunate and Reich convoy is somewhere up here, according to Tatiana." She swirled her fingertip in a circle in the middle of the gap between the two sides of the *V*. "Assuming they continue in this direction, following the valley…" She ran her finger up through the gap, then stopped at a jumble of *X*'s clustered near the coast. "…they will end up smack in the middle of volcano territory."

MacNeal nodded thoughtfully, recalling his briefings on Kamchatka. "Active volcanoes, right?"

"*Very* active." Ivan glared and rubbed his chin beard. "The closer we get, the more you will *feel* it."

"What else is up there besides volcanoes?" asked MacNeal. "Do you have any idea what the Shōgunate and Reich might be looking for?"

Oksana shrugged and looked at Ivan. "We never found anything of value there."

"What about the ancient legends you mentioned?" MacNeal leaned farther forward, drawing Oksana's gaze away from Ivan. "The ones you thought might have something to do with the voïvodes overheating."

Oksana sighed and put down the map. "According to Tatiana, the local Koryak tribes have legends of a great power source hidden deep within the volcanoes. An *eldritch* power source left behind by the gods themselves."

Ivan stopped rubbing his beard and threw up his hands. "We assumed the legends were just primitive attempts to explain the source of the volcanic activity. We thought nothing of them."

"But the way the voïvodes have been reacting…" Oksana shook her head. "It is as if some force is affecting them. Perhaps there is some truth to the legends after all."

MacNeal narrowed his eyes. "An eldritch power source." He turned to Brown. "That would account for Zermann and Von Heïzinger being here."

Brown smiled grimly. "It's their kind of target, all right."

MacNeal returned his gaze to Oksana. "You don't have any more details on the possible location of this power source?"

Oksana retrieved the map and pointed at the biggest *X* in the cluster near the coast. "This volcano is mentioned most often: *Kronotskaya Sopka*. It is not the largest in Kamchatka, or even the most active, but it seems to have some significance to the Koryaks."

Ivan nodded. "According to Tatiana, the local tribes refer to it as the home of the god Kutkha."

Brown frowned. "Kutkha? Never heard of him."

"He is some kind of god," said Ivan. "Very powerful and very revered. You will see his image on carvings and monuments throughout Kamchatka."

"What else do we know?" asked MacNeal.

Ivan shrugged. "I cannot think of anything else."

"You are welcome to talk to Tatiana." Oksana dropped the map in her lap emphatically. "If you can find her, that is."

"She is performing a rite," snapped Ivan. "Seeking wisdom from Baba Yaga."

"I wonder if this Baba Yaga's got a line on Kutkha." Brown smirked at MacNeal.

"She does not." Ivan was dead serious, his voice forceful. "The goddess does *not* know this local so-called deity."

"Okay, okay." Brown patted his hands in the air as if to say "calm down." "We get the picture."

MacNeal saw Ivan glare angrily and broke in. "I'll talk to Tatiana in the morning. Maybe she'll think of something else."

"It is worth a try." Oksana got up from her stool and gestured toward the tent flap. "And now, gentlemen, if you please, let us adjourn until tomorrow."

Ivan popped up from his stool and saluted in her direction. "Until tomorrow, Kapetan." He didn't bother donning any kind of rain gear before whisking out of the tent.

Brown got up next and nodded at Oksana. "Thanks for the hospitality." Then he went for his wet, green slicker on the dirt floor.

MacNeal moved to leave, too, but Oksana reached up and stopped him with a touch to his wrist. "Actually, MacNeal, do you have another minute or two? A discussion of strategy might be in order."

"Sure." MacNeal settled back onto the stool. "Evening, Boomer."

"Evening, Major." Brown pulled his hood over his head and ducked out into the rainswept night.

As Brown left, MacNeal watched as Oksana retrieved a thermos from a pack on the floor and unscrewed the cap.

She smiled as she raised the thermos. "Vodka, MacNeal?"

He nodded.

* * *

"Watch your step, ma'am." Hiruko gripped Nadia's elbow with one hand and held an umbrella over her head with the other. He was doing a good job of keeping the rain off her, though his own back and shoulders were soaked.

Nadia carefully put down one foot and adjusted her weight before daring to lift the other. Her black boots were already half-covered in mud, though she'd only walked ten steps from the amphibious vehicle. "It is a bit slippery out tonight." She spoke German, though her accent was much less harsh than Von Heïzinger's.

Looking ahead, Hiruko saw they had at least twenty more steps to get to Von Heïzinger's big tent in the middle of camp. Nadia was going to have dinner with the generalleutnant, and it was Hiruko's responsibility to get her there safely.

"Sorry to move so slowly," said Nadia as she planted another step…only to slip a little forward in the muck. She was holding on to Hiruko's arm where he braced her elbow, and she instantly tightened her grip. "Old age has taken its toll. I'm ninety-seven, you know."

Hiruko's eyes widened. "Ninety-seven?"

Nadia firmed up her footing, then started another step. "Have you known people this old, Mr. Orochi? Older, perhaps?"

"A few." Hiruko adjusted his grip on her elbow. "The oldest person I've known is my grandfather, who is ninety-eight."

Nadia dropped her left foot, then leaned her weight on it. "Is he in good health?"

"Very good, thank you," said Hiruko.

"Good for him." Nadia patted his arm. "Though, of course, health and longevity aren't everything. Not if they come at the expense of one's soul."

Hiruko wasn't sure what to say.

"You've already met someone older than your grandfather." Nadia took another achingly slow step. "We are on our way to dine with him now."

Hiruko frowned. "The generalleutnant?" He kept his voice low, though the roaring rain was probably loud enough to drown it out. "Older than ninety-eight?"

"Oh my, yes." She lowered her right foot, lifted her left. "Very much so. But there is the matter of his soul…or the lack thereof."

Hiruko knew the best policy was to mind his own business, but curiosity got the better of him. "What happened to it?" Still, he kept his voice low. "His soul, that is?"

Nadia sighed heavily. "It is long gone, Mr. Orochi. As if it had never been."

She stopped and stood under the umbrella, clutching Hiruko's arm, staring at the mud as the rain pounded it full of divots. Hiruko watched her shriveled face as some ancient despair flickered across it. "Ma'am? Are you all right?"

Nadia shook her head as if to dispel the gloom. "Perfectly." Right foot up. "But I do have a problem, Mr. Orochi." Right foot down. "Can you guess what it is?"

"No, ma'am," said Hiruko.

Her bright blue eyes glittered as she gazed up at him. "My memory is better than my eyesight."

Hiruko tipped his head to one side. "Ma'am?"

She tapped her left temple with one quivering fingertip. "I remember the man he once was better than I can see the man he is now."

"He was different?"

"As different as an angel can be from a demon." With that, she took another infinitely slow step, holding on to Hiruko as if he were the last tree standing in the middle of an earthquake zone.

* * *

MacNeal raised his tin cup along with Oksana and repeated her Russian toast. "*Na zdarovye!*" Then he joined her in throwing back a shot of burning, bracing vodka.

It was his third drink since Brown and Ivan had left, and he knew it should be his last. As long as Zermann and the blue-skinned devil were at large, he should keep his wits about him at all times.

So why did he let her refill his cup once more? The fact of it was, he enjoyed her company, and he thought there was value in spending time with her to gather intelligence.

As she poured more vodka from her thermos, he continued the thread they'd been discussing. "So what you're saying is, there's a power behind the Matriarchy throne?"

"*Da.*" She tipped up the mouth of the thermos, then tipped it back down and splashed a little more into the cup for good measure. "Have you heard of a man called 'The Black Angel'?"

MacNeal shook his head.

"You might know him better as Tsar Grigori Yefimovich Rasputin, MacNeal." She filled her own cup and put the thermos down on the ground beside her. "He is the husband of Tsarina and Grand Matriarch Anastasia Romanova, yes?"

MacNeal frowned. "You're saying he's also the Black Angel?"

She nodded emphatically. "The Black Angel is the true supreme power in the Motherland. He controls Grand Matriarch Anastasia's every move. He rules from the shadows with an iron fist, twisting our nation to suit his own reprehensible appetites."

"I knew the Matriarchy government was repressive," said MacNeal, "but I didn't know it was *that* bad."

"Well, it is." Her nose crinkled in disgust. "The Black Angel is systematically crushing all opposition."

"Including the New Guard?" asked MacNeal.

"He *tried*." Oksana smiled grimly. "But the best he could manage was to exile us. We are too *strong*. Our cause is too *just*." Her voice was impassioned as she raised her cup. "We will not *rest* until we have pried free the dog Rasputin's grip on our beloved Motherland." With that, she swung the cup to her lips and tossed back the vodka.

MacNeal did the same, then turned the cup upside down on his knee. He knew he could drink more and stay sharp, but he couldn't take the chance of losing his edge.

"So, MacNeal." Oksana narrowed her eyes at him. "Tell me, why does your freedom-loving Union support the Black Angel's tyranny?"

MacNeal considered his next words carefully. "I can't speak for the Union, Oksana." He tapped the bottom of his upended cup with one finger. "All I know is, I've fought alongside the Russian people on many occasions, and I'm proud to call them my allies."

Oksana smirked. "Spoken like a true diplomat, MacNeal."

MacNeal met her gaze with all the forceful sincerity he could muster. "Spoken like a true friend of the Russian people, you mean."

"Well said, MacNeal." Leaning forward, she tapped his cup with the mouth of the thermos. "We should drink to that."

He shook his head. "Save some for next time."

Suddenly, somebody outside started yelling.

In a heartbeat, MacNeal and Oksana shot to their feet and launched into crisis mode. As the yelling continued and spread, Oksana grabbed her Vesper scepter and switched it on. MacNeal yanked the revolver from the holster at his hip and charged out through the tent flap, instantly ready for anything.

Outside, Russians and Union men bolted through the rain with flashlights and rifles swinging. They were all heading in the same direction, toward the loudest yelling.

MacNeal joined them, and Oksana quickly caught up. They hurried through the rain-drenched night, feet splashing in puddles, clothes soaking wet.

As they approached a cluster of men at the far side of camp, MacNeal's heart hammered. Blazing adrenaline coursed through his bloodstream, burning off every trace of the vodka's effects. What would he see when he got to that cluster? What were those men looking at?

Suddenly, Brown's voice rang out. "Major!" He looked over from the crowd. "We have a situation!"

MacNeal rushed to Brown's side, and men made way to clear his view. There, in a shifting patch of flashlight beams on the muddy ground, lay a heap of red clothing with a set of silver dog tags gleaming atop it…and something else beside it.

Oksana, when she flew up beside him and had a look, sucked in her breath. "What *is* that?"

MacNeal stepped closer to the mess on the ground and squatted for a better look. Beside the clothing lay a glistening, steaming pile of what looked like bloody entrails.

"Whose uniform is that?" Oksana said it loud for the crowd's benefit.

Ivan stepped forward and spoke up. "It is a New Guard uniform, Kapetan. The identification tags belong to Private Smolensk."

"Genedi Smolensk?" Oksana's eyes widened. "Who was the last to see him?"

"I saw him just under an hour ago," a short man said quietly.

"Where, Private?" asked Oksana.

"Over there." The Russian soldier turned and pointed at a jumble of brush some thirty yards away. "He was walking toward the latrine as I was walking back from it."

"All right." Oksana pushed her soaked blond hair behind her ears and sighed. "Let us assume nothing. We will send out search details and comb the area." She looked at Ivan. "Groups of no fewer than three, understood?"

Ivan nodded. "Understood."

"Tatiana, examine the…evidence." Oksana gestured at the clothes and entrails. "See what you can learn."

Without a word, Tatiana stepped away from Ivan and crouched by the piles in the mud.

MacNeal turned to Brown. "We're joining the search, Boomer."

Brown nodded once and blasted a string of orders. "Marines, form up! I want teams of two, deployed in a standard grid search pattern. Lock and load!" He swung up his massive flash machine gun and activated its power supply. Then he pulled down his HB-5 night vision goggles from his forehead and switched them on.

As the Union and New Guard search parties moved out, MacNeal watched Tatiana pick at the remains. She gently lifted a fold of red cloth, rubbed it between her fingers, and closed her eyes.

Ivan walked up and stood behind her, reaching down to rest a hand on her shoulder. She shrugged it off with a scowl and bent down away from him; he lingered another moment, then shook his head and stomped off through the slop with a hurt look on his face.

Just then, Oksana drew up beside MacNeal. "This is terrible." She kept her voice low. "We are being hunted."

"But by whom?" asked MacNeal. "Or what?"

At that moment, Tatiana interrupted. "A wild animal did not do this. I can tell you that much. An animal would not organize the remains so neatly…or leave food behind." She gestured at the heap of entrails.

"It could not be Zermann or Itami," said Oksana. "You told us they ran off to rejoin the convoy, yes?"

"Unless they doubled back." Tatiana frowned at the red cloth between her fingers. "But this does not look like their work, either. It is still too orderly."

"Someone else then." MacNeal rubbed his stubble-covered chin. "An agent of the Reich or Shōgunate? Or could it be a local threat? The Koryaks perhaps?"

"They have never attacked the New Guard," said Tatiana. "I do not know." She let the cloth fall back on the pile. "I must pray on this. Perhaps Baba Yaga will show me the truth." She gestured with both hands at MacNeal and Oksana, waving them off.

As they turned away from her, MacNeal meant to head to his tent to retrieve his flash-gun and night vision eyepiece, then join the search. But Oksana caught his arm and held him.

Even in the rain and darkness, he could see the sadness in her eyes. "Genedi is a good man. I recruited him personally." She took a deep breath, then let it out slowly. "He is my cousin, MacNeal."

MacNeal nodded firmly. "We'll find him." He didn't see the need to state the obvious. Of course Oksana already understood, after seeing the evidence on the ground.

Of course she already knew how unlikely it was that she would ever see her cousin alive again

CHAPTER 13

UNS Pershing
Off the coast of Kamchatka
18 April 1952
0535 Hours

As soon as Admiral Suerte stepped through the hatch into sickbay, he saw the report had been true. For the first time since Hoax had been brought on-board, her eyes were open—halfway open and fluttering, to be sure, but still open.

Commander Tennyson, the ship's doctor, looked up from her bedside and nodded. "She's in and out," he said in his elegant-sounding British accent. "But it's the most progress we've seen so far."

"Thank God." Suerte posted himself on the side of the bed opposite Tennyson. As he gazed down at Hoax, her eyes flickered shut. "She's going to pull through, isn't she?"

"I believe so, yes." Tennyson scribbled something on his metal clipboard. "Her vital signs are improving. She still has a long road ahead of her, but she does seem to be on the mend."

"She'd better be." Suerte smiled grimly. "Otherwise, MacNeal will kill me when he gets back."

At the mention of MacNeal's name, Hoax's eyes snapped all the way open and focused on Suerte. "Where is he?" Her voice was weak and hoarse from days without speaking. "Where's MacNeal?"

Witnessing her burst of energy filled Suerte with a sense of relief. Her consciousness was an excellent sign. "He's ashore on a mission, following up on the intel your team brought back from Tokyo."

Hoax's eyes fluttered shut, then slid back open. "Ashore… where?"

"Kamchatka, Russia," said Suerte. "The Shōgunate has landed an expeditionary force. MacNeal's attempting to determine their objective and prevent them from attaining it."

"No." Hoax rolled her head slowly from side to side. "Bring him back."

"Bring back MacNeal?" Suerte frowned. "Why do you say that, Lieutenant?"

Hoax's eyelids fluttered, then opened steady again. "I had a terrible dream." Her lips moved silently before more words emerged. "It was…so real."

Tennyson spoke then, for Suerte's benefit. "We've been giving her morphine for the pain. It certainly could have caused vivid hallucinations."

Suddenly Hoax's hand shot up and grabbed Suerte's wrist. "Not… hallucinations. They need me."

Her grip tightened so hard, it hurt, but Suerte didn't try to break it. "You can't help them until you recover, Lieutenant. That's your only mission right now."

"You don't…understand." Hoax tried to pull herself up, then winced and slumped back on the pillow. "So much…darkness. It's waiting for them."

"MacNeal can take care of himself and his men." Suerte nodded firmly. "That *hombre* has cheated death more times than I can remember."

"No, please." Hoax shifted restlessly under the blanket and bed sheet. "You've got to take me to him…before it's too late."

"All right, all right." Suerte looked at Tennyson, who was injecting something from a syringe into the intravenous bag hooked to Hoax's arm. "It'll be okay, Lieutenant. Don't worry."

"So much darkness." Hoax continued to thrash under the covers.

Tears ran from her eyes down the sides of her head. "So much terrible *darkness*. I have to *help* them."

"You will, you will." Suerte's heart went out to her. She seemed so vulnerable, so scared for her teammates, so different from her usual hard-bitten self.

"No…please, no." Slowly, Hoax's movements calmed as whatever Tennyson had given her took effect. "Save them…got to…save them." Finally her eyes closed and she fell silent.

Tennyson lifted her arm and checked her pulse at the wrist. "Vital signs are steady. She's all right."

Suerte stared regretfully down at her face. "Seems like a shame to put her back under after waiting so long for her to come out of it."

"She became too agitated." Tennyson gently laid Hoax's arm down on the bed. "I was afraid she might damage some stitches and reopen the wound in her side."

Suerte patted her shoulder and stepped back. "Well, you take good care of her. Keep the progress reports coming." He reached for the wheel on the hatch, then scowled. "And let's hope those nightmares of hers are just that—bad dreams."

Tennyson shrugged. "I told you, it's the morphine."

"I know what you told me." Suerte took a last look at Hoax's face. Even asleep, her brow was knotted, her expression troubled. He wasn't a superstitious man, but he couldn't help but wonder if she'd seen something other than a dream in her near-death visions.

He couldn't help but feel a nagging ache in his gut as he turned the wheel, opened the hatch, and stepped out into the corridor. MacNeal was famous—and infamous—for cheating death.

Could this be the time his luck finally ran out?

CHAPTER 14

Kamchatka
18 April 1952
0554 Hours

Hiruko was breaking camp, stowing his folded pup tent in his pack, when Von Heïzinger glided up to tower over him. "I find this morning most agreeable."

"Yes, Generalleutnant." As always, Hiruko tried to keep his fear of the man as carefully stowed away as his gear. And he kept his opinions to himself, though he saw nothing at all "agreeable" about that morning.

Torrential rains had belted the valley all night, leaving the ground a super-saturated, muddy mess. Chilly drizzle still shivered out of the grey skies, and a murky mist clung to the ground. Most normal human beings would consider it the exact opposite of agreeable, but, well…

Von Heïzinger was Von Heïzinger.

"And how is Nadia this morning?" he said.

"I am on my way to see her, sir." Hiruko spoke German to Von Heïzinger, as usual, as he finished stowing the tent and reached for his bedroll.

Before he could touch it, Von Heïzinger bumped it out of reach with the toe of his muddy black boot. "Then I will join you."

Hiruko spotted the Daimyō nearby, watching the scene play out as he talked to the lab-coated scientist, Dr. Kondo. Without hesitation, Hiruko abandoned the bedroll and marched briskly toward Nadia's tent with Von Heïzinger in tow.

It was one of the largest tents in camp, second only to Von Heïzinger's. As they walked toward it, Von Heïzinger fell into step behind Hiruko, letting him reach the tent flap first.

"Go ahead." Von Heïzinger gestured at the flap. "Summon her."

Hiruko cleared his throat and called into the tent. "Ma'am? It's Mr. Orochi."

There was no answer from inside. Von Heïzinger grunted. "Again."

"Nadia?" This time, Hiruko spoke louder. He waited a moment, but no answer came. "Would you like me to give you a hand?"

Still, Nadia did not respond.

Hiruko kept trying. "Nadia? Are you all right?" Still nothing. "Nadia?"

"Nadia! Open up!" Von Heïzinger stomped forward as he snapped out orders. He smacked his hand against the canvas wall of the tent. "I demand that you let me in."

When that didn't get an answer, Von Heïzinger pushed Hiruko aside and reached for the zipper pull at the upper left corner of the flap. He yanked it over and down, and the flap fell outward, away from the seam.

As soon as Von Heïzinger had unzipped the entire flap, he plunged through the open entrance in a ripple of black leather. Hiruko leaned in for a look, but at first couldn't see past Von Heïzinger's tall cap and long overcoat. Worried for Nadia, he decided to step through after the generalleutnant and hope it didn't get him punished or killed.

"Nadia! No!" Suddenly, Von Heïzinger dropped to the ground. "I warned you!"

Finally, Hiruko could see the old woman, curled up like an overcooked prawn on a bamboo mat. Her eyes were closed, her mouth open, her hands knotted into fists. Her colorful babushka head scarf was on the mat beside her, and the long black dress she wore was smudged with patches of damp brown dirt.

"You know the rules!" Von Heïzinger grabbed her shoulder with his black-gloved hand and shook her. "You will not *leave* unless I *permit* it!" He shook her harder.

Hiruko's heart pounded like a piston in his chest. Was Nadia dead?

Von Heïzinger reached between the red lapels of his overcoat and drew out a gold object hanging from a chain around his throat. The object looked like a wedge of a circular amulet or medallion, three inches along its arcing edge, engraved with strange and intricate symbols. "You *will* come back to me!"

Hiruko watched as Von Heïzinger raised the amulet, placed a hand on Nadia's temple, and closed his eyes. Bowing his head, he whispered something Hiruko could barely make out in a language he didn't recognize—a stream of sibilant syllables hissing from his pale, chapped lips.

Suddenly, Nadia twitched on the bamboo mat. The fingers of one hand fluttered.

Von Heïzinger kept chanting. He raised the amulet higher and pinched his eyes more tightly shut.

Nadia twitched again, then moaned softly. A deep frown creased her heavily wrinkled face, and she shook her head.

Von Heïzinger's chanting grew louder…and that was when the amulet started glowing with a pulsing golden light. As the glow from the amulet grew brighter, he began to sway back and forth, his gloved fingertips kneading Nadia's temple.

Nadia groaned and thrashed on the mat. Von Heïzinger rocked and chanted, and the amulet's light intensified. The combination of movement, chanting, and pulsing reached a crescendo.

And suddenly, Hiruko saw a spiral streamer of golden light flash down from above and dive into Nadia's head. When all the light had passed into her, she sucked in a deep, shuddering breath, as if life had returned to her body all at once.

Von Heïzinger let the amulet fall to his chest. "She is back." Angrily, he snatched his fingers away from her temple. "She should have known better."

Hiruko watched as Nadia's eyes flickered open. At that moment, he glimpsed something so familiar, it made him ache—a sadness so deep, a hopelessness so powerful, they cast an impenetrable shadow on her heart.

With a snarl, Von Heïzinger drew back one gloved hand and struck her across the face. "You thought you could *escape* me? Did you forget about the Patmos Amulet in my possession?"

Nadia glared up at him defiantly.

Von Heïzinger struck her once more. "The amulet gives me the power to dominate *minds*. I will use it again, if I have to…and next time, it will not be so *pleasant* for you!"

Nadia drew in a steadying breath and spoke through quivering lips. "Why can't you let me go, Hermann?"

Von Heïzinger got to his feet and straightened his overcoat. "Clean her up," he snapped at Hiruko. "I expect her to be ready for breakfast in fifteen minutes."

"*Hermann.*" Nadia snapped out the words. "If you still love me, let me *go*."

Von Heïzinger looked down at her with his death's head smile. "Why of course I love you." He ran his gloved thumb and forefinger along the leather brim of his cap. "Which is why I will not allow your body *or* soul to stray from my loving arms for long."

With that, he spun and swept out of the tent, his black overcoat whipping behind him.

As soon as Hiruko was alone with Nadia, he rushed to kneel beside her. "What can I do? How can I help?"

Slowly, she lifted her head from the mat. "Get me out of here, Mr. Orochi." Her voice was a broken whisper. "Whatever it takes, get me away from him."

His heart went out to her. The side of her face was already black and blue from Von Heïzinger's blows as she looked up at him. Again he saw that terrible depth of sadness and hopelessness in her eyes, that looming shadow enwrapping her captive soul. And in that instant, to his surprise, he realized how truly alike they were.

* * *

Taki and Tala crouched behind the tumbled boulders in front of the mountainside recess where they'd spent the night. Gaps between the boulders made perfect peepholes to spy on the enemy forces sixty feet below.

"Some kind of commotion down there." Tala kept peering through the peephole as she narrated. "Von Heïzinger just stormed out of someone's tent and started yelling at people. Boy, does he look mad."

"I'm sure that's putting it mildly," said Taki.

"Now he's screaming at Zermann." Tala shifted position, trying for a better angle through the peephole. "What do you think has him so worked up?"

"Lack of cooperation?"

"But the Shōgunate troops have been bending over backward to accommodate him, from what I've been able to see."

"Maybe he just got some bad news," suggested Taki.

"Hey, look at the amphib truck parked at the back of the line." Tala moved to another peephole. "What's with the guy in the lab coat?"

Taki wedged his face against the rocks and peered down through another peephole. Sure enough, a middle-aged Japanese man in a white lab coat stood outside the open hatch of the third amphibious vehicle. He wrote something on a clipboard, then turned toward Iroh Minamoto, who was standing next to him. Taki could see the name tag on his lab coat.

"His name's Dr. Kondo. They're talking about whatever's in the truck." As Taki watched, Dr. Kondo and Minamoto talked and gestured at something in the boxy cargo compartment of the vehicle. The way the transport was turned, he couldn't get a look at what was inside.

"I'd love to know what's in there," said Tala. "I'll bet it would give us a clue to what they're after."

Taki continued to watch Kondo and Minamoto discuss the contents of the transport. "Is it some kind of equipment, do you think? Something a scientist would have to monitor?"

Before Tala could reply, the mountainside rumbled underneath them—another tremor like the one the night before. Instantly, they both scooted back from the boulders on the ledge and into the recess.

The rumbling died down, and Taki started to relax…but then it started up again and intensified. Loose pebbles tumbled from above and fell past the recess, reminding him that an indentation in the mountainside might not be the best place to seek shelter. What if more than pebbles fell, enough to block the entrance and trap them inside?

Tala looked like she might be thinking the same thing. "This is worse than last night. I wonder if one of the volcanoes is getting ready to blow?"

"I wonder," said Taki. "Or maybe it's something else."

"Something else?" She frowned. "Like what?"

Taki shrugged. "Something we don't know about yet. The reason the Shōgunate and Von Heïzinger are here, maybe."

* * *

MacNeal wasn't the only one who felt dead on his feet. Every time he looked into the eyes of one of his men, or one of the New Guard, he could tell they were equally exhausted.

The lot of them had spent the night searching the area in all directions for the missing man, Genedi Smolensk. The rain had poured and the ground had quaked as they'd combed the meadow and surrounding woods for miles, rifling every tangle of brush, lighting up every hole, pit, and thicket. In spite of the evidence of his death—the uniform and entrails left behind—they had dared to hope against hope that Smolensk might somehow have survived.

Now, as the latest shift straggled back to camp in the wan light of what passed for morning, the results of all their searching were evident on their haggard faces.

He could see the resignation in Oksana's eyes when she slogged toward him through the mud, empty-handed except for her glowing Vesper scepter. "No sign of him?" Even as she said it, there was no hope in her voice or expression.

MacNeal shook his head. "Nothing." Even Tatiana with her Baba Yaga prayers and supposedly mystical connection to the wilderness had found no trace of Genedi. No trace, at least, other than the piles of clothing and entrails.

Oksana stopped in front of him and sighed deeply. "My poor cousin." She looked around at the men plodding back into camp, all equally dispirited. "He was a true believer in the work of the New Guard. He wanted to make the Motherland a better place." Her eyes glistened with the moisture of tears. "He followed my lead."

MacNeal wanted to reach out and comfort her. She'd known from the start that Smolensk must be dead, but she'd mounted a search anyway. Now the hard truth had settled in…but could she accept it?

"The next detail is ready to go out."

Oksana sighed again and rubbed her eyes. When she pulled her hand away, the tears were gone. "No more searching." Her face was grey as the dismal morning sky and twice as grim. "We have a mission."

"I can take my men on alone, if you want to extend the search," said MacNeal. "We can rendezvous later."

Oksana drew a deep breath and let it out slowly. "Absolutely not. We refuse to abandon our allies. Besides…" She managed a weak approximation of a smile. "…it would be a shame if we missed out on our fifty percent share of the objective, wouldn't it?"

"Yes, it would." MacNeal saw Brown leading in a search team and waved him over. "Wrap it up, Boomer. We need to move on."

"Yes, sir." Brown looked as discouraged as everyone else, but not as tired. In a pinch, he could go without sleep for ages without showing fatigue. "Ma'am." He met Oksana's gaze. "I want you to know we did our best looking for him."

"Thank you." A shadow crossed her face briefly and was gone, replaced by a mask of smooth professionalism. "Please tell Ivan I need to see him."

"Will do." Brown touched the brim of his cap and moved on, the big flash machine gun swinging at his hip.

Oksana turned to MacNeal. "There is another reason not to split up, my friend."

MacNeal raised his eyebrows. "What's that?"

"Whoever has killed my cousin, he or she may be among us." She fixed him in a gaze laden with dark meaning and intensity. "New Guard, Union, or otherwise, I intend to find that person or thing and punish them to the fullest extent of my hatred." With that, she turned and walked off to meet Ivan, who had spoken to Brown and was marching toward her through the muck.

* * *

Unseen, Wolf whisked through the foothills on his way to a rendezvous, tracing shortcuts and back routes unknown to the invaders. Did he feel regret for putting his sometime friend MacNeal through the wringer? A little, but it had to be done for the sake of the mission.

Suddenly, a bird-like shadow crossed his path and he stopped cold. His gaze shot skyward as he looked for the source of the shadow, wondering if it was a hawk gliding past on currents of air.

But no. It was his ally, the driving force behind the whole operation, arrived for the rendezvous. It was the Dark God himself.

Wolf watched as he descended, spiraling down from the heights. He radiated enough barely contained power to strike at anyone who crossed him, to make his wishes a reality, to carry the game forward against formidable opponents.

He was the one who would make the next strike. It wasn't enough to wreak havoc with MacNeal's Union team and the Russian rebels.

Now it was time for the Shōgunate and Reich to feel the bite, too. Never mind that snaring an asset of theirs would be more dangerous, given the predatory creatures Itami and Zermann.

The Dark God, a predator himself, no more feared them than he might fear a rabbit. Wolf knew that nothing would stop him from claiming the next piece on the board.

CHAPTER 15

Kamchatka
18 April 1952
0736 Hours

There had been no breakfast for Nadia.

It had taken Hiruko a while to clean her up after Von Heïz-inger's attack. When she was finally presentable, he'd helped her struggle across camp through the mud to Von Heïzinger's tent. It had been no easy task; she'd moved even more slowly than usual. She'd planted her twisted canes one after the other with painstaking care—the black one, then the blond one, then the black.

At first, when they'd reached their destination, Hiruko had thought all was forgiven. Von Heïzinger had greeted them with a plate of steaming food: scrambled eggs, sausage, and fried potatoes. The smell of it had been enough to make Hiruko's stomach growl.

But then, Von Heïzinger had dumped the plate in the mud at Nadia's feet. "You must learn, there are consequences for your actions."

Nadia had stiffened, glaring as Von Heïzinger had stretched toward her like a snake. Hiruko had shivered along with her as the pale, sinister visage had drawn closer.

"No breakfast for you, Nadia," Von Heïzinger had said. "And no comfortable coach ride, either. Today, you *walk*." He'd snatched away the black cane and broken it over his leg. "You walk without *these*." He'd grabbed the blond cane from her grip, though she'd tried to hold on to it, and broken that one in pieces, too. "Enjoy your exercise!"

That was why, now, as the expedition set out, the old woman staggered behind the last vehicle, holding on to Hiruko for dear life.

"Ma'am?" Hiruko's voice was tentative. He wasn't sure if he should pry. "What did he mean when he said you were trying to escape?"

"Just that." Nadia was breathing heavily from the effort of trudging through the mud. "I was trying to get away from him."

Hiruko frowned. "But you never left the tent. You were lying there when we came in."

"I was far away, Mr. Orochi." Nadia slipped on a sloppy patch and fell against him. It took her a moment to regain her footing. "But not quite far *enough*, apparently."

"I don't understand," said Hiruko. "How could you be far away if your body was in the tent?"

"My *body* was there, but my *spirit* wasn't."

"Do you mean you were dying?" asked Hiruko.

"No." She shook her head slowly. "I mean my spirit was traveling separately from my physical form. My body was trapped there, but my *soul* was free…until he pulled me back, at least."

"How is that possible?"

"The goddess Baba Yaga makes all things possible to a priestess of the order." Nadia sighed. "*Almost* all things, that is. She has yet to liberate me from my captivity."

Just then, Itami bounded back from the convoy, kenabō club over his shoulder. "Greetings, my friends." His voice was dripping with false sincerity. He even bowed his head at Nadia.

As always, Hiruko felt a wave of fear overtaking him in the presence of the blue-skinned devil. "*Hai*."

"Very good, very good." Itami smiled, speaking Japanese. "How are you finding your hike? Not too slippery, I trust? No falling in the mud?"

"No, sir." Even as Hiruko said it, Itami lunged forward and

knocked him down with a flick of his hand. Since Nadia was holding on tight to him, she tumbled with him into the muck.

"Until now, it seems." Itami bowed. "But do not worry, my friends. I have done you a favor. When the generalleutnant sees the shape you are in, he will surely decide you have suffered enough and will let you back aboard your vehicle."

Hiruko didn't dare show his anger or disgust. Instead, he focused on dredging himself out of the mud and getting Nadia back on her feet.

"You are most welcome." Itami smirked. "It has been my pleasure to serve you." With that, he turned and marched back toward the convoy, which by then had drawn farther away from them all.

In the midst of his bounding stride, however, he stumbled. He landed on his feet but seemed off balance, staggering as if the world was tilting under him.

Hiruko was standing, in the process of lifting Nadia. "Something's wrong with him," he said, switching back to German for Nadia's benefit. Grunting, he hefted her up beside him. "He looks dizzy."

"Get me over to him." Nadia said it firmly, in spite of her recent trauma. "Do it now."

Hiruko was puzzled but did as she said. As quickly as he could while still being careful, he led Nadia over the muddy ground to Itami, who was still staggering.

When they reached the horned hulk, she snapped at him. "You! Stand still!"

Itami froze, more or less, though he couldn't have understood her German. Even as he stood there, his body kept weaving from side to side like a sapling in a stiff breeze.

"I need to touch him," said Nadia. When Hiruko did not immediately comply, she smacked his wrist. "*Now*."

Hiruko guided her the last bit forward, and she reached out with one quivering hand. Her fingertips landed lightly on the pale blue skin of Itami's back, and she closed her eyes.

"I see," she said softly. "Yes, I see."

Suddenly, Itami whirled to face her. "Old woman! Remove your hands! My condition is not your concern!" With that, he charged away from her, heading once more for the now-distant convoy. His movements were steady again; he no longer looked like he was dizzy or off balance.

"I see now," said Nadia. "I know what we're looking for."

"What?" asked Hiruko. "What is it?"

"Some kind of heavenly power." Nadia raised her shaking hand as if she were still touching Itami's hide. "The closer he gets to it, the more it disorients him."

Hiruko remembered the Shōgun saying they were going to retrieve a "heavenly prize." "Why does it disorient him?"

"There is something...*demonic*...in his nature." Nadia frowned. "I *think*. He is difficult to read. Something about him disrupts my insight."

"Demonic." Hiruko had no trouble believing it.

"So there are otherworldly forces in play here." Nadia nodded and rubbed her chin. "It would explain why Von Heïzinger needed me for this expedition."

"Why he abducted you?" asked Hiruko.

"Exactly." Nadia glared at him with unexpected fire for a ninety-seven-year-old. "Because I have *been* to other worlds, Mr. Orochi. I am one of the few to have gone there and *come back* to tell the tale."

* * *

Tala had wanted to toss a grenade at the blue-skinned freak after the way he'd knocked down the soldier and the old woman. She and Taki, following the convoy through the valley, had watched the scene from a mountain ridge above.

Now, she was glad she hadn't blown him up after all. Because the erratic behavior she'd just witnessed might be the most important piece of intel she'd gathered since making landfall at Kamchatka.

"Something's wrong with Itami," she said. "Either he's had a few too many drinks..."

"Or he's coming down with something," chimed in Taki, who was lying beside her on the ridge.

"Or something else is affecting him." Tala watched through her binoculars as Itami loped back to the convoy, good as new. But the memory of him staggering around like a punch-drunk fighter stayed with her. "We need to find out what it is."

"Whatever it is, it knocked him for a loop," said Taki from behind his own binoculars. "Could it have something to do with the tectonic activity in the area? Animals can sense tremors and quakes long before humans can. Maybe Itami's the same way."

"Maybe." Tala switched her view from Itami to the old woman and Hiruko. "Or maybe there's something else altogether going on here. Something we can't even guess at."

Taki pulled the radio from his belt. "We need to call this in, don't we?"

"You better believe it," said Tala as she continued watching Hiruko and the old woman.

* * *

Taki's call came in just as the Union and New Guard forces were getting ready to move out. His information on Itami's impairment was potentially crucial; MacNeal was glad to know there might be a chink in that powerful creature's armor.

But MacNeal's news was bigger, its impact more immediate. Smolensk's murder meant that everyone—including Taki and Tala—was at a greater risk. Taki was a cool customer, but even so, MacNeal heard the worry in his voice as the details of the murder flowed over the radio channel.

After the call, the Union and New Guard forces got back underway on the trail of the Shōgunate and Reich. One thing was clear to MacNeal as he and Brown marched at the head of the column: it was going to be a hell of a long day.

It wasn't even 0830 yet and the heat was already high. The steamy air was so thick with humidity, it was practically solid. Drizzle fell off and on from the shelf of dark grey clouds stalled overhead. The ground was so muddy, the voïvodes couldn't scuttle through it on their segmented legs and had to be carried on makeshift stretchers. Occasional tremors rippled underfoot, raising the fear that something bigger was on the way.

And one more thing: at some point overnight, it seemed that millions of mosquitoes had been hatched and turned loose.

"Damn bugs!" Brown scowled and slapped the back of his neck. "They're biting like crazy!"

"Tell me about it." MacNeal glared at the swollen red spots on his forearms. "I've got bites *on top* of my bites. Mosquitoes're coming out of the woodwork."

"All it took was one good rainy night, I guess." Brown stared at the hand he'd slapped his neck with, then suddenly smacked his bare bicep. "It brought out *all* the little bloodsuckers, didn't it?"

MacNeal took a quick look around to make sure none of the New Guard was nearby. "How's the surveillance going, Boomer?" He'd instructed Brown and the other Union men to watch the New Guard for anything suspicious. He guessed Oksana had done the same with her people.

"Nothing new," Brown said quietly. "But my money's on Ivan. Talk about a grade-A *chump*."

"Maybe this alliance wasn't such a great idea." MacNeal felt a tickle on his cheek and slapped it. "Our profile's too big. We're too good of a target."

"I still think it was the right play, Major. Zermann and Itami left us five men down. The alliance gave us the firepower we need to finish the mission."

"And then we get to fight over the prize." MacNeal checked his hand, which was bloody from the last mosquito slap, then wiped it on his pants. "Boomer." He'd been talking softly, and now he dropped his voice even more. "We need to be ready in case they won't honor our agreement."

Brown casually looked away. "Already on it, sir. We'll be ready when the time comes."

"*If* it comes," said MacNeal. "Maybe the New Guard won't be a problem."

"One way or another, we both know they *will* be." Brown's expression was grim, his voice matter-of-fact. "The Matriarchy is a Union ally. They won't approve of us handing over any percentage of what we find to a rebel organization. *Especially* if it's any kind of weapon."

"Then again," said MacNeal, "what the Matriarchy doesn't know won't hurt it. Maybe we can keep the situation under wraps."

Brown shrugged. "Or maybe it won't matter if people keep *dying*."

"You don't think we've seen the last murder?"

Brown looked at MacNeal like he was crazy. "You saw those leave-behinds, didn't you? Whoever did that to Smolensk is highly organized and severely twisted. I'd be more surprised if he *didn't* kill someone else."

MacNeal thought about it, swatting away gnats and mosquitoes. He knew Brown was right; they were being stalked. The only question was, who would die next?

"We can always break away if you like," said Brown. "We know we can trust our own men. Might improve our chances."

MacNeal shook his head. "Let's see how this plays out a little longer first."

Brown raised his eyebrows. "Even if we lose more 42nd Marines?"

"That won't happen." MacNeal looked at him gravely. "Because you won't let it, will you, Boomer?"

"No, sir." Brown snapped off a crisp salute.

They both knew it might be an empty promise, but MacNeal was satisfied that he'd gotten his message across. "That's what I thought."

* * *

Hiruko and Nadia steadily fell farther and farther behind the convoy. Finally, near a bend that fed into a ravine, they lost sight of the expedition completely.

"I don't understand," said Hiruko. "I thought the generalleutnant didn't want to let you go. Why would he abandon you like this?"

"He wouldn't." Nadia pointed at a tumble of boulders along the base of the ravine wall. "Take me over there, will you, Mr. Orochi? We might as well rest a bit."

Hiruko hesitated, looking in the direction of the convoy. "But shouldn't we try to catch up?"

She brushed an angry wave through the air. "I'm done playing his game for now. I've let him punish me enough. Now get me over there."

Hiruko did as she asked. When they got to the boulders, he helped her sit back against a big one in the shadow of the rock wall. Then he set about pacing the muddy ground in front of her, worrying over what he should do next.

"Everything will be all right, Mr. Orochi," said Nadia. "I promise. Hermann would never leave me alone long enough for me to escape."

Hiruko stopped pacing. "The Union and Matriarchy are following us. What if they found you? You could escape him then, couldn't you?"

She shook her head. "Hermann won't let that happen. He still *needs* me. For what reason, I don't know."

Hiruko started pacing again. "But what if he decides he doesn't need you after all? What if he leaves you here to die?"

"That will never happen."

"Him leaving you here?" asked Hiruko.

"No, no, the other part." Nadia shook her head. "The part about me dying."

"Why?" Hiruko stopped. "Why do you say that will never happen?"

"Because I have…resources." She smiled.

"What resources?"

Nadia spread her hands. "All of it. All of nature around us."

Hiruko folded his arms over his chest. He liked Nadia, he felt she was a kindred spirit, but he couldn't see the sense in what she was saying. "All of nature?"

"Hand me those weeds." She pointed at a clump of spindly plants with little daisy-like flowers in the mud at Hiruko's feet.

Bending down, he wrapped his hand around the clump and pulled it out, roots and all. Then he brought it to her.

"Thank you, Mr. Orochi." Nadia took the weeds in her fist, closed her eyes, and chanted something under her breath. The plants shivered in her shaky grip as she raised them to eye level. Then, with as sudden a movement as a ninety-seven-year-old woman could manage, she swung her arm sideways and back, plunging the plants toward the boulder against which she leaned.

She held them there and continued chanting for a long moment. When she pulled her hand away, the weeds stayed behind, standing up straight on the surface of the rock.

Nadia opened her eyes and pushed away from the boulder. "Now watch, Mr. Orochi." She waved her hands over the weeds, and they fluttered.

Hiruko moved in for a better look. At first, he thought the weeds were just stuck to the rock…but the closer he got, the more they looked like they were actually rooted *into* the rock, as if she'd somehow *planted* them inside it.

"Here it comes." Nadia smiled and snapped the fingers of both hands. Then, she let out a sharp little cry of delight that surprised Hiruko.

He was even more surprised by what happened to the boulder. Suddenly, the weeds started growing at an insane rate, bursting from the spot where they'd been rooted and fanning out over the big rock. They rolled over it in all directions, becoming a mat of green vines that twisted and twined and grew thicker with each passing second.

When the boulder was completely enshrouded, the blanket of green sent down two sturdy shoots that flattened and broadened like feet against the muddy ground. Nadia stumbled back, laughing, weaving her hands in the air like an orchestra conductor...and one of the feet moved. It slid forward through the muck, pulling the right side of the boulder along with it. Then the other foot did the same, bringing the left side forward to meet the right.

Gaping in shock, Hiruko staggered away from it. What he was seeing was impossible, utterly *impossible*. It had to be some kind of bizarre *trick*.

But it certainly looked *real* enough, didn't it?

Nadia kept conducting the green-covered rock as it continued its wobbly shuffle forward. "The goddess Baba Yaga could join things together and bring them to life." She swept her arms apart with fingers fluttering wildly, and the boulder walked faster. "She joined chicken legs to a house and made it her home. So too can a true priestess of her order join weeds or flesh and blood to a stone."

Hiruko rubbed his eyes hard, but the rock was still walking when he opened them again. Had she hypnotized him, somehow? True magic didn't exist...did it?

"Do you see now, Mr. Orochi?" Nadia kept conducting the rock forward. "Do you see why we would not die in the wilderness?"

"This can't be real," said Hiruko.

"As real as you or I standing here!"

"B-but why?" asked Hiruko. "If you can really *do* this, why haven't you used it to escape the generalleutnant?"

She guided the stone a moment more, then let her hands fall limp at her sides. The boulder fell, too, dropping to the mud between its makeshift feet.

The brief, savage joy that had filled her was gone. Her gaze lowered, her shoulders slumped. "He has the Patmos Amulet, which enables him to dominate my mind."

"What if someone took it away from him?"

"There is something else," said Nadia. "Another reason."

"What reason?" asked Hiruko.

"I'm ashamed to say it." Her eyes were filled with tears as she looked up and met his gaze. "Part of me still cares about him. Even after everything he's done." Her quivering fingers touched the black and blue bruise on the side of her face.

Hiruko went to her. He put his arm around her frail shoulders and let her lean against him. He wanted to tell her to let go of her feelings for Von Heïzinger; he wanted to tell her that the general-leutnant wasn't worth it.

But she already knew all that.

Just then, before either of them could say another word, the ground rumbled. He tightened his grip on her shoulders, holding her steady against the quake.

All the while, his eyes kept drifting back to the green-covered boulder, the rock that only moments ago had been walking through the mud at Nadia's command. Had the withered old woman leaning against him really made all that happen? If so, what *else* could she do?

Just how powerful *was* she?

CHAPTER 16

Kamchatka
18 April 1952
0908 Hours

As the ground rumbled, the Dark God watched from shadows in the rock face and picked his moment. Sidestepping the old lady and the bear charmer, he'd spotted perfect targets a half-mile on: two Japanese soldiers trekking back from the convoy to retrieve the people they'd left behind. When the soldiers marched into the bend at the mouth of the ravine, they would be out of sight of the convoy.

The Dark God's heart beat faster as he listened to the soldiers' boots approaching and prepared for action. He would have to strike like a whirlwind, leaving no time for either man to get off a shot, whisking them out of sight before anyone was the wiser. Then, he would lay out the remains, setting the stage as he'd done with the New Guard's man.

The footsteps were getting closer. He tensed, alternately tightening and relaxing his muscles. He took a deep breath and got ready to spring from his hiding place. Was it foolhardy, striking in midmorning like this instead of darkest night? Not for someone with his extraordinary powers and fighting skills.

Most importantly, taking two men in broad daylight would be demoralizing and infuriating to the Shōgunate expedition…precisely the effect he wished to create. He needed them to hurry, to act without thinking, to make mistakes. And he needed the Union and New Guard to do the same.

Smoothly, he stepped out of the shadows. He assessed the two soldiers with one swift glance and took down the both of them without breaking his stride. The man closest to him got a chop to the throat and a blow to the sternum. The other man whipped around his rifle and took a kick to the head for his trouble.

Within seconds, the Dark God was standing alone over the two bodies in the ravine. He lifted his face to the sky and let out a cry that sounded for all the world like the screech of a crow.

* * *

Hiruko heard the rumble of rolling treads long before he saw the amphibious vehicle emerge from the ravine. He'd had his doubts about Nadia's theory, but she'd been right; the convoy had sent someone back for them after all.

"Finally." Nadia pushed away from the rock she'd been leaning on and dusted off her hands. "It took them long enough."

Hiruko was just glad they'd come at all. Protecting and providing for the ninety-seven-year-old in the wilderness would have been a challenge, even if her power to merge organic and inorganic things was more than just some kind of trick.

The vehicle pulled up and stopped twenty feet away. The main hatch flew open, and two of Von Heïzinger's men marched out—his black-clad Schocktruppen with their dark goggles and death's head faceplates.

Von Heïzinger himself followed them out, then swept between and past them. His eyes were wide, his pasty face frozen in a furious glare. "You have gone too far! You have crossed the line and will suffer because of it!"

Hiruko had just put his arm around Nadia's back to brace her. He froze, staring at the ghoulish generalleutnant.

Nadia let out a heavy sigh. "What is it this time, Hermann?"

"Two Shōgunate men were sent to retrieve you." Von Heïzinger jabbed a finger toward the ravine. "They never returned. Their *remains* were found piled on the ground at the base of the rock wall. The I.D. tags found among those remains match the men sent after you—Fukuzawa and Hamada."

"We had nothing to do with that," said Nadia. "We've been standing here waiting for someone to come back for us."

"Is this your revenge play, *witch*?" Von Heïzinger gestured at the Schocktruppen, who stormed over to grab Nadia and Hiruko. "Pick us off one by one until I finally release you? Well, it won't happen! You will never sway *me*."

"*Hermann*." Nadia's voice was firm. "Take me to the remains."

Von Heïzinger lunged over and pushed his face close to hers. "So you can *gloat*?"

"So I can look for clues to the killer," said Nadia.

Von Heïzinger sneered. "Throw suspicion on someone else, you mean?"

"Hermann." Nadia's voice darkened. This time, it was her turn to crowd him, pushing her face so close to his that their noses touched. "If I *wanted* to kill someone to gain my freedom, would I waste my time killing anyone else but *you*?"

Von Heïzinger stayed locked with her, staring into her eyes like a vulture trying to will someone to die. Then, slowly, he drew back. "Consider yourself under arrest. *Both* of you." He flashed a look at Hiruko. "All privileges have been rescinded."

"Do your worst." Nadia glared at him. "I've been under arrest since the day you showed up at my village in the Ukraine and kidnapped me from my own home."

Hiruko wanted to suggest she not taunt Von Heïzinger; he had no desire to see the worst the generalleutnant could do. But he continued to stay silent.

Unlike Nadia. "Now are you going to show me those remains, Hermann, or shall we just stay here and dance around the point some more?"

Von Heïzinger stewed for a moment, then spun on his heel and marched toward the amphibious vehicle. "Bring them!"

As soon as he snapped out the command, the two Schocktruppen moved mechanically after him, hauling Hiruko and Nadia in his wake.

* * *

Ivan and Tatiana were having a knock-down-drag-out. They didn't seem to care who witnessed it, either.

As the Union and New Guard column marched along through the muck and mosquitoes, the two supposed lovebirds had it out. Unfortunately, the fight was in Russian; MacNeal could only make out a few words of it, though it was enough to give him the general idea. Most of what he understood from their exchange was ferociously obscene.

The shouting continued, rising to a fevered pitch, until Oksana finally intervened. She rattled off a string of clipped orders, and just like that, the fight was over…for the time being, at least. Tatiana charged past and disappeared around a bend; Ivan started after her, then reconsidered and dropped back to join MacNeal.

"Why must she be so difficult?" Ivan said under his breath, just loud enough for MacNeal to hear. "Why must she always test me?"

MacNeal shrugged. He wondered why, after all Ivan's hostile posturing, he was opening up to him all of a sudden. "Beats me, pal."

"She claims I do not appreciate her abilities." Ivan laughed ruefully. "*I* am the one who encouraged her to use them in the Guard!"

"That's what you're fighting about?" MacNeal couldn't have cared less, but Ivan was still a murder suspect. Tatiana was, too, for that matter. If Ivan suddenly wanted to confide in him, he might as well take advantage of the situation and find out everything he could.

"She was trying to tell me the murderer is some kind of supernatural force or being." Ivan sighed. "She got angry because I questioned her conclusion."

"You don't think it's possible?" asked MacNeal.

"I am a man of reason," said Ivan. "I believe, first and foremost, in what I can see with my own two eyes. What I can *prove*." He smacked his fist into his palm. "Not what is superstitious and supernatural and unprovable."

MacNeal nodded. He'd once been like Ivan, but had since seen too much to stay close-minded. His missions with the 42nd had taken him down some very dark paths without rational explanations.

"I cannot deny that her rituals for communing with Baba Yaga have been most effective." Ivan raised his hands, palms up, and shrugged. "But I question that they are solely based in the supernatural. And even though I admit the possibility that the supernatural can touch our lives, I do not accept it as the first, best explanation for *all* unexplained phenomena."

"If you don't think the supernatural is to blame," said MacNeal, "who do *you* think murdered Private Smolensk?"

Ivan looked at him with a glint in his eye. "I believe it could be anyone, Major. One of us, one of the Koryaks, a very stealthy Japanese ninja, anyone. The killer could be right under our noses at this very moment, do you not agree?"

MacNeal smiled. "You never know."

"Let me know when you find him," said Ivan, "or her." With that, he stomped off after Tatiana—to apologize or continue the fight, MacNeal didn't know.

But what he *did* know was that if a supernatural force were to blame for what had happened to Private Smolensk, the situation had just gotten much more complicated. And dangerous.

And unpredictable. Any time he got involved with the supernatural, the standard playbook went out the window. He never knew what to expect.

Suddenly, he found himself wishing he hadn't sent his resident shaman, Tala, on that far-forward scouting mission after all.

* * *

"Look at that." Tala adjusted her binoculars. "Two piles of guts, two piles of clothes. Just like what MacNeal said happened to Private Smolensk."

Taki lay on the ridge beside her, watching the scene in the ravine below. "I guess that's all that's left of the two men they sent back from the convoy."

"What I want to know is, how the hell did it happen without us seeing anything?" Tala lowered the binoculars and sighed. "We couldn't see this one section from our earlier positions, but we should've seen anyone coming in or out." She'd been at one end of the ravine, watching the convoy, and Taki had been at the other, watching the old woman and her attendant.

"Unless they went straight up." Taki raised his binoculars and scanned the sky.

"Not a chance." Just then, Tala spotted activity down below and swung her binoculars back in place. "Look. The vehicle's rolling back through…stopping at the piles. Von Heïzinger's getting out, and the old woman, too. Plus her valet."

As she and Taki watched, the old woman examined the piles in the mud. With help from her valet, she hunkered down and passed her hands over them.

Tala squinted into the binoculars. "She's saying something…in German, is it?"

"It's German, all right. Something about a 'god'?" Taki kept watching. "'They were touched by a god'?" He grunted in frustration. "Hard to tell from up here."

"What kind of god, I wonder?" Tala frowned as Von Heïzinger hauled the old woman to her feet and kicked one of the piles of clothes, scattering them. "And where are the rest of the bodies?"

"I hate to think about it," said Taki. "Could the locals have done this? They haven't put up any resistance so far. Maybe they decided to handle it guerilla-style."

"Whoever did it, they're good. *Really* good." Tala stared at the piles of guts glistening in the overcast morning light. "It isn't easy to pull off a pair of gruesome murders right under Von Heïzinger's nose."

"In broad daylight, no less," said Taki. "A real ninja."

"As long as they keep chipping away at the Shōgunate forces, I'm all for it." Tala lowered her binoculars and took a long look over her shoulder. "But I guess we should watch our backs more carefully just in case."

"A wise precaution," said Taki.

Tala returned her attention to the view through her binoculars. Just as she did, more people ran up to join the crowd around the remains. "Taki, look. Iroh Minamoto just arrived."

He scrambled to get his own binoculars back in place. "Along with Itami and Zermann."

"Iroh doesn't look happy," said Tala. "He's yelling at Von Heïzinger. Can you tell what he's saying?"

"I'd rather not repeat it," said Taki. "The words 'cursing up a storm' come to mind."

* * *

"What do you mean 'we're not searching for the killers'?!" The Daimyō's face was flushed as he snapped at Von Heïzinger. Hiruko had never seen him so angry before.

"Exactly that." Von Heïzinger spread his hands. "I could not have been more clear. It is imperative that we press on toward our objective."

"But we could still apprehend them!" The Daimyō's voice was rising steadily. "We must punish them for what they have done! We must have justice!"

"Does this man care about justice?" Von Heïzinger gestured at one of the piles of clothing. "Does this one?" He gestured at a pile of entrails.

The Daimyō surged toward him, veins twitching in his temples. "These are *my* men we're talking about. I won't let their killers escape at your *whim*."

"They are *my* men, *Daimyō*." The word curled out of his brittle lips with pure disgust. "By order of your most *esteemed* Shōgun. And I say justice has no meaning to them. I say they are disposable." Leaning forward, he cast a glowering gaze at the Daimyō, exuding hatred with blazing intensity. "Much like *yourself*."

The Daimyō glared back at him for a long moment. Hiruko thought he could see a battle raging within him, a struggle between the desire for action and the need for restraint. Was he finally going to challenge Von Heïzinger? Hiruko took a step back just in case.

But it turned out he didn't need to after all. The Daimyō kept his gaze locked on Von Heïzinger and slowly shook his head, but there were no fireworks.

"Damn you," he muttered. "Damn you straight to whatever hell you crawled out of."

Von Heïzinger summoned up an icy, mirthless smirk. "Perhaps you would prefer to stay behind and search for the killers yourself," he said, "while I continue onward in *sole* command of the expedition."

The Daimyō uttered a stream of curses, then turned to Hiruko. "At least gather up their uniforms, Jōtōhei Orochi."

"*Hai*." Hiruko saluted and moved to comply. He was worried

Von Heïzinger might try to stop him, but he didn't.

The Daimyō turned back to Von Heïzinger. "If you will excuse me, Marquis Generalleutnant, I must prepare my *remaining* men to 'press on.'"

Von Heïzinger didn't answer. He was too busy staring at Zermann. "Is something the matter?"

Zermann was clutching his skull with both hands. "*Head.*"

Itami, who was standing nearby, was rubbing his own head and scowling. "How extraordinary. I have been experiencing exactly the same symptom."

"Ah, yes." Von Heïzinger nodded. "The farther we travel, the worse it gets?"

"Correct," said Itami.

"And are there other…symptoms?" asked Von Heïzinger.

"Occasional dizziness," said Itami, "and nausea."

"*Head,*" Zermann repeated, shaking his head hard as if to clear it of cobwebs. "*Doom…*" He raised his infamous Luger with its glowing barrel. "*…misses.*"

"Splendid." Von Heïzinger pulled the black leather glove from his left hand and gazed at the glowing red ring on his index finger. Hiruko remembered he'd called it the *Orbis Christus*; he couldn't be sure, but it seemed to be glowing brighter than before. "Then we must keep moving."

"Our illness is *splendid*?" asked Itami.

Von Heïzinger ignored him and marched toward the amphibious vehicle. "Move out! No further delays!" He paused at the hatch for another look at his glowing ring. "The trail is getting warmer!"

CHAPTER 17

**Kamchatka
18 April 1952
1309 Hours**

The bugs were getting worse. MacNeal was slapping at them as if there were a dozen tiny brush fires on his neck and arms and face. The whole time he was talking to Tala on the radio, getting the story on the two Shōgunate men who'd been killed Private Smolensk-style, he was smacking at the insects nipping his flesh.

It took a scream piercing the air after the call ended to take his mind off the bugs. It was a woman's scream—not Oksana's, since she was walking nearby, so it had to be Tatiana's. Without saying a word, MacNeal leaped into action, swinging up his flash-gun and charging toward the jumble of little hills where the cry had originated.

He heard footsteps running behind him, though he didn't turn to see who was back there. He was far more focused on Tatiana and whatever danger she was in. Had the killer returned to claim his second victim?

Heart pounding, MacNeal hurtled among the hills with his flash-gun at the ready. Just as he lost the direction, another scream followed the first, and he instantly homed in on it.

Barreling between two slopes, he burst into a gap among the hills and stopped in his tracks. Directly ahead, fewer than twenty feet away, he saw Tatiana sprawled on the muddy ground, clutching her arm. Ivan hunched over her with fists and teeth clenched, heaving and glaring.

Without hesitation, MacNeal raised the flash-gun and pointed it right at Ivan. It seemed pretty obvious to him what had just happened here. "Stand down, Ivan!"

Ivan scowled with apparent confusion. "Do not just stand there, MacNeal! He is getting away!"

MacNeal had no intention of letting him out of his sights. "*Who's* getting away, Ivan?"

Just then, Oksana ran up and stopped beside MacNeal, panting softly. "Explain yourself, Pervyja Lejtenant!"

"The killer! He attacked Tatiana!" Ivan gestured vaguely at the hills behind him. "I got here just in time and scared him away!"

He was lying. MacNeal was sure of it. After all, the killer had just been miles away, murdering two Shōgunate men. "Is that so?" The flash-gun in his grip didn't budge the slightest fraction of an inch.

"You must *apprehend* him!" Again, Ivan gestured at the hills. "He is getting away!"

At that moment, Brown and a contingent of Union and New Guard soldiers arrived, weapons in hand. "*Who's* getting away?"

MacNeal shot him a look. "He claims the killer attacked her."

Brown nodded and sized up Ivan. MacNeal could tell he'd caught the underlying meaning in his words: *her boyfriend gave her a beating.*

Oksana went to Tatiana and crouched down beside her. "This is true? You were attacked?"

MacNeal took his eyes off Ivan long enough to see a flicker of fear cross Tatiana's face. Her gaze slid from Oksana to Ivan, then back again. One of her eyes, MacNeal realized, was black and blue. So were the sides of her throat.

Tatiana hesitated, then nodded slowly. "He came out of nowhere. I do not know what he might have done if Ivan had not come along when he did."

MacNeal didn't believe her for a second. "What did the killer look like?" He already knew what she would say before she said it.

"I do not know." Tatiana shrugged. "He grabbed me from behind. I did not get a look at him."

Of course you didn't. He was miles away. MacNeal finally lowered the gun, though he wanted to fire a few rounds in frustration. Everyone there knew the truth of the matter, but no one was willing to take action unless Tatiana changed her story.

"What about your weapons?" MacNeal gestured at her sawed-off shotguns, which were still in their holsters on her hips.

Tatiana shook her head. "He restrained me from behind. I was in shock the whole time. When he ran off, I could not react fast enough to shoot before he reached cover."

"Think hard, Tatiana." Oksana put a hand on her shoulder. "Do you remember anything at all about the man who attacked you?"

Tatiana closed her eyes. "He was very strong." Her brow creased as she frowned from the strain of remembering…or lying. "He had an accent I did not recognize."

"What did he say to you?" asked Oksana.

"That he was going to kill me and rip out my guts." Tatiana opened her eyes. "That was all he said. Then Ivan scared him away."

Oksana made a point of leaning closer and meeting her gaze. "You are sure you do not have anything else to tell me? Anything at all?"

Tatiana shook her head. Then Ivan stepped in and helped her to her feet.

"All right." Oksana sighed. "Let us get those bruises treated, at least."

"I will take care of them, Kapetan." Ivan snaked an arm around Tatiana's shoulders and started leading her in the direction of the Union and New Guard column. "You can depend on me."

MacNeal's fingers twitched on the stock of his flash-gun as Ivan guided Tatiana past him. The men locked eyes, exchanging volleys of unspoken hostility in an instant.

Then, Ivan moved on to Brown, who was blocking his path. They stayed like that for a moment, facing off, until MacNeal spoke up. "Let them through, Boomer." Even then, Brown was slow to step aside, and kept his eyes glued on Ivan until he and Tatiana were out of sight.

When they were gone, MacNeal turned to Brown. "Keep an eye on him."

"You know I will." Brown nodded and stormed off after Ivan and Tatiana. The other Union men fell in behind him.

Oksana ordered the New Guard contingent to return to the unit, and then she and MacNeal were alone.

"So that's it?" asked MacNeal. "We just let him walk away."

"Yes." Oksana let out a long sigh. "We let him walk."

"But his story can't be true. I've learned from my scouts that two Shōgunate men were just murdered the same way as Private Smolensk. The killer was far away when *this* happened." MacNeal gestured around him at the scene of the crime.

Oksana raised her eyebrows. "That is interesting information, MacNeal...but it does not influence my decision."

"You don't think Ivan's *guilty*?" asked MacNeal. "You don't think he *did* that to her?"

"Of course he did," said Oksana. "Obviously, he is lying about the killer attacking Tatiana. She is lying, too...covering up his misdeed. But there is more going on here than you know. Tatiana is following my orders to protect Ivan."

MacNeal scowled. "Why the hell would you order her to do *that*?"

Oksana moved close and dropped her voice. "Because he is a *spy*, MacNeal, and I am in the process of *using* him to my advantage."

* * *

Wolf watched from his hiding place and smiled grimly at the unfolding drama. As usual, all he'd had to do was snatch a piece from the board, and the pawns themselves took care of the rest.

With Private Smolensk gone, tensions had risen among the Union and New Guard allies. One of them, Ivan, had taken advantage of the situation for his own purposes, and that had ratcheted up the tension even higher.

The alliance between the Union and New Guard was just starting to show the strain. As fractures spread, mistrust and cross-purposes would intensify and multiply.

In other words, Wolf was meeting his goals and setting the stage. Now that everyone was moving in the right direction, he just had to keep pushing them along.

A couple more mysterious attacks ought to do the trick quite nicely.

* * *

"Ivan is a *spy*?" asked MacNeal. "And you *know* about it?"

Oksana nodded. "He is working for the Black Angel. Tatiana has been able to confirm this."

MacNeal frowned. "You assigned her to get close to him?"

"What kind of a leader do you think I am, MacNeal?" Oksana looked offended. "She *volunteered*."

As MacNeal considered what she'd told him, the ground rumbled underfoot. He looked up at the peak of *Kronotskaya Sopka* towering in the distance and wondered if it was about to erupt.

Then, he returned his gaze to Oksana. "How exactly are you using him to your advantage?"

"I…and Tatiana…have been feeding him certain information." Oksana narrowed her eyes. "*Misleading* information, which we *want* him to report back to the Tsar. We are laying the groundwork for our next moves against the Directorate, you see?"

MacNeal stared at the peak of *Kronotskaya Sopka* again. "This is starting to make sense now." Raindrops fell on his face as the ground rumbled once more. "Tatiana's a tough cookie…reminds me of my own demolitions specialist. I couldn't believe she'd take a beating from him."

Oksana nodded. "You are right about the 'tough' part. But she is under orders to hold back unless her life is threatened. We want to keep this misinformation channel open as long as possible."

"There's just one problem," said MacNeal. "His orders may have changed. Spying might not be his primary goal anymore."

"What do you mean?" Oksana frowned.

"Has he ever attacked Tatiana before?"

"No, never." Oksana's voice allowed no room for doubt.

"That's it then," said MacNeal. "He's moved up to sabotage." He swatted at a mosquito on the side of his neck, then wiped his hand on his hip. "He's becoming increasingly disruptive. Seems to me he's doing what he can to torpedo this mission."

"Including murder?"

"I wouldn't put it past him," said MacNeal. "But the fact remains, he was with our unit during the Shōgunate murders, and they happened miles away." He frowned. "Maybe our list of suspects has changed."

Oksana nodded. "Maybe it has."

MacNeal stared at the ground and thought for a moment. "I still think we should take Ivan out. He's a danger to the mission."

"No." Oksana shook her head. "If he disappears, the Black Angel will send someone to look for him. I will not risk our objective falling into Rasputin's hands."

"That's a mistake," MacNeal said firmly. "If he isn't the killer, he might still be *working* with the killer."

"But he might not be," said Oksana. "In which case, if we can contain him from completely disrupting the mission, he could still be of use."

MacNeal looked at her and nodded. "That's it, isn't it? If all else fails, you want him as a bargaining chip."

She shrugged. "I neither confirm nor deny anything." Snapping around, she started toward the unit. "We had better get back, MacNeal. I suggest we resume our progress before the Shōgunate expedition gets too far ahead."

MacNeal followed her. "So you're taking responsibility for any additional murders he might commit or assist with?"

"If it suits you." She sighed loudly. "Unless *I* am among the victims, of course. It might not be so easy to accept responsibility in that case."

* * *

Since the murders of *Nitōhei* Fukuzawa and *Ittōhei* Hamada, the men had started to grumble. Hiruko overheard them whenever they came near—always out of earshot of the Daimyō, Von Heïzinger, or any of the Reich's goons, of course. He was marching on foot while Nadia slept inside the amphibious vehicle, and the other men would approach from time to time.

The latest to come near him was *Ittōhei* Chiba, Hamada's best friend. Chiba strolled over to Hiruko when the convoy stopped to set up camp in the settling twilight. "Jōtōhei Orochi, may I have a word with you?"

Hiruko took a quick look around and saw that no superiors

were nearby. He and Chiba were alone alongside the vehicle. "Of course."

Chiba bowed. "Orochi, you have the ear of the Daimyō. You also work closely with the generalleutnant and his woman."

"You are too kind." Hiruko shook his head. "I am but a servant to them. I have no influence."

"You are too modest," said Chiba. "Perhaps you have more influence than you realize. I have seen you speaking often to the old woman."

"Because I am her servant," said Hiruko.

"You are on friendly terms with her."

"Even if that were true," said Hiruko, "she has no authority. She is being held against her will."

"Nevertheless." Chiba moved closer and lowered his voice. "Would you be willing to ask on our behalf if we could send out a search party for the killers of Hamada and Fukuzawa?"

Hiruko shook his head. "I can't do it. I wish I could, but I can't."

Chiba looked irritated. "What's the worst that could happen? They tell you no?"

"The *worst* that could happen? You don't want to *know* the worst that could happen."

"Come on, Orochi. Do us a favor." Chiba reached out and patted his shoulder. "This is Hamada and Fukuzawa we're talking about here. They deserve *justice*." He looked around furtively. "And we cannot let their sacrifice have been in vain. We must ensure that the killers do not claim any more lives."

"Chiba, listen, I want to help." Hiruko dropped his voice to a whisper. "But this could get me *killed*."

Chiba's face crawled with disgust. The ground rumbled as he hissed out his words. "I should've known you wouldn't help us. You think you're too good for us now, don't you?"

Hiruko blew out his breath in frustration. "Chiba, no, that's not it."

"Maybe you're just too scared. Is that it?" asked Chiba. "Or are you a Union or Matriarchy sympathizer? Because the killers could very well be part of that gang of villains on our trail, couldn't they?"

"No, Chiba," said Hiruko. "I swear to you, I'm not a sympathizer."

"The hell with you." Chiba reached out again, this time to give him a shove. "You coward. You pampered lapdog. Go to hell."

"Chiba, please!"

"We'll do it without your help," snarled Chiba. "And we'll do it without permission. And I swear, if you let a single *word* slip to your masters, I will make you pay when it's all over."

With that, he spun and hurried over to a pair of soldiers waiting not far away. When he'd finished talking to them, they all looked in Hiruko's direction at once, faces etched with cold hatred.

Then they turned their backs on him and went off to prepare for their unauthorized mission, leaving Hiruko to stand there and watch with a terrible sick feeling in the pit of his stomach.

CHAPTER 18

Kamchatka
18 April 1952
2133 Hours

Hours after the Union and New Guard unit had set up camp, MacNeal and Brown patrolled the perimeter along with multiple other two-man teams. As long as the killer was out there in the wilderness—or somewhere in camp—no one would be left alone as easy pickings. Not after what had happened to Smolensk.

As they patrolled the mountain forest where they were spending the night, MacNeal filled in Brown on the Ivan situation. Boomer wasn't the first person he'd briefed, though: MacNeal had already radioed Tala and told her Ivan was a spy. She and Taki needed to know in case anything happened to MacNeal and they found themselves dealing with Ivan. Blindly trusting him could lead to disaster.

Now that Tala and Taki had been brought in on the news, it was Brown's turn. "You're telling me Oksana knows he's a spy, and she's not shutting him down?" Brown smirked and shook his head. "If you ask me, she won't have a *choice* in the matter pretty soon."

"Roger that." MacNeal adjusted his HB-4 eyepiece over his left eye, improving the resolution of the glowing green night vision images. "Ivan's stepping up his game. Even if he isn't the killer, he's a threat to the mission."

"Here's a thought, Major." Brown raised an eyebrow at MacNeal. "If he gets much worse, someone might end up having to take some kind of independent action."

MacNeal nodded. He didn't care for the idea, but he knew he had to consider it. "You might be right, Boomer. But not without my order, understood?"

"Understood." Brown scanned the beam of his flashlight back and forth, revealing rain-drenched hemlock branches quivering under the latest downpour. "Unless he gets you first, of course."

"Wishful thinking, Boomer." MacNeal elbowed him hard in the side through his olive drab slicker. "I've got eyes in the back of my head, Sergeant. And did I mention I breathe fire?"

"You didn't have to," said Brown. "You're in the 42nd Marines, aren't ya?"

MacNeal saluted. "Semper fi." As the words left his lips, he heard an outburst of noise and shouting not far away. Without hesitation, he charged toward it. That was Brown's signal; instantly, he was on MacNeal's heels, pounding through the mud behind him.

A small crowd had formed out past the perimeter, near two toppled spruces whose trunks had fallen across each other in the shape of an *X*. MacNeal's heart sank as soon as he saw the six men gathered there; he knew only one thing could have halted their patrols and brought them to that spot.

When the men moved aside to give him a look, he was just as shocked and repulsed as if it had all been completely unexpected. He'd been hoping there would be no more ambush murders…but there they were, in the dancing beams of six flashlights.

More piles of clothing and entrails. And not just two this time.

"There are four piles, Major." Alpha Commando Private Beaudreau spoke first. "Looks like two men's uniforms, sir. One Union, one New Guard."

MacNeal plowed past everyone and crouched by the piles. He and Oksana had agreed to integrate some of the teams, putting together a Union man with a New Guard man. Had that been a huge mistake?

A set of dog tags lay on each pile. MacNeal pulled up his eyepiece; he didn't need night vision with all the flashlight beams bathing the scene. Reaching for the set of tags atop the Union uniform, he read the name aloud. "Hamilton, Paul." Another one; he'd lost another one.

One of the Russians picked up the tags from the other pile. "Kandinsky, Sergei."

Everyone stood there a moment more as the realization of what had happened sank in. All their double-teaming and preparation had been for nothing. By working in teams of two, they'd made it harder for the killer to snatch them one at a time...so instead, he'd taken two of them at once.

The ground rumbled, and that snapped MacNeal back into action. He rose from the piles, ready to charge off in search of Hamilton and whoever had killed him.

But then more figures rushed up from the rain-soaked night, and he caught himself. Someone shone a flashlight beam on the newcomers, and one face of particular interest jumped out at him.

It was Ivan. "What is going on here?" He was right beside Oksana, gaping at the terrible handiwork on the ground.

MacNeal strode forward to meet them. "Two more victims. Just like Smolensk. Just like the two Shōgunate men who were killed, according to Tala and Taki."

Oksana frowned. "How could the killer have gotten from Smolensk's murder scene to that of the Shōgunate men to here so fast?"

"Maybe he's working with someone who has infiltrated our unit," said MacNeal. "By the way, where have you been lately, Ivan?"

Ivan glared. "On patrol with Kapetan Gusarenko. Where have *you* been, Major?"

MacNeal didn't dignify the question with an answer. Instead, he swung his gaze to Oksana. "You can vouch for him?"

She nodded. "He has not been out of my sight in two hours."

"Beaudreau," MacNeal said over his shoulder. "When was the last time you saw Hamilton?"

"About an hour ago, sir," said Beaudreau. "I saw him and Kandinsky moving in this direction."

"All right then." MacNeal kept his expression neutral, avoiding even the appearance of admitting he was wrong. Ivan was still an abuser and a spy; for all MacNeal knew, he could still be a killer.

"We should mount a search party for the killer. Groups of no fewer than three."

"Agreed," said Oksana. "It has not been long since the attack. We could still apprehend the perpetrator. *However*…" She raised an index finger. "…we must not continue the hunt all night again. Our people are starved for sleep, MacNeal."

"They're doing all right. They're used to it, aren't they?"

"What if this has been the goal all along?" asked Oksana. "To deprive our forces of sleep and wear us down? With each sleepless night, we become more vulnerable to attack."

She had a point. MacNeal had applied a similar tactic himself a time or two. But limiting the search still went against his grain. "I don't like it."

Oksana's face was set with grim determination. "It is settled then? We call it after two hours?"

MacNeal glanced at Brown, who shook his head. No support there…but MacNeal's gut told him Oksana might be right. "*Three* hours," he said.

Oksana nodded and started barking out orders, sending her people to gather up the rest of the unit. MacNeal wasn't about to wait until they got there, though.

"Boomer, Beaudreau, with me!" Before anyone could get in his way, MacNeal tugged his eyepiece back into place and bolted off into the forest. He heard his men falling in step in his wake, joining him in a hunt that could be dangerous indeed. For whoever had been deadly enough to take out an armed Marine and a New Guard soldier at the same time—without a sound, no less—might be able to take the three of them out, too.

* * *

The Daimyō charged through camp, barking out orders to his Shōgunate unit. He was scrambling every able-bodied man to join search parties for the latest men to go missing—namely, Chiba and his two comrades. He even gave Dr. Kondo a rifle and sent him out with one of the search parties.

The three missing men had failed to report for their sched-uled duty shift at midnight. No one knew where they were except Hiruko, who'd been threatened into secrecy by Chiba. As far as the

Daimyō and the rest of the unit were concerned, Chiba and the other two had been attacked by the killer who'd taken out Hamada and Fukuzawa.

"You too, Jōtōhei Orochi!" The Daimyō jabbed a finger at Hiruko as he passed. "Form up with the rest of the unit! Search parties leave in three minutes!"

Hiruko couldn't tell him the search would be a waste of time. "*Hai*, Daimyō." Without another word, he ran after the Daimyō.

When they reached the middle of camp, Hiruko split off to join the line of men standing at attention in the rain. No one spoke to him or even spared him a glance; maybe Chiba wasn't the only one who looked down on him for serving the Reich. Didn't they understand he was only acting under orders? Didn't they realize it was the *last* thing he wanted to do?

"Attention!" The Daimyō marched up and stopped in front of the men. Rain poured off his black slicker, running in rivulets down to the muddy ground. "Chiba, Ikeda, and Kokowa are missing. We must assume they have been taken against their will. Therefore, time is of the essence. We will divide into teams of four and…"

"Return to your duties." Von Heïzinger's gravelly rasp interrupted the Daimyō. "Go on." Von Heïzinger made shooing gestures with one hand as he glided up behind the Daimyō.

The Daimyō whirled to face him. "You won't stop us from searching for our missing men."

"We cannot afford to waste the manpower," snapped Von Heïzinger. "The Union and Matriarchy dogs are still out there. What if they're closer than we think? What if they mount an attack?"

The Daimyō thrust his face forward and glared at Von Heïzinger. "I would *welcome* such an attack. I have not yet had the chance to test my sword in battle in this wilderness."

"*Zermann*." When Von Heïzinger called the name, Zermann emerged from behind a tent and lumbered over to join him. "Tell them no searching."

"*No searching*." Zermann's voice was a menacing roar.

All eyes turned to the Daimyō. He stood for a moment, gaze locked with Von Heïzinger's…and then he, too, called out a name. "*Itami*!"

Seconds later, the blue-skinned behemoth arrived at his side.

"Yes, Daimyō?"

"Would you please tell our Reich allies that we *will* be searching for our missing men," said the Daimyō, "whether or not they approve?"

Itami bowed and cleared his throat, then turned to Von Heïzinger and Zermann. "Gentlemen. I have been asked to inform you that we will be conducting a search for our missing colleagues." A wicked smirk curled around his up-curved tusks, and his voice took on a darker edge. "I trust you have no…objections?"

Von Heïzinger glared at him, then swooped away without another word. Zermann lingered a moment longer, swaying a little—still dizzy, perhaps?—and then he too left the scene.

Hiruko wanted to cheer. It was the first time since the start of the expedition that he'd seen the Daimyō stand up to the Reich… and win.

But there was no time to dwell on it. The Daimyō didn't miss a beat; as soon as Von Heïzinger and Zermann left, he leaped to the task of assigning teams and quadrants for the search.

Hiruko loved seeing him fully take charge again. The Daimyō was so inspiring, Hiruko wanted to seek out the missing men with all his heart and resourcefulness.

If, of course, they'd been in any kind of danger in the first place.

* * *

The ground rumbled as MacNeal, Brown, and Beaudreau dragged themselves back into camp empty-handed.

The three hours allotted for the search had passed too quickly. MacNeal had wanted to keep going, but Oksana's argument against it had made sense. Too many nights without sleep, and the unit's effectiveness would be impaired. That could make them even more vulnerable to whoever was picking them off.

Still, it galled him to give up on Hamilton and Kandinsky. It felt like defeat, and MacNeal didn't like to lose.

Neither did Brown. "Let's turn around and go back out there." He grabbed MacNeal's shoulder when he spoke. "The hell with the Russians. I'm not ready to call it a night."

MacNeal was tempted to take him up on it, but he knew that he shouldn't. "We're done, Boomer."

Oksana hurried over to meet them. "You are the last team back. I see you have had the same results as all the others."

"*No* results, you mean," said Brown.

MacNeal sighed and pulled up the eyepiece from his left eye. "I was hoping someone else had better luck."

Oksana shook her head. "And now we have a *new* problem, I am afraid."

"What's that?"

"Someone else has disappeared," said Oksana. "Ivan."

"*What*?" asked MacNeal. "*How*?"

"He was out with a search party and he slipped away." Oksana shrugged. "Or he was taken."

"Unbelievable," said Brown.

MacNeal frowned. "Any new piles of clothing or internal organs?"

"We have not found any yet, no," said Oksana. "Which leads me to think he may still be alive."

Beaudreau spoke up. "So we're going back out to search more after all?" He sounded eager.

"No," said Oksana. "We are pulling in the perimeter and locking down camp for the night. No more disappearances."

"I don't understand," said MacNeal. "Why would the killer go from two victims in his last two attacks to just *one* this time? Why just Ivan?"

"Maybe he didn't plan it that way," said Beaudreau. "Maybe Ivan found him, and he had to shut him up."

"Or maybe Ivan's been working with him all along." Brown raised his eyebrows. "Maybe he was involved with the other murders."

"Or maybe," said MacNeal, "his disappearance has nothing to do with what happened to Hamilton, Kandinsky, Smolensk, or the two Shōgunate men. Maybe this is related to something else altogether."

* * *

Following the Daimyō's orders, Hiruko was searching with three other men: Nakashima, Takeuchi, and Uchida, all privates. Together, they combed the wooded foothills for some trace of Chiba, Ikeda, and Kokowa—but all they found was more rain, rumbling, and mosquitoes.

Hiruko worked just as hard as the others at beating the bushes and turning over rocks, though he knew they wouldn't find a thing. That was why the shock was doubly great when he *did* find something.

He almost *fell* into it, actually. He was away from the team, thrashing through some dense brush, when he stumbled over an exposed root. As he tripped, he flew forward through a tangle of thorny branches that scratched his face and hands and gave way under his weight.

Hiruko toppled toward the ground, only catching himself by grabbing a low-hanging tree branch at the last instant. If he hadn't, he would've fallen right into the piled mess in front of him.

He smelled it before he could see it: something putrid. Scrambling back, he swung around his flashlight and cast its beam into the rainswept darkness.

There they were on the ground, arranged in the shape of an *X*: three piles of entrails and three piles of clothing. Each pile of clothing was topped with a set of gleaming I.D. tags.

Easing forward, he reached for the tags atop the closest pile. Even before he read them, he knew what the name engraved on them would be.

"Orochi!" His teammate, Uchida, hurried up beside him, then swept his own flashlight beam over the scene. "No! More murders!"

Hiruko turned the tags over in his hand in the beam of his flashlight. "Looks like it."

"Whose are those?" Uchida crowded in and squinted at the tags in Hiruko's hand.

Hiruko sighed. "Chiba." All along, he'd thought Chiba was fine, on his way to search for Hamada and Fukuzawa. He'd thought the Daimyō's search parties were useless and would come up empty-handed no matter how hard they looked.

Hiruko had been wrong.

Just then, Nakashima and Takeuchi burst through the brush and added their lights to the scene. Nakashima scooped up the tags from another pile and read them in front of his flashlight. "These are Kokowa's."

Takeuchi read the third set of tags. "Ikeda." He sounded like he was about to be sick.

"Three more," said Uchida. "This thing's going to get us all."

"'Thing'?" asked Nakashima. "More like a death squad if you ask me. A Union or Matriarchy death squad."

"Whatever it is," said Uchida, "we're all as good as dead."

"The Daimyō won't let that happen." Nakashima dropped Kokowa's tags on the pile of clothing. "He'll mobilize our own kill team and eradicate the enemy."

"If the Reich lets him," said Uchida.

Then they all fell silent. Hiruko became aware that all eyes were on him, expecting him to say something as servant of the Reich, Von Heïzinger's lackey.

But he didn't say a thing.

* * *

Later, Von Heïzinger appeared at the site where Hiruko had found the remains of Chiba, Ikeda, and Kokowa. Zermann accompanied him, carrying Nadia in his arms like a child.

Hiruko and the others made way as Zermann put Nadia down near Chiba's folded uniform. She looked angry and averted her eyes from the piles of clothing and innards, refusing to look at them— but then Von Heïzinger stormed over and forcibly turned her head. When he removed his hands, she did not look away again.

"Read them." Von Heïzinger made an aloof gesture toward the piles. "Do it now."

Nadia moved her hands over Chiba's clothing. Swaying in the flashlight beams, she closed her eyes, chanting words Hiruko couldn't hear.

Finally, she slumped. Everyone stood silently and waited to hear what she said next.

Except Von Heïzinger. "Tell me," he snapped. "What have you found?"

She gazed at Chiba's tags as she spoke. "He was touched by the same god who touched Hamada and Fukuzawa."

"This god," said Von Heïzinger. "He must be powerful."

"I suppose that goes without saying," said Nadia.

"Tell me something about him." Von Heïzinger clapped his gloved hands together. "Something I can use."

Nadia took a deep breath and let it out slowly. When she met Hiruko's gaze, he could see the weariness in her eyes. "He has wings," she said. "Great, dark wings."

Von Heïzinger scowled. "Like an angel? A demon?"

Nadia shrugged. "His wings are big and dark. That's all I can tell you. That's all I'm getting."

Von Heïzinger snorted. "Keep trying."

"There's nothing else," insisted Nadia. "But I can start making things up, if you like."

"I need *more*." Von Heïzinger shook his fist at her. "For tomorrow, we shall *capture* this god of yours."

"Capture a god?" asked Nadia. "Good luck to you."

"Wish your little *friend* luck instead." Von Heïzinger pointed at Hiruko. "For he shall be the bait in the trap."

CHAPTER 19

Kamchatka
19 April 1952
0637 Hours

Tala was jamming in bites of breakfast between glances through
her binoculars. Not that a can of mush was much of a breakfast,
but beggars couldn't be choosers in a field op like the one she was
working. Still, with all the advances the Union seemed to be making, she sometimes wondered why they couldn't make an advance
in field food.

She and Taki were watching the action from a hill less than a
quarter-mile from the Shōgunate camp. They'd spent the night on
the back side of that hill, trying like hell to figure out what was happening down below. The darkness, rain, and tree cover had made it
difficult to scope out the details of the enemy's movements.

But they were having better luck in the light of day. "They're
moving out." Tala had another spoonful of mush, then took another
look. "Not sticking around to investigate the murders, apparently."

She and Taki had seen just enough the night before to know
more killings had happened. There'd been search parties fanning out

through the area, then a mad scramble as everyone, including Von Heïzinger and Zermann, had converged on a single location. After that, Tala and Taki had seen Shōgunate personnel burying some kind of remains and hauling piles of clothing back into camp—*three* piles, from what they'd been able to see.

If only they'd been able to get closer and find out more...but it was better to stay at a distance unless something critical demanded an up-close presence.

Once things had calmed down, they'd radioed MacNeal and told him what they could. He, in turn, had told them about the latest victims on the Union and New Guard side. Tala hadn't known Paul Hamilton well, but losing any member of the 42nd Marines was a tragic occasion. After hearing the news and ending the call to MacNeal, she'd pulled a few items from her medicine bag and had a small Navajo ceremony in his honor.

But now the time for mourning had passed. It never did last that long in the field.

"The column's advancing." Tala scanned the length of the formation of men and machines...then stopped. "But not all of it."

"What are you talking about?" Taki stared through his own binoculars.

"I don't believe it." Tala focused on the lone figure remaining stationary behind the column. "They're leaving him behind again! The same guy!"

"You're kidding." Taki shook his head. "Now why would they do that?"

"Last time, they left him to wait for Zermann and Itami," said Tala. "But I don't think they've left the convoy, have they? So what possible reason could the Shōgunate have for leaving him behind *this* time?"

"He's just *standing* there," said Taki. "At attention, yet..."

"He doesn't look sick or injured. He's not heading back to the beachhead." Tala's heart went out to the Shōgunate soldier who'd been abandoned for the second time. She'd been the odd woman out often enough in her life. Even now, though she'd earned the acceptance of her peers, she sometimes felt like an outsider.

"So why do you think they're leaving him behind?" asked Taki.

Tala thought it over, then nodded. "This has Von Heïzinger written all over it. Another one of his damn schemes."

"Whatever the reason, it can't be good for that poor guy," said Taki.

* * *

Hiruko wasn't cold, but he shivered anyway. He had a feeling he was being watched.

Standing at attention in the little clearing, he was completely exposed. All he could do was stand and wait…and pray. But he didn't think his chances looked good.

Whatever had taken the five men from the unit, it was still out there. How long would it be until it finally pounced on the bait in the trap? How long until it came after Hiruko?

Von Heïzinger and the Daimyō had taken measures to capture the culprit. As soon as it—or he, or she—took the bait, the trap would close. The threat would be ended.

But what would happen to Hiruko, the bait? How much damage would the culprit inflict before being captured? For that matter, how much damage would the trap itself inflict on Hiruko? Would he survive the killer, only to fall victim to friendly fire?

The heat of the day had not yet ratcheted up, but sweat trickled down his back nevertheless. His heart pounded against his ribs like a mallet striking a gong.

And the poetry rose, unbidden, in his worried mind.

> Water, cupped in a hand unseen, gathers, contained,
> Yet always working at the cracks, at the flaws,
> Drawn down always into loamy earth,
> Descending like the hawk, like the lightning,
> Like the flesh and bone and blood,
> Into ever-tightening spirals of iridescent life,
> Meant always to flow down and down and then
> Rise up again, sighing and singing
> That single, quivering chord sustained in sky and sea,
> Humming as a formless thread through the interwoven
> Strands of every living thing,
> Be it man or bear or plant or things yet to come,
> Yet to be dreamt of in the foamy tides of slumber
> Like a handful of water.

Hiruko frowned. Why had it come to him again at that moment? Why did his mind flow in that direction when he was in the most danger? Was it his way of keeping from going mad? Did it even matter, if he would be gone soon, gone for good?

Suddenly, he heard crackling sounds in the woods around him. He looked to one side but retained his rigid posture as required by the Daimyō's orders. He was to do nothing that would scare off the killer, even if his own life was in immediate danger.

There it was again. The crackling.

Hiruko wanted to run, but he stood his ground. He tried to steel himself for what was to come, though he couldn't quite manage to find the courage he was looking for.

* * *

The Dark God circled in the sky, relishing the rising thermal currents as the sun's heat bathed the earth below. The rain clouds that had blanketed the region had finally crawled off, paving the way for a clear day with lots of sun and plenty of thermals on which to glide.

Far below, the Shōgunate convoy was pulling away, continuing its journey toward the great volcano, *Kronotskaya Sopka*. One man had been left behind, though, standing alone in a clearing...why? Was he guarding something? Was he being punished? Was he a sacrifice offered up in the hope that the Dark God would not take anyone else? Perhaps he had been left behind to negotiate, as if the Dark God would ever consider a truce.

Whatever the reason for his abandonment, the man presented an opportunity that could not be ignored. Taking him would require no effort at all. Even if he tried to fight back, he was alone and could be easily overcome. Even if he hadn't been alone, the Dark God was confident in his power and would not have hesitated to claim him.

Fixing his gaze on the man, the Dark God spiraled downward. A familiar thrill surged through him as he closed in on his prey, who waited helpless beneath him.

* * *

As the Union and New Guard forces broke camp and headed out,

MacNeal was half in a daze. The Russians' strong coffee had gotten him moving, but hadn't come close to blowing away the cobwebs. If the enemy's goal was to wear him down, they were making progress.

MacNeal hadn't been able to sleep much, given the situation. Whoever was picking off the Union and New Guard troops seemed to be unstoppable...but had to be stopped. If MacNeal couldn't find a way to do it soon, the mission would have to be aborted. He and Oksana would simply run out of manpower...if the two of them weren't killed first, that is.

Just as he thought of Oksana, she appeared, hurrying up beside him as the column continued forward. Her two voïvoides scurried along behind her; now that the rain had finally stopped and the ground was less sloppy, the three-legged automatons could get around without help. "Have you seen anything unusual, MacNeal?"

"Other than that big yellow thing up in the sky?" MacNeal managed a smirk as he pointed at the sun. "Nothing."

She squinted up at it. "It has been a while since we have seen it, yes?" Then she returned her gaze to him. "I wonder how long it will be until we see our other prodigal son."

MacNeal shrugged. She was talking about Ivan, of course. "I wish I knew."

"We have found no piles of clothes or organs, at least," said Oksana. "That leads me to think he is still alive. Perhaps he left the unit of his own accord, for his own reasons."

MacNeal rubbed his bristly chin. He had a pretty good beard coming in; he hadn't shaved since leaving the sub. "That makes him a suspect again, doesn't it?"

"How so?" Oksana frowned. "He was with me during those last two murders. He could not have killed those men. And he certainly could not have raced across Kamchatka and killed the three Shōgunate men who were murdered last night, too."

"Maybe he didn't," said MacNeal, "but he could have been working as the inside man for somebody else. Maybe it had something to do with his spying for the Black Angel."

Oksana raised an eyebrow at him, then slowly looked away. "I suppose it is possible."

"If only we had a lead on where he is," said MacNeal. "What about Tatiana? Does she have any insight?"

Oksana grunted. "No, but she wants very badly to commune with Baba Yaga and hunt Ivan down like the dog that he is." She chuckled a little. "It has taken all my powers of persuasion to keep her from charging off on her own."

"Good for you." MacNeal smiled. "But I still hope she gets the chance to give him what he's got coming to him."

"She will." Oksana nodded. "When this is all over, I will make sure of it."

"Meanwhile, we're still at square one. Where's Ivan?"

"And who is he working with?" Oksana added. "What do they want? Why are they picking us and the Shōgunate off a few at a time instead of all at once?"

"And how the hell do we stop them?" MacNeal said grimly.

* * *

The hairs on the back of Hiruko's neck stood up when the crackling in the brush grew louder. Slowly, he turned his head to look in that direction, expecting to see the killer hurtle out at him.

Instead, a lean, brown-furred rabbit loped out of the brush. Ears pointing skyward, it sat for a moment in the dirt, staring at Hiruko with eyes like little black marbles.

Hiruko felt relieved. If this was the worst thing he encountered while serving as bait, maybe he would get through the ordeal in one piece.

He imagined going over to try to pet the animal. It would certainly calm his nerves, though he knew it would never sit still long enough. He couldn't even try to get it to come to him, because he wasn't allowed to move. All he could do was watch the creature and...

Suddenly, the rabbit took off like a shot and sprinted into the woods. Heart racing, Hiruko looked around for some trace of what had driven it off, but saw nothing. The ground shook. Was that what had alarmed the rabbit?

Then, a huge shadow passed overhead. At first, he thought it might be a low-flying plane...but if so, why was there no engine sound?

He was about to look up and see the full picture when something plunged from the sky and knocked him down.

Hiruko landed on his back, gazing up at the thing that had collided with him. It was some kind of bird-like creature, an enormous figure towering over him with ebony feathers. Its head was like that of a giant black bird, darkly feathered with bright red eyes and a golden beak. It spread its wings wide and cried out to the heavens above. Hiruko guessed it was at least seven feet tall standing up.

In other words, it was more than big enough to slaughter him where he lay.

* * *

When the ambush happened, it caught the Union and New Guard alike by surprise. It happened suddenly, as the column of allies proceeded northward through dense woods on the trail of the Shōgunate convoy. MacNeal was marching near the front of the line, discussing strategy with Oksana. Brown was a few steps behind, offering insights and suggestions as needed. It was business as usual.

Then, as the column snaked around a bend, a man came into view up ahead, standing in the middle of the path. He was bald, with a black mustache and goatee, and MacNeal recognized him instantly.

"Ivan!" Oksana called his name. "Where have you been?"

Ivan said something MacNeal couldn't make out.

Oksana couldn't understand, either. "What did you say?"

Suddenly, a new voice spoke up from nearby—the voice of a woman with a Russian accent. "He *said*, put down your weapons or we will shoot you where you stand!" In spite of the threat, the voice was high and melodic, with a clear, bell-like tone.

And it was familiar. MacNeal hadn't heard it in a while, but it was a voice he couldn't forget.

All at once, armed men dressed in shades of brown and deep scarlet emerged from the forest with rifles and flamethrowers held high, all aimed at the Union and New Guard forces. Ivan swung up a revolver, too, pointed right at MacNeal himself.

"We're surrounded." Brown kept his voice low, for MacNeal's ears only. "But I say the hell with it. Give the order and we'll start knockin' 'em down."

"Hold your fire," said MacNeal. "I think these are friendlies."

"Not friendly at all, MacNeal." Oksana's voice was a growl. "Not even close."

"We'll see about that." MacNeal took a breath and called out. "It's been a while, hasn't it, Irina?"

"John?" Hemlock bows parted, and a woman emerged from the forest. She was slender, with a narrow waist and long legs tucked into knee-high black leather boots, and she radiated sensuality. Even pointing her trademark double-barreled 1920 Nagant revolver at MacNeal, she moved with the feline grace and brazen confidence of Cleopatra or Mata Hari.

"To what do we owe the honor?" asked MacNeal.

Irina strode languidly toward him, never letting the revolver waver in her grip. Her short, platinum blond hair fluttered in the breeze. "Sweet, sweet John. You have not changed a bit."

MacNeal smiled. "Thanks, I guess."

"It was not a compliment." She stopped a few feet away, close enough for him to see the glints in her glittering blue eyes. "I meant that you still do not know how to listen to a woman." She eased the gun forward and pressed it to his chest. "When I say put down your weapon or I will shoot you, that does not include a 'maybe' at the end."

MacNeal kept his hand tight on the grip of his flash-gun. He wasn't about to let go of it, even on the say-so of someone who'd been an ally of his more than once. "You haven't changed, either, have you, Irina?"

"That is correct, John." Irina raised the revolver to his forehead and cocked the hammer. "I still keep my promises, no matter what."

CHAPTER 20

Kamchatka
19 April 1952
0749 Hours

As the seven-foot-tall bird-thing cried out again, Hiruko frantically scrambled backward, trying to get away from it. He knew he was bait, and the trap was supposed to spring shut any second now, but all he could think of was escaping the fearsome creature.

Rolling over, he fumbled to his knees and nearly got his feet under him to make a run for it. But the creature latched onto his leg with a claw and dragged him back. Hiruko scrabbled at the ground, trying for a handhold, but could do nothing to fight the furious pull.

And the bird-thing didn't stop there. It hoisted him off the ground, holding him upside down by his feet. It was then, as Hiruko dangled helplessly before it, that he realized the creature had a set of human arms to go with its huge wings. The arms were swathed in swirling black stripes and spirals that ran all the way to the razor-sharp claws on its fingertips.

The creature had human legs, too, also covered in elaborate black markings…but the three-toed feet were all bird, ending in gleaming, hooked claws.

Even as Hiruko's mind swirled with panic, he wondered what kind of beast he'd had the misfortune to encounter. What kind of bird was seven feet tall with human arms in addition to huge wings—and what did it want with him? Was this the "god" Nadia had sensed when she'd passed her hands over the men's remains? If so, would a trap set by mere mortals be any match for it?

Hiruko would find out soon enough. As he hung there with the blood rushing to his head, a heavy net suddenly fell over him and the bird-thing, enclosing them both.

Screeching, the bird-thing let go of him and clawed at the net, trying to break free. Supported by the tight mesh, Hiruko slid to the ground and came down on his shoulders. Still half upside down, he watched through the net's grid work as his rescuers charged out of the woods.

Itami came first, with the massive kenabō club perched on his shoulder, ready to swing. Zermann was two steps behind him, holding on with both hands to a line connected to the net. Behind them both strode Von Heïzinger, the Daimyō, and Dr. Kondo, all business, eyes fixed on the creature they'd caught.

As the group of them got closer, the bird-thing thrashed with increasing desperation, buffeting Hiruko with its knees and wings in the process. Hiruko pulled his legs down and curled up in a fetal position, hoping to wait out the worst of the creature's agitation.

It passed more quickly than he'd expected. One minute, the bird-thing was going crazy, straining at the net; the next minute, it was utterly calm. Just like that, it stopped screeching and thrashing and fighting. It cocked its head, with its obsidian feathers and red eyes, and watched as Itami and the others arrived.

"Incredible!" Dr. Kondo hurried forward with a bag full of scientific instruments, his face alight with wonder. "I have never seen anything *like* it!"

Itami bounded up and stopped in front of the creature, gazing into its eyes. "I have finally found a being as unique as I."

Hiruko uncurled on the ground and looked up to see Von Heïzinger leaning toward the creature. "You will submit." As he said it, he reached between the lapels of his overcoat and pulled out the Patmos Amulet on its chain around his neck. "This outcome is preordained."

* * *

Tala was glued to the view through her binoculars. She couldn't look away, not even for a second.

Neither could Taki, who was watching at her side on the edge of the hill. "So that's why they left the poor guy behind. He was *bait* in a trap...again."

Tala didn't answer. She was too busy gazing at the black-feathered bird-thing under the net.

She couldn't believe what she was seeing. A piece of her heritage, an aspect of her most deeply held beliefs, had seemingly come to life before her eyes.

As a Navajo shaman, she had faith in the legendary powers of the world, incredible powers that held sway over human destiny in manifold ways. She had heard many stories of those powers, seen paintings and costumes portraying their physical manifestations. But she had never seen one in the flesh.

Until now.

"What *is* that thing?" Taki said in a hushed voice. "It's like some kind of giant *crow*."

"Not a crow." The bird-creature cocked its head. Its red eyes flashed behind its sharp yellow beak, seemingly staring back at her through the binoculars. "I believe that is *Raven*."

"Giant crow, giant raven. What's the difference?" asked Taki.

"Raven is a trickster god," said Tala. "He is known to the Navajo and other American aboriginal tribes."

"A god?" Taki frowned. "I don't know about that, Tala."

"I admit, it's hard to believe," said Tala. "But we can't ignore the evidence of our eyes."

Taki shinnied a little farther forward for a better view. "If that's a Navajo trickster god, what's he doing all the way out here in Kamchatka?"

Tala scowled. "And what the hell is Von Heïzinger trying to do to him?"

* * *

"Will you submit, John?" Irina pressed the double barrels of her revolver more tightly against MacNeal's forehead. "Or will you die for nothing?"

MacNeal locked eyes with her, meeting her cold, glittering stare… and then he smirked. "Neither." Reaching up, he grabbed the double barrels and pushed them up to point at the sky instead of his head. "I'll ask you to kindly order your men to stand down before something happens that we all regret."

Irina sneered. "I will do no such thing." Then, she hummed a little high-pitched tune, a flowing melody of crystal-perfect notes.

MacNeal felt his resistance wavering. Irina had a gift: the ability to control minds with the songs she sang and chanted. Her "Liturgies" could turn the tide of battle…or simply bend a strong man to her will.

It helped that MacNeal recognized her power and had successfully fought it before. As her humming grew louder, he wavered but did not surrender. "Is this how you treat your *allies*?" he said. "You *have* heard of the UMTOMA treaty, haven't you?"

Irina stopped humming. "It is how I treat my *subordinates*." She snatched the gun from his grip and waved it at Oksana. "I have been instructed to assume command of this operation. You report to *me* now. *All* of you." She shot a nasty glare in MacNeal's direction.

Oksana surged forward, looking defiant. "The New Guard does not recognize your authority!"

"But the *Directorate* recognizes *your* incompetence." Irina jabbed a finger at Oksana's chest. "At the rate you are going, your entire unit will be *murdered* before you ever get near the Shōgunate's objective. That is why these elite *Bogatyrs* and I were sent to take over the task force."

"*You* are the one who engineered this turn of events." Oksana thrust her Vesper scepter forward accusingly. "Your *spy* has been sabotaging our mission." She waved Vesper in Ivan's direction.

For once, Irina looked as if she'd been caught off guard. "You knew there was a spy?"

"I know more than that!" snapped Oksana. "I know he has been working with the killer who has been stalking us."

Ivan had walked over and now stood beside Irina. "Not true!"

"I now believe that killer was more than one person," said Oksana. "I believe it was *you* and your so-called Bogatyrs."

"How *dare* you! I would *never* order the murder of a fellow officer."

"Who said you *ordered* it?" Oksana smiled grimly. Irina drew back a hand to slap her, but Oksana caught the hand before it could connect.

MacNeal, as he watched the scene play out, wondered what his next step should be. Irina was a hell of a soldier, but unprovoked murder didn't seem like her style. And the truth of it was, since the killings had diminished his team, an infusion of manpower would be a godsend.

But could he envision the New Guard and Directorate working together without blowing each other to pieces? Not really...but the reward could be worth the risk. He'd just have to worry about the consequences later.

"Irina. Oksana." He stepped up and placed a hand on each of their shoulders. "I have a proposition to make. It does *not* involve submitting to your authority." He raised an eyebrow at Irina...then Oksana. "*Or* yours."

They both looked outraged and opened their mouths to say something.

But MacNeal wouldn't let them get a word in edgewise. "What it *does* involve is an alliance of equal partners, working toward a mutual goal." He smiled ruefully. "*Without* killing each other along the way."

* * *

"I think we should get closer." Tala was getting to her feet. "Maybe we can help."

"We can't." Taki jumped up and grabbed her arm. "We'll jeopardize the whole mission. If we're captured or killed, the 42nd will lose its advance intel."

Tala shook free of his grip. "Don't worry. I have no intention of putting us in harm's way." She swung her pack off her shoulders, dropped it on the ground, and dug out two of her improvised dynamite bombs. "With any luck, I can just lob in some explosives and shake things up a little."

"It's too risky." Taki made a grab for her again. "You don't even really know what that bird-creature is."

"Does it matter?" Tala sidestepped. Taki didn't know her well, or he'd have known better than to try to change her mind. Once the Tala train started rolling, nothing and no one could stand in her way.

Taki stepped back, fixing her in his unwavering gaze. His hands hovered over the handles of the tonfa clubs strapped to his thighs; for a moment, she thought he might try to use them.

Then, the look in his eyes changed, and he relaxed. "I have my doubts about that thing being a god." He swung his flash-gun off his shoulder and braced it in both hands. "But if you're that determined, then let's go."

"All right." Tala shoved the bombs into her hip pockets. She hefted her pack, pushed her arms through the straps, and adjusted the weight on her shoulders. "Let's see if we can render assistance without being captured or killed."

Taki snorted. "Nothing to it."

* * *

The Patmos Amulet glowed with pulsing golden light as Von Heïzinger held it up to the bird-thing. Eyes closed, he chanted otherworldly syllables and swayed from side to side, trying to exert his power as he had with Nadia.

From what Hiruko could see, he was failing. The amulet glowed more brightly with each passing moment, but it had no visible effect on the bird-like creature. The bird-thing just stood there under the net and stared with its bright red eyes, looking from Von Heïzinger to Itami to the Daimyō to Zermann to Dr. Kondo, then back to Von Heïzinger.

And once in a while, it looked down at Hiruko, still huddled at its claw-like feet. When it gazed at him, Hiruko felt certain there was intelligence in its eyes, equal to that of a human, not an animal. He truly believed the bird-thing fully understood what was going on and being said around it.

But it might as well have been an animal, as unreachable as its mind and motives seemed to be. Its features lacked any expression that Hiruko could recognize. It was implacable, unreadable, and utterly alien. Hiruko had no idea what it wanted.

At least, until it finally made its move.

Just as Von Heïzinger's chanting rose to a fevered pitch, the bird-thing suddenly tucked its wings and arms in tight against its body. The weighted net followed suit, drawing tight around it like a cocoon.

Then, with a loud grunt, the bird-thing flexed its wings and muscles outward all at once. The net gave way instantly, its reinforced mesh bursting apart.

Von Heïzinger stopped chanting and flung up his arms to protect himself from the flying debris. As he and Dr. Kondo stumbled back, Itami and Zermann surged forward.

Itami literally kicked Hiruko aside, sending him rolling, and grabbed hold of one of the creature's wings. Zermann latched onto the other wing and threw his strength into pinning it down.

But the bird-thing, now that it was out in the open, would not be easily restrained. Screeching, it flexed the wings against Itami and Zermann, dragging them back and forth. They grappled with the wings to no avail; one big swoop and Zermann was knocked to the ground.

Itami still held on, but Hiruko could see he was having a problem. He blinked and shook his head hard as the wing continued to flex in his grip. He lost his footing and staggered a few steps before digging in again. When the creature swung around and raked his chest with its talons, he lost his grip. He fumbled to get it back, but it was too late; the wing had broken free.

With a few mighty flaps, the bird-thing rose into the air. It took a last look at Hiruko, then turned and churned higher, gaining speed.

Zermann fired three rounds with Doom, but his aim was off, and none connected. The creature raced off into the bright blue sky, wings sweeping up and down with great, majestic strokes.

* * *

"You expect me to work with a *murderer*?" Oksana trained a look of intense hatred on Irina, who was looking just as hatefully back at her. "We cannot *trust* her, MacNeal."

"How do we know *you* are not the murderer?" Irina folded her arms over her chest and sneered. "Maybe *you* are the one sabotaging the mission, to keep the Union from reaching the objective."

"Who said anything about trust?" MacNeal shrugged. "I'm simply proposing a temporary marriage of convenience."

"How can you even *consider* it, MacNeal?" Oksana shot him a wide-eyed stare. "You *know* where her loyalties lie."

"*I* am loyal to her majesty the Tsarina Anastasia Romanova," snapped Irina. "*I* serve the Directorate and the Matriarchy of Mother Russia, as do *you*…or is that not true?"

Oksana took a deep breath and let it out slowly. MacNeal could imagine the conflict in her mind: the Black Angel Rasputin was the power behind the throne of the Matriarchy, and Oksana opposed his will…but could she say she wasn't loyal to the Tsarina, the Directorate, and the Matriarchy? Would it be smart, surrounded by armed Bogatyrs, to disavow her loyalty to the ruler and nation in whose name she still technically served?

Oksana gathered herself up, squared her shoulders, and stuck out her chin. "Of course it is true. My loyalties lie *only* with my Tsarina and the defense of the Motherland over which she presides."

MacNeal smiled to himself in admiration. She'd reiterated her support of Tsarina and country without openly declaring the treasonous intentions of the New Guard. "Sounds to me like you're both working for the same people, in which case we're all on the same page here. I can't really see a good reason not to move forward with this alliance."

"What about spoils?" Irina took his measure through narrowed eyes. "We will share them equally?"

MacNeal shrugged. "Goes without saying." Even as he said it, he had no intention of giving over a deadly power to the Black Angel if he could help it.

"Then perhaps an alliance will be tolerable," said Irina. "After all, thanks to UMTOMA, we are *already* allies, are we not?"

Oksana was still glaring at her. "This was your plan all along. The murders were a way for you to undermine us and insinuate yourself into the operation."

Irina shook her head sadly. "Paranoia does not become you, Kapetan Gusarenko."

MacNeal interrupted before tempers could rise any further. "It's settled. The 42nd Marines, New Guard, and Bogatyrs will work together as allies for the duration of this mission."

Oksana looked like she was fuming, but she managed a curt nod. Irina sighed and nodded, too.

"Great." MacNeal smiled. "Then do you think you could tell your Bogatyrs to stop pointing their weapons at their new allies?"

* * *

The Dark God flapped his massive wings, carrying himself farther from the mortals who had caught him. He watched as they scurried below, shouting and firing weapons, trying to bring him down.

When they finally gave up, he smiled to himself. The outcome of their encounter had never been in doubt. Though he had to admit, they *had* tricked him, which was *never* an easy feat. And he was flying away empty-handed, without the victim he'd sought.

But at least he'd made them angrier, which, after all, was his primary goal. They'd be more determined than ever to reach his lair and have their revenge.

As for being empty-handed, he suddenly realized that condition could change. Soaring over the land below in a widening spiral, he saw what appeared to be a perfect new target: a dark-haired woman running through a clearing.

She was just what he needed. Truly, the signs and omens were aligning to ensure the success of his task.

The Dark God banked on a rising thermal current and swept around, gracefully gliding down from the heights toward the running woman far below.

* * *

When the bird-creature started to descend, Tala stopped running and watched its gently looping flight path. Her heart pounded in her chest, and not just from the run; Raven, if that *was* Raven, was a sight to behold, truly majestic in his command of the skies.

Tala had gotten the jump on Taki, but he finally caught up to her. He looked all around, his head flicking nervously from side to side, before he finally joined her in looking up. "I guess the raven doesn't need a rescue anymore." His voice was tense. "We should find some cover before Von Heïzinger spots us."

"No, look." Tala pointed upward. "He's coming this way."

"You're right," said Taki. "Then like I said, we should find some cover."

"But what if that *is* Raven?" Tala kept watching as the descent spiral brought the bird-creature closer. "I know it seems impossible, but *look* at it." She shook her head in amazement. "Half-bird, half-man.

I've seen that exact image in ancient paintings and carvings."

"We're not here to commune with gods," said Taki. "Or whatever that is."

"But maybe that's *exactly* what we need to do," said Tala. "Maybe it can help us. Maybe it can lead us to the objective before the Shōgunate or Reich can reach it."

"Or maybe," said Taki, "it's the reason those men have been taken. Maybe *it's* doing the taking."

"It's possible." Tala shrugged. "It could be trying to defend itself. But a trained shaman like me could get through to it."

The bird-creature was about thirty feet overhead, still approaching in its lazy-looking spiral. Taki grabbed Tala's elbow and tried pulling her with him, but she rooted her feet and wouldn't budge. "Tala, please."

Tala turned to shake free of him. "Let go of me!"

In that instant, the bird-creature tucked its wings against its body and suddenly accelerated. When Tala and Taki looked up again, it was dive-bombing straight at them; they didn't have enough time to get out of the way, fire a weapon, or say a word.

It swooped toward them like a fighter plane, and then it pulled up, extending its leg claws in the process. The claws grabbed hold of Tala's shoulders, clamping down tightly, wrenching her forward as the bird-creature continued its path.

Then the creature swooped upward, and Tala's feet left the ground.

As Raven continued climbing, Tala heard Taki shouting below. His voice grew ever fainter as the creature gained altitude, leaving him earthbound in its wake.

* * *

Taki ran after the airborne creature a moment more, then stopped. If he kept running in that direction, he'd end up face to face with Von Heïzinger and the rest.

Instead, he turned and ran back the other way, looking for cover…and the privacy he needed to radio MacNeal. As he ran, he kept looking back over his shoulder, watching the bird-thing recede into the distance with Tala in its grip. He thought of pulling out his binoculars, but he didn't need them to see where the creature and Tala were headed. It was impossible to miss.

They were flying straight for the massive volcano looming over everything, the perfect snow-streaked cone towering hundreds of feet above the landscape: *Kronotskaya Sopka.*

The Shōgunate and Reich—and everyone following them—had been heading there all along anyway. According to Brown on their last check-in, Oksana had said it was the likely location of a legendary eldritch power source, and Tatiana had called it the home of the god Kutkha.

Now the bird-creature was making a beeline for that volcano. If Tala was right, and the giant raven was some kind of god, or some bizarre creature mistaken for a god, what were the chances that it and Kutkha were one and the same?

Pretty good, in Taki's opinion.

As for the chance it would hurt her somehow, he couldn't say. But he wasn't about to give it much time to consider its options. As soon as he reached cover and called MacNeal, he would triple time it to *Kronotskaya Sopka.* He would find Kutkha's lair and do whatever it took to free Tala.

One way or another, he would get her back safely. Because as much of a rattlesnake as she could be, and as rocky as their partnership had been at the outset, he realized he couldn't stand the thought of anything bad happening to her.

CHAPTER 21

**Kamchatka
19 April 1952
0905 Hours**

When the call came in from Taki, and MacNeal heard about Tala's abduction, his first words were, "Is she hurt?"

"Not from what I could see." Taki's voice crackled with static. "But she's no longer in visual range, sir."

The signal should have been clear, thanks to the radio's Ilirium. MacNeal wondered what could be causing the interference. "You say this thing looks like a seven-foot-tall raven?"

"Yes, sir," said Taki. "Tala thought it was a raven *god*, actually. Didn't the Russians mention a god who supposedly inhabits *Kronotskaya Sopka*?"

Suddenly, Tatiana leaned over MacNeal's shoulder and spoke. He hadn't even realized she was back there. "*Kutkha*. It is said he lives in an aerie inside the volcano."

MacNeal turned to her. "What else do you know about this Kutkha?"

"He is a tragic figure," said Tatiana. "Everyone he ever cared about has been lost to him. They say the volcanic eruptions and quakes are caused by his weeping."

"Anything else?" MacNeal stared at her expectantly. "Anything that could help us defeat him?"

"The order may provide guidance." Tatiana pulled a polished onyx pendant on a chain from the neck of her uniform. The black stone was etched with the image of a mortar and pestle…with wings. "If anyone can defeat a god, the goddess Baba Yaga can."

"Von Heïzinger *tried* to defeat him." Taki had heard Tatiana over the radio channel, which MacNeal had kept open. "He used a Shōgunate soldier as bait and caught Kutkha in a trap, but Kutkha broke free."

"So he's formidable enough to escape Von Heïzinger," said MacNeal. "A force to be reckoned with."

"Absolutely," said Taki.

"All right." MacNeal spoke into the radio. "Taki, start heading our way. We're going to rendezvous with you."

There was a pause on the other end of the call. "Did you say I should triple time it to *Kronotskaya Sopka* and initiate retrieval of Corporal Aponi?"

"Negative," said MacNeal. "Do *not* attempt retrieval without support. We're going after her together, over."

"Roger that," said Taki. "I will initiate retrieval and await your support."

"I said *negative*," snapped MacNeal. "Listen to me, Taki! We've got additional manpower now. A Matriarchy unit has joined forces with us. There's no reason for you to go in alone."

Taki's voice crackled back to him. "Affirmative, Whiskey Foxtrot. The Matriarchy unit will provide additional backup after I've retrieved Corporal Aponi. Victor Tango, roger and out."

"Negative!" said MacNeal. "Your orders are to *rendezvous* with us before approaching *Kronotskaya Sopka*. Do *not* initiate retrieval."

But it was too late. Taki had closed the channel, leaving nothing but static to fill the radio speaker.

"Damn." MacNeal hooked the radio on his belt. "That insubordinate SOB is going in after her."

"Never figured him for headstrong." Brown shook his head, then smirked. "But I guess that makes him true 42nd material, doesn't it?"

Brown might have been right, but MacNeal didn't want to talk about it. "We need to get a move on. This Kutkha, whatever he is... if he's powerful enough to break away from Von Heïzinger, Zermann, and Itami..."

"...he's the kind of guy we want on *our* side," offered Brown.

"I was going to say he could be more than Taki can handle." MacNeal smacked a bug on the side of his neck, then turned back to face the at-rest column. "I need to get Irina and Oksana to get us moving again."

Brown grinned. "Good luck with those two. I can hear them arguing from here."

* * *

Wolf watched and listened from the shadows, very pleased with the way things were developing. He'd overheard MacNeal's conversation over the radio and was happy to know his ally, the Dark God Kutkha, had taken another victim.

Irina and the Bogatyrs could be a problem, though. He wasn't sure how their influence would affect MacNeal and Oksana and the unit. He couldn't afford to let them lose momentum at this stage.

It would be best to control the newcomers' impact with some carefully tailored intervention. In other words, Wolf would give the Bogatyrs a kick in the ass the same way he and Kutkha had done for the other factions.

* * *

"Look!" The Daimyō pointed at the dark figure gliding through the sky with a woman dangling from its claws. "It has a captive!"

"A Union soldier," said Von Heïzinger. "I recognize her."

"From here? Without binoculars?" The Daimyō shot him a withering look. "Of course you do."

Hiruko, who was standing behind them, squinted at the sky. He too was surprised that anyone could make out any details of the distant woman or bird-thing.

"She is Corporal Aponi." Von Heïzinger wrinkled his nose in evident distaste. "One of MacNeal's bitches."

The Daimyō shielded his eyes and took a step forward, still

watching the flying figures. "So the Union forces are closer than we thought."

Von Heïzinger shrugged. "Or perhaps just she is."

"It must be taking her away to kill her like the others," said the Daimyō.

"Or," said Von Heïzinger, "perhaps it has found a new *ally*. Aponi is some kind of 'shaman,' supposedly."

The Daimyō turned to him, looking alarmed. "We cannot allow that to happen. Especially now that we have *proof* of what we seek."

Von Heïzinger slipped his glove from his left hand and held up the ring with the red stone, which was glowing brighter than ever. "The light of the *Orbis Christus* wasn't proof enough for you?" He gestured at Itami and Zermann, who were both swaying, looking woozy. "The growing illness of our unusual friends wasn't enough? My *word* wasn't enough?"

"Your word and your tricks have been most encouraging." The Daimyō's voice was thick with sarcasm. "But now, with my own two eyes, I have seen an *angel*. A heavenly creature. Now I know without a doubt that we are near the great prize. The treasure of *Heaven*."

Von Heïzinger put the glove back on his hand. "You would be nowhere without me, without the Bering Map."

The Daimyō ignored him. "We must hurry to *Kronotskaya Sopka*. We must seize the heavenly power before the angel makes a deal with the Union."

Suddenly, Von Heïzinger flung out a claw-like hand and grabbed hold of the Daimyō's arm. "You are fortunate our goals happen to coincide…for now." He gave the Daimyō a hard shake. "Pray that is always the case, Minamoto."

The Daimyō's hand rested on the hilt of the sword in the scabbard at his hip. "You would not care for my prayers." He drew the sword halfway out and pressed his face close to Von Heïzinger's. "*You* are often the subject."

The two of them stayed like that for a long moment, locked together in seething opposition. Hiruko watched for the slightest movement that could herald open conflict, but there was nothing. They remained frozen like statues, perfectly balanced by mutual hatred and equal force of will.

Then, finally, they both disengaged at the same time. Von Heïzinger released the Daimyō's arm, and the Daimyō slid the sword back down into the scabbard. They'd made a mutual decision to step away from the brink...for now, anyway.

But there was no doubt in Hiruko's mind that they would return to it sooner or later. The enmity between them, which had grown since the start of the expedition, was just too strong.

* * *

The column of Union, New Guard, and Bogatyr forces was back in motion again. Now if only MacNeal could keep it that way.

Hostilities kept threatening to break out again between Oksana and Irina. They could barely stand the sight of each other...and then there was the Ivan-Tatiana problem. Now that Ivan's role as a spy was out in the open, Tatiana saw no need to hold back her true feelings.

In fact, MacNeal heard them going at it again somewhere behind him—this time in English for some reason, which just meant he understood every word. Ivan kept trying to explain and apologize, which was just making matters worse.

"Get away from me!" Tatiana's voice was shrill with rage. She kept her hands on the stocks of the sawed-off shotguns on her hips. "I do not want you anywhere *near* me!"

"Do you not understand?" Ivan was pleading for all he was worth. "I was only obeying the orders of Grand Matriarch Romanova! I was serving the needs of the Motherland!"

"If you think I could *ever* trust you again, you are sadly mistaken!" said Tatiana.

"You are just as untrustworthy! You were *handling* me for Kapetan Gusarenko, were you not? Feeding me bad information?"

"*I* did not *beat* you!" said Tatiana. "Not *yet*, anyway!"

The fight ended there, at least for now. Tatiana marched forward and joined Oksana and MacNeal near the head of the column.

"We should have fought off these Bogatyrs, MacNeal," said Oksana. "Mark my words, this will not end well."

"Or maybe it will." MacNeal shrugged. "Maybe the extra personnel will make the difference. Maybe you'll even get through to these people."

Oksana snorted. "They are loyalists to the core. The Black Angel has them in his power."

"But isn't it possible you might bring them around?" asked MacNeal. "Maybe this is a golden opportunity."

Tatiana leaned in and spoke. "A golden opportunity to strike a blow against the Black Angel, maybe." Her voice was almost a snarl.

MacNeal shook his head. "We have a *mission*. You need to focus on that."

"And maybe *you* need to focus on the big picture," said Oksana. "Ask yourself this: will you be better off if the *Black Angel* or the *New Guard* controls the Matriarchy?"

She had a point, but he didn't answer her question. It was just as well, because Irina chose that moment to strut up and join them. "I have completed my inspection. This ragtag team of yours is not fit to fight."

MacNeal smirked. "Then it's a good thing we ran into you and the Bogatyrs, isn't it?"

Irina tossed her head, flicking her platinum blond bangs out of her eyes. "How long will it take to reach *Kronotskaya Sopka*?"

"Seven hours," said Oksana, "approximately."

Irina sighed. "I fear for your Tala, John. Perhaps a detachment of my Bogatyrs should go on ahead. They can get there much faster on their own, without the dead weight."

Oksana and Tatiana both glared dagger eyes at her. MacNeal could almost see steam coming out of their ears…but he wasn't going to let the situation erupt. "How considerate of you. What a great idea, Irina."

Now Oksana and Tatiana were glaring at him instead.

But Irina was all smiles. "Wonderful! They will leave immediately." She turned to go.

Before she could take a step, MacNeal cleared his throat loudly. "Wait!"

"Yes, John?" Irina slowly turned his way.

He put on his best poker face. "You did say the non-Bogatyrs aren't fit to fight, didn't you?"

Irina nodded. "I did say that."

MacNeal sighed. "Then we'd better keep all your men close, for the sake of the rest of us." He looked perfectly deadpan as he said it. "I don't think we'll feel safe otherwise. Especially with that murderer roaming around."

"Oh." Irina cocked her head. "If you feel that strongly about it…"

"I do." He nodded firmly. "*Very* strongly."

"All right then." Her smile, as always, was dazzling. "Anything for you, John." She hummed a sweet melody as she turned and strutted away, returning to her men in the column.

MacNeal had to catch himself. The little tune was working its way into his head, masking his true feelings toward her with a layer of artificially imposed warmth.

The musical mind control completely lost its hold on him when Oksana started swearing. She was standing right next to him when she unleashed a stream of Russian curses and spat on the ground. "You are too diplomatic, MacNeal." She slid a sidelong glare in his direction. "I am starting to think you are in her sway."

"Not a chance." MacNeal glared at her. "My number one priority at this point is retrieving my abducted demolitions specialist. If kissing Irina's ass a little increases my chances of doing so, then by damn that's what I'll do."

Oksana stared at him for a moment, her expression unreadable. "This Tala. She is special to you?"

"Like a daughter." MacNeal tightened his grip on the flash-gun. "I'm trying not to think about the fact that she could end up like the others who've been taken."

Oksana looked down. "Like my cousin, you mean."

MacNeal nodded. "I'll do whatever it takes to save her."

"Perhaps I can help," said Tatiana. She was holding the onyx pendant etched with the image of the winged mortar and pestle. "I have been meditating and praying to Baba Yaga. She has put me in mind of a certain ritual that might help us against Kutkha."

"Whatever it takes," said MacNeal.

"Also, I know these woods and mountains better than anyone in our group." Tatiana narrowed her eyes. "There is a shortcut to *Kronotskaya Sopka.*"

"Point the way," said MacNeal.

"The terrain is rough," said Tatiana. "And the geologic activity can be unpredictable."

MacNeal raised an eyebrow. "Will it get us there faster?"

"If everyone keeps up, yes."

"We'll keep up," said MacNeal. "Just get us to that volcano in time to rescue Tala."

* * *

When Hiruko rejoined the convoy after the debacle with the bird-thing, he found Nadia sitting on a folding chair outside her amphibious transport. She was sitting in the shade; the sun was hitting the other side of the vehicle.

"Back so soon?" She glanced at Hiruko, then watched Von Heïzinger storm past with the Daimyō in tow. Itami and Zermann followed a moment later, looking unsteady. "No luck, I take it, Mr. Orochi?"

Hiruko marched up and stood beside her. "We encountered a creature, Nadia. Some kind of bizarre being."

She raised her eyebrows. "What did he look like?"

"He looked like a seven-foot-tall raven with human arms and legs," said Hiruko. "Even those two couldn't hold him for long." He gestured in the direction of Itami and Zermann.

"Were you hurt, Mr. Orochi?" She reached over and brushed her fingertips over his wrist.

"No, ma'am." Hiruko smiled. "I am fine."

"What about the giant raven? Was *he* hurt?"

"Von Heïzinger tried to use the Patmos Amulet on him, but it had no effect," said Hiruko. "Then the raven burst free of the net and flew off. Zermann tried shooting him down, but every shot missed."

Nadia snorted. "He tried to shoot it *down*?"

"Yes, ma'am," said Hiruko. "And the raven just kept flying toward the big volcano, *Kronotskaya Sopka*." He hiked a thumb in the direction of the snow-streaked, smoldering peak. "He grabbed a woman on the way and took her with him."

"A *woman*?" Nadia scowled up at him. "Where on earth did *she* come from?"

"Von Heïzinger recognized her. He said she's Corporal Aponi from the Union, and she's some kind of shaman."

"A shaman." She nodded as if it all made sense now. "And a giant raven. A raven *god*, I'm sure. No wonder he didn't kill her on the spot."

Hiruko frowned. "I don't understand."

"She is what every god needs, Mr. Orochi. A *believer*." Nadia folded her hands in her lap and gazed up at the giant volcano. "And her belief will give him *power*."

CHAPTER 22

Kamchatka
19 April 1952
1316 Hours

One of the Bogatyrs was missing.

The mixed Union, New Guard, and Bogatyr unit had been making great time, jogging along through the low scrub and gravel of Tatiana's shortcut. But when they made their first stop at the mouth of a winding river valley, there was suddenly a great outcry. Everyone converged at once, including MacNeal, as the word went out.

"Where is he?" Irina was pacing with her hands on her hips. "Where is Dobrynin?"

One of the flamethrower troopers turned and gestured in the direction from which they'd come. "He was behind me the whole time, Holy Commissar. He fell back a little as we ran up that last incline."

"He fell out of your *sight*?" snapped Irina. "And you did not bother to go *back* for him?" Her voice didn't sound so melodic anymore.

The trooper hung his head. "I am sorry, Holy Commissar."

Irina sent back a detachment to search for Dobrynin while the rest of the unit milled around the river bank. Everyone was nervous, looking over their shoulders, expecting the killer to strike again.

MacNeal wasn't unsympathetic, but Tala was still his top priority. He tried to call Taki on the radio and got no answer, which made him more worried. His people were in danger, and the clock was ticking.

So now it was his turn to make a proposal. "Irina." He walked up to her as she was looking at a map with Ivan. "I'm thinking I should take my team forward while you continue the search."

She didn't look up from the map. "And *I* am thinking the search will go faster if we put *everyone* in the field, John. Your people and Oksana's as well as mine."

MacNeal was about to protest when a flurry of action drew his attention. A squad of four Bogatyr troopers had just returned, and one of them carried a pile of clothes.

"It's Dobrynin's uniform." The trooper held up a pair of silver I.D. tags on a chain. "We found something else, too." He looked pale and swallowed hard. "A heap of…guts."

Irina walked over and laid her hand on the uniform. "Well, then." Her face was utterly emotionless as she looked over her shoulder at MacNeal. "I guess you do not need to leave us behind after all, do you?"

"I guess not," said MacNeal.

Irina cleared her throat. "None of us is safe. The killer strikes the 42nd Marines, the New Guard, the Shōgunate, and now the Bogatyrs with equal prejudice."

"Yes." MacNeal nodded. "It seems we're all in the same boat."

"How strange." Irina gave him a funny look, then took the uniform from the trooper. "In that case, I will sing a sacred Liturgy in honor of poor Dobrynin, after which we shall go forth and save those who can still be saved in his name, whatever their allegiance."

* * *

As Taki watched the soaring raven god through his binoculars, he wished he had wings just like him. He'd been running hard over open terrain, and Kutkha and Tala were already miles ahead of him. From where he stood, it looked like they had almost reached the great volcano, in fact. It wasn't humanly possible for Taki to catch up before they landed.

All he could do was follow them and the trail they were leaving—objects from Tala's backpack that had dropped from above and scattered on the ground. He saw her canteen, her binoculars, her ration cans…and he left them where they lay. The trail could help MacNeal and the others stay on track. Besides, gathering Tala's gear would slow Taki down; he had to keep moving, even if he couldn't catch up to her in time.

He just had to hope Kutkha wouldn't do anything to her—or if he tried, that she would fend him off. If anyone could take care of herself, it was hard-nosed Tala; she was a born brawler through and through. Not to mention, her backpack was full of explosives, and she had dynamite bombs in her hip pockets. But all that might not be enough if that bird-creature really was a god, or something just as powerful.

Taki had never met a god before, and he wasn't a religious man. But that didn't mean he didn't believe a god might exist. And he wasn't about to leave Tala at the mercy of one.

So he stuffed the binoculars back in his pocket, had a quick drink from his canteen, and started running again. He still had a few miles to go before he'd reach the base of *Kronotskaya Sopka*. Then came the hard part: scrambling up the side of the enormous peak and fighting a god to set Tala free. If, of course, she hadn't freed herself already and kicked Kutkha's ass by then.

Taki couldn't help smiling as he imagined it. God or no god, his money was on Tala.

But he ran faster just in case.

* * *

Taki wasn't answering. MacNeal called him once more for good measure, then gave up and clipped the radio back on his belt.

The whole time, he never stopped running. The Union, New Guard, and Bogatyr unit was double-timing it through the river valley, racing toward the towering volcano.

The closer they got, the more violent the rumbling became, to the point that it jarred their footing. MacNeal had almost fallen twice already—but he wasn't about to slow down. Not with Tala kidnapped by a raven god and Taki going in alone, on radio silence, to stage a rescue.

"This so-called 'god' we're going after. This Kutkha." Brown talked as he ran beside MacNeal, looking grim. "He couldn't have taken that Bogatyr, could he?"

MacNeal shook his head. "He was flying off with Tala at the time."

"So he isn't working alone," said Brown. "You think there's another one like *him*, picking us off?"

"He has a partner, all right." The ground rumbled under MacNeal again. He stumbled, then regained his steady footing. "There's no way one person, even with wings, could travel back and forth so much between us and the Shōgunate forces. I don't care *how* much of a god he is."

"Uh-huh." Brown wiped his forehead on his sleeve. "So here's a thought. Von Heïzinger trapped Kutkha with human bait, right?"

"He trapped him but couldn't hold him," said MacNeal.

"Has it occurred to you that Kutkha might be doing the same thing to *us*?" Brown raised his eyebrows. "Only this time, Tala's the bait?"

"Yeah." MacNeal nodded. "It's occurred to me, Boomer."

"And you think we're ready for this trap?" Brown bobbed his head back toward the rest of the column. "You think *they're* ready?"

"Does it matter?" MacNeal shrugged and kept running. He and Brown both knew the answer to the question without saying it aloud.

Those people were all they had to work with. One way or another, they were rushing forward together. And if they weren't ready, and things didn't work out, well…

None of it would matter in the end, would it?

* * *

The Shōgunate convoy was moving forward with new speed and purpose. Ever since the Daimyō had returned from attempting to capture the bird-creature, he had seemed reinvigorated. His drive and sense of urgency had been reborn. He pushed his men harder than ever to reach their objective and seize it for the Shōgun and Emperor.

He was like a different man…the man he *used* to be. And Hiruko, for one, was glad to see it.

Had the chain of command changed, restoring his full authority over the Reich's representatives? Probably not. But the Daimyō acted like he was in full control again.

Von Heïzinger seemed content to let him lord it over the troops and get the job done. It must have suited him that the convoy was moving faster than ever toward what had been his goal from the start of the expedition.

And so, the men and vehicles kept moving toward the massive bulk of *Kronotskaya Sopka*, spurred on by the Daimyō's shouts. Only Itami and Zermann dragged their feet, growing more sluggish and unsteady with each passing mile. Whatever was waiting at the volcano, it had a potent effect on those two.

Hiruko wondered if the Daimyō was right about the heavenly nature of the treasure they sought. He could believe it, the way it affected Itami and Zermann so profoundly—and there most certainly seemed to be something *un*-heavenly about *them*.

However, he wasn't so sure the giant raven was a heavenly creature. The Daimyō had called it that, but it hadn't impressed Hiruko as being particularly angelic. He'd sensed intelligence behind its red eyes, and the strangeness of its form had struck him as unearthly, unlike anything he'd ever seen before. But as he'd watched it fly to *Kronotskaya Sopka* with the woman dangling from its claws, he'd thought it looked more like a bird of prey than an angel.

He shivered as he looked up and found the spot on the side of the volcano, about three hundred feet up, where he'd seen the raven land. There was a ledge and a hole in the slope, the mouth of a cave. It was the perfect lair for a winged creature, the perfect place to take its prey.

But he wondered what the raven would do to her there. Was Nadia right about it being a god and needing the power of her belief? Or were the raven's designs darker than that? If so, what unspeakable things might be about to happen to that abducted woman?

* * *

The first thing Tala saw when she opened her eyes was a pile of bones at her feet. Without thinking, she scrambled back away from them, elbows and feet churning through twigs and dirt.

She broke through a tangle of brush...and suddenly, the ground dropped away under her right elbow. Reacting quickly, she pushed off with her left arm and lunged forward, away from the drop-off.

Only when she looked back did she realize she was on a ledge, and how close she'd come to plunging off it. Ashen grey hills and plains fanned out far below, vast dry pans scrawled with networks of cracks and dotted with specks of scraggly scrub.

All at once, the memories rushed back to her. She remembered the flight with Raven, soaring through the sky toward the massive volcano. She remembered closing in on a cave in the mountainside, bobbing toward it on the warm thermal currents. There'd been a broad ledge lined with brush, and she'd seen it rise up to meet her.

Then she remembered Raven's claws releasing her. She remembered falling out of the sky toward the brush-lined sliver of rock jutting out of the side of *Kronotskaya Sopka*.

The last thing she remembered thinking was that she'd hoped she wouldn't blow up. Between her explosive-filled pack and the dynamite bombs in her pockets, she'd literally been a human bomb.

Amazingly, she was still in one piece…though she must've been knocked unconscious in the fall. At the thought of it, she realized her head was throbbing; reaching up, she found a tender lump above her right ear. She was lucky that was the worst that had happened; if she'd scuttled a few more inches over the edge just now, she would've fallen a hell of a lot farther and ended up with much worse than a bump on the head.

Heart pounding, adrenaline blazing through her bloodstream, she carefully eased herself forward. She slid her legs under her, then levered herself up onto her hands and knees.

Now she was facing the pile of bones. Taking a closer look, she wrinkled her nose and shivered.

The bones were fresh and blood-streaked, not picked clean and sun-bleached. Most still had meat and cartilage stuck to them. The smell of rancid, rotting flesh permeated the air, which was buzzing with flies.

Tala's stomach lurched. She crawled away along the curve of the ledge, then braced herself against the rock face and got to her feet.

Once she was standing, she saw that the ledge widened closer to the cave mouth. There was more brush piled around, highest near the drop-off and matted down farther in like a nest. She saw more bones scattered around, too, and a pile of something she didn't want to go near. From a distance, it looked like a mass of skins or carcasses— also bloody, also swimming with flies.

Tala felt her stomach lurch again and looked away. She'd imagined the bird-creature to be a relative of Raven, or perhaps an incarnation of the god himself—but this gruesome roost wasn't at all what she would have expected as the home of such a being. According to the lore, Raven was a trickster, not a murderer.

Gingerly, she walked among the bones and matted brush, watching all around for surprises. As she rubbed her throbbing head, she wondered where her pack was; she was dying to gulp down the aspirin in the first aid kit she kept in there.

Unless the pack was under the pile of skins—and there was *no way* she was going to check—but it definitely wasn't out in the open on the ledge. So maybe inside the cave was a safer bet.

Of course, Raven—or whatever he was—might be in there, too. And though Tala had been excited when she'd first seen him through the binoculars, expecting a sacred kinship because of her shaman background, the signs she was seeing in his nest were all bad. Meeting him alone in a dark cave might not be such a good thing.

Still, as she moved slowly toward the mouth of the cave, she heard no telltale sounds from within. Maybe, after dropping her off, Raven had gone back out in search of more prey.

Inching up to the rim of the opening, she realized she'd need a light to see inside the dark space. Her flashlight was gone with her pack…but at least she had a backup method of breaching the darkness. Explosives specialists like her made it a habit to have plenty of lighters on hand at all times.

Pulling one of her lighters from a shirt pocket, she snapped it open with her thumb. Holding her breath, she eased inside the mouth of the cave. She ran out of sunlight a few yards in and found herself facing a gulf of pitch blackness.

Swallowing hard, she raised the lighter and planted her thumb on the switch. Then she flicked it down, raising a tiny flame.

As the glow of the flame penetrated the darkness around her, Tala gasped. They were hanging from the ceiling in front of her, naked and pale. Silent and still as corpses.

Bodies. The bodies of *men.*

CHAPTER 23

Kamchatka
19 April 1952
1507 Hours

Until the shooting started, the Shōgunate convoy was making great time. Men and machines alike were charging through the forest, unfazed by the heat of the day as the sun blazed down from above.

The Daimyō's new drive and determination continued to inspire the men. It was as if the entire unit was inexhaustible as long as their leader's willpower burned bright. They would not be slowed from seizing the heavenly prize that awaited, the priceless treasure protected by that singular dark angel they'd briefly captured.

Hiruko was just as inspired as any of them. For a time, at least, he stopped worrying about Von Heïzinger and what he might do next. He just kept running alongside Nadia's vehicle, rifle at the ready, happy to play his part.

But he was still surprised when the shooting started.

Everyone was moving along briskly when a sudden *crack* echoed through the woods. Suddenly, a Shōgunate soldier's head snapped back violently. The man twisted and fell in the dirt, landing fewer than ten yards from Hiruko. A pool of deep crimson formed under his head and quickly expanded as his lifeblood rushed out of him.

"Incoming fire!" Even as Hiruko yelled the words, the troops were already in motion. Years of training and drills kicked in as the men up front swung their weapons around in the direction of the first shot and opened fire.

As the men at the point of the formation cut loose, the rest of the unit took action, too. Some threw themselves into covered positions, ducking behind vehicles and trees before returning fire. Others lobbed smoke and fragmentation grenades into the kill zone. Gunners atop the amphibious vehicles swung their turrets around and kicked out high-caliber rounds of their own.

Hiruko stood his ground, crouching alongside Nadia's vehicle. The blasts of the vehicle's large gun hurt his ears, but he still thought it was the best place for him. The vehicle had cover, a big gun cranking off round after round, and an old woman whose well-being was his responsibility.

The word flew down the line: "Hold your fire!" The Shōgunate barrage stopped immediately, and the echoes of gunshots faded after it.

Hiruko kept a tight grip on his rifle and watched the surrounding forest. He couldn't see very far because of the smoke from the grenades.

Just when Hiruko thought the skirmish might be over, Von Heïzinger's feral Stosstruppen hurtled past, growling behind his muzzlelike mask. As he bolted into the drifting smoke, the two robot-like Schocktruppen ran after him, side by side.

As the three Reich warriors disappeared into the smoke, the gunner atop Nadia's vehicle called down to Hiruko. "What do you think they'll come back with? Matriarchy or Union corpses?"

Hiruko shrugged and kept watching and listening for danger. The word went down the line to stay alert, but he didn't have to be told.

Suddenly, fierce snarling and thrashing exploded in the forest. It sounded like a dog or wolf attacking its prey, tearing it to ribbons. Then, there was a booming double shot that sounded like a single shot—two rifles blasting rounds simultaneously. As the echo fell away, bestial howling filled the air.

Moments later, the Stosstruppen bounded out of the smoke,

threw back his head, and howled the same inhuman howl. The two Schocktruppen emerged after him, each hauling an arm of the corpse they towed between them.

"So which is it?" the gunner asked Hiruko. "Matriarchy or Union? I can't tell from here."

The Daimyō and Von Heïzinger strode up to examine the body. Some of the men gathered at a distance, and Hiruko joined them. He got just close enough that he could see the corpse and hear what the leaders were saying.

The body was that of a dark-haired, middle-aged man with coppery skin. He was wearing a long-sleeved shirt and britches that looked like they'd been stitched together from some kind of tanned hide. The Daimyō took his chin between thumb and forefinger and turned it slowly from side to side. "Looks like a local. I wondered why none rose up against us after the landing."

"Cowards." Von Heïzinger glared at the body with icy contempt. "They hide like vermin and take potshots from the shadows." He nudged the dead man's leg with the tip of his boot. "They cannot comprehend true power and purpose."

The Daimyō looked up at him with a dark, guarded gaze. "Nothing can stand in the way of that. He should have known."

Von Heïzinger held his gaze a moment, then looked into the smoky woods. "There will be more."

The Daimyō leaped to his feet and turned to his troops. "We are now on high alert status. This lone sniper is our first contact, but I anticipate increased resistance as we near our objective.

"Change formation from column to wedge! Distribute the armor in front and on the flanks! Prepare to engage at any time!" The Daimyō drew his sword and shook it overhead. "And remember, we must not let them slow us down! We must get to the objective before the Union and Matriarchy scoundrels! We will not be kept from our rightful destiny!"

The men, including Hiruko, cheered. Meanwhile, Von Heïzinger gathered the agents of the Reich off to one side and issued his own orders. Without a word, they bounded into the forest ahead—Zermann, the two Schocktruppen, and the Stosstruppen, like a silent squad of monsters.

The Daimyō summoned his own heavy-hitter, Itami, and ordered him to stay close. Itami still looked a little shaky, but slammed his club on the ground in acknowledgement.

The unit erupted in a flurry of activity, shifting men and machines into a new formation. As for Hiruko, he carved out his own task while the others scrambled around him. He went to the body of the dead Shōgunate soldier, crouched down beside him, and hefted him up in his arms with a grunt.

He carried the dead soldier to the vehicle with the secret payload and no passengers, but the driver told him he couldn't bring the body aboard. The drivers of the other two vehicles said the same thing.

So he carried his comrade's corpse into the woods, snapped the dog tags from his neck, and piled rocks over him. He had to replace some twice, because the rumbling ground knocked them loose. It was the best he could manage; by the time he was done, the unit was already moving forward again.

* * *

Giant geysers roared to life on either side of MacNeal as he ran through the river valley. He'd passed at least a dozen of them already, flinging up great plumes of hissing spray from holes in the salt-crusted earth. There were many more arrayed before him, shunting up steaming fountains of water in syncopated alternation.

He'd never seen so many geysers in one place; if he'd had more time, he would have loved to slow down and savor the beauty of the natural wonders. But as it was, all he could do was briefly take note while he kept churning his way toward *Kronotskaya Sopka* and Tala.

MacNeal ran at the head of the column, leading the cross-country charge. No one else in the unit came close to his level of sheer determination. Tala was family, plain and simple; he might be too late to save her, but he was sure as hell going to try.

At least he was sure he was heading in the right direction. He kept finding pieces of Tala's gear along the way—a flashlight here, a ration can there, a walkie-talkie up ahead. Had the trail been left intentionally? He couldn't be sure, but he knew it was leading him to her, and that was all that mattered.

He was already soaked from sweat and the spray of the geysers when the next one hit, shooting up right in his path when he was almost on top of it. The blast knocked him for a loop, popping up when he was in mid-stride and sending him stumbling. At least it wasn't a giant—it threw him off-pace but didn't bowl him over.

Still, the ground lurched as he stumbled, and he thought he might go down after all. He heaved left, fighting for sound footing, and flew toward the point of completely losing his balance.

Then, just as he nearly dropped to the hard-packed earth, someone grabbed him by the shoulders. Strong hands caught him before he could fall, then wrenched him upright.

Panting, MacNeal turned to see the face of his rescuer. He fully expected it would be Brown, who'd been close behind—so he couldn't help looking surprised when he realized it was Irina instead.

"All right, John?" She was just as drenched as he was.

"Yeah." MacNeal steadied himself and nodded. "Thanks for the backup."

She gave him a flirty smile. "Always happy to strengthen our alliance." She squeezed his shoulders, then drew her hands away a little too slowly. It was a sensuous move, another of Irina's trademarks. She was great at playing men, no doubt about it.

But spotting her game was half the battle. Once upon a time, MacNeal had fallen for her routine, but he wouldn't let it happen again. "I'll be more careful where I step from now on." He gestured at the geyser that had blown up in his path; it was still going strong.

"Major!" Just then, Brown thundered up, with the rest of the unit close behind. "What's your status?"

"Good to go, Boomer." MacNeal nodded once and started running again. The longer they stood around, the less chance they'd have of finding Tala alive.

This time, Irina matched his pace, staying right alongside him. "We have some strange bedfellows in our little alliance, do we not, John?"

"I say the more the merrier," said MacNeal. "Political differences aren't my concern right now."

"Nor are they mine, believe it or not," said Irina. "Trustworthiness, on the other hand, is." She bobbed closer and bumped him with her elbow. "Oksana Gusarenko is not who you think she is, John."

"Who is, these days?" MacNeal picked up his pace.

So did Irina. "How much do you really know about her?"

"All I need to at this point," said MacNeal. "She saved my life."

"That may be," said Irina, "but she is also the wrong woman for this mission. If there is a god involved, she cannot be trusted."

"Not interested, Irina. Why don't you save your breath for running?"

"Did you know she was once an *archimandrite*, John? A *gifted* one, at that." Irina reached up and pushed her platinum blond hair behind her ears. "She was even chosen to participate in Project SVAROG, to be the vessel for the incarnation of the god Vetchorka when she was summoned to Earth. Can you imagine? Aside from the Tsarina herself, there can be no higher honor in the Matriarchy."

MacNeal scowled. "An incarnation of a god?" He'd encountered bizarre phenomena before, but this one sounded crazy. He'd never heard of Project SVAROG or Vetchorka before. The idea of a god being forced to incarnate inside a human vessel seemed ridiculous. "Well, good for her, I guess."

"Not so good, John. She tried to bend Vetchorka to her will. She tried to *control* her." Irina shook her head in disgust. "An entire research facility was destroyed in the struggle that ensued."

The whole story sounded preposterous—an effort on the part of Irina to poison his partnership with Oksana. MacNeal had no intention of giving it any credence whatsoever. "So no incarnation of a god, then."

"Correct," said Irina. "And we have not been able to restore contact with Vetchorka since. We can only pray Oksana did not do some kind of permanent damage to her."

Four new geysers sprang to life fifty yards ahead, occluding the view beyond with towers of mist. MacNeal kept running, thinking the towers might recede by the time he reached them. "Why exactly are you telling me all this, Irina?"

"Because you need to be aware of whom you are dealing with," said Irina. "She is a god hater, John. Does that make her fit for this mission, now that at least one god is involved?"

MacNeal shot her a sideways look. "And I suppose you and your men *are* fit?"

"In every way, John." Irina nudged his elbow again. "Do you know where the name 'Bogatyr' originates? The first Bogatyrs were Russian knights of the Middle Ages—noble warriors renowned for their power, courage, faith, and devotion to the Motherland." She gestured in the direction of the men and women running behind them. "The modern-day Bogatyrs are no less devoted, powerful, and courageous. Their faith—their greatest might—is at least as strong as that of the Bogatyrs of yore. *They* will not *fail* you, John. *They* will not *shirk* their duty to the Motherland when faced with the incarnation of a *god*."

MacNeal grated his teeth. Whatever her angle might be, he was ready to shut down the whole line of discussion.

Before he could say another word, though, something flashed out of the geyser mist, flying straight toward him. Reflexively, he leaped aside; as the object whizzed past, he got the quickest flash of a glance at it.

An arrow. Someone was shooting at him through the geysers up ahead.

"Down!" He dropped as he said it, swinging up his flash-gun to return fire in a big way. He cranked off a few rounds into the mist, then hollered over his shoulder to the rest of the unit coming up behind him. "*Incoming!*"

* * *

Wolf watched the action in the geyser valley below as the Dark God, Kutkha, flew him toward the great volcano. His and Kutkha's efforts to chip away at the Union, New Guard, and Bogatyr unit, and the Shōgunate and Reich group had been very successful. Both factions on the ground were racing to *Kronotskaya Sopka*, driving harder than ever.

The last of Wolf's victims, in fact, dangled from Kutkha's other claw. It was the fastest way to get him across the miles to the aerie. After ambushing the lone Bogatyr, Wolf had called in the local version of air support, and Kutkha had given them both a lift above the fray.

Now it was time for the next stage of the game. The two factions were highly motivated and moving in fast. Both sides were being attacked by the native Koryaks, who were trying to hold them off. The Koryaks were acting in their own interest, which was opposite the Dark God's, but their half-hearted fumblings would end up serving Kutkha's interest after all.

Because the factions heading for *Kronotskaya Sopka* would push harder than ever now.

The Koryaks might slow them briefly, but they would move faster than ever after defeating them. It was a law of human nature that Wolf understood all too well from past experience: the greater the resistance, the greater the human desire to overcome it.

As Kutkha soared toward his aerie on the side of the great volcano, Wolf smiled to himself. The opening gambits were over, the strategies exposed, the pieces positioned for their inevitable final struggle. Soon, he would see if his planning would pay off the way he expected…or if that one factor that no man could predict in any human endeavor would upset his careful preparations.

That one factor being luck.

* * *

Taki heard shots in the distance, but didn't look away from his binoculars. He was too busy watching Kutkha fly back to his nest with more human cargo.

He'd seen the giant raven race out after dropping off Tala. Now he was back, flapping slowly toward the volcano as he toted the weight of two full-grown men.

One was awake and clothed, the other unconscious and naked. Taki saw their faces clearly but couldn't identify them.

He snapped the binoculars shut and stuffed them in his pocket, then took a deep breath. He was about to leave the forest and strike out across the barren plain around *Kronotskaya Sopka*. From that point on, he would be out in the open, exposed to attack. The only cover he saw for the remaining miles to the base of the volcano was an occasional boulder or scruffy bush.

That exposure made the sound of distant gunfire more worrisome. He would have to be on even higher alert for the slightest sign of danger. But the lack of cover could also work in his favor: there would be fewer places for ambushers to hide.

Not that it mattered. Not that anything would keep him from running to rescue Tala.

Adrenaline surged through him at the thought of the task ahead. Heart pounding, blood rushing, he set out across the volcanic plain, running over the cracked, grey earth as the sun blazed down on him.

* * *

When Tala first glimpsed the bodies hanging from the cave ceiling, she gasped. As tough as she was, the sight still surprised her. She stumbled back out and leaned against the rock face for a moment, steadying herself.

MacNeal and Brown had told her about the ongoing murders, and she'd seen the remains of the Shōgunate victims herself. Now, she knew where the victims had ended up. They were just around the corner, strung from the cave ceiling like sides of beef. The killer had dragged them here after disemboweling them, leaving behind piles of uniforms and guts as a warning. Sure enough, the bodies were all naked now.

But wait. Tala frowned as she realized something didn't jive. She'd only glimpsed the bodies for an instant before backing out of the cave, but...

Swallowing hard, she went back in and ignited her lighter. It was then she knew that all was not as it had appeared to be.

The men had not been disemboweled.

A spark of hope flared within her like the flame of her lighter. What if the lack of disemboweling wasn't the only thing unexpected about them? Tala went to the one she knew from the 42nd—Paul Hamilton—and placed her hand against his chest. The heartbeat within his rib cage confirmed her suspicion.

Still alive.

She went from man to man, raising the lighter to check all eight of them. The results were all the same. The men were unconscious—drugged, maybe?—but still alive. The whole murder campaign had been some kind of elaborate hoax.

But where had the piles of guts come from? Tala had a thought and stormed out of the cave. She went straight to the pile of skins on the ledge and took a closer look. Sure enough, telltale traces were visible among the hides: faces and claws of animals, including bears and deer. Next, she went to the pile of bones and found more of the same when she kicked through it: antlers and non-human skulls.

So that was how Raven had done it. He'd taken the guts from animals and kept the men intact and alive. Whatever his rationale, he'd only pretended to kill off those men.

Now it was up to her to free them and get them out of there.

Tala turned and headed for the mouth of the cave, pocketing the lighter and reaching for her medicine pouch. She thought she might have something to wake the men.

But before she could get inside, she heard the beating of giant wings. Turning, she saw Raven's great black wingspan swoop over the ledge.

He was carrying a naked, unconscious man in one claw and a clothed, conscious one in the other. He released them as soon as he'd cleared the lip of the nest. The unconscious one fell and rolled into the pile of bones. The conscious man dropped down in a crouch right in front of her.

As soon as he looked up, she recognized him. His black hair, dark gaze, and shadowy intensity hadn't changed a bit since the last time she'd seen him. Just like before, there were weapons strapped to almost every inch of his body: guns, ammo, grenades, and knives of all shapes and sizes.

"Hello, Tala." His voice was as deep and gravelly as she remembered. "Small world, isn't it?"

"Wolf?" The mercenary had worked with the 42nd on several missions. He'd worked *against* them a time or three, as well. She wondered whose side he was on *this* time. "What the hell are you doing here?"

Rising, he unsnapped one of the many holsters he wore. "Oh, a little of this, a little of that."

Tala dropped her hands to hover near the bombs in her pockets. Her mind was ticking along, considering the possibilities. "Does that include blowing my ass off this mountain?"

"That depends." Wolf drew a Colt .45 pistol from the holster and slowly raised it.

"Depends on what?" asked Tala.

Wolf smiled grimly. "On whether the god can talk me out of it."

CHAPTER 24

**Kamchatka
19 April 1952
1613 Hours**

More arrows zipped out of the geysers, and MacNeal kept cranking off rounds. He was firing blind, thanks to the mist; he only knew he hadn't hit anyone because the arrows kept coming.

Irina didn't seem to be having any more success. She fired shots from her double-barreled revolver, but there was no sign that she'd made any kind of contact.

The rest of the unit was fanned out behind them, firing from various points of cover. MacNeal heard Brown's flash machine gun booming away, somewhere off to the right, pumping ammo into the concealing mist.

Still, there were more arrows. At least they all sailed wide of any human targets; MacNeal guessed the mist must be making it just as hard for the attackers to take aim as it was for the unit under attack.

Finally, Irina lowered her gun and cleared her throat. When she opened her mouth, a song issued forth—one of her amazing Liturgies. MacNeal had heard them in action before; hell, he'd been on the receiving end more than once. Her bell-like voice rose and fell, weaving an intricate melody of dreamlike notes with the power to mold men's minds. Irina's Liturgies could make dispirited soldiers fight with fresh vigor, bring hope and faith and fortitude to those who had lost it, or, as in this case, make an enemy stop shooting.

Suddenly, one of the geysers fell away, exposing a man with a bow. He just stood there, gazing at Irina, with a spellbound look on his face. Before he could shake off the daze and get off another shot, MacNeal swung his flash-gun around and cut him down.

Irina stopped singing and took a breath. The brief interruption in her Liturgy seemed to set the dead man's comrades free, as more arrows flew from other positions in the remaining mist. MacNeal focused his fire on one of the still-spraying geysers and was rewarded with a direct hit. A man cried out in pain and fell forward through the spray, dropping face down on the ground.

Two of the other geysers switched off at the same moment, leaving another man exposed. Brown blew him away with a blast of high-powered ammo, and the fight was over.

Brown whistled and waved, and two men from the 42nd followed him toward the bodies. Before they could reach them, however, Tatiana dashed past with red hair flying.

She threw herself down to crouch among them, staring at their faces. "They are all Koryaks!"

Irina and MacNeal jogged after Brown's squad. Just as they drew near, Oksana sprinted up and stopped beside them. "We have injured." She sounded half out of breath. "One of the New Guard took an arrow in the shoulder."

"Leave him here," said Irina. "He will only slow us down."

Oksana wouldn't even look at her. "We have treated his wound. He is fine to keep going."

"I do not understand." Tatiana was staring at the dead Koryaks. "Why would they shoot at us?"

"Maybe they didn't have a choice." MacNeal stepped forward and crouched beside Tatiana. He checked the body for a pulse and found none. "Maybe it's their duty to protect whatever's inside that volcano." He placed his fingers on the dead Koryak's eyelids and slowly drew them shut.

"The duty of *all* the Koryaks, perhaps." Oksana planted Vesper at her side and looked down at the other two corpses. "These will not be the last, will they?"

MacNeal checked the two bodies for pulses. They were as dead as the first one had been. "My gut says no." He looked at Tatiana.

She shrugged. "I am surprised they attacked us at all. The Koryaks have mostly steered clear of us." Her frown deepened and she looked up at Irina. "Until now."

Irina gave her a withering look. "If you want to point fingers, point one at *yourself*. I have never even *met* these people."

Tatiana got to her feet. She glared at Irina, then slowly turned to face Oksana. "I do have history with the Koryaks. Perhaps I should try to make contact. Perhaps I can negotiate with them."

"It's too late for that." MacNeal rose. "You'll end up a hostage… or worse."

"Maybe I do not care." Tatiana's gaze was steely. "Maybe I am willing to take the chance."

Oksana moved in and put her hand on Tatiana's shoulder. "We need you with us. I do not think we can finish this without you."

Tatiana clenched her jaws and stared down at the body of the man she'd known. She flashed a look at Irina, then MacNeal, then turned back to Oksana. "You are right. It might be better if I am with the unit, ready to help the next time we encounter the Koryaks."

"All right then." MacNeal clapped his hands together. While they were standing around, who knew what could be happening to Tala? "Let's get moving, people. We need to make up for lost time."

Without hesitation, Brown whirled and barked out orders to the rest of the 42nd, instantly kicking them into gear. The New Guard responded quickly, too; they'd learned to fall in line with the Union men, at least unless Oksana told them otherwise. The Bogatyrs, however, watched but didn't move a muscle. They were waiting for specific instructions from Irina or Ivan.

MacNeal took it all in, as always. His observations would flesh out the battle plan he was already building in his mind. The key to devising any strategy was to turn flaws and fractures into strengths.

Or at least not to be taken by surprise when they blew up in your face.

* * *

The ground rumbled when the Shōgunate convoy left the forest and set foot on the barren plain surrounding *Kronotskaya Sopka*.

Hiruko, marching at the point of the wedge formation alongside Nadia's vehicle, gazed out over the emptiness. There was nothing but flat, grey terrain for the next few miles, cut by jagged fissures and littered with lumps of rock. The area around the volcano had been covered over with lava flows so often, submerged under molten rock that had cooled and hardened over time, that a big, grey plate had built up around it.

The vast bulk of the volcano's cinder cone towered over it all, bathed in the light of the afternoon sun. As Hiruko peered up at it, a shiver raced along his spine; being so close, he could not help but marvel at the enormity of the mountain...and his awe was tinged with fear as it rumbled with greater force the closer he got. He hated to think what it would be like to be so close when *Kronotskaya Sopka* erupted.

As soon as the convoy crossed over onto the plain, the Daimyō ordered a full stop. He proceeded to scan the area ahead with binoculars—looking for signs of the enemy, no doubt. Hiruko couldn't see any hiding places out there.

Instead of staring at the emptiness along with the Daimyō, he decided to check on Nadia. He knocked on the hatch of the amphibious vehicle and waited, but no one answered from inside. He tried again with the same result, then announced he was coming in and turned the handle.

"Nadia? Hello?" Hiruko opened the hatch and leaned in for a look. "Are you all right?"

Nadia looked back at him from the dim light within the compartment. A battery-powered lantern mounted on the ceiling was the only illumination. "I'm fine, Mr. Orochi." As usual, she was strapped into a padded couch with her back to the cab. "Thank you for the fresh air. It was getting stale in here."

Hiruko bowed. "We are nearly there. We will soon reach the base of the volcano."

She sighed loudly. "And then Hermann will finally have what he wants. I can only hope he will let me go, then."

"*Hai*." Hiruko hesitated. "What is it he wants?"

"I wish I knew." Nadia shook her head. "Or maybe it's better I don't."

Hiruko frowned. "What do you mean?"

"I mean he brought me here for a *reason*, Mr. Orochi." Her hand twitched in her lap. "And I don't think it has anything to do with old times' sake."

Hiruko nodded silently.

"I have a terrible feeling, Mr. Orochi," said Nadia. "Why do you think I have wanted so badly to escape?"

"What reason could he possibly have for bringing you here?" asked Hiruko.

Nadia shrugged. "I have power, Mr. Orochi. You've seen it in action."

Hiruko remembered the boulder she'd grown over with weeds and made mobile, and he nodded.

"Perhaps he plans to call on that power," said Nadia, "or drain it from me. Or perhaps he hopes to use me as a conduit to tap the heavenly power that he expects to find in the volcano. Who knows?" She sighed. "His machinations are intricate and impossible to predict. The evil that has taken hold of him will not allow him to be straightforward."

"So what will you do?" asked Hiruko.

"You'll see." Nadia's eyes narrowed, and a smirk filtered onto her wrinkled face. "I still have a few tricks up my sleeve, Mr. Orochi."

* * *

Taki ran across the volcanic plain under the blazing sun, soaked in sweat. He was less than a mile from the base of *Kronotskaya Sopka*.

So far, no one had leaped out of a camouflaged foxhole and surprised him, but that could still change. Periodic gunfire raged in the distance, so he knew the mountain was defended. He just had to hope that the approach he'd chosen fell between the lines of the defense grid.

He would have enough trouble on his hands without stumbling into a firefight. For one thing, he'd have to climb the side of the volcano. It wasn't too steep or sheer, so it could be done without mountaineering gear...but it would be significantly harder than running across a mostly level plain. And once he reached the ledge, he'd have to fight for Tala's life.

And the odds on that ledge would be against him. Moments ago,

Kutkha had swooped down and dropped off the two men he'd been carrying. The conscious one had landed nimbly; Taki had seen that he was armed to the teeth.

As for Kutkha, he'd looped around and was gliding back in with legs extended, about to land. By the time Taki got up there, he'd have to face two opponents—one of them a god, or at least a freak of nature strong enough to break free of Von Heïzinger's trap.

Taki was glad he'd brought so many of his personal weapons—the tonfa, jitte, and nunchaku. If the flash-gun failed, he would have to rely on his kobudō skills to bring Tala out alive.

If she wasn't already dead, that is.

* * *

Raven swooped down in a rush of wind and landed on the ledge behind Wolf. When his claws touched down, he fanned his huge wings back and forth dramatically, then drew them in tight against his body.

"Speak of the devil," said Wolf, who was still pointing the Colt .45 at Tala's head. "I guess it's time to get a verdict on whether you live or die."

Tala scowled and kept her hands near the bombs in her hip pockets. If Wolf started shooting, they wouldn't do her much good; it would take too long to pull them out, light them, and throw them. But maybe they would serve as a distraction. "I don't get it, Wolf. Why kill me?"

"Good question." He looked over his shoulder at Raven. "Why kill her?"

As Tala watched, Raven's head changed shape. It was like watching taffy being pulled in a vat, twisting from one shape to another, shifting from the head of a giant black bird to that of a man with coppery skin and short, black hair. "We will not." His voice, when he spoke, was high and clear, like that of a tenor singer at the opera. "She is one of my people."

"In that case…" Wolf lowered the Colt .45 and slipped it back into the holster.

Meanwhile, Raven kept changing shape. "Welcome to my aerie." He spread his wings, and they melted, compressing into two human arms covered with swirling black tattoos. His bird-like body shifted, molding itself into the form of a muscular man. Instead of a bird's legs and claws, he suddenly had human legs and feet. Instead of feathers, he was covered from neck to toe in those black tattoos... but the more Tala looked at them, the more she realized they weren't tattoos at all, but some kind of living stain that constantly swirled and flowed over his skin.

Tala knew she was staring, but she couldn't help it. Of all the strange things she'd seen during her time with the 42nd Marines, this was the topper.

Wolf finally broke the spell. "I thought you were a shaman, Tala. Haven't you ever seen a shapeshifting god before?"

Tala shook her head to clear it, then shot Wolf a look. "You told him I'm a shaman? Is that why he picked me up?"

Raven answered. "It was a happy coincidence. I picked you up because you were there. Now that I have you here before me, I see you are one of mine. I can *feel* it from here."

Tala frowned. It was one thing to believe in beings like Raven, and quite another to be considered one of "his people." But she thought she might be better off if she didn't mention that just then. "I've heard many stories about Raven."

"I am called Kutkha in this place." He smiled and nodded. "But I am also Raven. You might think of me as an *aspect* of him."

The mountain rumbled as Tala considered what Kutkha had said. He might be telling the truth—the evidence of his raven-like altered state was persuasive. Then again, Raven had a reputation as a trickster god. She needed to stay on guard with him...and Wolf was not to be trusted, either.

"So tell me, Kutkha." Tala hiked a thumb over her shoulder toward the cave full of men. "What's with the prisoners?"

"Think of them as guests," said Wolf. "Think of yourself as one, too, because you're about to join them."

"No, Wolf," said Kutkha. "She has a different role to play. She's going to help us. Isn't she?" He tipped his gaze toward her.

"That depends," said Tala. "What exactly do you want me to help you *with*?"

"Completing my quest." Kutkha flapped his arms as if he'd forgotten they were no longer wings. "Ending my loneliness."

"Loneliness?" asked Tala.

"That's all you need to know," said Wolf.

"Is that why you brought those men here?" Tala gestured at the cave. "Why you faked their deaths? Because you're *lonely*?"

"In a way, yes," said Kutkha. "They are serving my quest."

"Well, you won't be lonely for much longer." Tala gestured toward the landscape beyond the ledge, in the general direction of the 42nd. "People are on their way here as we speak. They've been heading for this volcano all along."

"Good." Kutkha smiled. "I left them a trail to follow. I scattered the gear from your backpack in their path."

Just then, the sharp crackle of gunfire echoed in the distance; the sound carried clearly across the wide open expanse around the volcano. Tala could hear two sides exchanging fire, neither one of them the 42nd. Even from a distance, she would have recognized the unique retorts of her comrades' Union flash-guns.

Wolf cocked his head and listened as the fire continued. "Sounds like the Koryaks are putting up quite a fight down there."

"Putting up a fight for what reason?" asked Tala.

"To keep everyone away from this volcano," said Wolf.

Tala scowled. "But I thought getting people to come here was the whole point."

"The Koryaks aren't working for us," said Wolf. "They're the enemy."

"They're my *followers*…and my *jailers*." Kutkha's voice was full of anger. "They want to keep me from finishing my quest." He folded his arms over his chest. The tattoo-like designs on his upper body swirled faster, perhaps from the strong emotion he was expressing. "Why do you think we wanted *your* people to come here?"

The gunfire continued to chatter in the distance. "And the Shōgunate?" asked Tala. "And the Russians and the Reich?"

Kutkha nodded. "All of them. I need all of them."

"What for?" asked Tala. "They won't work together."

Kutkha chuckled. "But don't you see? That's *exactly* what they're doing. By working *against* each other, they're working *together* to accomplish my goal." He walked toward her, extending his hand. "And so will you, Tala."

CHAPTER 25

Kamchatka
19 April 1952
1718 Hours

As soon as a Shōgunate round took out the latest native fighter to appear from a hidden foxhole, another one popped up twenty yards away and opened fire. Hiruko, crouching alongside the amphibious vehicle at the point of the formation, churned out a stream of rounds in reply.

It turned out the barren volcanic plain was riddled with camouflaged tunnels and trenches. Locals armed with rifles, revolvers, and bows sprang up one after another in the Shōgunate convoy's path, firing with abandon.

The locals provided a fierce resistance; even with their outdated weapons, they'd already knocked down four men and slowed the convoy's progress to a crawl. The last few miles to *Kronotskaya Sopka* were turning out to be the toughest of the entire expedition.

Hiruko cranked off a few more rounds, and his target dropped out of sight. Just as he was wondering if he'd scored a kill shot, fresh fire burst to life from another direction, blowing in from two o'clock.

Hiruko spun and got a bead on the latest shooter, only to realize it was the same shooter as before. Once again, the damn tunnels had worked to the locals' advantage.

As Hiruko and the shooter traded fire, the gunner atop the amphibious vehicle launched high-caliber rounds at a cluster of archers at twelve o'clock. The other gunners were busy at the flanks of the wedge, dealing with other targets.

As for the Daimyō, he'd lost none of his drive and momentum. Clad in his crimson armor, he charged foxholes like a vengeful demon, sending heads flying with sweeping strokes of his *katana* sword, the legendary *Dyuaru-Kontan*.

Itami roamed the battlefield fearlessly, too, pulverizing natives with his enormous kenabō club. Many times, the enemy howled in terror and disappeared before he reached them. Other times, their fear made their shots fly hopelessly wide, opening them up to quick annihilation.

Like the Daimyō, Itami slaughtered with ruthless precision, dancing gracefully between arrows and bullets. His inhumanly tough blue hide was his own version of armor, deflecting many strikes and absorbing others without major damage. Bullets stuck in his flesh without penetrating deeply; sapphire blood oozed around them, but never poured out. Hiruko was starting to wonder if *anything* could kill him.

Then there was Von Heïzinger, who seemed not so much unkillable as *untouchable*. Striding along the lines in his black overcoat, he clutched the Patmos Amulet in his left hand and gestured at local fighters with his right. Instead of opening fire on him, they turned their weapons on each other and blasted away. The air filled with screams as men killed their comrades next to them, then killed themselves, too. Not once did a single round come anywhere near Von Heïzinger.

As deadly as Von Heïzinger and the Shōgunate forces were, the natives still outnumbered them and refused to retreat. For every head the Daimyō lopped off or Itami crushed, two more popped up farther forward.

If only the Shōgunate soldiers had some countermeasure that would let them take away the natives' tunneling advantage. Then their superior skills and firepower would surely enable them to shut down the enemy defenses.

And it wouldn't be so hard dealing with a single shooter like the one battling Hiruko. Instead of disappearing from Hiruko's line of sight yet again, then reappearing moments later in a different foxhole thirty yards distant, maybe he'd stay in one place long enough for Hiruko to blow him to smithereens.

Frustrated that the same shooter kept evading him and continuing to pump out rounds, Hiruko decided to follow the Daimyō's example. Taking a deep breath, he tightened his grip on his rifle and ran forward, planning to get close enough to nail the shooter before he could duck.

He swung up the barrel of his gun, ready to fire on the run. The shooter was in his sights.

Hiruko's finger touched the trigger.

But before he could squeeze it, the ground caved in under him. Bullets streaked past as he dropped; they would have punched right into his chest if he hadn't fallen out of the way when he did.

* * *

MacNeal knew he'd been lucky. He could hear the echoes of a distant clash from the direction of the Shōgunate's route, and he realized his unit had been getting off easy.

From the sounds of it, there was a lot of action going on out there—a sustained battle with a hell of a lot of rounds expended. By comparison, the Valley of Geysers had stayed relatively calm. While following Tatiana's shortcut to *Kronotskaya Sopka*, the 42nd and its allies had run across five small teams of Koryaks. The first team, using a cluster of geysers for cover, had been the biggest challenge; none of the others had presented more than a minor delay. The 42nd, New Guard, and Bogatyrs possessed superior numbers and firepower. They also had Irina, who sang Liturgies that inspired her men and confused the enemy, making them easy targets.

Apparently, the bulk of the Koryak forces was concentrated on the main approach to the volcano, the one the Shōgunate had followed, while only scattered ancillary squads spilled over into the secondary approach; the Koryaks must have expected all the factions to follow the main route instead.

As a result of the light opposition, the allied unit had been making great time. They were nearly at the end of the valley, about to cross the border of the grey plain around the volcano. A few last pieces of Tala's gear were scattered on the ground ahead, pointing like an arrow at *Kronotskaya Sopka*.

That was when MacNeal's luck turned sketchy. Sudden gunfire erupted along both flanks, drawing the unit's attention. The 42nd and New Guard opened fire on the left, while the Bogatyrs focused on the right. Irina joined her men on the right, singing what she said was a Liturgy of Fortitude while cranking off shots with her double-barreled Nagant revolver.

MacNeal was firing left with his men when someone suddenly leaped down from a tree and slammed him to the ground.

MacNeal was pinned face down with his gun under him. He strained to boost himself up and throw off his attacker, but he couldn't do it. Whoever was up there knew how to keep him down, not to mention what came next.

As MacNeal struggled to free himself, the attacker's hands swung down and wrapped a wire around his neck. Instantly, the wire tightened and pulled tighter still, digging into his windpipe with crushing force.

* * *

As Taki raced toward the base of the volcano, two men scrambled out of a hole in the ground thirty feet away and charged toward him. It was the ambush he'd been hoping to avoid; it seemed the approach he'd taken wasn't completely undefended after all.

But wanting to *avoid* a fight didn't mean he wasn't *ready* for it.

His eyes flew over the enemy, assessing the threat they represented. One man had an old revolver; the other carried a bamboo staff.

First things first. Ducking down, Taki snapped up a rock the size of a grapefruit, then wound it back and whipped it in one smooth motion. The rock hurtled straight for the man with the gun and crashed into his skull just above his left temple.

The gunman stumbled and fell, but the other attacker kept coming. He gripped the staff with both hands, spinning it clockwise, then counter-clockwise, as he ran.

Taki smiled grimly and reached for his tonfa clubs. His flash-gun stayed slung at his back, unneeded. A kobudō master like him knew a little light exercise when he saw it.

Not that the Koryak fighter wasn't giving it his best effort. He charged in with staff spinning, shearing through the air toward Taki's head.

Taki bounced back, bobbing out of the path of the twirling staff, then lashed up a tonfa to block it on the return stroke. He held it there, resisting the attacker's attempts to force it free, and used the other tonfa to clip the side of his head.

Howling with rage, the Koryak hauled the staff back and swung it around at Taki's lower body—but again, a tonfa shot into place to block it. The other tonfa landed hard on the Koryak's forearm, making his grip spring open and drop the staff.

Whirling, Taki planted a kick square in the man's belly, bringing him down. But before he could follow up with a final strike, he glimpsed movement out of the corner of his eye.

As he flung himself around, he saw the gunman had regained his feet and was pointing the revolver at him. He saw the man's hand squeeze the trigger and heard the thundering crack of the shot exploding from the muzzle in his direction.

* * *

When Hiruko looked up from the trench into which he'd fallen, the first thing he saw was blue sky. *Bright* blue sky, actually, so crisp and clear and sharp it almost hurt his eyes. At that moment, a burst of poetry rose, unbidden, to his mind:

> *Blue light stretches over the horizon*
> *Like canvas on a frame, still and steely blue,*
> *Thinnest curtain concealing black glorious*
> *Madness, stars reeling in eternal lovers' dances*
> *Astir as by the ladle of the night, the brush of*
> *Push and pull and spinning always never and*
> *If, in an eye of bear or man, one teaspoon of that*
> *Limpid firmament swirls, all things become as crystal,*
> *Far-flung, faceted, prismatic, consecrated*
> *And shattering.*

As the last words flowed through him, Hiruko sat up, shaking his head at the strangeness of the lines. Why did they come to him at moments like this, when his life seemed to be nearest the end?

Just as he sat up, he heard footsteps on the packed ash of the trench behind him…then the unmistakable *clack* of a gun being cocked.

Looking back over his shoulder, he found himself facing the barrel of a rifle held by the native man he'd been trading fire with before the fall. A second man stood behind him, also armed with a rifle, looking on with cold intensity.

Now that he was close, Hiruko could see that the man he'd been fighting was younger than he'd thought—barely out of his teens, unless he looked young for his age. He was just a kid, it turned out, probably no older than Hiruko's own nephew back home.

Even with the gun pointed at him at point-blank range, Hiruko still found himself feeling grateful he hadn't killed the kid.

Taking a deep breath, he turned away from the gun and closed his eyes, preparing for the end. There was no way he could fight it; the kid had him in his sights. It would be better to face his fate with dignity and honor.

Then, suddenly, he heard a sound like an animal running toward him at a high rate of speed. His eyes shot open, and he realized he hadn't been far wrong.

Von Heïzinger's feral Stosstruppen was racing toward him on all fours. Hiruko ducked as the creature launched himself off the ground in front of him, leaping over his head at the gunmen.

After that, the air filled with the Stosstruppen's snarls and the screams of the local fighters as he tore into them.

Hiruko wished he could block out the screams, but at least they didn't last. Within seconds, both gunmen fell silent; only the snuffling and growling of the Stosstruppen remained.

As Hiruko braced himself against the wall and got to his feet, more company came charging down the trench. The two Schocktruppen ran mechanically toward him, followed by Zermann. So now Hiruko knew where Von Heïzinger had sent his squad of monsters after the first attack by one of the locals. It turned out there *was* a countermeasure against the enemy's trenches and tunnels after all.

Hiruko flattened himself against the trench wall as the Schocktruppen barreled past without a word or a glance. Zermann, at least, flashed him a brief glare on the way past, as if Hiruko was only worthy of contempt.

Von Heïzinger's monsters stormed through the remains of the two gunmen and continued on down the trench. Soon, it was like they'd never been there at all…except for the dead gunmen.

And the living Hiruko.

* * *

The wire pulled tighter, ever tighter, around MacNeal's neck. He started to see stars as his oxygen supply was restricted by the pressure on his windpipe. Soon, all he would see would be the pitch blackness of death.

Gathering his will and strength for one last push, he pictured himself rolling hard off his belly and pitching the attacker off his back. He had to act fast, or it would be too late; he counted down from five…

But before he got to three, he heard a woman's voice shouting, "Hold your fire!" Then: "Gol! *Poluchit' ot nego!*"

Instantly, the pressure on MacNeal's throat let up. The next voice he heard was that of the man on his back. "*Tatiana*?" He spoke a few more words in Russian, which MacNeal couldn't follow.

Then MacNeal heard Tatiana's footsteps whisking toward him. "I *said* get *off* him! *Poluchit' ot nego!*" There was the sound of a blow being struck. "*Syeïchas!*"

Finally, the wire moved away from his neck. The weight on his back shifted to one side, then went away.

Before something else could knock him down, he scrambled to his feet. The whole time, he never took his eyes off the skinny young man with the blond hair and loop of wire around his fists.

Once MacNeal was back up, he lunged at Gol and snatched the wire away from him. Gol glared but gave up the weapon without a fight.

Now that MacNeal was on his feet, he could see that Brown was front and center, training his flash machine gun at the blond Koryak. He must have been the one Tatiana had told to hold fire. Oksana, Irina, and Ivan were gathered alongside him, watching with interest.

Tatiana spoke to the Koryak in Russian. Her voice was sharp, as if she were reprimanding him.

Gol scowled at her. His answer was in rapid-fire Russian, too fast for MacNeal to follow.

Tatiana translated Gol's words into English. "He wants to know why *I* am working with *you*." She gestured at MacNeal, then Brown, then Irina. After another exchange with Gol, she translated once more. "I told him you are my friends, as I thought he and I once were. Gol says we are still friends, but he has his own mission to complete."

"What mission is that?" asked MacNeal.

Tatiana and Gol chattered through another exchange, which Tatiana then translated. "Gol says his people must stop the invaders from taking away their god, Kutkha. I told him that is our mission, too, and we are on the same side. I told him that is why we are heading for *Kronotskaya Sopka*…to keep great power from falling into the hands of the invaders."

In spite of the assurances of a shared mission, MacNeal thought Gol still looked suspicious. "Tell him our current priority is rescuing our people. Kutkha carried one off to a cave in the mountain."

Tatiana and Gol went back and forth several times before she translated again. "Gol says there is no need for a rescue. Kutkha is a benevolent god. He would never hurt a friendly visitor."

"Then it's more important than ever that we get to her fast," said MacNeal. "Her teammate has gone after her, and he thinks Kutkha wants to harm her."

After the next exchange with Tatiana, Gol's eyes flew wide open. "Then we need to stop him," translated Tatiana. "He cannot be permitted to attack Kutkha."

"Why?" asked Brown. "Because he might hurt Kutkha?"

Tatiana shook her head emphatically. "Because Kutkha might hurt *him*. Benevolent he may be, but he is also quick to wrath. And that wrath is *terrible* to behold."

* * *

Kutkha glared when Tala didn't take the hand he'd offered. He pushed it toward her again, looking deeply offended.

Still, Tala didn't reach for him, though she knew it would have been smarter to play along with the god's every move. "Hold on now," she said, which only made his glare deepen. Seeing the angry glint in his eye, she tensed but tried not to show her fear. "What exactly is this goal you want me to help you accomplish?"

Kutkha's voice was stern. "You are one of my people. All you need to know is that it will please me."

Tala cleared her throat. "The more I know, the better I can please you." She met his gaze, trying not to think about the fact that she was dealing with a powerful shapeshifter who could toss her from the ledge in a heartbeat...or do much, much worse, for that matter. "What is your goal? What does it have to do with ending your loneliness?"

Kutkha cocked his head. The movement looked bird-like, though he was still in human form. "When Raven answered the prayers of your people, did he interrogate them like this?"

Tala sighed. "All right." She reached out and took his hand. "At least tell me what you want me to do. Give me something to work with here."

Kutkha folded his hand around hers in a grip that was almost too tight. His glare seemed to harden, and Tala worried that he was about to do something to hurt her.

Then, suddenly, a grin spread over his face. "You *are* a born warrior, aren't you?" He chuckled and raised her hand to give it a light kiss. "I truly made a marvelous choice when I picked you, didn't I?" He kissed her hand again.

Tala managed a little smile of her own, but it was forced. The battle sounds from the volcanic plain below kept drawing her attention. She found herself wondering if Taki was in the midst of that action, and if he was, if he could prevail without her.

"Fine." Kutkha shrugged. "I will tell you this much: I need you to stay by my side, to draw your comrades closer." He gave her hand a squeeze. "And when the time comes, I will need you to pray and perform rituals as a shaman to help me break into Heaven."

* * *

When the round exploded from the muzzle of the Koryak's revolver, Taki couldn't move fast enough to escape it.

The bullet was streaking toward his chest before he even thought about dodging it. By the time his muscles tensed, preparing to propel him out of the way, it was too late. The projectile had already made contact in the vicinity of his heart.

If not for the Ilirium vest he was wearing, he would have been dead. As it was, the miraculous Ilirium plates inside the vest enabled it to generate a counter-flux field. The field turned the bullet's own kinetic energy against it, stopping it before it could penetrate Taki's body.

Instead of piercing his heart, the bullet simply fell away, spinning down to hit the ground at his feet. Then, before the gunman could recover from his shock at seeing the shot fail, Taki leaped into action.

Charging the gunman, he smacked the revolver from his grasp with a blow from a tonfa. He used the other tonfa to whack the side of the man's head, sending him reeling to the ground.

When the gunman lay motionless beside his unconscious comrade, Taki dared to stop moving. He stood for a moment, catching his breath after the close call. Staring into space, he touched the spot on his vest where the bullet had hit.

He knew he'd made a mistake. He'd underestimated the Koryaks and waded in to let off some steam…but the "light exercise" had almost gotten him killed.

He should have known better. He was in a combat zone, and his teammate's life was at stake. He should have stuck with traditional firearms instead of showing off his kobudō.

There was a time and place for martial arts, and his latest fight had been neither. He wouldn't make the same mistake again.

Slipping the tonfa clubs back under the straps on his thighs, he scooped up the Koryak's revolver and set off running again. He ran harder than ever, closing the gap to the base of the volcano where Tala had been taken.

CHAPTER 26

Kamchatka
19 April 1952
1743 Hours

When Hiruko climbed up out of the trench, he saw that the tide of battle had changed. The convoy had moved about fifty yards past his position and was rolling along slowly but steadily. Koryaks were still shooting from foxholes and trenches dug into the volcanic plain, but there weren't nearly as many as before. Von Heïzinger's monsters had apparently done a thorough job of clearing the enemy from their hiding places. Now it seemed there weren't as many obstacles between the convoy and the volcano.

Hiruko adjusted the pack on his back and ran to catch up. He wanted to rejoin the action and continue to do his part; he also wanted to stay close to Nadia.

Gripping his rifle tightly, he leaped across a trench. He ran twenty yards farther and jumped another one, clearing it fine. He was just about to leap a third when a Koryak popped out of it, looking the other way, and took aim with a pistol at the convoy.

Hiruko stopped a few feet away and swung up his rifle. Without thinking, he fixed the crosshairs on the Koryak and cut loose three rounds. One of them pierced the back of the Koryak's skull and punched out his right eye, sending up a blossom of blood. Instantly, he let go of the revolver and dropped back into the trench, a load of dead weight.

Hiruko stood there a second as his shaking hands calmed and the significance of what had happened sank in. He'd done a lot of shooting that day, but this was his first kill.

His first kill *ever*. He had never before taken another man's life.

Taking a deep breath, he stopped thinking about it as much as he could and pulled himself together. He backed up a few steps, then took a running leap over the trench...all without looking down at the body inside.

His feet touched down on the opposite edge. He clenched his teeth and locked his gaze on the convoy, getting ready to start forward again.

It was then that one of the amphibious vehicles exploded in a blazing fireball, casting shrapnel in all directions.

* * *

Now that he wasn't trying to strangle MacNeal with a garrote, Gol was turning out to be a major asset to the 42nd and its allies. Tatiana had convinced him to help the unit get to Kutkha faster, and he was really coming through.

From the Valley of Geysers, Gol led them on a special route across the volcanic plain, one that took them through a network of trenches and tunnels. It had taken a little work hauling the voïvodes down with them, but it had been worth it to stay out of the line of fire on the surface.

Gol also helped them get past Koryak checkpoints, either by following alternate routes or talking his way through them.

Since Gol only spoke the Koryak language to the Koryaks, MacNeal couldn't understand the conversations...but Tatiana listened and translated. Once, Gol referred to the Union, New Guard, and Bogatyr unit as his captives. Another time, he said they were Koryaks in disguise, just back from infiltrating the invaders. The next time, he tried the truth, that they were allies on the way to Kutkha's aerie, but really they meant him no harm; that was the one time they ended up having to fight their way through.

There were two guards at that particular checkpoint, one armed with a pistol, the other a spear. As the conversation grew more heated, MacNeal saw them both move to raise their weapons, and he signaled Brown. Before the spear could be thrown or any shots could be fired, MacNeal and Brown rushed the guards and disarmed them with fierce efficiency. Then they subdued them with matching sleeper holds and gently laid them along the side of the trench. If MacNeal planned to keep Gol cooperative, he knew he had to do as little damage as possible to any Koryaks along the way.

Gol stared at the unconscious men and sighed. He said something in Russian, which Tatiana translated into English. "Gol says we have to move faster now. When the others find these two, they'll raise the alarm and close down this quadrant."

So the unit picked up its pace as he guided them onward through the maze. MacNeal thought they couldn't be far from the base of the volcano now, but it was hard to tell. Looking up from below ground level through the periodic holes and trenches, he saw nothing but blue sky and an occasional tree overhead.

But if the rumbling was any indication, they were closing in. It kept getting stronger and louder as they went, shaking down dirt from the trench walls and tunnel ceilings. If it got much worse, MacNeal thought the walls and ceilings might just collapse and bury them all alive.

The rumbling faded from time to time, allowing MacNeal to hear the distant crackling of battle noise leaking in from the wide open expanse of the volcanic plain. The exchanges of gunfire sounded closer than before, but more sporadic and one-sided.

Then, suddenly, there was a huge explosion, one that sent a tremor through the trenches and shook down more dirt. MacNeal braced himself against the walls, wondering what the hell had just blown up...praying it wasn't a blast from the volcano.

Because once the lava started flowing, those trenches and tunnels would make the perfect riverbeds for thousands of tons of molten rock.

* * *

Taki didn't look back or slow down when the explosion hit. He was too busy scrambling up the side of *Kronotskaya Sopka*, aiming for the ledge where Kutkha had taken Tala.

He'd only gone a little ways up by that point—about fifty feet from the base. He still had a long way to go, and couldn't afford a delay or distraction.

Not paying attention could cost him his life. The volcano wasn't steep that far down, so the climb wasn't bad; most of the time, he could run leaning forward. But the shallow slope was scattered with loose scree. One slip, and he could end up sliding back down the mountain, out of control, and cracking his skull open on a rock.

So he couldn't worry about the blast down below, whatever had caused it. He had to stay focused and watch his step, driving harder than ever to save the woman held captive above. The woman who'd been taken away from him just as he was getting to know her.

The woman he now realized he cared for deeply and would fight with all his strength to protect.

* * *

When the vehicle exploded, Hiruko panicked. He'd come to care about Nadia; the thought of her being blown up was like a hot needle piercing his heart.

He started running toward the flaming husk of the amphibious vehicle…and then his initial panic fled. The decimated vehicle was on the right flank of the convoy's wedge formation. The one carrying Nadia was at the point, and intact. She was still alive.

If anyone in the exploded vehicle was as lucky, they needed immediate help. So Hiruko kept running, thinking he could help pull men from the wreckage…but the closer he got, the hotter the fire became.

Squinting into the flames, he quickly realized there was no one left alive in there; the gunner and driver had most certainly died on impact. The vehicle had been blown to smithereens by whatever explosive device had gone off in its path.

The question now was, could another device already be waiting along the convoy's route, perhaps set to destroy Nadia's vehicle this time? Were the locals working to plant and activate more such booby traps?

Keeping his rifle at the ready, Hiruko looked toward the nearest trench, wondering if he might glimpse one of the fighters setting the traps…and maybe he did, because the ragged, bloody body of a local flew out at that instant.

Another fighter tried to scramble out on his own, and he nearly made it—but just as he started crawling away, the bestial Stosstruppen lunged up and grabbed him with his clawed hands. The Stosstruppen dragged the screaming fighter back down over the edge. Seconds later, the fighter's shredded corpse came hurtling out and landed on the grey, sun-baked plain beside the corpse of the first local.

Von Heïzinger's monster squad was cleaning up the attackers from below; Zermann, the Stosstruppen, and the Schocktruppen were making the rounds.

Determined to rejoin the lead vehicle, Hiruko skirted the explosion site and headed forward. He kept his rifle at the ready and moved cautiously, checking each trench and foxhole for signs of the enemy. He found local fighters in the third trench and opened fire as they ran, pushing them to run faster, but not hitting any of them. In the next trench, he found a pile of bodies, all locals, all torn or blown apart.

"Jōtōhei Orochi!" The Daimyō was calling him from the distance, from the point of the formation. Hiruko saw him waving for him to join him.

Hiruko picked up his pace as much as he could without getting careless. He kept his rifle pointed downward and continued checking trenches as he came upon them, but only saw more corpses, no sign of trouble. The convoy must have cleared out a lot of locals on its advance to the volcano.

When Hiruko reached the point and saluted, the Daimyō gestured behind him with *Dyuaru-Kontan*. "We must change formation from a wedge to a single column." He waved the sword in the direction of the left flank. "Bring all elements together in a single file."

Hiruko nodded. "Because of the booby trap, sir?"

"Because of *that*." The Daimyō swept *Dyuaru-Kontan* around to point at the base of *Kronotskaya Sopka*. It was less than a half-mile away now. "A wedge cannot fit through that *door*."

Peering at the volcano, Hiruko saw a rectangular sliver of blackness carved from the base directly ahead. He hadn't noticed it before, perhaps because it was seated between two curved outcroppings that obscured the view from either side.

Hiruko's brows lifted. "This is it, sir? The way in?"

"You tell me." The sudden interruption of Von Heïzinger's raspy croak made Hiruko jump. "Does it *look* like we're heading the right way?" Von Heïzinger thrust the *Orbis Christus* ring in Hiruko's face. The crimson gemstone was glowing brighter than ever, so bright it made Hiruko shut his eyes against the blinding glare.

"Yes, sir!" said Hiruko. The glare was so strong, it blazed red through his closed eyelids. He felt the warmth of the ring, too, pulsating against his face. Only when both faded did he dare open his eyes again.

When he did, he saw Von Heïzinger shaking the *Orbis Christus* at the Daimyō. "Why are we *waiting*? Have you lost your stomach for *victory*, Minamoto?"

In a sudden swirl of motion, the Daimyō swung around *Dyuaru-Kontan* and stopped it against the side of Von Heïzinger's throat. He held it there, staring coldly into the Reich officer's eyes. "The only thing I have lost my stomach for is *you*."

"Weakling." Von Heïzinger sneered at him. "You think you are up to the task?"

"I have been up to it since I first met you." The Daimyō pressed the blade more tightly against Von Heïzinger's throat. "Now is as good a time as any."

Hiruko watched as Von Heïzinger slowly reached up and touched the Patmos Amulet on its chain around his neck. He had used it to stop Nadia from escaping; how could the Daimyō resist its power?

"Use it on yourself," said Von Heïzinger. "Cut your own throat and get out of my way."

The Daimyō stood his ground at first, keeping his gaze locked with Von Heïzinger's. But then his sword began to quiver. He shook his head hard, as if to clear it.

"I order you to die," said Von Heïzinger. "Make way for the true order of the future."

"*Never*." Even as the Daimyō snapped out the word, his blade quivered harder. Slowly, it moved away from Von Heïzinger's throat.

Hiruko saw sweat rolling down the Daimyō's face as he struggled against Von Heïzinger's mind control. Briefly, he forced the blade back toward Von Heïzinger's throat...but then it drifted toward the Daimyō's throat instead.

The ground rumbled. Someone screamed in the distance—another victim of the monster squad, perhaps? Still, the Daimyō's own blade floated closer to his throat. It was starting to look as if Von Heïzinger might actually force him to kill himself.

Hiruko was paralyzed, afraid to do anything lest Von Heïzinger turn on him next. But that was *the Daimyō* he was about to kill. He was Hiruko's commanding officer. How could Hiruko just stand by and watch him die?

He couldn't. But what could he do to intervene? Making threats wouldn't work. Taking action would be just as ineffective. So what *could* he do?

Make it look like an accident.

Hiruko fumbled with his rifle, swinging it around to hoist it over his shoulder. When the barrel was pointing straight up, he reached back as if to adjust it...and pulled the trigger instead.

A round discharged with a loud *crack* that left his ear ringing. It also broke the spell the Daimyō was under. With a grunt, he wrenched the katana away from his throat and shoved Von Heïzinger backward.

Breathing hard, the Daimyō glared at Von Heïzinger. "You...and your tricks. I'd like to see you...face me...without them."

Von Heïzinger's eyes glinted under the brim of his black cap. "Waste of time." He snorted and shook his head. "Pathetic." Then he turned and marched away from the Daimyō.

On his way past Hiruko, Von Heïzinger muttered softly, "Misfires can be *fatal*, Orochi."

Hiruko's blood chilled.

* * *

Meanwhile, on the ledge two hundred feet above, another battle of wills continued. As Wolf looked on, Tala kept trying to get information out of Kutkha, and Kutkha just wasn't giving it.

"I don't understand," said Tala. "If you're a *god*, why do you need to break into *Heaven*?"

Kutkha sighed. "It's a long story." Just then, Wolf walked over and whispered something in his ear. As Wolf stepped away, Kutkha shrugged. "Unfortunately, I don't have the time to tell it right now."

Tala was beyond frustrated. She could feel her temper fraying, and she had to work doubly hard to keep from exploding. "All right." She took a deep breath and let it out slowly. "Why don't you have time right now?"

"So *inquisitive.*" Kutkha grinned, then walked past her toward the cave. "Come with me, Shaman Tala."

Tala watched and waited as he entered the cave. Wolf, meanwhile, walked to the edge of the ledge and leaned out to look down. "What about you?" she asked him.

Wolf spared her the briefest glance over his shoulder. "You two go ahead. I'll catch up."

CHAPTER 27

**Kamchatka
19 April 1952
1810 Hours**

Taki paused on the slope of *Kronotskaya Sopka* and wiped the sweat from his brow with the sleeve of his uniform. He took care to lean forward, balancing on his knee as he reached for the canteen hanging from his belt. He was over two-thirds of the way up now, and the mountain was steeper. It wouldn't take much to slip and backslide all the way to the bottom.

So much for running up the slope; he'd been reduced to working his way up on all fours, crawling through the scree from handhold to foothold. Looking up as he drank from the canteen, he wished he'd brought mountaineering equipment after all. The volcano wasn't going to get any less steep as it rose toward the ledge.

Not that Taki would let the steepness or anything else stop him. He'd come so far already; he had no intention of getting so close to Tala, and then failing to save her.

As he screwed the cap on his canteen and hooked it back on his belt, he thought of her face and voice. Would he fight a god to get her back? Hell, yes. He thought he was ready to fight just about anyone.

But what he wasn't ready for were the bullets that whizzed down from above.

* * *

Wolf watched Taki through his rifle sight and squeezed the trigger again. The shot jumped wide to the left, missing his target by several inches...on purpose.

The whole idea was to make Taki work harder on the way up, not take a bullet. Why kill the new meat from the 42nd without playing with him a little first?

Would he be a challenge in hand-to-hand combat? The 42nd had a tradition of turning out excellent opponents—or allies, depending on the mission—not that he'd ever tell MacNeal that.

Wolf would find out soon enough how much of a challenge Taki would be. While Kutkha took Tala inside and set the plan in motion there, Wolf would put Taki through his paces on the ledge and see if he measured up. By then, the other players would reach their new positions on the board, setting the stage for the next phase of the game...a game that Wolf controlled at all levels, as always.

Smiling, he lined up his rifle sight again and pulled the trigger. He laughed as Taki ducked and scurried aside, never realizing his life was not in danger.

Yet.

* * *

Tala followed Kutkha into the cave, then stopped when she heard the gunshot out on the ledge. She turned toward the entrance, intending to run outside...but she wasn't going anywhere. Right before her eyes, a wall of rock slammed down from above, blocking the opening.

"Hey!" She whirled to face Kutkha. "What's the big idea?"

He just stood there and stared at her, his face lit by the torch he carried. "You're about to find out, Shaman." Then he turned away.

Tala darted over and grabbed his arm. "Wait a minute! What about these men?"

Kutkha looked around at the eight bodies hanging from the ceiling and shrugged. "What about them?"

"Aren't you going to free them?" asked Tala. "You didn't kill them, so you must not mean them any harm."

"They'll be fine. They have a role to play." He shook free of her grip and moved toward the rear of the cave. "Just as you do." Without looking back, he entered a tunnel and kept walking.

Tala stayed behind and spun in a frustrated circle. She looked at the men, then the rock wall over the entrance, then the men again…then Kutkha's retreating form. She considered using one of her bombs to crack a hole in that wall, then realized the blowback could be fatal to everyone in the cave. What if she freed the men and teamed up with them against Kutkha? It might work…if they weren't unconscious.

That left her with two options: stay in the cave in the darkness, or go with Kutkha. Either option was lousy.

"Are you coming?" Kutkha's voice was getting farther away. The flickering light from his torch was fading from the cave.

Tala stomped her foot and went after him. She wouldn't accomplish anything standing around in a dark cave. But maybe, wherever he was taking her, she could do some good.

Just not the way Kutkha expected.

* * *

When the 42nd and its allies reached the base of *Kronotskaya Sopka*, Gol was the first one out of the trench. He waved for the rest to follow, and reached down to give Oksana a hand.

"*Spaceba*, Gol." Oksana pulled herself up without his help.

Irina, however, grabbed the helping hand without being offered it. Gol gaped at her, looking shocked…but his expression changed when she sang a lilting little melody in her mesmerizing style. As she cooed the chiming notes especially for him, his face shifted from a look of shock to one of pure adoration. He beamed at her as if she were the long-lost love of his life. Instead of just helping her up with one hand, he used both, hauling her up with great enthusiasm so she didn't have to exert even the slightest effort.

The rest of the unit scrambled out around her. MacNeal was one of the first up, and he helped drag out the two voïvodes alongside men from the 42nd, New Guard, and Bogatyr groups. Oksana did the same, while Irina dusted herself off and strolled around.

"John?" she said after a while. "The man we're looking for? You said he's Japanese, didn't you?"

"Japanese-American," said MacNeal.

"That's what I thought." She paused. "Is that him up there?"

When MacNeal turned and looked where she was pointing, he saw Taki scaling the slope of the volcano, two hundred feet up. He was working his way toward the ledge where Kutkha's nest was located—his aerie. He couldn't have been more than twenty feet below it.

And he was under fire. Someone—MacNeal couldn't see who—was taking pot shots at Taki from the ledge…but the shooter's aim was off. The shots came close, but none of them hit the target. Either he was a hell of a poor shot, or he was trying to miss.

"Well?" Irina was by his side, leaning close. "Is that him?"

MacNeal nodded as he unsnapped a pouch on his belt and pulled out his binoculars. "Yep." He swung up the binoculars for a look at the shooter on the ledge. At first, the man's scope and gun obscured the details of his face; then, as Taki moved out of range under the ledge, he lowered the weapon, and his features came into view. "Son of a bitch." MacNeal knew him well…*too* well. He had a habit of turning up, sometimes as an ally, sometimes an enemy, always an irritant. "*Wolf.*"

"Really?" Of course Irina knew him. He'd betrayed her to MacNeal once in Istanbul…and done the reverse six months later in Canberra. Rumor had it, in spite of his shifting loyalties, that they'd been quite a hot item.

MacNeal continued to watch as Wolf pulled back from the edge and disappeared. Taki, meanwhile, was ascending the slope along the left side of the ledge with fewer than ten feet to go. He had his flash-gun in one hand, but if Wolf was waiting for him, he wouldn't have a chance. It was time to call in a sharpshooter. "Beaudreau!"

"Yes, sir!" Private Beaudreau ran up beside him. He must have anticipated MacNeal's request, because he already had his rifle off his shoulder, ready for action.

"Watch that corner of the ledge." MacNeal pointed at the side Taki was approaching. "If the shooter rears his ugly head, take him out."

"You mean you want to *wound* him, don't you, John?" asked Irina.

"I mean I want a *kill shot.*" MacNeal glared at her. "And don't you *ever* countermand one of my orders again."

Irina muttered something obscene in Russian and strutted away.

Beaudreau took up a position nearby, bracing his sniper rifle on a boulder. The guy had an eye like the farthest-seeing hawk of all time; even without Zermann's enchanted Luger, he never missed.

"Gol!" MacNeal needed to talk to the Koryak, but couldn't look away from the scene unfolding above. Taki was fewer than four feet away from the ledge now.

Within seconds, Gol and Tatiana arrived at MacNeal's side. As usual, Tatiana was doing the talking. "Yes?"

MacNeal kept watching through the binoculars. "How fast can we get up there?"

Tatiana repeated the question in Russian, then translated Gol's answer. "Not so fast if we stay outside. But *inside* is a different story."

MacNeal kept watching. "Inside the volcano?" Taki was three feet from the ledge. Then two feet.

Again, Tatiana spoke to Gol in Russian and translated his answer. "There are secret ways to ascend. It is the Temple of Kutkha."

Just as he said it, *Kronotskaya Sopka* rumbled ominously. Watching through the binoculars, MacNeal saw Taki lose his grip and start to slide on his belly. His gun strap broke under him, and his flashgun slid free, spinning down the slope out of reach.

As Taki fell, MacNeal involuntarily held his breath, wishing he were there to pull him to safety. Before Taki had gone more than a few feet, though, he caught an outcropping and stopped his fall. Slowly, he climbed his way back up to where he'd been before.

Reaching up, Taki latched on to the lip of the ledge. Gripping the rock with both hands, he smoothly swung himself to one side, then threw his legs up over the lip of the edge. Not once did MacNeal see Wolf look down from above.

Which didn't mean he wasn't waiting for Taki, of course. MacNeal would have bet good money he *was* there the second Taki arrived, ready to pounce in typical Wolf fashion.

* * *

Hiruko was worried. Ever since his misfired weapon had stopped

Von Heïzinger from killing the Daimyō, he'd been looking over his shoulder. He kept expecting to see Von Heïzinger there, waiting to murder him for daring to interfere.

But other concerns distracted him as the Shōgunate convoy drew up to the rectangular doorway in the base of *Kronotskaya Sopka*. According to the Bering Map, the heavenly treasure awaited within. The goal of the entire expedition was finally within reach.

Not that anyone other than Von Heïzinger seemed to care much. The conflict between Von Heïzinger and the Daimyō had cast a pall over the unit; the group's earlier enthusiasm was gone. None of the Shōgunate soldiers were eager to serve Von Heïzinger after the way he'd treated their commanding Daimyō. But they still followed the Daimyō's orders, even if those orders meant doing what Von Heïzinger wanted. If that meant marching into the unknown inside a rumbling volcano, all of them would do it.

Almost all of them, that is. As the convoy hovered at the threshold, about to roll forward, Itami sat on the ground and rocked, groaning and clenching his teeth. Occasionally, he thrashed his head and roared like a bull in a state of agony.

The Shōgunate's powerhouse wasn't alone. Zermann paced in circles, clutching his skull. The Stosstruppen howled and clawed at the volcano's rock wall until his claws were bloody.

The Daimyō tried to order them to enter first and clear away any resistance.

"Itami!" The Daimyō drew *Dyuaru-Kontan* from its scabbard and stabbed its point at the doorway. "You must complete the mission! It is your *duty*!"

Itami dragged himself to his feet and stood there, heaving. "There is so much *pain*, Daimyō. Like ten thousand red-hot *spikes* driven into my body."

"Honor demands you overcome it!" The Daimyō swept *Dyuaru-Kontan* through the air. "The Shōgun and the Emperor expect no less of you!"

"I am trying." Itami shook his head hard and pounded his club on the ground. "But it hurts so much, I cannot even *see* straight! I keep bumping into things!"

"Then I know what you need." The Daimyō spun, and his eyes sought out Hiruko. "You! Orochi! Get over here."

Hiruko hesitated, dreading whatever duty the Daimyō had in mind. If it involved Itami, he wanted nothing to do with it. But then the Daimyō called his name again, and he had no choice but to march over and receive his orders.

"Guide him," snapped the Daimyō. "Help him find the targets he must eliminate to guarantee our safe passage."

"*Hai*." Hiruko wanted to turn around and walk away. Being anywhere *near* Itami was enough to fill him with fear…and hatred, too, after the way he'd killed the bear. But instead of leaving, he saluted, bowed his head slightly to the Daimyō, then turned and approached Itami, resigned to the task.

This time, however, the terror didn't rise up in him when he got close. Perhaps the same phenomenon that was causing Itami's pain was also dampening the fear he always seemed to exude.

"Follow him, Itami." The Daimyō barked the words, then whirled on the Reich's own other-worldly beings. "And the rest of you do the same! Now move! Do you *want* the Union and Matriarchy to seize the objective *first*?"

Hiruko took a deep breath and bowed to Itami. "Come with me, sir." Then he turned to face the doorway. He saw Itami's shadow rise over him; then he felt Itami's hand clamp down on his shoulder. "Here we go."

With that, he took his first step over the threshold into the darkness beyond.

CHAPTER 28

Kamchatka
19 April 1952
1844 Hours

As soon as Taki set foot on the ledge, he leaped into a fighting stance and armed himself with his tonfa clubs. He fully expected an attack from the man who'd been shooting at him on his way up.

But at first, he saw no one around. The shooter wasn't visible, and neither was Tala or Kutkha. Taki seemed to be alone.

Giving each tonfa a spin by the handle, he wandered the ledge, looking for signs of life. Was the shooter behind the pile of bones? The pile of skins and entrails? Only one thing was certain: he wasn't in the cave, because the cave entrance was gone. As far as Taki could see, the mountainside was solid rock where the opening had once been.

He continued to explore. Frowning, holding on tight to the tonfa, he eased across the ledge. There were piles of brush along the edge, like the rim of a nest; maybe someone was hiding in among them.

Taki's heart pounded as he worked his way to the middle, waiting for something to happen. Why wasn't the man shooting at him already? Why hadn't Kutkha swooped down and scooped him up in his giant talons?

Kronotskaya Sopka rumbled violently, and Taki staggered. Just as he recovered his balance, he heard a sudden clattering sound from somewhere nearby. He whirled around in time to see a tumble of bones roll down from the pile. Taki watched for a heartbeat, expecting someone to burst out of the pile...but no one did.

Suddenly, it occurred to him that the pile of bones had been a distraction. He whipped back around just as the shooter dropped from a crack in the rock wall above the former mouth of the cave and tackled him down to the surface of the ledge.

* * *

"Right this way, Shaman." Kutkha turned left down another dark corridor, lit only by the torch he carried. "We're getting closer."

Tala was lost. She was a decent enough tracker, but Kutkha had taken so many turns, she'd given up trying to memorize the route. Wherever he was taking her, she was at his mercy as far as finding her way back out again.

"Where did you say we're going again?" she asked, hoping he'd let his guard down enough to finally give her a straight answer.

"Don't worry." Kutkha smiled over his shoulder at her. "I know the way."

Tala rolled her eyes. For what seemed like the thousandth time since they'd left the cave and set out through the tunnels, she thought about blowing her payload. The dynamite bombs in her pockets were sure to wipe the smile off Kutkha's face. Maybe they would even break him into Heaven, just not in the way he expected. As powerful as he seemed to be, the years of the Great War were long past the glory days when so-called pagan gods were large and in charge...and invincible.

But no, she couldn't take the chance. Maybe he was tougher than she imagined and would strike back with a vengeance. Or maybe he'd just leave her to rot in the maze of tunnels.

Not to mention, she had a mission to complete. The best way of doing that might just be to follow him right now and see what he meant about breaking into Heaven. After all, there was supposed to be a heavenly power source in the volcano, and the Shōgunate and

Reich were headed right for it.

She was better off staying the course, at least for now. Even if he kept being evasive about where he was taking her.

"All right, Shaman." He stopped at the end of the corridor; an iron door blocked the way, caked with rust. "Close your eyes."

Tala scowled. "Why?"

"It's a surprise." He raised his eyebrows. "Now trust me."

Tala's heart raced. What was he planning? "That's okay." She shrugged. "I don't think we need to do that."

His expression turned cold. His face seemed to ripple in the flickering torchlight...or was he on the verge of shapeshifting back to his deadly raven form? "Close your eyes." His tone was stern and insistent.

Tala realized she had no choice if she wanted to move forward. "All right already." Her flippant voice belied how nervous she felt. "Eyes closed. Got it." She took a deep breath and shut her eyes as he'd ordered.

"Don't open them until I say so," said Kutkha.

"Got it."

Seconds later, Tala heard the sound of metal creaking and groaning—it had to be the ancient iron door opening on its rusty hinges. A hot breeze surged up in her face, taking her breath away; the breeze smelled like sulfur and smoke, like asphalt baking in the hot sun on a summer's day. She got a vaguely metallic taste in her mouth, as if she'd licked a copper penny.

She had the sense of a great space opening up before her, so different from the cramped confines of the corridor. A bell chimed, sounding very far away, and gave birth to a rush of keening echoes.

What *was* that, out there in front of her? She wanted to look so badly, she could barely keep her eyes closed.

Kutkha took her by the elbow. "Come with me."

She let him guide her forward, even as her heart hammered for fear that he might heave her into the great space to die. She took two shuffling steps forward; on the third step, she felt herself emerging from the enclosed corridor. On the fourth step, the hot breeze engulfed her, swirling all around her body.

Then, they stopped. She stood there a moment, listening to the bells chime and Kutkha breathe deeply by her side.

Finally, he said it: "Open your eyes."

And she opened them.

And she gasped when she saw what lay before her.

* * *

Hiruko continued walking forward, leading Itami into the darkness. They were alone; the creatures of the Reich hadn't joined them as the Daimyō had ordered.

Hiruko squinted, straining to see what lay ahead, but couldn't make out a thing. Unclipping his flashlight from his belt, he thumbed the switch. A cone of yellow light streamed from the lens, and he aimed it into the darkness. All he saw was a grey dirt floor strewn with gravel, framed by rock walls on either side.

"What is it?" asked Itami. "What do you see?"

Hiruko jumped a little. Amazingly, even with Itami's hand on his shoulder, he'd briefly forgotten he was back there. It was hard to believe; Itami had always instilled such pure fear in him...but the fear was gone now. Was it because Itami was unwell? Or had Hiruko simply overcome the fear—worked through it on some deep level of which he hadn't been aware?

"I don't know, sir." Hiruko swept the light back and forth as he moved forward, exposing more of the same. "Nothing much."

"Tell me as soon as you see something." Itami's voice was still deep and powerful, but it sounded strained; obviously, he was in a lot of pain. "Especially something I need to kill."

"I will, sir." Hiruko continued forward—flashlight in one hand, rifle in the other. His heart was going crazy in his chest; his fear of Itami had faded, but he still worried about whatever unknown awaited them in the darkness.

Taking another step, he felt his foot hit something which he assumed was a lump of gravel. But then he heard a creaking sound from above, like a tree about to fall, and he stopped in his tracks. He swept the beam of the flashlight up in front of him and saw what looked like a giant wooden mace studded with spikes swinging toward him.

"Look out!" Even as he shouted the words, he flung himself to the ground. He felt a rush of air as the spiked mace swooped past behind him...and then he heard an explosive *crash*, followed by the clattering of wood and the clanging of metal falling to the ground.

Rolling over on his back, he fumbled with the flashlight, then finally shot out a beam to illuminate the scene. He saw Itami standing there, gripping his kenabō with both hands. Bits of wood and metal, the remnants of the falling mace, littered the ground around him.

"Thank you for the warning," said Itami. "That could have done some damage otherwise."

"You're welcome, sir." Hiruko got to his feet and trained the flashlight on the ground ahead. He resolved to be more careful from that point on…at least as careful as he could be in a dark tunnel with only the beam of a single flashlight by which to see.

Maybe it wasn't so bad having Itami around after all.

* * *

Gol pressed his hand against a stone plate on the rock wall, and the volcano opened before him. A triangular slab dropped away, sliding straight down to reveal a doorway into darkness.

He stepped through without hesitation, followed by Tatiana. MacNeal was right behind them. Speed was imperative if they were to reach the ledge by secret routes inside the volcano and save Taki from Wolf.

Irina came through next, staying close behind. "I have your back, John, do not worry."

MacNeal didn't answer. He just kept following Gol and Tatiana as the rest of the unit pushed in after them, forced by the close confines to march single file.

What a perfect place for a trap, MacNeal thought. If someone wanted to take down the entire unit, the close quarters of the tunnel would make it easy. All it would take were a few strategically arranged gun emplacements aiming down from the ceiling, or up from the floor.

Just as they got far enough in that the light from outside faded into shadow, Gol stopped and grabbed a torch from a sconce on the wall. He lit it with a beat-up silver cigarette lighter from his pants pocket, then continued onward.

MacNeal kept his hands on his flash-gun as he followed. "We need to get up to the ledge. Our friend needs help right away."

Tatiana translated into Russian for Gol, then translated his response back to MacNeal. "Where do you think I am taking you?"

"A sewer, maybe?" Irina whistled. "It sure stinks down here."

MacNeal wrinkled his nose; she was right. The tunnel was suffused with the strong smell of sulfur.

The mountain rumbled and MacNeal felt dust trickling down from above. As usual, he was heading into the heart of greatest danger—in this case, a volcano that sounded ready to blow.

At least they got out of the tunnel before long. Gol led them through a few twists and turns, squeezing through some tight spots along the way, then guided them into a cave.

The light from Gol's torch picked out the cave's low ceiling, then found the bottom of a swaying rope ladder. The ladder hung from a hole in the center of the ceiling, and Gol led Tatiana and MacNeal over to have a look. When Gol held his torch under it, the flame danced and flickered, and revealed that the hole was the base of a long shaft.

Irina joined them for a look; so did Oksana. When Oksana aimed her flashlight into the shaft, MacNeal could see it stretched up into distant heights.

Gol rattled off some words in Russian, which Tatiana translated into English. "This is it. This is the way up."

"All right then." MacNeal shouldered out of his pack and dropped it on the ground. He slung his flash-gun over his back and rubbed his hands together. "I'd better get climbing."

"I'm coming with you, Major." Brown stepped forward and lifted the strap of his flash machine gun over his head.

Just then, the volcano rumbled with the greatest ferocity yet, sending men and equipment tumbling. Brown staggered back, fighting to stay on his feet. Oksana and Irina were thrown together, then hastily pushed away from each other as soon as they realized they were touching.

MacNeal gripped the ladder with both hands, using it to keep his balance. Rocks and dust fell around him...and then the rumbling got worse. The cave floor suddenly bucked, slamming him hard to one side, nearly knocking him over.

And then he did lose his footing and went down, but not because he let go of the ladder. In fact, he never lost his grip on it.

But the ladder itself came loose. Wherever in the heights it was anchored, the shaking broke it free and sent it plummeting down the shaft. Seconds after MacNeal hit the floor, the ladder flopped down in a huge heap at the base of the shaft, piling up right in front of him.

So much for the fastest way of getting to the ledge. Taki was still on his own.

* * *

As soon as his attacker jumped him from above, Taki pushed up hard, but couldn't throw him. The man's weight pressed him down, keeping him pinned to the sun-baked rock.

But at least one of Taki's hands was free, and a tonfa was in his grip. In a twinkling, he pumped it up and back, whacking the attacker in the head.

The man's weight shifted slightly, just enough for Taki to get some traction. Gathering his strength, he let go of the tonfa and used the hand that had been holding it to heave himself to one side. The sudden move pitched the man off his back…but he grabbed Taki's collar and pulled him over with him.

The man used his momentum to roll the rest of the way over and swing Taki down hard on his side. Taki winced when he hit, but kept his head and scrambled to his knees. He scooped up a rock the size of a grapefruit and used it to block the man's incoming punch.

As the man yanked his fist back, Taki leaped to his feet. Instinctively, he reached for his jitte in its scabbard on the left side of his belt and pulled it free. The weapon had one long metal prong with a much shorter hook at the base, near the wooden handle. As a kobudō master, Taki was trained to wield it with deadly skill.

The second the jitte was in his hand, he swung it back to strike and charged his attacker. The weapon swept forward, its heavy shaft aimed at the man's throat.

But before it could hit its target, the man dove aside and came up with a knife in his hand. Taki swung the jitte back around, but the man slid under the arc of its flight and lunged the knife at Taki's belly.

The point of the knife jabbed into the bulletproof Ilirium vest just as Taki jumped back away from it. He jumped back again, then snapped out a kick that knocked the knife from the man's grip, sending it flashing through the air and off the ledge.

Before Taki could lash out another kick, the man drove a shoulder into his abdomen and plowed him backward, forcing him off his feet. He tackled Taki into the pile of rancid animal skins and leaped away just as Taki took another swing with the jitte.

Taki tried springing up fast from the pile, but the skins were slippery. He had to scramble his way off the putrid heap.

Just as he staggered to his feet, he saw his opponent unclip a grenade, pull the pin, and roll it in his direction.

CHAPTER 29

**Kamchatka
19 April 1952
1909 Hours**

As the live grenade rolled toward Taki, he drew back his jitte, instantaneously took aim, and let it fly. The two-pronged knife collided with the grenade, sending it rolling back the way it had come, straight toward the man who'd thrown it.

Before it could reach him, he bolted out of its path, heading for the rock wall that stood where the cave entrance had once been. He looked like he was going to slam into it at a dead run.

But instead of hitting solid rock, he went right through it. He passed through it as if he were running through thin air, and then he was gone.

Taki ran the other way, getting as far from the grenade as he could. When he ran out of ledge, he turned away from the expected explosion and ducked, shielding his head with his arms.

But the explosion never came.

After a long moment passed without any blast, Taki stopped ducking. After another moment went by, he scooped up his jitte and tonfa, then ran over to the rock wall where the man had disappeared, giving the grenade a wide berth in case it still blew.

When he reached out to touch the rock wall, his hand passed through like a knife through water. The wall was just an illusion, a perfect mirage covering the entrance to the cave.

Taking a deep breath, he plunged through it, determined to catch up to his attacker…and find Tala, wherever she was.

* * *

Tala's heart raced as she gazed at the structure inside the volcano. She had never seen anything like it.

Cubes and spheres in a multitude of sizes, sculpted from what looked like obsidian and diamond, filled the vast vault. They were stacked in a seemingly haphazard way around a great stone circle ringed with a moat of bubbling lava. Gleaming silver spires jutted up among the structures, supported by intricate webworks of glittering silver cords wired to the inner walls of the mountain.

Lush, green vegetation crawled everywhere, twining around the structures and bursting from open park-like squares. Birds flew in all directions, flocks of brightly colored songbirds swooping on hot breezes like schools of airborne tropical fish.

All of it was awash in the rippling red light streaming from a translucent core that towered at the center of the structure. The core reached all the way to the top of the volcanic cone, throbbing with swirling red liquid that could only be lava. Even from a distant ledge along the wall, Tala could feel the tremendous heat it was giving off.

Kutkha stood beside her, smiling, hands clasped behind his back. "Not bad, yes?"

Tala shook her head slowly. For once, she was at a loss for words.

The place was spectacular. During the course of the war, she had traveled the world with the 42nd and seen some incredible things… but this was unique. It literally sent chills up her spine just to look at it.

The buildings of alternating black glass and clear crystal…the silver spires, strung from glittering webs…the lush billows of deep green foliage…all of it bathed in the rippling red light of the lava tube…

It was stunning to behold.

She drank it in for a long moment as distant bells chimed and the hot, sulfurous breeze washed over her. Then, finally, the imperative tug of duty brought her back to reality. "If you say so." She turned to Kutkha. "So what now?"

He looked her in the eye and chuckled. "You like it." He nodded. "I know you do."

Tala shrugged. She wasn't going to give him the satisfaction.

Kutkha spread his arms wide. "This is my temple, Shaman. The Temple of Kutkha, over ten thousand years old." He stepped forward until his toes hung over the edge of the ledge, then threw his head back and let out a piercing cry. "I was in my glory when I built this! The height of my godhood!"

"You've been living here all this time?" asked Tala.

"Yes." Kutkha visibly slumped. His arms fell at his sides. "But not by choice."

Tala frowned. "What do you mean, not by choice?"

His expression, when he turned to face her, was grim. "I mean I am a prisoner."

"A prisoner?" Tala's frown deepened. "But you fly wherever you like, don't you?"

Kutkha looked away. "There are many kinds of prisons, Shaman." When he looked at her, the misery in his eyes was plain to see. "I cannot tell you how much I hate my life. I have been trapped here for a thousand years. Held against my will without the company of my loved ones."

Tala frowned. "Held by the Koryaks, you mean?"

"Yes," said Kutkha. "I've been held prisoner by my own worshippers. Like most humans, they are happiest when they can *control* their god."

"But how could they?" asked Tala. "With all your power, how could they control you?"

"They took control of the most important thing in the world to me." Kutkha stretched out an arm, pointing to the temple. "The only thing that matters."

"What's that?" asked Tala.

"The key to all that I love." Kutkha's voice cracked as he said it. "They took it and threw it away forever. But they didn't count on something." He snapped his fingers. "They didn't count on me finding a *new* key."

"What new key is that?" asked Tala.

Kutkha pointed at her. "*You*. They didn't count on *you*." He chuckled grimly. "And very soon, after a thousand years of imprisonment, I will finally put that key to use."

* * *

Hiruko and Itami stood before a massive metal door at the end of the tunnel. Hiruko ran the beam of his flashlight over it, searching for a latch or a lock, finding nothing but rivets and cast iron ribs.

Dead end. It didn't seem fair, after the gauntlet of booby traps they'd gone through.

The giant spiked mace had been the first of many. After Itami had destroyed it, Hiruko had led him farther down the passageway, where one trap after another had sprung in their path. Waves of daggers had shot out of the walls at them. Giant axes had swung down from the ceiling, whistling as they slashed through the air. Rows of spears had punched up through the ground like the teeth of a massive beast. Clouds of darts, no doubt poison-tipped, had burst from hidden launchers in the walls. Slabs of rock had dropped down from above. Holes had opened up in the ground to pull them in.

Each time one of the traps had struck, Hiruko had shouted out directions for Itami, who still couldn't see right. Itami, in turn, had deflected and obliterated whatever menace had been set loose on them. He hadn't failed even once; Hiruko didn't have a scratch on him.

But now they had to get through the door.

"This must be the last obstacle." Itami winced when he touched the metal surface. "The force that is painful to me is strongest on the other side." He pulled back and gnashed his teeth.

Hiruko examined the ribbing with the beam of his flashlight. "Can you break through, sir?"

"I do not want to." Itami rubbed his skull with one huge, blue hand. "It will be very bad for me over there."

"But can you do it?" asked Hiruko.

Itami groaned and gave his head a rough shake. He stumbled away from the door, dragging his kenabō club with him, and groaned again.

Hiruko lit him with the flashlight, watching his back as it heaved up and down. "Are you all right, sir?" The blue-skinned giant was in obvious pain. Hiruko couldn't believe it, but he actually felt sorry for him.

"Yesss." Itami hissed the word over his shoulder. "Now get out of my *way*."

Hiruko's eyes flew wide open. Just as he scrambled away from the door, Itami spun and charged, hauling back the kenabō as he ran. When he reached the door, his mighty swing plowed the club into the metal surface, leaving a massive dent at eye level.

With a great roar that sounded like a mix of rage and pain, Itami swung the kenabō again, deepening the dent. Another swing pushed the dent even deeper. After the next blow, when Itami pulled the club away, Hiruko could see red light pouring through a jagged fissure. Itami had broken through to the other side.

He seemed to need a rest, then; maybe it was the influence of whatever was affecting him from over there. He lowered the kenabō and leaned against the rock wall, scowling and rubbing his head.

A moment later, to Hiruko's surprise, relief arrived. Booted footsteps scuffed down the corridor; as Hiruko stared in their direction, he glimpsed familiar glowing scars approaching through the darkness. When he aimed the flashlight at them, the perpetual glare of Zermann appeared in the beam.

Why had he stayed behind before and only came forward now, at that particular moment? Hiruko didn't have a chance to find out. Zermann hurtled past him as if he didn't exist and headed straight for the dent Itami had put in the door.

Drawing his Luger, Doom, Zermann aimed the glowing barrel at the fissure. "*Ghnoss'Goloss*, tear open door." Then, from fewer than three feet away, he pulled the trigger.

A glowing round leaped at the fissure, leaving a trail of golden light. Whatever its special properties, it blew the fissure wide open when it made contact, leaving a smoking hole three inches in diameter.

Three more rounds chewed the hole even wider, big enough to push a fist through. Zermann turned to Itami and gestured with the gun, pointing the barrel at his kenabō. "Continue."

Itami bowed and stepped up to the door. When he swung the big club and wrenched it free, the hole was at least three times bigger.

As he swung it again and again, Zermann used Doom to weaken

other spots. Each glowing round pitted the metal or left a fresh fissure for Itami to exploit.

Soon, the door was full of big holes. Hiruko was able to gaze through them and see the structure inside the volcano. It was all so beautiful—the stacked blocks and spheres of obsidian and crystal, the gleaming silver towers, all bathed in red light—it made chills run up his spine.

So this was what they'd been heading for since leaving Tokyo. This remarkable, secret place had been waiting for them from the start. It looked like Shangri-La to him, a hidden temple cut off from the corruption of the outside world since time immemorial. What would this paradise be like when Von Heïzinger and Zermann got through with it?

He would find out soon enough. As Zermann shot out the last bits of metal between the holes, Itami thumped Hiruko on the shoulder. "Shall we return outside to inform the Daimyō that the way is clear?" His face was knotted with obvious pain as he spoke. His voice was different—higher, more strained than before.

"*Hai.*" Hiruko turned from the red-tinted vista of the volcanic temple to face Zermann. "We will be back momentarily. Please wait here and guard this portal."

Zermann slumped against the wall, rubbing his head. The glowing scars on his face and arms were pulsing brighter, rippling with crimson light now. "I…go." He sounded shaky, not at all his usual harsh-voiced self. "Pain *worse*…since smashed door."

Hiruko doubted Zermann would stay behind if he insisted, so he didn't try to stop him from coming along. The three of them walked out together to summon the unit forward, even as Hiruko wished he could leave Shangri-La pure, and not summon Von Heïzinger at all.

* * *

MacNeal stood at the base of a stone stairway and shook his head. Forty-some stairs up from the bottom, a big section had crumbled, leaving a gap of at least twenty-five feet. So much for Gol's latest route to the ledge.

"Well, this is a no-go." MacNeal turned and glared at Gol. He was starting to get the feeling Tatiana's friend didn't want to help so much after all. "Where's the next shortcut?"

Gol said a few words and Tatiana translated. "That way." Gol bobbed his head to one side and Tatiana pointed at a tunnel in the wall. "It is not far."

MacNeal's frustration was mounting. Taki had been on that ledge a long time with Wolf. With each passing minute, the likelihood of Taki's survival became more remote.

And the discontent of the Bogatyr faction became more pronounced. "You cannot be serious." Irina, who was standing nearby with Ivan, let out a long sigh. "Whatever happened to our supposed *mission*, John?"

MacNeal wasn't in the mood for her attitude. "If you're in such a hurry, feel free to finish it yourself."

"Maybe I will do just that." Irina planted her hands on her hips. "In which case, our alliance is out the window. All bets are off."

MacNeal stayed focused on Gol. "Are you *sure* about this next shortcut, Gol? Because we're running out of time."

Tatiana translated his words for Gol, who nodded and spoke. "Unless something has changed, I am sure," she translated back to MacNeal. But then, her expression shifted to a frown, and she shook her head. "*He* is sure." She gestured at Gol. "But I am not." She placed the palm of her hand against her chest.

"Why do you say that?" asked MacNeal.

Tatiana looked grim. "The Shōgunate force is closing in on the objective."

MacNeal frowned. "How exactly do you know this?"

"I have been communing with a priestess of Baba Yaga," said Tatiana. "She is part of the Shōgunate expedition."

"She waited until *now* to reach out to us?" asked MacNeal.

"She might have been trying for a while, but I did not hear her until now. Something about this place amplifies my sensitivities." Tatiana's frown deepened as she stared into space. "Perhaps something given off by the objective."

"The heavenly power source." MacNeal nodded and rubbed his bearded chin. He had to make a choice: keep trying to reach and rescue Taki, possibly failing to complete the mission in the process, or leave Taki to his own devices, and head for the objective.

He could keep trying to save one man, who might already be dead, or he could change the course of the war. When he thought about it in those terms, he realized it wasn't much of a decision after all.

"All right." He nodded at Tatiana, then Oksana, who nodded back at him in agreement. Finally, he turned to Gol. "Can you take us to the power source that's located here?"

Tatiana repeated the question in Russian. Gol scowled and answered, which she translated: "The volcano itself is the only true power."

"Is there something else then? Something of value?" asked MacNeal. "Something an army might want to take?"

"Only one thing." Gol hesitated, scanning the faces that surrounded him. His gaze settled on Tatiana, who nodded encouragingly. "I will take you to it."

"Thank you," said MacNeal.

Gol spoke once more through Tatiana. "If you will help keep the great god Kutkha safe, that will be thanks enough."

CHAPTER 30

Tala followed Kutkha down the sloped path toward the temple. "You said the Koryaks took away the most important thing in the world to you. What does that have to do with breaking into Heaven?"

Kutkha's black tattoos swirled faster over his muscular shoulders. "Heaven is where they put it. Put *them*. And then the Koryaks locked me out."

"But how could they do that?" Tala wiped sweat from her brow; it had been a long walk down. "You're a *god*."

Kutkha sighed. "They tricked me."

Tala frowned. "But you're a trickster, aren't you? I mean, *Raven* is, and you're an *aspect* of him, right?"

"Sometimes a trickster is *easiest* to trick." When Kutkha turned his head toward the temple, his dark profile glowed with red light from the lava column. "I became overconfident. I made fools of the Koryak elders, and then I let my guard down, and they had their revenge. They couldn't kill me, but they took away what I loved most."

"What was that?" asked Tala.

"You'll see soon." Kutkha faced forward and pointed into the distance. "The guests are starting to arrive."

Squinting, Tala gazed in the direction in which he was pointing. Sure enough, a column of men was flowing through an opening in the volcano wall and over an arching stone bridge toward the temple. Five of the men were clustered around a large, blocky object covered in a grey tarpaulin; they must have unloaded it from one of the vehicles they'd left outside, and now they had to carry it by hand. "The Shōgunate."

"This is good." Kutkha nodded excitedly, and his black tattoos grew more animated. "The others can't be far behind. Everyone is coming together as expected. The Union and Russians can't let their arch enemies steal the prize."

"You're not going to let the Shōgunate get it, are you?" asked Tala. "Or the Reich? Whatever it is, Von Heïzinger will use it to spread death and destruction."

"I doubt it." Kutkha laughed with a bitter edge. "Don't worry, Shaman. I've planned it so *no* man will win this game. The only reward will be *mine* at the end of this contest."

* * *

Von Heïzinger was at the head of the line as the column crossed the bridge over the lava moat into the temple. The Daimyō and the creatures of the Reich were not far behind. The rest of the convoy was moving slowly; the vehicles had not been able to fit through the doorway, so now the men had to carry the equipment that had been stowed aboard them.

Von Heïzinger's boots clacked over the paving stones of alternating black and crystal with the brisk rhythm of a metronome. His left glove was off, revealing the *Orbis Christus* on his finger; the gem in the ring throbbed with a crimson light so bright it hurt Hiruko's eyes to stare at it.

He had to look away as he followed across the bridge, still guiding Itami. Zermann stumbled along beside them, looking woozy, and the Stosstruppen at his heels didn't seem much better off. The feral creature howled and whined and ran in circles; it scratched at its hands, arms, and face until it drew blood. Whatever was up ahead, it was powerful…and getting closer every minute.

The *Orbis Christus* confirmed it when Von Heïzinger stepped off the bridge on the other side of the moat. As soon as he put his foot down, the ring flared with an even more intense light, stopping everyone in their tracks.

Von Heïzinger shouted incoherently and grabbed for the ring. He turned in a circle as he pulled at it, fighting to wrench it from his finger. All the while, its light grew brighter and throbbed faster, like a signal lamp at sea rattling off Morse code.

Finally, with a loud grunt, Von Heïzinger managed to free the ring. He dropped it as if it were scalding hot, then fluttered his pasty hand as if he'd just burned it.

Hiruko watched from the bridge without saying a word or making a move. The Daimyō rushed up beside him to see what was holding things up…but when he saw what was going on, he stayed silent, too.

Nobody moved or spoke as Von Heïzinger cursed and flapped his hand. Maybe it was because none of them had seen him hurt before; maybe, Hiruko thought, none of them had realized he was a human being until that moment.

But the moment didn't last. Von Heïzinger stopped flapping his hand and drew himself up straight as a flagpole. He pulled on his glove, bent down stiffly to pick up the still-blazing ring, and slid it on over one leather-clad pinky.

Casting his darkly glittering gaze over the column, he curled his pale lips away from his grey tombstone teeth. "Our shining hour is at hand." With that, he turned and resumed his march into the temple of diamond and obsidian.

The Daimyō followed in his wake, waving his sword overhead to signal the column. Hiruko and the others fell in step behind him, continuing their long advance into the unknown.

* * *

When Taki ran through the rock wall mirage, he found himself in a dark space on the other side—a cave. He reached for the flashlight he kept on the side of his pack, but the flashlight was gone; it must have fallen off during his climb up the volcano.

With no light to see by, he took one tentative step forward, then another. A few steps later, he bumped into something hanging from the ceiling; when he touched it, he found it was warm and familiar—a human leg.

Before he could puzzle it out, a torch flared to life on the far side of the cave, illuminating the chamber with flickering light. Blinking as his eyes adjusted, Taki saw that the man he'd been chasing was holding the torch; he also saw that more than one body was hanging from the ceiling between them.

"Don't tell me you've given up already," the man said in a mocking tone. "Your girlfriend Tala would *not* be impressed."

Taki breathed deeply, steadying himself in preparation for battle. "Where *is* she, you bastard?"

"First of all, the name is *Wolf*, not 'bastard.' Second of all…" He shook the torch, throwing shadows around the cave. "…if you want *her*, you have to catch *me* first."

Suddenly, Wolf whirled and sprinted into a tunnel. Taki could hear his laughter echoing through the passageway behind him.

Without hesitation, Taki raced after him, following the sound of his footsteps. Even as he did, he was all too aware of the fact that Wolf *wanted* him to follow. And that meant, more than likely, that he was leading Taki into a trap.

* * *

When Tala was near the bottom of the slope, distant movement caught her eye. Stopping, she looked toward the back of the temple, the side opposite the Shōgunate and Reich's entry point.

There, for the first time since she and Taki had set out on their scouting mission, she saw the men of the 42nd. MacNeal and Brown marched at the head of the group, along with a frosty-haired woman she recognized—Irina, that piece of work—and a woman she'd never seen before. There were lots of other unfamiliar faces in the unit, too—all Russian, judging from their uniforms.

Tala wanted to call out to them at that instant, but giving away her position, and theirs, could be a huge mistake. Kutkha seemed to share that opinion; he stood inches away, watching her with hands hanging at his sides, as if he might clamp one over her mouth at any time.

"It is as I planned." He looked off into the distance at the latest intruders. "Everyone is coming together at once. The stage is almost set. Our hard work is finally paying off."

Tala had an impulse to pull out one of the dynamite bombs, light it, and lob it. MacNeal would come running at that kind of signal. If anyone could break her free from the scheming god, it was him. MacNeal would find a way; he always did.

But maybe, this time, he'd be better off staying clear. "What are you planning to do to them?" She met Kutkha's gaze. "What will you do to my friends?"

"I will do nothing to them." Kutkha tipped his head to one side. "The question you should ask is, what will *they*..." He gestured at the 42nd and its allies, then swung his arm back to encompass the Shōgunate and Reich. "...do to *each other*? And *that* is entirely up to *them*."

* * *

MacNeal was on the highest alert possible as he crossed the bridge over the lava moat. His heart was pounding in his chest, his blood swirling with hot adrenaline. All his senses were tuned to maximum intensity, registering every detail of his surroundings: the black and crystal paving stones, the smell of sulfur, the blistering heat, the sound of bubbles popping in the lava.

Up ahead, a tall, silver door stood waiting, split down the middle, gleaming with reflected crimson light. Whatever the Shōgunate had come for, it had to be inside; if a heavenly power existed in Kamchatka, could there be any grander place to contain it?

"I wish I had a camera right now." Brown's eyes were fixed on the gleaming gates. "That's one for the photo album there."

MacNeal nodded. As he drew closer to the door, the light playing over it rippled and flowed. If just the *door* looked so incredible, he couldn't wait to see what lay beyond it. Turning to Gol and Tatiana, he asked, "How do we get inside? Knock?"

Tatiana translated his question and Gol's response. "That knowledge is unknown to me. Only the elders can break the holy seal."

MacNeal stopped in front of the door and reached out. In spite of all the heat in the surrounding area, the metal was cool to the touch. It was firm, too; he pushed, and the door didn't give in the slightest.

"You can't *push* them open," Gol said through Tatiana. "The elders never even *touch* them."

"Whatever you say." MacNeal put his shoulder into it, grunting with the effort…but the result was the same. Brown joined him, and they both pushed with all their might, but still the door held firm.

The rest of the men of the 42nd marched up and added their strength to the big push. Then Oksana barked an order in Russian, and the men of the New Guard threw their backs and shoulders into it, too.

Still, the door would not budge.

Sweat poured down MacNeal's face as he redoubled his effort. He couldn't feel even the tiniest bit of give from the cool, silver metal.

"Somebody get me the horn of Jericho!" said Brown as he dug in and struggled to push harder. "I think that's what it's gonna take to bring these damn doors *down!*"

* * *

At the Daimyō's command, the men—including Hiruko—opened fire, blasting the great silver door of the temple with rounds from their rifles. When the shooting stopped, and the smoke cleared, Hiruko could see the results.

Nothing had changed. Not a single round had pierced the metal.

The Daimyō cursed. Ever since the unit had crossed the bridge over the lava moat and reached the door, they had been trying to get inside. First, Itami and Zermann had failed to smash their way through; then, all the men in the unit had pushed together at once, with the same result. Now, concentrated firepower had also failed to make a dent.

Hiruko wondered if they would ever get through. Had they come all this way just to run into a dead end?

The Daimyō seemed ready to admit defeat. Throwing up his hands and shaking his head, he spun and walked away from the door.

But there was still one other person who would not give up, even then. Von Heïzinger, who'd been lurking off to one side, glided up with Nadia holding on to his arm. She'd been forced to enter the volcano on foot since the entryway had been too small to accommodate the amphibious vehicles.

Hiruko was instantly worried. He moved closer, but Von Heïzinger brushed past him, guiding Nadia toward the door. "Time to earn your keep, Priestess."

Frowning, Hiruko followed them. What was Von Heïzinger planning?

"Please, Hermann." Nadia hobbled clumsily as Von Heïzinger dragged her along. "Leave me alone."

"You know what you need to do." Von Heïzinger hauled her up in front of the door and held her there. "Open them. I know you can do it."

"Why, Hermann?" She glared at him. "So you can use whatever is in there to make the world *suffer*?"

Von Heïzinger shook her by the shoulders. "Would you have me *kill* you, woman?" He pulled her up to face him. "I can do it, you know."

"Then why haven't you already?" Nadia hissed out the words, meeting his gaze with her own hateful stare.

"Because I have need of you," said Von Heïzinger. "But the moment that need *ends*, so does your *life*." He spun her to face the door. "Unless you do not value that life."

Nadia stood there, gazing at the gleaming silver panels of the sealed entryway. She shook her head slowly, and tears trickled down her withered face.

Hiruko wanted to run to her side, but he didn't dare try it. He feared what Von Heïzinger might do if he—or anyone—tried to get between the generalleutnant and the prize beyond the door.

After a long moment, Nadia raised a hand and pressed it against the metal. Then she turned and cast a hateful scowl in Von Heïzinger's direction. "I rue the day I helped you find that first artifact. That was the day your dark future was set in stone."

"And now it is about to lead to your death." Von Heïzinger drew his Walther P38 from its holster and jammed it against her back. "How ironic."

Nadia stood and scowled another moment, then seemed to come to a decision. She lifted her other hand and pressed it to the metal, then closed her eyes.

Almost immediately, the vegetation growing at the base of the door sprang to animate life.

CHAPTER 31

The door wouldn't budge. The men and women of the 42nd and the New Guard had given it their all, with no success. Even the Bogatyrs had joined in, adding their strength to the effort, but the door had stayed firmly in place.

The sound of weapons fire from the far side of the massive temple, from what had to be Shōgunate guns, had spurred MacNeal to order up some heavy fire of his own. Brown had emptied a small ammo dump's worth of flash machine gun rounds at the door, but still there had been no change.

It was then that Oksana made her suggestion. "I would like to try my voïvodes." She gestured with the Lucifer control glove, and the two automatons skittered up on their segmented triple legs. "I believe they can penetrate the armored doors."

Irina strolled over. "Why would your defective clockwork toys have any more success than anything else we have tried?"

"You know as well as I," said Oksana, "these voïvodes are infused with the energies of the gods themselves."

Irina snorted. "I would not be so sure of that. These are inferior prototypes. They could no more contain the energy of the gods than *you* could."

"Enough!" MacNeal stepped between them, waving his flash-gun at the voïvodes. "If there's a chance they can break through, let's give them a try."

"I will do that, MacNeal." With that, Oksana flexed Lucifer, turning the mechanical gauntlet palm up. When she wiggled two fingers, the voïvodes ran toward the door.

Oksana stopped wiggling her fingers and the voïvodes stopped. When she clenched Lucifer into a fist, the voïvodes sprang into action.

MacNeal watched as the voïvodes went to work on the silver door. Tesla coils flaring with bright blue light, the three-legged pods attacked the metal with robotic efficiency. One blasted it with bolts of crackling energy; the other flashed out an electrified blade and spun at high speeds, letting the knife skim the metal like a whirling propeller.

At first, the door seemed unchanged. The energy bolts scattered over the surface and splashed off like jets of water. The spinning blade seemed to glance off the metal without making the slightest cut.

"You see?" Irina shook her head. "These inferior things cannot measure up to the instruments of the true god, Zor'ka."

Oksana ignored her and continued manipulating Lucifer. Each twitch of the glove made an adjustment in the angle and intensity of the voïvodes' attack.

And after a moment more, MacNeal finally began to see a difference. The blade began cutting into the metal, screeching and shooting off bright sparks. The electrical blasts made the great silver panels course and arc with streams of dancing blue energy.

Wielding Lucifer with one hand, Oksana thrust her Vesper scepter forward with the other, unleashing another crackling surge against the door. As Vesper's blast joined the voïvode's, the streams of current raced over the door with ever-increasing speed and intensity. The knife-wielding voïvode, meanwhile, scuttled back and forth while its pod kept spinning, slicing its blade in a deepening cut across the bottom three feet of the door.

Finally, the team was making progress. MacNeal checked his

flash-gun and gear, making sure he was ready to enter the temple. Glancing over his shoulder, he saw Irina standing with arms folded over her chest, staring at Oksana and the voïvodes.

She didn't say another damn word about how inferior they were.

* * *

At Nadia's command, a patch of stubby weeds had grown to engulf the entirety of the towering silver door. The weeds had become mighty vines that clung to the metal surface, climbing higher and growing thicker with each passing moment.

Hiruko had seen Nadia work such magic before, so he wasn't as surprised as the rest of the Shōgunate unit to see her in action. The other soldiers gaped in silent awe as the vegetation, in a matter of moments, did what should have taken it years to do. Even the Daimyō looked stunned.

The weeds continued to thicken and sprawl, wrapping around nearby pillars and buttresses. Soon, the only clear spots on the door were the two places where Nadia's hands made contact.

Then, when the wall of green had completely overtaken the door, Nadia pulled her hands away, and the growing stopped. Eyes closed, she slowly took a hobbling step backward…then another. All the while, her lips never stopped moving in a chant Hiruko couldn't hear.

When Nadia was seven steps back, she swung her hands together in a clap so loud, it surprised Hiruko. Immediately, the wall of vines began to twist and contract.

The mass of vegetation was so huge, its rustling filled the sulfurous air. Soon, Hiruko heard the creak and groan of straining metal; the vines twitched and shivered as the door resisted their pull.

Then, all at once, the door gave way. Dividing in half along the split down the middle, the two sides shot open and slammed hard against the obsidian walls. A blast of hot air rushed out of the dark space beyond and washed over the convoy. When Hiruko breathed it in, he got the taste of dust and fire in his mouth.

When it was over, Nadia slumped to the ground. Von Heïzinger swept past her without a downward glance. Legs flicking back and forth under his long, black coat, he stormed straight into the open doorway of the temple without the slightest hesitation.

As Von Heïzinger disappeared into the darkness, Hiruko ran to

Nadia. He knelt beside her, taking her head in his hands. "Nadia?" Her eyes were closed, her mouth wide open. He wondered if she might be dead. "Nadia? Are you all right?"

Her eyes finally fluttered and she coughed. "What have I done, Mr. Orochi? Oh, what have I done?"

* * *

Taki chased Wolf through a maze of dark tunnels, following the light from his torch and the sound of his footsteps. He was hopelessly lost; if not for Wolf, he'd have had no idea how he'd gotten where he was or how to find his way out.

If only he could catch up and get his hands on his quarry…but Wolf was always a few steps ahead. He had the advantage of knowing where he was going; every time Taki rounded a corner, Wolf was already gone.

Until, finally, he wasn't. Taki charged around one more turn in the tunnels, and there he was—standing in the heart of a circular space thirty feet in diameter. It was a juncture between tunnels, an intersection with exits all around, spaced five feet apart.

Wolf grinned and waved. "Think you can catch me, Taki?"

Taki stood for a moment, surveying the chamber, expecting a trick. Nothing jumped out at him, no sign of an obvious trap.

Then, Wolf stomped his foot, and a hole fell open in the floor between them. "Think again!" With that, he jumped into the hole feet-first and disappeared.

Taki ran over and gazed into the opening. He could see nothing but darkness below, just the pitch black unknown.

But that was where Wolf had gone, and Wolf was his only hope of quickly finding Tala. Clearly, he was leading Taki right where he wanted him to be, but Taki could think of no better option than to follow.

Gulping a deep breath, he leaped off the edge of the hole and plunged feet-first into the darkness after Wolf.

* * *

Moments had passed since Von Heïzinger had stormed into the temple, and the rest of the expedition still waited outside. No one, not even the Daimyō, had been quick to follow him inside. Everyone just waited and gazed through the open door into the darkness, straining to see what was in there.

Hiruko stood up front, supporting Nadia with an arm around her middle. The effort of prying open the door had taken a lot out of her; she slumped against him, face slack, breathing shallow.

The Daimyō paced in front of them, rarely taking his eyes off the temple's interior. Was he waiting to see if Von Heïzinger might be devoured by whatever he'd found inside? Hiruko couldn't tell; his face was unreadable.

"What should we do?" Hiruko muttered under his breath, not intending it for anyone's ears in particular.

The words had barely left his lips when the temple lit up inside. Bright light drove away the darkness, exposing the solitary figure of Von Heïzinger marching out toward the assembled forces of the Shōgunate and Reich.

"Get in here! All of you!" His voice echoed in the giant chamber beyond the threshold. "*Now!*"

Immediately the unit stirred to life. Men began moving again, adjusting their gear.

"Orochi!" Von Heïzinger pointed one black-gloved finger at Hiruko. "Bring the witch first! Do it now!" Without another word, he spun and whisked away from them, back into the depths of the temple.

The Daimyō waved his sword and snapped out orders. "Let's go! *Sousou*! Hurry!"

Hiruko looked at Nadia, who seemed to be reviving. Her breathing was growing stronger, and the spark of life was fanning brighter in her eyes.

"I'm so sorry." Her voice was still weak. "I should have let him kill me."

"You did what you had to," said Hiruko. "Don't berate yourself."

"Mr. Orochi." Her gaze met his and she frowned. "What if I asked you to kill me? Would you do it?"

Hiruko ignored her questions. "Can you make it inside?"

"I would rather die," said Nadia.

"You two!" The Daimyō shook his sword at them. "Get in there *now*."

"We have to go, Nadia." Hiruko gestured at the open door of the temple. "I will help you."

Nadia sighed. "If you truly wanted to help me, you would take me away from this place." Her voice rose with stubborn willfulness…but then she started to move forward anyway.

One hobbling step at a time, she walked into the temple, braced by Hiruko's arm around her waist. As much as she clearly wanted to be anywhere else but in that ancient place, she went forth to face whatever destiny Von Heïzinger had cooked up for her.

CHAPTER 32

**Kamchatka
19 April 1952
2207 Hours**

Taki hurtled down a steep, polished chute, rocketing through absolute darkness. Leaping into the hole in the floor in pursuit of Wolf had sent him on this wild ride. Now, with nothing to slow or stop his fall, the only thing he could do was endure it.

At least he knew he wasn't far behind Wolf; he could hear Wolf's taunting shouts up ahead, down below. Maybe, if Taki flew fast enough through the chute, he would actually catch up and get his hands on the lunatic…or get his feet on him first, since they would be closest.

Trying to speed up, Taki tucked his arms against his body and squeezed his legs tightly together like a bobsled racer. Heart pounding, he worked his body through the cut, climbing the curves and shooting down the straightaways. He could feel himself cruising faster, getting closer to his quarry.

Then, suddenly, the chute dropped out from under him, and he was zooming through pitch black space like an arrow. He kept his body stiff and straight, hoping to cross as much emptiness as possible before he fell, though he had no idea what waited ahead or below.

He continued to cruise through the air, and then his acceleration slowed. His stomach lurched, and he felt himself begin to lose altitude.

As Taki stalled and dropped, adrenaline surged through his bloodstream. Panic clawed at him, setting his heart racing. He was falling out of control—to his death, probably. He was about to fail his personal mission—to rescue Tala—and lose his precious life in the bargain.

The feeling of falling overwhelmed him with dread. He fought to block out the rush of air against his skin, the smell of brimstone, the sound of his heart thundering in his ears. But he had no success.

Then, he turned to the Diamond Sutra to calm himself, reciting the words in his mind.

> *Bodhisattvas should leave behind*
> *all phenomenal distinctions*
> *and awaken the thought of*
> *the Consummation of Incomparable Enlightenment*
> *by not allowing the mind to depend upon*
> *notions evoked by the sensible world—*
> *by not allowing the mind to depend upon*
> *notions evoked by sounds, odors, flavors,*
> *touch-contacts, or any qualities.*
> *The mind should be kept independent*
> *of any thoughts which arise within it.*
> *If the mind depends upon anything*
> *it has no sure haven.*

As always, the words of the Buddha brought Taki a measure of peace. They swirled in his head as he continued to plunge, distracting him from the sensations flaring with vivid intensity at what he knew might be the end of his existence.

Then, suddenly, his body crashed onto another chute. He landed in a tumble of arms and legs and resumed the slide that had been interrupted by his fall.

This time, he spun as he raced onward, rolling over and over on the chute's slick surface. His head bounced as he blasted around a tight turn, then sailed through a dip.

Finally, a circle of light became visible in the distance. He flew up to it like a dive-bombing plane, swooping through one high hairpin after another. All the while, the circle grew larger, expanding as his distance from it dwindled.

He soared closer, ever closer to the light. Waves of heat pressed toward him as he plummeted toward the opening in the darkness.

And then, like a bullet from the barrel of a gun, he shot through it.

* * *

As Hiruko guided Nadia past the threshold of the door, he stared in open wonderment at the vast interior of the temple unfolding before him.

From the outside, it had looked like a stack of cubes and spheres, a modular structure consisting of separate, self-contained units. But on the inside, it was smooth all around—a domed vault with walls of blended obsidian and diamond. The inward-facing edges of the cubes and spheres had been flattened and molded into one continuous, glittering surface.

Crimson light from the towering lava column streamed in through the diamond sections of the walls and ceiling. A circle of translucent crystal in the middle of the dome projected a ring of crimson rays around a massive stone dais in the temple's heart.

The raised dais was surrounded by a moat of bubbling orange lava. Three stone stairways crossed the moat, equidistant from each other; Hiruko wondered if there was a fourth he couldn't see on the far side, in which case the stairways would be like compass points. They arched over the liquefied rock and reached up to the black surface of the dais, which was raised at least ten feet above the superheated moat.

Atop the dais was something Hiruko could not entirely see. From a distance, all he could make out was the rounded top of an object mostly hidden by the angle of its elevation.

Von Heïzinger stood at the bottom of one of the stone stairways, waiting with hands clasped behind his back. "Congratulations." His raspy voice echoed through the massive chamber. "You are about to make history."

Nadia paused and sighed, then resumed hobbling forward. "You and your grand gestures, Hermann. There are easier ways to impress me, you know."

Von Heïzinger held out his hand. "Come to me, Nadia." The faintest trace of a smile played over his death-white face. "Come and see why I have brought you here."

"But don't you see, Hermann?" Nadia shook her head sadly. "I don't care."

When she reached him, he took her hand and drew her away from Hiruko. "But you will, my sweet." His voice was devoid of any affection; the endearment seemed to catch in his throat, and he coughed. "Believe me, you will."

* * *

Kutkha stood at the bottom of the long switchbacked slope and stared at the temple. His head cocked one way and then the next with a bird-like motion, as if he were listening to sounds beyond the range of Tala's hearing.

On one side of the temple, the Shōgunate troops were marching through an open door. On the opposite side, the 42nd Marines and their Russian allies were still stuck outside, watching as a pair of robots worked on breaking through their own door.

In other words, it wasn't going well for the Union and Russians. Von Heïzinger had already charged inside, and now the rest of the Shōgunate and Reich forces were joining him. They would get first crack at the objective, leaving the 42nd at a disadvantage.

"I need to get over there." Tala pointed in the direction of MacNeal's team. "They need my help, Kutkha."

Kutkha brushed her aside with a wave of his hand. "They're doing just fine, Shaman. They don't need you."

"Yes, they do." She walked around to stand in front of him. "They're my *friends*. They're *good people*." She pulled out one of her dynamite bombs and shook it at him. "I'll bet I could blow those doors wide open, if you'd just get me over there."

"Stop worrying." Kutkha reached past the bomb and patted Tala on the head. "Your friends will get through. I *believe* in them."

Tala scowled. She wanted to stuff the bomb in his mouth after that patronizing head-patting. "I thought you said the Shōgunate wouldn't get the prize."

Kutkha flicked an index finger back and forth. "I said *no* man would get it. That includes the Shōgunate, the Reich, the Russians, and your beloved Union."

"But don't you see?" asked Tala. "We're the *good guys*. We just want to stop the *bad guys* from getting what they're after. Then we'll give you *all* the help you want. I'll pray and perform rituals for you. We'll help you get back what the Koryaks stole and put in Heaven. We'll do whatever it *takes*."

Kutkha smiled lovingly at her. "Thank you for the offer, Shaman. It's very sweet." Reaching out, he made contact again…but this time, he pinched her left cheek. "I think you genuinely care about me, which is flattering. But the truth of the matter is this." He let go and spread his arms wide. The black swirls that covered his body began to twist and churn with new life. "I have the situation under control." Dark wings sprouted from his arms, and black feathers flowed over his flesh. "You will do what *I* want. *All* of you will."

* * *

Oksana and the voïvodes were almost through.

The bolts of energy kicked up by Vesper and one voïvode were dancing more erratically over the door. The other voïvode's cutting blade was buried in the gash it had been digging, slicing ever deeper into the silver metal surface. The screeching from the blade was getting louder all the time.

"How much longer?" MacNeal shouted the question to Oksana over the crackling of Vesper's energy beam.

Oksana held up her Lucifer glove and raised a single finger in reply. *Just one minute.*

Pulse pounding, nerves humming with their own building electrical overload, MacNeal stepped closer to the door and tightened his grip on the flash-gun. Sweat trickled down his back and sides as he waited for the minute to pass.

Brown stomped forward and waited beside him, aiming the muzzle of his flash machine gun dead-on at the deepening fault line in the silver metal. "Almost in the soup again, Major. Seems like we just got out of it not too long ago, doesn't it?"

"We're *always* in the soup, Boomer." MacNeal smirked ruefully and took another step forward. "We spend our whole *lives* in the damn soup."

Brown laughed. "I wouldn't have it any other way, Major."

CHAPTER 33

**Kamchatka
19 April 1952
2213 Hours**

After shooting out of the hole at the end of his wild ride, Taki found himself soaring through the interior of the volcano. Blistering hot air wrapped around him as he flew over rivers of lava, heading for a massive structure that looked like it had been built out of crystal and onyx cubes and spheres.

A collision seemed imminent...but then he lost momentum and started to drop. The arc of his flight stopped short of the structure; instead, he plummeted toward a mound of grey ash on the bank of a smoking pool of lava.

Taki plunged headfirst into the mound, his fall broken by the huge drift of powder. He sent up a grey cloud when he hit, then blew out another when he punched through on the other side. He rolled down that side of the mound gracelessly, coughing out lungfuls of ash. When he reached the bottom, he finally came to a dead stop.

Still coughing, Taki wiped both hands down the length of his face. They came away with a dark film of ash, much like the grey layer covering the rest of him.

He struggled to his feet and dusted off what he could, raising mini-clouds every time he brushed another spot. Not that he wasn't grateful for landing in the ash mound instead of a lava river or a pile of rocks. It was better to be a little dusty than dead.

Suddenly, Taki heard a shrill whistle from the direction of the crystal and onyx structure. Looking toward it, he saw Wolf running away, grinning and waving over his shoulder.

Taki coughed out more ash, then took a deep breath and gathered his strength. Wolf was playing a game, but he was also the key to finding Tala. There were no two ways about it; Taki knew what he had to do.

Squaring his jaw, he set his eyes on Wolf and ran after him, heading for the mysterious structure in the middle of the great volcano.

* * *

As Von Heïzinger led Nadia up the stone staircase over the lava, Hiruko followed close behind. If Nadia slipped or stumbled, he wanted to be there to catch her; he didn't trust Von Heïzinger to do the same.

At the top of the stairs, they stepped onto the huge raised dais that occupied the heart of the temple. For the first time, Hiruko got an unobstructed view of what was up there.

In the middle of the dais, fifty yards away, stood a single object: some kind of elliptical metal framework. Hiruko had glimpsed its rounded top edge from below, though its full shape and size had been concealed from him where he'd stood on the ground. As Von Heïzinger led him and Nadia closer to it, he could see more detail.

The frame was seven feet tall, made of a silvery metal that was tinted with the colors of the rainbow. The multi-hued highlights seemed to shift as Hiruko watched, playing over the metal's skin in the red light from the volcano's towering lava core.

The metal hoop of the frame was stamped with elaborate markings—design accents or a language that Hiruko didn't recognize. In some places, the metal was split into strands that were braided and interlaced like wires or vines.

The hoop rested in a base that kept it standing erect. Legs like upside-down V's supported either side, ending in broad, clawed feet.

The base was made of the same rainbow-hued metal as the frame and stamped with the same intricate markings.

But the most interesting part to Hiruko was what was *missing*—namely, what the framework was supposed to be *framing*. There was no mirror or pane of glass inside that frame; Hiruko could have walked right through it without stopping.

It was an empty frame…so why was it standing alone on a dais at the heart of the temple? Why was it in such a place of importance?

And more importantly, what did Von Heïzinger want with it?

"Do you *feel* that?" asked Von Heïzinger as he drew up to the framework with Nadia. "The *power* calling out to us?"

Nadia didn't answer at first. Her eyes, like his, were fixed on the intricately crafted hoop of metal. "How much more power do you *need*, Hermann?"

"Tell me!" He shook her by the arm. "Tell me you feel it!"

Nadia sighed and nodded. "Yes, I feel it."

Von Heïzinger stepped away from her. Raising his left hand, he gazed at the blazing red ring on his black-gloved pinky. The gem was burning so bright it bathed his face in pulsing crimson light. "The *Orbis Christus* responds to the call. It demands *completion*." With that, he released Nadia's arm and stormed toward the framework alone.

Hiruko stepped forward and took hold of Nadia. She slumped against him. "Mr. Orochi." Her voice was a whisper. "You should run."

Hiruko whispered back to her. "I can't leave you here."

"*Now.*" Nadia pushed at his chest, trying to push him away. "While he is distracted. This could be your only chance."

Hiruko stood firm and shook his head. "I won't do it."

"Look at him." Nadia raised a shaking finger to point in Von Heïzinger's direction. "Don't you understand? Whatever twisted goal he has been working toward, this is the *culmination*. This is when he gets what he *wants*." She jabbed Hiruko's shoulder with her finger. "Do you think that will be *good* for you? For *any* of us?"

Hiruko's gaze returned to Von Heïzinger. He stood before the framework now, chanting something that Hiruko couldn't understand. Slowly, he raised his left hand and slid the *Orbis Christus* from his pinky.

"I fooled myself into thinking there was something inside him left to save." Nadia waved a hand dismissively at Von Heïzinger. "But there isn't. Everything I once cared about is long gone."

The chanting grew louder. Von Heïzinger reached up and plugged the crimson ring into an eyeball-shaped socket in the middle of the top edge of the framework.

For a long moment, nothing happened. Von Heïzinger stood with his hands at his sides, chanting as he gazed into the opening at the heart of the framework.

Then, the air within the frame *rippled*.

"Please, Mr. Orochi." Nadia's voice was urgent. "You must leave here while you still have time."

But Hiruko was too busy watching to pay attention to what she was saying. The rippling was intensifying, rolling from the top of the frame to the bottom like waves on a wind-blown lake.

Von Heïzinger's chanting got louder with each passing moment. Then, suddenly, he hit a dramatic crescendo and thrust both arms in the air.

At that instant, the rippling transparent gap within the framework flared with brilliant white light. The light surged, then dimmed, and Hiruko could no longer see through to the other side. Now the frame was filled with a milky, shimmering skin; little arcs of what looked like electrical current crackled over it, sparking and dancing like lightning roaming over a thunderhead.

"I don't understand." Hiruko's voice was hushed when he spoke. "What is he doing?"

"Opening a doorway," said Nadia.

Hiruko frowned. "A doorway to where?"

"For now, only he knows." Nadia glared at Von Heïzinger, who was turning to face her. "And I wish we could keep it that way."

Von Heïzinger's eyes glittered from the shadows beneath his cap. "Oh, Nadia." He extended one index finger toward her, then slowly curled it back toward himself. "Come here. I have something to show you, my *liebchen*."

* * *

As Kutkha flapped his great ebon wings, Tala took a step back from him…then another. His transformation from a man covered in swirling black markings to a winged creature covered in black feathers was startling to see up close.

His body became that of a giant bird again except for his head, which stayed human. "The wheels are in motion, Shaman." He grinned when he said it. "It is time for us to go."

Tala took another two steps back. Her heart was bashing against her ribs like a battering ram. "Go where?"

"To end my suffering, of course." Kutkha flapped his wings and his clawed feet lifted off the ground. "To get back what was taken from me so long ago."

"But you still haven't told me what that is." Tala kept backing away from him. "I still don't know exactly what you want me to do."

"What you're told." Kutkha kept flapping and rose higher. "It is as simple as that."

"I could be more use to you if I knew more," said Tala.

"All will be revealed, and you will do just fine." Kutkha flapped and rose some more. "Trust me, Shaman Tala."

Suddenly, he flapped harder and shot upward. When he reached thirty feet off the ground, he angled his wings and dove toward Tala.

He might have been an incarnation of the god Raven, but her instincts still sent her running. With a better head start, she might have made it to cover.

But she didn't. Before she got far, Kutkha's claws snapped around her shoulders and hoisted her upward.

Her feet left the ground and she sagged in his grip. He was taking her with him to play out whatever drama he'd been planning, whether she liked it or not.

But maybe things would still work out for the best. After all, he wasn't just taking her toward the Temple of Kutkha.

Every flap of his wings carried Tala closer to the 42nd Marines as well.

* * *

Sweat rolled down MacNeal's back as he waited for the door to open before him. It was supposed to happen any minute now, and he was determined to be the first one through.

Oksana continued to blast away with her Vesper scepter. Her voïvodes kept up their work, too, directed by her Lucifer control glove. One fired a steady stream of focused energy, the other sliced a spinning, screeching blade through the metal door as if it were a tin can.

Vesper and the voïvodes had made great progress since they'd started, but the fact remained: they were taking too long for MacNeal's liking. Oksana had held up an index finger, indicating the job would only take one more minute, several minutes ago. Meanwhile, for all MacNeal knew, the Shōgunate and Von Heïzinger could already be inside the temple.

MacNeal looked at Brown, who was standing beside him. Brown rolled his eyes impatiently.

The two of them weren't the only ones running out of patience. Irina marched forward, hands on her hips, and stopped beside Oksana. Irina shook her head with dismay, but Oksana just ignored her and kept firing Vesper at the great door.

Looking back at MacNeal, Irina gave him a confident nod...and a wink. Turning to face the door, she squared her shoulders and took a deep breath.

Then, she opened her mouth and started to sing.

* * *

Von Heïzinger gestured impatiently for Nadia to hurry and join him at the framework. Hiruko, with an arm around Nadia's waist, tried to push her forward...but she would not be rushed.

"*Now!*" barked Von Heïzinger. But nothing he said made her budge. Nadia seemed to be determined to delay him as much as possible.

Suddenly, Hiruko heard the Daimyō's voice behind him. "So there it is." Turning, Hiruko saw the Daimyō walking toward them. "Finally, we have it."

"Be gone, Minamoto!" Von Heïzinger snapped out the words. "You are interrupting a delicate procedure."

The Daimyō ignored him. "We have come so far. At last the heavenly prize is within reach." Smiling, he clapped his hands.

Von Heïzinger spun and snarled at him. "You *applaud*? Are you *mocking* this great achievement?"

This time, the Daimyō did look at him. "Not at all, Generalleutnant." He bobbed his head over one shoulder as he kept clapping. "I was simply summoning the others, so they might share in our triumph."

Just then, two Shōgunate soldiers slowly moved into view at the far edge of the dais, backing up the stairs with shoulders hunched. They were carrying one end of the mysterious blocky object that had been transported to the volcano in one of the amphibious vehicles. Even as the men grunted and muscled it up the stairs, its true nature was still hidden from sight, shrouded under a grey tarpaulin.

"No! Send it back!" said Von Heïzinger. "Get it out of here!"

"Easy, men." Again, the Daimyō ignored him. "One step at a time, that's it."

Hiruko held on to Nadia and watched as the two men heaved their end of the object up to the dais. Three more soldiers brought up the other end, straining and grunting as they pushed. Sweat poured down their faces from the strain and the heat of the lava moat below.

When all five men had topped the stairs, the Daimyō waved for them to bring their cargo closer. "Over here." He pointed at the framework.

As the men hauled the object closer, Von Heïzinger stormed over and blocked the way, clutching the Patmos Amulet. "I said get it out of here!" He held the gleaming amulet out in front of him, aiming it at the men. "Throw it into the lava and throw yourselves in after it!"

The men looked confused. They fumbled around, clearly unsure what to do next.

Suddenly, the Daimyō drew *Dyuaru-Kontan* from its scabbard and flashed across the dais like lightning. Before Von Heïzinger could say another word, the Daimyō swept the katana around and stopped its point just below Von Heïzinger's right eye. "That's enough!" He flicked the tip of the sword, blotting Von Heïzinger's pasty flesh with a streak of bright red blood. "Revoke your commands!"

Von Heïzinger's nose curled in contempt. "Do not throw the device or yourselves into the lava." The whole time he said it, his eyes never left the Daimyō.

"We had an agreement." The Daimyō scowled. "I suggest you honor it." The point of the Daimyō's sword did not stray from Von Heïzinger's cheek. "We will not interfere with your procedure, and you will not interfere with ours. Understood?"

"Wait until I'm done," said Von Heïzinger.

The Daimyō smiled grimly and shook his head. "Why don't *you* wait until *we're* done?"

Von Heïzinger stared at him for a long moment. Then, without a word, he stepped back from the blade, leaving the tip to drift in empty air, and marched back to the framework. "Nadia! I have waited long enough for you!"

As he and Nadia were forced to join Von Heïzinger in front of the frame, Hiruko's attention was focused on the Daimyō's men bringing the object the rest of the way. They carried it over and put it down near the framework, six feet from the right edge of it. Then, they set about loosening the straps that held the tarp in place.

When they were done, they pulled off the tarp. Finally, Hiruko got a look at what had been hidden aboard the transport ship and the amphibious vehicle for all that time.

It was a device of some kind, mounted in a rectangular case. The case measured six feet long by four feet wide by three feet high, and it was bursting with instrumentation. Dials and knobs and meters covered the long sides, and the top was lined with glass tubes. A glossy black dome bulged on either end of the case, smooth as glass and as big as a man's head. As for the bottom, it sprouted legs when the men picked it up and punched a button on the side, leaving it to stand on its own.

And so it stood revealed, whatever it was...whatever it did. It had been delivered and set up by Hiruko's own people, yet it was as mysterious to him as the framework. He could not imagine either one's purpose, let alone how they might interact.

At least he was bound to know soon. Dr. Kondo marched up the stairs and headed for the device. As always, he wore his white lab coat and carried a clipboard.

He started hitting switches and buttons as soon as he reached the device. The volcano rumbled as if in response.

And the electrical arcs danced more frantically over the milky skin within the framework.

CHAPTER 34

**Kamchatka
19 April 1952
2245 Hours**

MacNeal had heard Irina sing many times. He had seen her work miracles with her Liturgies, turning the tide in even the darkest of battles. But he had never heard her sing like she did that night.

Whatever lay at the root of her ability, whatever trick of sonic manipulation let her do what she did, MacNeal had only ever seen it affect living creatures. He'd seen her inspire them, seduce them, terrify them, put them to sleep, and change their minds. He'd seen her turn enemies into slaves with little more than a simple tune. Because of that, she was one of the most dangerous operatives he'd ever encountered in the field. But he had never known her singing to affect an inanimate object.

Until that night.

As she sang before the temple door, her voice soared to operatic heights. Each note burned like the cry of an angel, rising above even the crackling energy blasts from Vesper and the voïvode, and the shriek of the other voïvode's cutting tool.

Irina's voice swirled and changed with inhuman agility. It ululated and quavered, shifting tones and keys and pitches so fast that it seemed as if she were singing with two or three voices at once instead of just one.

Still, MacNeal couldn't see what she hoped to accomplish…at first. But as moments passed, and her Liturgy grew wilder and more complex, he did notice a change. The metal of the door began to ripple; it started slowly, then sped up, rolling through the great silver panels like shivers through mercury.

Irina closed her eyes and sang harder, offering up wave after wave of skirling, piercing tones. Just when it seemed she couldn't hit a higher pitch, she climbed to another key. Just when it seemed she couldn't get any louder, she poured out more power and boosted the volume.

Brown clamped his hands over his ears. MacNeal tried not to do the same, but didn't hold out much longer. The Liturgy filled him to the point of bursting; he covered his ears, and still it pumped into his head unabated.

Finally, Irina struck the highest note yet, a silver needle of a note that spiraled upward with unfailing ferocity. She held it without breaking for what seemed like a very long moment; where she was getting the breath to sustain it, MacNeal couldn't guess.

Then, suddenly, the great door to the temple split open along the seam cut by the voïvodes. The gleaming metal peeled apart, puckering like lips from left to right. The top and bottom halves rolled open further, curling like wet paper in the sun. When Irina finally cut off that last keening note, and the metal stopped warping, the opening was big enough for men to fit through without bending over.

Irina slumped like a puppet with cut strings. MacNeal darted over to catch her, and she fell into his arms.

She gazed up at him with amusement in her glittering blue eyes. "Well?" She raised her eyebrows. "Do I not at least deserve a round of applause?"

MacNeal smiled. The two of them had a history, and a boatload of differences…but he couldn't help being impressed with her work. Maybe he hadn't been giving her enough credit. Maybe her intentions were better than he'd thought. "Hell of a performance, Irina. Thanks for the extra push."

"A higher percentage of the prize will be gratitude enough, John."
She pushed away and stood up straight. *So much for good intentions.*
"Now let us go get it before someone takes it away from all of us."

* * *

The ground rumbled so hard it nearly knocked Taki off his feet.
He flailed his arms, fighting to regain his balance; when he had
it again, he continued chasing Wolf toward the black and crystal
structure.

They weren't far from it now. Wolf was less than a quarter-mile
from the gleaming cubes and spheres of its walls. Taki, in turn, was
fifty yards back from Wolf.

Determined to catch up, Taki redoubled his efforts. Arms and
legs churning like propellers, he closed some of the distance between
him and Wolf, then closed some more. If he could just run a little
faster, maybe...

Wolf fiddled with something on his belt as he ran. Suddenly, a
rectangular slab of the ebony cube directly ahead shot downward,
leaving an open doorway in Wolf's path.

He was nearly upon it. Would he leave it open once he got
through? Taki wasn't willing to bet on it.

Grabbing the jitte from its scabbard on his belt, he flicked it back
and hurled it forward, aiming for Wolf's head. But the running
throw didn't connect as hoped; it missed Wolf's head and clipped
his shoulder, bouncing off as he kept running.

Wolf was only yards away from the doorway now. Focusing all his
strength on one last sprint, Taki hurtled toward him.

The distance between them shrank...but the distance between
Wolf and the doorway shrank faster. He bolted through and disappeared inside the cube, leaving Taki outside.

As Taki had predicted, the door shot up and closed as soon as
Wolf had passed through it. When Taki reached it, the entrance was
sealed tight; the surface was so smooth, he couldn't even tell where
the seam had been.

He pounded his fists on it and cried out in rage and frustration.
Then, he took a deep breath and turned away, determined to find
another door elsewhere.

As soon as he walked away, though, the door flew open again. He heard the whooshing sound of the panel sliding downward, and he spun toward it.

Without questioning why it had reopened, Taki charged through it, running inside before it had a chance to slide shut again.

* * *

Hiruko stood there beside the frame, still supporting Nadia, and watched as Dr. Kondo pushed buttons and spun dials on the mysterious device. Indicator lights flashed to life—little bright green bulbs scattered over the control panels. The device emitted a low hum, like the buzz of an electrical generator.

Kondo moved fast, popping open a panel and tugging out a pair of black cables with clamps on the end. As he rushed over with the clamps, the cables fed from inside the device behind him. When he reached the framework, he squeezed in front of Hiruko and Nadia and clamped one cable to the right edge; then he pushed in front of Von Heïzinger and clamped the other cable to the left edge. Von Heïzinger glared, but Kondo ignored him and scurried back over to his device.

Von Heïzinger watched Kondo as he went. Hiruko thought he might do something to the scientist…but then he simply cleared his throat and turned to Nadia. "You are an astral traveler. You have experienced many worlds in your astral form." He gestured at the sparking, milky skin within the framework. "But you have never seen the Superior Realms, have you? You have never seen Heaven?"

"I've been in *hell* ever since you kidnapped me, but no." Nadia shook her head slowly. "I haven't seen Heaven."

Von Heïzinger nodded and smiled, showing his grey teeth and purple gums. "Would it surprise you to learn you are standing on an intersection of the Axis Mundi, specifically a bridge from the material to the Superior Realms? Earth and the Superior Realms coexist here."

"You've found a back door into Heaven because they'll never let you in otherwise," said Nadia. "Is that it?"

"I'm glad you're here, *liebchen.*" Von Heïzinger's smile was like the smile on a dead man's face: devoid of any emotion. "After all, you started me down this road long ago. It's only right that you share my crowning glory."

"Go to Hell." Nadia snapped out the words. "Or Heaven. I don't care. But leave me out of it."

The hum from Kondo's device intensified, distracting Hiruko. There was another noise, too—a loud hiss—followed by a sound like turning gears. Hiruko couldn't help looking over to see what was happening.

The glossy black dome on one end of the device was sliding out of sight. It rotated into a semi-circular slot, revealing a bunch of spiky silver antennae sticking out of a hole where the dome had been.

As Kondo pulled down a lever under the hole, the bunch of antennae pushed forward and fanned out. Clicking and clacking, the spiky antennae unfolded, expanding like a slow-motion umbrella without canvas between the spines. When the antennae were done moving, they'd formed a skeletal dish four feet in diameter, pointing directly at the framework.

Kondo flipped a series of switches, and the tubes on top of the device flared to life, glowing with bright purple light. He spun a knob, and the hum began to oscillate, alternately turning stronger and weaker.

Suddenly, Von Heïzinger shouted at Kondo at the top of his lungs, making Hiruko jump. "Do you *mind*?"

Kondo looked up briefly without reacting, then fished a pair of black-tinted goggles out of his lab coat pocket. As he pulled them on, he turned his back on Von Heïzinger.

"You are *disrupting* history in the *making*!" Von Heïzinger's voice had a vicious edge. Hiruko thought he was about to see Kondo being slaughtered in cold blood.

That was when the Daimyō spoke up again. "Leave him alone!" He'd been off at the edge of the dais, giving orders to the men who'd carried up the device. Now, he was rushing back with his long katana drawn. "Mind your own business!"

"How *can* I with all that *racket*?" Von Heïzinger gestured angrily in Kondo's direction. "If you know what's good for you, you'll tell him to turn that thing off!"

Kondo turned and the Daimyō slashed his sword through the air. "Keep working! Don't listen to a word that corpse of a German says!"

Kondo returned to his controls. The oscillating hum fluctuated faster, and the antennae crackled as a web of glittering golden energy surrounded it.

"Don't say I didn't warn you!" said Von Heïzinger.

"Go to hell." The Daimyō sneered and whipped his sword back into its scabbard with a flourish. "Your role in this is over. Be grateful I allow you to bear witness to the *true* shape of history in the making."

Von Heïzinger said nothing in reply.

"Daimyō!" Kondo called out from the controls of the device. "I am nearly ready to open the link."

"Then do it," said the Daimyō. "As soon as you are ready, let the purification begin."

"I hope," Kondo said over the noise. Kondo turned a dial, checked a gauge, and pressed a series of buttons. The glowing tubes atop the device changed from purple to blood-red crimson. "If I can purify this instrumentation, there will be much glory ahead for the Shōgunate."

"It *will* work!" said the Daimyō. "The angel was a sign of our assured success."

Suddenly, a loud *crack* split the air inside the temple. At first, Hiruko thought it had come from the device, which was already making so much noise. But then he heard the sound again, and realized it hadn't been made by the device or the framework or anyone on the dais. Because he recognized it as a very familiar noise, one that had come to be part of his daily life.

It was a gunshot.

* * *

Cakewalk. That was what MacNeal had dared to hope for when he'd charged into the temple.

After scrambling through the opening in the door, he'd led the 42nd down a long passageway, followed by the New Guard and Bogatyrs. The passageway had been deserted, which he'd taken for a good sign.

Even when they'd emerged into the big open heart of the temple, things had looked promising. There hadn't been an enemy soldier in sight.

But then, the situation had changed. Shōgunate soldiers had

appeared, marching out around either side of a great lava moat. As soon as MacNeal had spotted them, they'd caught sight of him and the rest of his unit.

So much for the cakewalk. The 42nd and their allies were out in the open with no good cover nearby, completely exposed. There was only one viable option that might keep them alive long enough to reach the objective.

That was why, without hesitation, MacNeal swung up his flash-gun and pulled the trigger. A high-powered round blasted into one of the Shōgunate men, catching him in the chest.

As the man went down, MacNeal cranked a round into another Shōgunate soldier, right through the forehead. The soldier spun into the man next to him, knocking him down.

That was enough to give the 42nd and the Russians a fighting chance. Now all they had to do was keep up the offensive.

Which they did, automatically, without a word or gesture from MacNeal. Brown unleashed his flash machine gun, scattering the soldiers with a flurry of rounds. Oksana sent the voïvodes skitter-ing forward and laid down crackling energy blasts with her Vesper scepter. Tatiana fired shots from her pair of sawed-off shotguns while Irina followed closely with her double-barreled Nagant revolver, and Beaudreau picked off men with his sniper rifle.

The Shōgunate men returned fire and tried to regroup, but they couldn't pull together. A stone stairway leading up to a huge dais split their forces, preventing them from massing for a proper coun-terattack. MacNeal pressed the advantage, pushing forward while pumping off rounds alongside Brown, Oksana, and Tatiana.

More Shōgunate men fell, and then the rest finally pulled back. As the last of them retreated around the moat, MacNeal continued forward, heading for the stone stairs. They arched up over the lava and connected to the surface of the dais, which was elevated ten feet overhead.

Looking up from below, MacNeal couldn't see much of what was happening up there, but he knew it was where he needed to be.

CHAPTER 35

Kamchatka
19 April 1952
2319 Hours

When Taki entered the temple, Wolf was nowhere in sight. The outer door, which had shut briefly after Wolf's entry, had delayed Taki just long enough to give Wolf a chance to elude him.

Not that Taki was alone, however. Once he'd sprinted through the door in the side of the temple, he came face to face with a Shōgunate soldier.

The soldier swung his rifle around and opened his mouth to shout at the same time. Before he could shoot or call out, Taki leapt into action.

Snatching a tonfa from the strap on his right thigh, Taki swept it around, wrenching the rifle barrel hard to one side. He followed that with a chop to the man's throat, catching his call before it could escape. Then he kneed him in the belly, making him double over.

Keeping the rifle pushed aside with the tonfa, Taki latched his other hand on the gun and tore it out of the soldier's grip. The man lurched forward, trying to throw his weight into Taki, but Taki sidestepped. The soldier flew to the ground, where Taki clocked him in the head with the rifle butt, rendering him unconscious.

Taking a quick look around, Taki saw that the rest of the Shōgunate unit was in the temple, but no one was looking in his direction. Everyone's attention was focused on an elevated dais inside a lava moat in the middle of the temple. The lone soldier he'd encountered must have been patrolling the perimeter, or maybe he'd wandered off to relieve himself.

Whatever the man's reason for being there, he'd given Taki an opportunity. His uniform looked like it would fit Taki just fine.

Which was a good thing, because he was guessing he had to go through those Shōgunate troops to find Wolf…and get to Tala. Whatever was drawing everyone's attention, it must be important enough for Taki to get a closer look.

Maybe it was the so-called raven god. Maybe Kutkha was already there…in which case, Tala would be there with him.

The volcano rumbled, and the ground shook underfoot. Taki grabbed the soldier's ankles and pulled him back into the recess around the doorway. Then, mostly hidden from the eyes of the Shōgunate troops, who were all looking the other way anyway, he set about stripping the soldier out of his uniform and putting it on himself.

* * *

Hiruko watched as a soldier hurried over from the edge of the dais and rattled off a report to the Daimyō. Hiruko couldn't hear a word over the hum and crackle of the device, but the Daimyō took it all in and nodded. Then, he ran to the edge and leaned over to have a look down. He quickly withdrew and ran to the opposite edge, where he shouted orders to his men on the floor of the volcano.

This time, Hiruko heard what he said. He called for Itami and a squad of men to set up a cordon on the dais, and he ordered the rest to defend the dais from below. Itami was the first one up, but he moved sluggishly, as if he were dead on his feet; this close to the heavenly power, he was weaker than ever. As soon as he topped the last step, he slumped to his knees, then collapsed on the dais. Shōgunate soldiers had to crawl over him and drag him to one side to clear the way for the others.

Meanwhile, the Daimyō rushed over to Von Heïzinger. "The Union and Matriarchy forces have arrived." The Daimyō raised his voice over the noise from the device. "They've already killed some of my men."

"So I heard." Von Heïzinger smirked when he said it. "That MacNeal. Always so reliable."

"My forces are moving to quell the threat," said the Daimyō. "Still, perhaps we should continue our research when things have quieted down."

Just then, the oscillating hum from the device became a piercing whine. The glow of the tubes on top of it switched from crimson to bright white.

"Too late." Von Heïzinger shrugged.

"Daimyō!" Kondo shouted over the noise. "This it it! The link is opening! The purification of the device is about to begin!"

More shots were fired. The Daimyō turned toward them, then scowled. "We should wait." He marched over to the device. "Shut it down, Kondo."

"But Daimyō!" Kondo looked frantic behind his smoked goggles. "We could damage the refacsimilator!"

"Which will be no use to us if the damned Union and Matriarchy storm this dais." The Daimyō chopped his hand through the air. "Now shut your mouth and shut it down!"

Kondo shook his head emphatically. "You don't understand!" The whine was increasing, forcing him to shout ever louder. "The feedback could…"

Angrily, the Daimyō lunged at the control panel on the side of the device and started hitting buttons. "Enough! If *you* won't shut this down, then *I* will!"

Suddenly, a shot rang out, so close it made Hiruko's ears ring. A round blasted into the Daimyō's left shoulder, spinning him away from the controls.

Hiruko looked down and saw the Walther P38 pistol in Von Heïzinger's hand, the smoking barrel pointed at the Daimyō. Hiruko was stunned; he hadn't even seen Von Heïzinger draw the weapon.

"Don't you dare." As Von Heïzinger said it, he fired another shot. This one blew into the Daimyō's right thigh. "This research stops for *no one*."

* * *

MacNeal headed for the stone steps, planning to run up to the dais…but he didn't get far. Just as his foot touched the first step, he heard the sounds of movement from above. Looking up, he saw a line of Shōgunate rifles poking over the edge of the dais, pointing down at him and his team. The Shōgunate soldiers manning the guns were lying on their bellies, presenting as low a profile as they could.

But it wasn't low enough. Someone behind MacNeal got off a shot, and it was a good one. A nearby enemy shooter went limp, and his rifle clattered down and splashed into the lava moat.

MacNeal followed that by cranking out suppressor fire with his flash-gun. If he couldn't get a clean shot at the prone shooters from where he was standing, at least he could keep them from shooting, maybe even push them back.

Brown joined in with his flash machine gun, pouring out a squall of his own, and other shots flowed up from the rest of the unit. As wave after wave washed over the ledge of the dais, Beaudreau used the screen of high-powered rounds to calmly sight in on the Shōgunate snipers and pick them off one by one.

Not that the snipers didn't claim a body count of their own. MacNeal heard a man's scream behind him as someone took a round. The same thing happened two more times as the unit's numbers dwindled.

But the Shōgunate snipers were thinning out faster, by far. Soon, there were only a handful left and none near the stairs, that MacNeal could see. Taking a deep breath and keeping his head down, he put his foot back on the first step and started climbing slowly toward the surface of the dais.

* * *

"*Why?*" The Daimyō sat on the ground, holding his shoulder and thigh where he'd been shot. Sweat stood out on his brow as he glared up at Von Heïzinger. "Why did you *shoot* me?" The whine of the device nearly drowned out his voice.

"Because you sicken me." Von Heïzinger sneered. "And it was the quickest way to stop you."

The Daimyō sucked in his breath and winced at the pain. Hiruko felt an impulse to go to his aid, but thought better of it. He feared that Von Heïzinger might shoot him too if he did.

"But I thought you *wanted* the device shut down," the Daimyō said between gasps of pain.

"You only thought that," said Von Heïzinger, "because I *wanted* you to. *This* was my intention from the start." He gestured at the framework, the clamps on its sides, the cables leading to the device. "Now, finally, the stage is set."

"Shut it down, Kondo!" The Daimyō shouted the words over his shoulder. "Hurry!"

"I already *told* you," said Kondo. "The feedback…"

"The hell with the feedback!" Gritting his teeth, the Daimyō struggled to his knees. "Just do it!"

"All right, all right!" Hunching over behind the device, Kondo started flipping switches on the control panel. As long as he stayed down, the device would block Von Heïzinger's view and any shots from his Walther P38. "I'm doing it!"

Forcing himself up to his feet, the Daimyō drew *Dyuaru-Kontan* and stood between Von Heïzinger and Kondo. "You think I'm no threat anymore? Just *try* getting past me!"

Von Heïzinger said nothing. Instead, he jammed two fingers between his pale lips, threw his head back, and let loose the shrillest, loudest whistle Hiruko had ever heard.

The volcano rumbled as if in reply. *What next?* Hiruko wondered, looking around. *What could possibly happen next?*

* * *

Taki took up position along the lava moat with the Shōgunate soldiers. So far, he was doing a good job of blending in; he made it a point not to meet anyone's gaze or to do anything attention-getting.

There was still heavy fire on the opposite side of the dais, which he guessed involved MacNeal. Taki wanted to race over there and do his part against the Shōgunate…but he didn't dare. In his disguise as a Shōgunate soldier, he'd been ordered, along with the other men, to protect the access points on that side of the dais. Breaking ranks might get him shot.

But then there was a shrill whistle from above, and the situation changed. The Reich contingent had been standing off to one side, silently staying out of the way. When they heard the whistle, they all perked up at once—the Stosstruppen, the two Schocktruppen, and Zermann.

Immediately, the Stosstruppen and Schocktruppen charged through the Shōgunate troops toward the stairway leading up to the dais. Zermann stayed behind, rubbing the sides of his head; he looked woozy and sick.

Then, some kind of green light flickered over his face, and he shook his head hard and roared. His glowing scars flared from within as he ran, bolting past the Stosstruppen and Schocktruppen and taking the stairs two at a time on his way to the dais.

Taki saw his chance to move and took it. While everyone was staring in confusion after the Reich's nightmare warriors, Taki broke from the defense line and darted up the stairs himself.

He'd called it perfectly: no one shot him on the way up.

* * *

Hiruko saw the danger before Kondo and the Daimyō knew it was there, but he didn't warn them. How could he? Opening his mouth would have gotten him killed, he was sure of it.

So he watched with horror as Zermann lurched across the dais toward them, followed by the Stosstruppen and Schocktruppen.

Von Heïzinger saw them too, of course—he'd whistled for them. When they were close, he whipped the glove from his right hand, revealing a glowing emerald ring on his index finger. Rays of bright green light streamed out from the ring and played over the faces of his approaching nightmare squad. As the light touched them, they seemed instantly energized and picked up their pace; Zermann straightened, and his scars glowed brighter.

The Daimyō looked over his shoulder, following the rays of light to their targets. Von Heïzinger jabbed a bony index finger toward Kondo while drawing the side of his hand across his neck in a slicing gesture. The meaning was clear.

Raising Doom, Zermann pointed the pistol at the scientist and pulled the trigger. A single glowing round flashed toward Kondo, leaving a trail of light as it swerved *around* the device.

The Daimyō called Kondo's name, telling him to duck, but it was too late. The bullet punched through Kondo's left temple and exited through the right. Then, it turned in midair and doubled back, this time plunging into his heart and staying there.

Kondo lurched backward and dropped to the ground, motionless. His eyes were frozen open, staring in Hiruko's direction.

The Daimyō raised his katana overhead and charged the nightmare squad, disregarding his wounded thigh. Von Heïzinger pointed at him and called out to his creatures, "Subdue him!"

The words had barely left his mouth when the Stosstruppen leaped at the Daimyō, kicking *Dyuaru-Kontan* from his grip. The Daimyō pulled out *Hoka-Kontan* and managed one slice across the Stosstruppen's chest…but the Stosstruppen grabbed his wrist on the follow-through and twisted it hard, forcing him to drop the blade. Before the Daimyō could erupt in hand-to-hand combat, the Stosstruppen swept around him with unearthly speed and wrapped his arms about him in a powerful hold.

"How?" The Daimyō forced the words out through clenched teeth as he struggled to break free. "How could your creatures attack like this? How could Doom strike a target? The heavenly power—"

"—can be countered by *this*." Von Heïzinger shook his fist, the emerald ring flashing on his finger. "The Eye of Tages restores the health of those I choose! Its power is limited and can only be used infrequently…but aren't you glad I saved it until now?"

Von Heïzinger turned back to the framework. Kondo hadn't managed to shut down the device before his death; it was still emitting a screaming whine, and it was having an effect.

The milky skin within the framework was turning silver, and the electrical arcs dancing over it were building in intensity.

"*Now* then." Von Heïzinger put an arm around Nadia's shoulders and gave her a squeeze. "Where were we?"

CHAPTER 36

Kamchatka
19 April 1952
2335 Hours

MacNeal made it up the stairs and onto the dais in time to see Zermann kill the scientist in the white lab coat. Then, he saw Von Heïzinger's feral Stosstruppen disarm and capture Iroh Minamoto.

Apparently, the Reich and Shōgunate alliance was a thing of the past.

Crouching down, MacNeal took a moment to observe and evaluate. Von Heïzinger was standing in the middle of the dais a good fifty yards away in front of some kind of frame with a mirror-like surface. Cables ran from the frame to a device that was putting out a piercing whine and a nimbus of white light.

Near the device, the Stosstruppen had Iroh imprisoned in a tight hold, arms pinned against his sides. Zermann and the Schocktruppen protected Von Heïzinger with weapons raised.

Then there were the Shōgunate troops who ringed the dais, except for the section where MacNeal had come up. They seemed to be at a loss, perhaps because their commander had been subdued.

No one was rushing over to plug the hole in the ring opened up by the 42nd and its allies. No one was rushing to help Iroh, either…for the moment, at least.

It was the calm before the storm. Everything was suspended on the brink, awaiting the signal to swirl into chaos. Anything could still happen; anyone could turn the tide.

He had been here so very many times before.

The volcano rumbled as MacNeal pulled the spent clip from his flash-gun and jammed in a fresh one. He knew exactly where he was going to go, and what he had to do.

Obviously, the silvery frame was the objective of Von Heïzinger's quest. The device was doing something to it, or drawing something from it.

The fact that Von Heïzinger was anywhere near that frame and device—and had come so far and gone to such trouble to reach it—told MacNeal everything he needed to know. One way or another, he had to stop Von Heïzinger.

If he lived long enough to do it, that is. Just as MacNeal rose and took three steps forward, a sudden movement sparked his attention from the corner of his eye. Whipping around, he saw a Shōgunate soldier running toward him with rifle raised, aiming in his direction.

Instinctively, MacNeal swung up his flash-gun and curled his finger around the trigger. Before he could squeeze it, however, the soldier called out to him.

In perfect English with an American accent and a very familiar voice. "Major, get down!"

MacNeal did not hesitate to fling himself to the ground. Gunfire slashed past overhead, before he'd even finished his fall. Somewhere behind him, a man cried out, and then a body thudded to the surface of the dais.

MacNeal looked back to see a Shōgunate soldier lying on his side, not twenty feet away. Blood gushed from a hole in the middle of his forehead, dripping onto the black rock underneath him.

"Are you all right, Major?" There was that familiar voice again, the voice of the man who'd saved MacNeal's life.

MacNeal looked up and grinned. "Nice shooting, Taki."

Taki didn't smile as he reached down to help him up. "Thank you,

Major. It's not a regulation weapon—I took it from a Shōgunate man—but I guess it still did the trick."

Suddenly, another shot rang out. A bullet passed close enough for MacNeal to hear it hissing through the air.

He and Taki both swung toward the shooter—another soldier approaching from the perimeter—but neither got off a shot. This time, a bolt of searing blue energy leaped out from behind them, lashing at the soldier like a tongue of divine flame. The energy lit him up, sending him into a paroxysm of jittering spasms…and then it cut off, and he slumped to the ground like a pile of clothes without a man inside.

"Oksana!" MacNeal looked back to see her marching his way from the top of the stairs with the Vesper scepter in hand. Brown, Tatiana, Gol, Irina, and the rest were not far behind.

"Are we too late, MacNeal?" A look of cold intensity burned on Oksana's features as her gaze zeroed in on Von Heïzinger and the framework.

"We're about to find out." He was well aware that other Shōgunate men were becoming interested in his team and drifting toward him from their positions along the edge of the dais.

Just then, Irina swept between him and Oksana with a knowing smirk. "You were not thinking of cutting me out of my share of the objective, were you?"

MacNeal shook his head once and pushed past her, watching the Shōgunate soldiers size up his team. "It never crossed my mind."

At that instant, Taki shouted a single word and stormed past MacNeal, pointing up at something in the heights of the temple.

He shouted the word again as MacNeal followed his gaze. "Tala!"

Sure enough, it was Tala. Even from a distance, MacNeal could see her familiar form and trademark long, black hair. He could also see that she was dangling from the clawed foot of a giant raven.

"Kutkha!" Gol sounded terrified when he said the name. A moment later, he ran for the stairs and was gone.

Kutkha glided down from a wide open window in the temple ceiling. The bird-creature's wings were fully extended, spread wide to carry him along the thermal currents from the lava moats and pools. He carried Tala in one claw, and in the other, he held a dark-haired man in a black uniform, a man who looked more familiar the closer he came.

"*Wolf?*" When MacNeal said it, Taki nodded without taking his eyes off Tala long enough to look back.

"He's the raven's partner." As Taki said it, he cocked the rifle in his hand. "I followed him in here."

"The bird is coming down," said Ivan. "Coming down *fast.*"

He was right. As MacNeal watched, Kutkha soared in a spiral, picking up speed as he lost altitude. His target was obvious and mere moments away.

Without another word, Taki started running toward the framework…and Von Heïzinger and his henchmen. The Shōgunate soldiers watched him go but didn't lift a finger to stop him; after all, he was wearing the same uniform that they were. Maybe they thought he was one of them.

And maybe they thought, instead of running toward Tala, that he was running away from MacNeal and the others. Because as Taki started running, the soldiers started shooting at MacNeal and his allies.

* * *

The whine from the device had gotten so loud, Hiruko thought it would break his eardrums. The cluster of antennae on the end of the device shot off sparks, and the twin cables hooked to the framework glowed bright cherry red.

Something was about to happen. Something *big.*

And Von Heïzinger was at the heart of it all. "*Look.*" He still had an arm around Nadia's shoulders and jerked her forward. "What do you see?"

Hiruko watched as Nadia stared into the framework. The interior had once been milky white, with dancing arcs of electrical current. Then it had turned silver like mercury. Now, the silver was breaking apart, yielding to a swirling, pearlescent mist.

"Tell me," snapped Von Heïzinger. "What do you *see?*"

Nadia breathed slowly as she frowned into the swirling mist. "Angels with harps."

"Try again." Von Heïzinger shook her roughly. "The *truth* this time."

"All right, all right." Nadia's eyes were fixed on the light. "I see…shapes." Slowly, she tipped her head to one side. "Amorphous shapes…drifting through the mist." This time, when she moved closer, she did it without a push from Von Heïzinger. "I can't tell what they are."

"*Yet*," said Von Heïzinger. "Not *yet*, perhaps. But very *soon*."

Hiruko stared into the mist over Nadia's shoulder, straining to see the shapes she was talking about. At first, all he could see was mist and more mist, swirling through the frame.

Then, suddenly, he saw what looked like a shadow in there. It moved through the upper third of the frame, dimly visible and poorly defined. But for a split second, part of it came almost into focus... just a piece, just one little segment...

And it didn't look human.

Hiruko shivered, and the hairs on the back of his neck jumped to attention. Catching that glimpse had been startling...yet he couldn't look away. He just kept staring as the thing in the mist shifted back out of focus again. And then he saw it.

An *eye* was staring back at him.

A wave of nausea coursed through him, and he stumbled back away from the frame. Finally, he was able to tear his eyes from the view inside it...but he couldn't get the image of that *eye* out of his mind.

Because it hadn't looked human.

Hiruko took another step back.

Meanwhile, Von Heïzinger was still talking over the whine of the device. "We are almost there, dear Nadia. The window is almost *open*."

"*You* are almost there, you mean." Nadia, with a burst of energy, pushed out from under his arm. "I'm leaving, Hermann. I'm done. I've seen enough."

"You're not done yet, *liebchen*." Von Heïzinger grabbed her upper arm. "You're just getting started."

Hiruko shook off his state of shock and moved to help Nadia. It was then that he heard the beating of giant wings and looked up. The bird-thing was there—the one he'd been trapped with; it held a dark-haired, dark-clad soldier in one claw and a black-haired woman in the other.

Hiruko had barely caught sight of the bird-thing when the soldier dropped from its claw. Hiruko ducked back out of the way as the man landed in front of him with a rifle pointed in his direction.

Hiruko threw his hands in the air. He wasn't a coward, but he wasn't sure what exactly was happening, either.

The soldier charged past him without a word, headed straight for Zermann. Meanwhile, Hiruko heard the giant wings getting closer and whipped around. The bird-thing held on to the woman with both claws and angled its wings back, pitching into a dive. Hiruko could see the bird was about to collide with Von Heïzinger...and anyone standing close to him.

In other words, Nadia was in danger.

Leaping into action, Hiruko lunged at Nadia and grabbed her around the waist. He wrenched her free of Von Heïzinger's grasp, spun her around, and carried her away from the framework.

He was just in time. As soon as he and Nadia were clear, the bird-thing swooped down, let go of the woman, and plowed into Von Heïzinger, knocking him to the ground.

As Von Heïzinger fell, the woman landed on her feet. She had to run a few steps before she could stop and catch her balance, but then she was fine.

Meanwhile, the dark-clad soldier was holding Zermann at bay by sprinkling clear liquid from a silver flask on him. As he sprinkled the liquid, which might have been acid—it burned on contact—the soldier filled the Schocktruppen with rounds from his rifle. One of the Schocktruppen twisted and went down screaming behind his death's head faceplate, followed by the other...and the soldier kept shooting, making sure they were dead.

While this was happening, the Daimyō struggled with renewed strength against the Stosstruppen, but still couldn't break free. Hauling up his uninjured left leg, the Daimyō kicked it back hard into the Stosstruppen's shin and finally got a reaction. The feral beast's leg buckled, and his hold weakened enough for the Daimyō to escape.

The Daimyō dove after his katana on the ground. His fingers almost touched the handle...and then the Stosstruppen dragged him away by the ankles. The bestial soldier wrenched him back from the blade, then pounced on him, bashing his head against the ground. The Daimyō slumped, unconscious, as the Stosstruppen raised his claws for a final slash at his throat.

At that exact instant, Hiruko heard a bellowing roar and saw a hulking blue figure hurtle across the dais. *Itami.*

The sapphire giant looked awful as he charged at the Stosstruppen, holding his kenabō club high. Without the healing rays of Von

Heïzinger's Eye of Tages, he was literally burning from the effect of
the heavenly portal's power. His blue skin was blistered and cracked,
his white horns charred soot-black.

But like a steaming freight train, he kept coming, driven by some
deep wellspring of indomitable willpower to rescue the Daimyō.
Roaring again, he covered the last remaining distance in one leap,
swinging the kenabō as he landed.

The blow swept the Stosstruppen off the Daimyō's back, sending him flying into the side of the device. He sprang up fast; now
that the Eye of Tages had negated the effects of the portal, he
seemed to have regained his intimidating immunity to pain and
his supernatural strength.

Howling with rage, the Stosstruppen hurled itself at Itami. The
feral beast ducked Itami's next swing with the kenabō and slashed
wildly with his claws. Normally, the claws would have barely
scratched Itami, but this time, as he remained under the portal's
influence, they opened gashes in his torso.

Itami stumbled back, shaking his head as if struggling to clear it.
The Stosstruppen pressed his advantage, raking Itami's chest, drawing more sapphire blood. He pulled his claws back for another strike,
this time aiming at the throat...

That was when Itami gathered himself up and unleashed a mighty
swat. The Stosstruppen shot to the ground at his feet.

And Itami stomped on him. He brought a foot down on the
Stosstruppen's belly with crushing force, bursting it like a balloon.

The Stosstruppen was as good as dead, but kept squirming...at
least until Itami smashed his skull with the kenabō.

Then, it was like the last of the fight had gone out of Itami. He
teetered over the body for a moment, and then he wobbled backward, holding up the kenabō to shield his face from the power of
the portal.

As Itami stumbled away from the framework, the whine from the
device kept building. The volcano rumbled constantly, as if in tune
with the piercing noise. Gunshots crackled from a firefight on the
other side of the dais.

Von Heïzinger scrambled up from the ground, pointing his
Walther P38 at the bird-thing, which was now standing in front
of him. He was fast enough to get off a shot, but it missed, and he

didn't get a second chance. Before Von Heïzinger could squeeze the trigger again, the bird-thing swatted the gun away with one sweep of his giant wing. Then, he whipped the wing back along its arc to bash Von Heïzinger's upper body, sending him crashing to the ground.

At that point, Zermann howled in agony. Turning, Hiruko saw the soldier splashing the rest of the acid-like liquid over Zermann's face and chest. Plumes of smoke curled up from his burning flesh as the substance cooked him alive.

As Zermann fell and tossed back and forth on the ground, the soldier raised the silver flask to his lips and took a drink. Hiruko winced...but the soldier didn't burn.

Because the liquid wasn't acid. "Wish I had more joy juice for you, demon," said the soldier as he pocketed the flask. "But it's hell finding true blue holy water these days."

Just then, the bird-thing threw back his head, opened his beak, and cried out, his keening shriek rising above the cacophony in the volcano. When he was done and lowered his head, the beak melted away, receding into the form of human lips. His entire face changed shape, shifting from the features of a giant bird to those of a man with short, dark hair and coppery skin.

The rest of his body transformed, too. His wings became human arms, and his chest and torso and legs became those of a man. He was covered in what looked like densely layered black tattoos, swirling in constant motion over his flesh.

When he spoke, his voice was a high-pitched tenor, and his words were in English, which Hiruko understood. "Shaman! It is time!"

The black-haired woman joined him at the framework, sparing a glance at Hiruko and Nadia along the way. "All right, Kutkha. What do you want me to do?"

"Pull out your medicine bag." The bird-thing called Kutkha cranked his hand in a circle, gesturing for her to hurry. "Pray and perform a ritual of opening for this doorway." He squinted as he gazed into the drifting mist within the framework. He reached toward it, nearly touching it with his fingertips...and tiny wisps curled out of the shimmering surface to caress each one.

The shaman looked like she was about to say something but thought better of it. She dug into her pants pocket and came up with a dark brown leather pouch.

She opened the pouch's drawstring and dipped in her finger and thumb. As she fished through the contents, she looked into the mist inside the framework and frowned. "You're sure this will work? You'll get back what you love most? What the Koryaks took away from you?"

Kutkha smiled at her. "I have planned very carefully for this moment. So has Wolf." He pointed at the dark-haired soldier. "He and I lured the various factions here, and they have played their parts. Without Von Heïzinger's mystical *Orbis Christus*, working in concert with the Shōgunate's machine, the door would not now be open a crack." His reached out and ran a finger along her jawline, stopping at her chin to tip her head back slightly. "Now your ritual—your *faith*—will open it the rest of the way. You are the *key*, remember?"

"I remember," said the shaman.

"Then the answer is yes. I am sure this will work." With that, Kutkha let go of her chin.

The shaman took a deep breath, let it out slowly, and closed her eyes. She pulled a small white feather out of her pouch, held it in front of the mist, and began to chant in a language Hiruko didn't recognize.

Almost imperceptibly, the mist began to swirl faster. So did the black tattoos on Kutkha's skin.

CHAPTER 37

Kamchatka
19 April 1952
2354 Hours

As Taki charged toward the framework, MacNeal and the others got bogged down under fire. Shōgunate soldiers converged on them from the rim of the dais, filling the air with rifle rounds.

MacNeal's team formed a back-to-back semi-circle, all shooting in different directions. Together, they were keeping the soldiers at bay, knocking down one after another without taking casualties. But they still couldn't run after Taki without breaking formation.

It wouldn't take long to clear out the worst resistance, especially with Brown's flash machine gun blasting away. They would move out then, but in the meantime, Taki was on his own. For precious moments, he would be without backup while facing a godlike creature...and Wolf. If only there was a way to speed things up.

"Irina!" MacNeal had to shout to be heard over the gunfire. "How about a Liturgy for these guys?"

Irina shouted back. "There is a lot of noise up here, MacNeal. It could interfere with the...signal." She cleared her throat. "But I will try."

With that, she started singing, Russian words with a carefully modulated tune. She sang higher and louder with each moment, weaving elaborate patterns very different from those she'd sung to bring down the temple door.

And the whole time, she never stopped shooting her double-barreled Nagant unless she needed to reload.

* * *

Tala chanted in Navajo, reciting a ritual her grandfather had taught her. It was meant to close off the past and make new beginnings possible—the closest she could come to a ritual of opening.

Even as she chanted and held up items from her medicine bag—a white feather, a striped pebble, a piece of burnt wood—she wondered if it would work. Even standing there with an incarnation of Raven beside her and what might be a heavenly gateway in front of her, she had her doubts that any of it was true magic and could be influenced by her skills.

Then, she felt it: a tingling in her fingers, spreading into her hands and arms. Soon, her whole body was tingling, a sensation like pins and needles.

The mist in the framework swirled faster and glowed brighter. It corkscrewed to a central point that slowly reached out toward her from inside the frame.

Eyes wide, she tried to step back, but Kutkha stopped her. "Almost there," he whispered in her ear, nudging her forward. "Don't stop now."

Tala swallowed hard and resumed the ritual. She pulled out a tiny bone from her medicine bag, cupped it in her palm, and continued chanting.

Suddenly, the tingling in her body changed to a chill so sharp it burned. The corkscrew of mist reached out farther, stretching and thickening—and then the end of it puffed up and flattened.

It was *taking shape*, she realized. It looked like a flattened disk on the end of a handle…or the head at the end of a snake.

Nervously, Tala kept chanting, and the mist kept changing. The edge of the disk sprouted growths like the stalks of a plant—four of them pushing straight out, and a fifth like a stump from the side. When they'd finished growing, they were instantly recognizable.

So Tala's magic had been enough to do the job after all. Because there, sticking out of the center of the frame, was a five-fingered hand and an arm made of mist. A *woman's* hand and arm, slender and tapered.

Suddenly, the whine from the device stopped. The only sound was the gunfire from the far edge of the dais, the rumble of the volcano…and Kutkha's voice. "Miti?" He said it softly, with a tone of abject joy and wonderment. "Is that you?"

The hand moved up and down in silent affirmation. It was transforming before Tala's eyes, changing from a thing of wispy mist to one of solid flesh and bone.

Kutkha eased Tala aside and reached for it. "It has been so long." His fingers twined with the fingers of the hand in the portal. "I've missed you so much." The two hands tightened their grip.

And then, a face pushed through the mist—the face of a beautiful, dark-eyed woman. "And I have missed *you*, my darling." She spoke a strange language, but somehow the words made sense in Tala's mind. "I have waited so *long* for you, my *husband*."

So this was what Kutkha had been trying to retrieve from Heaven, what the Koryaks had stolen away from him. This was the one thing—the one person—he loved more than anything in the world: his *wife*. After a thousand years, they were finally reunited.

"My love." Kutkha leaned forward and softly kissed Miti on the lips. "I have brought you back to me."

"We have another chance." Tears ran from her eyes. "It is more than I dared hope." Kutkha kissed the tears away.

Tala watched in amazement as the scene played out. Their faces radiated with powerful emotion. She wondered if she could ever love someone as deeply as the two of them clearly loved each other.

"You are almost through." Kutkha tugged on her hand, and her arm emerged from the mist up to her elbow. "Keep pushing, my love."

Miti's brows knitted in a frown. "It is slow going. Heaven has a hold on me."

Kutkha scowled. "But it shouldn't be *this* slow. Not for one person."

"Well…" Miti grinned sheepishly. "Did I mention there are *two*?"

"*What*?" Kutkha looked stunned. "There are *two*?"

Miti nodded. "I am bringing someone with me." She beamed as

she told him the rest. "Someone who loves you as much as *I* do. I could not *bear* to leave him behind."

Kutkha's face lit with rapturous joy. The black tattoos rippled and danced on his flesh. "Oh, my love! Oh, Miti! Oh, thank you!"

"He is right here with me." Miti nodded. "I am holding on to him with my other hand."

"Oh, Miti!" Kutkha kissed her on the lips and then each cheek and then the lips once more. "You have made this the happiest day in the last thousand years!"

Tala wiped away a tear of her own. She'd gotten caught up in the moment and couldn't help it.

Then, she heard the sound of a rifle being cocked and turned to see Taki taking aim at Kutkha.

* * *

Taki had Kutkha in his sights—no longer a giant bird, but unmistakably the so-called god he was after. From a distance, he'd seen him transform after swooping down with Tala and Wolf. Now, in the form of a man, he stood in front of the framework and talked to a woman in the mist. If he knew Taki was there, he gave no sign of it.

So Taki's strategy had paid off. After running most of the way across the dais, he'd resorted to stealth to get close, keeping low and sneaking around the dead and unconscious on the ground. The racket from the device had helped conceal him as he hid behind it, staying out of eyeshot and earshot of Wolf. It had helped that Wolf was distracted, closely watching the proceedings at the framework. But when the whine from the device had shut off, Taki had realized he needed to move.

Leaping up, he'd sighted in on Kutkha and cocked his rifle. "Kutkha!" Taki kept his finger on the trigger as he called the name. "Let her go!"

Kutkha turned with an angry scowl. "Stay out of this!"

"Come over here, Tala." Taki's steady eye never wavered as he kept the sight locked in on Kutkha. "If anyone else makes a *move*, I will blow their *head* off."

"Taki, wait," said Tala. "I'm fine. Let him finish what he started."

Why was she defending Kutkha? Had he done something to

her…or did she have a good reason? "I'm glad you're all right," said Taki. "But he can finish just fine with you over *here*, can't he?"

Just as the words left his mouth, someone leaped up from behind him and grabbed the rifle. An iron grip clamped around his hand on the trigger and squeezed.

The gun fired with a loud *crack*, launching a round straight at Kutkha. The hand that had grabbed the rifle wrenched it back into Taki's chin, stunning him, then heaved him aside.

As Taki fell, he finally got a look at his attacker: his black leather coat whirled around him as he ran, his wrinkled face focused on the misty framework in his path.

Von Heizinger.

Chapter 38

Kamchatka
20 April 1952
0014 Hours

When Von Heïzinger came for Nadia, Hiruko couldn't stop him. Everything happened too fast. The rifle shot hit Kutkha's head; Miti screamed in terror; Von Heïzinger charged Hiruko like a rabid dog, yanking out his Patmos Amulet and using it to paralyze Wolf as he ran.

Hiruko tried to fight back, but Von Heïzinger was too quick for him. He pistol-whipped Hiruko across the side of the head with his Walther, sending him plunging to the ground before he landed a single blow.

The shaman leaped into the fray next, unleashing a flurry of blows and kicks. She managed to push back Von Heïzinger, but not for long; he swung up the Patmos Amulet and did something to her mind, making her stop fighting and sit down on the ground.

Still reeling from the pistol-whipping, Hiruko struggled to get up, but he was already too late: Von Heïzinger had taken Nadia.

Through vision blurred by the blow to his head, Hiruko watched as Von Heïzinger whisked her to the framework. He tried to throw her in, but she fought him, holding on tight to the sides.

"Hermann, stop it!" She kicked him in the shin as he kept working to shove her into the mist. "Why are you *doing* this?"

"It's called a *sacrifice*." Von Heïzinger clubbed her hands with the butt of his pistol, trying to break her grip. "An offering to call down the power of Heaven."

"You can't summon the power of Heaven with a sacrifice!" Nadia kicked him again, harder than before. "Such corruption will only be *punished*!"

"*Exactly*." Von Heïzinger peeled away one of her hands. "*Now* you understand."

Nadia looked at him with horrified disbelief. "You *want* to bring Judgment Day down on yourself?"

"Who said anything about *myself*?" With that, he tore her other hand free and propelled her into the mist. The force of her entry thrust Miti back through the portal before her; their screams mingled as they disappeared into the misty realm on the other side.

When they were both gone, Von Heïzinger holstered his Walther, dusted his hands off, and smiled at Hiruko, who was still fighting to get up. "You should be happy, Mr. Orochi."

A wave of dizziness rolled through Hiruko. He felt like he was going to pass out.

"Our side has won." With a strange flourish, Von Heïzinger slid the fingertips of both hands along the brim of his hat from center to sides. "Victory is assured."

* * *

It had taken MacNeal and his team longer than they'd expected to dispatch the Shōgunate forces. Just when they'd gotten through most of the men who'd been stationed on the dais, reinforcements had arrived from the floor of the temple. Then they'd had a run-in with Itami; the blue-skinned devil had been vastly diminished from their first meeting in the forest, but he'd still given them a run for their money. If not for the special Liturgy that Irina had whipped up, he might have mashed them into paste with his giant club instead of falling asleep on the ground like a child in the middle of the battle.

So by the time MacNeal reached the framework, he was too late to stop Von Heïzinger from regaining control of the artifact. Just as he got there, Von Heïzinger was hurling Nadia through the portal. Once she was gone, the Reich's cadaverous mastermind was the last one standing in the middle of the dais. Everyone else was down: Tala, Taki, Wolf, Iroh, and a Shōgunate soldier. Corpses littered the scene, too: a lab-coated scientist, a Stosstruppen, two Schocktruppen, and Kutkha, who lay at Von Heïzinger's feet with a gunshot wound in the middle of his forehead. Although he could have sworn he'd seen Zermann earlier, the tattooed monstrosity was no longer at the center of things.

As MacNeal stood on the edge of the carnage, backed up by his team of allies, Von Heïzinger sneered in his direction. "*Guten Morgen*, old 'friend.' You are too late."

MacNeal kept his flash-gun aimed at his enemy. The trigger was warm from the heat of his finger, a twitch away from ending the villain's monstrous life. "It's never too late, Hermann. Haven't I taught you that already?"

"This time, *I* will teach *you*." Von Heïzinger glanced at the mist in the portal. It was growing darker and swirling faster with each passing moment. "Your first lesson is when to *hold on*." He gripped the edge of the framework. "And the answer is *now*."

Suddenly, the darkening mist surged out of the frame. It hung there in a cloud, churning and roiling in midair...and then, with a crackling roar, a massive bolt of pure black energy plunged down from it, lancing into the ground. The cloud held there, continuously feeding the dark bolt into the earth, charring the ground black as pitch at its entry point.

As soon as the bolt touched down, the ground started to shake. It quickly exceeded the rumbling of the volcano and kept going, building in strength.

MacNeal braced himself and held steady, but it took effort. "What have you *done*, Von Heïzinger?"

"Isn't it obvious?" Von Heïzinger shouted the words over the roar of the black energy. "I have signed your Union's *death warrant*."

"What are you talking about?" asked MacNeal.

"*Disaster*, MacNeal." Von Heïzinger gestured at the contact point for the energy bolt. "All that power pouring into an intersection of the mystical Axis Mundi...an intersection of geologic *fault lines* as well. It has triggered an earthquake that will unleash the biggest tsu-nami of all time—sweeping across the Pacific Ocean, aimed at the West Coast of your beloved North America!"

MacNeal listened and struggled to stay upright. The ground was shaking harder than ever. Looking over his shoulder, he saw that half his allies had already fallen, leaving Brown, Oksana, and Tatiana on their feet.

"Imagine the devastation, MacNeal!" Von Heïzinger shook his fist and bellowed over the roaring power. "*Millions* will be killed *instantly*. Your Pacific fleet will be *decimated*. The coasts of Canada, America, and Mexico will be *ravaged*. Then the forces of the Reich and Shōgunate will lay waste to what is left!"

"Is that the best you can come up with?" MacNeal looked around, trying to figure out his best chance for shutting down the energy flow. He thought about detaching the cables from the framework, but the device they led to seemed to have been shut down. Maybe if he started it back up again and caused some kind of feedback?

"You should *thank* me, MacNeal." Von Heïzinger jabbed a finger in his direction. "*Finally*, someone is breaking the stalemate! *Finally*, we will put an end to this never-ending Great War!"

The quake intensified. MacNeal eyed Kutkha's body on the ground and got an idea. If throwing an innocent mortal woman through the portal caused a destructive power surge, would throw-ing in a dead *god* do the opposite?

In lieu of better options, it was worth a try. Looking back at Brown, MacNeal nodded curtly and mouthed two words: *Cover me.* Brown set his jaw and nodded back at him.

Spinning, MacNeal ran toward the portal. As Brown cranked out a wave of cover fire, Von Heïzinger ducked behind the framework and shot back.

The ground kept shifting and buckling under MacNeal…and then, after he'd taken a few steps, it split open in front of him. He stumbled, trying to stop, but couldn't catch his footing on the quaking ground. It seemed inevitable: he was going to fall into the crevice.

CHAPTER 39

**Kamchatka
20 April 1952
0041 Hours**

Taki shook his head hard as he drifted back to full consciousness, awakened by the earthquake. He'd been curled up in a daze since Von Heïzinger shot Kutkha with his rifle and knocked him down.

What the hell had happened? The best Taki could figure was that he'd been zapped by Von Heïzinger's mind control amulet. One of the last things he remembered was seeing Von Heïzinger flash the thing around, putting Tala and Wolf under his spell.

Now, as the puzzle pieces of his awareness fell back into place, he realized how much he'd missed. Bolts of black energy were stabbing the ground from a churning cloud. Von Heïzinger was using the framework for cover as Brown fired at him with his flash machine gun. MacNeal was about to plunge into a crevice. And Tala...

She was sitting, looking dazed, as the ground fell away around her. She was about to be trapped on an island, encircled by a crevice. And how long would it be until that island, too, fell down into the lava below?

Instantly, Taki sprang to his feet. With no regard for anything else happening around him, he dashed toward Tala.

* * *

The rock surface of the dais was cracking and splitting all around, breaking under the stress of the intensifying earthquake.

The upheaval was enough to wake Wolf from Von Heïzinger's control. Jumping up, he saw people in jeopardy everywhere, and he had to make a choice. Whom, if anyone, should he help?

Ten feet away, the bald Russian, Ivan, slid into a sinkhole. At the last second, red-headed Tatiana lunged out a hand and grabbed his arm, delaying his final drop.

Wolf had watched them during his surveillance in the woods and knew the story of his betrayal. He thought of intervening…but decided to let the drama take its course. He thought he knew what was going to happen, what she was going to do, given the situation.

Besides, he had a more important fish to fry.

Just before he turned and ran toward the one he'd decided to save, he saw the conclusion of their story. It was a happy ending, just as he'd predicted.

"Tatiana!" Ivan swung free over the edge of the crevice, scrambling to find a foothold. "Thank Zor'ka! Pull me up!"

Tatiana's face was grim. "So you can betray me again? So you can betray *all* the New Guard?" Tears trickled down her cheeks. "So you can *beat* me again?"

"Tatiana, no!" Ivan reached for her with his free hand. "I had no *choice*! I've *always* loved you!"

"Never again." Tatiana spat on him, then cracked his fingers with the butt of her sawed-off shotgun. "Burn in hell, Ivan!"

With that, he lost his grip and fell. A cloud of steam sizzled up from the lava below as his body burned away in an instant.

So there was a happy ending after all…just not for Ivan.

* * *

As Taki ran toward Tala, more ground collapsed around her, widening the crevice. He was no longer sure he could leap across it to reach her little island.

Stopping in mid-stride, he saw the cables running from the device to the framework, and he grabbed one. He gave it a mighty heave, and the clamp on the end popped free of the framework.

Racing to the edge of the crevice, he spun the weighted end overhead, then hurled it at Tala. The clamp hit her in the shoulder and landed beside her.

The impact of his throw must have jarred her out of the daze inflicted by the Patmos Amulet. She blinked her eyes hard, then rubbed them with her fists.

As Taki looped the cable around his shoulders, he called her name, and she stopped rubbing. Her gaze fixed on him, and she frowned. "Taki? You look like hell."

"Grab the cable!" Taki gestured at the clamp beside her. "Jump as far as you can and hold on tight!"

Tala looked around, and awareness of the situation dawned in her eyes. Cursing, she grabbed the cable and got to her feet. "You better have a good grip over there! Is this thing anchored?"

Taki doubted the connection to the device would be much of an anchor. "Just do it! You're running out of time!"

Tala got the message. She took three steps back, the most she could on her shrinking island, looped the cable around her waist, and cinched it. Then, screaming a Navajo war cry, she sprinted and leaped.

She almost made it the whole way, but came up short. As she dropped and slammed into the crumbling rock face, Taki took the full weight of her on his shoulders. The cable dug in to the muscles along his shoulder blades, dragging him down as she hung suspended over the chasm.

Gritting his teeth, Taki shifted his grip and started pulling. Her hands appeared at the edge of the drop-off, clasped around the cable…but then the quake shook him off balance, and she slid down.

Quickly regaining his footing, he caught the weight and started hauling again. When he saw her hands this time, he reached deep and pulled backward with all his strength.

Suddenly, she lurched up and grabbed the ledge. He kept pulling until she'd rolled her legs up onto solid ground.

He let go of the cable and ran to her. As she scrambled to her feet, he wrapped his arms around her. He swung her farther back from the edge, and then he gazed into her dark eyes and smiled. He couldn't help himself.

He'd come so far and fought so hard to get her back. He was battered and bruised, dead on his feet, in the midst of a quickly deteriorating situation…but all he could feel was happy.

She frowned, but then her gaze softened. "Thank you," she said.

And then, impulsively, as the earth shook around them, building to the biggest quake of all time, he kissed her. And Tala…

Tala kissed him back.

* * *

MacNeal had been running toward the portal when the crevice had opened up before him. He'd stumbled as the quake rocked the ground, knocking him into a certain fall to his death.

Then, before he could topple over the edge, two hands caught hold of him. They pulled him back from the brink and planted him firmly on the ground—as firmly as possible with the shifting quake in progress.

That was when he stood eye to eye with his rescuer. "*Wolf.*"

Years of history flew between them in the space of a heartbeat. They'd battled side-by-side…fought each other just as often…betrayed each other again and again. Now here they were again, in the thick of it.

"What's the play, MacNeal?" Wolf drew his Colt .45.

"That depends." MacNeal held tight to his flash-gun, ready to fire at a second's notice. "Whose side are you on?"

"Whoever's against that German ghoul over there." He waved the .45 in Von Heïzinger's direction.

MacNeal smirked. As a mercenary pain in the ass, Wolf made a career out of driving him crazy. He'd almost gotten MacNeal killed a few times, too. Wolf changed sides so often, and pursued so many seemingly conflicting agendas, it was hard to keep track without a scorecard. But one thing had never changed between them and probably never would.

Mutual respect.

"Then here's the play," said MacNeal. "Kill the ghoul, stop the tsunami, save the Union."

"Sure. Why not?" Wolf shrugged. "I've got nothing better to do at this particular moment."

CHAPTER 40

Kamchatka
20 April 1952
0047 Hours

As the earthquake continued to build, MacNeal and Wolf charged toward the framework. A new fissure opened up to block the way and they leaped across it. They landed on the other side without missing a step, resuming their drive to the objective.

At least, until Zermann crawled out of another trench in front of them. As his hulking form clambered up over the rim where he'd fallen, he looked even more hellish than usual. His uniform was in tatters, shredded and scorched; his flesh was riddled with raw red burn blisters and charred black patches. His glare was beyond demonic, to the point of senselessly bestial. With a roar, he lurched to his feet and shambled toward Wolf.

"Keep going, MacNeal!" Wolf shouted the words as he cocked the Colt .45. "I'll catch up!"

MacNeal took him up on the offer. The Union itself was at stake; every moment was precious.

As he bolted forward and leaped the next trench, he heard Wolf unload the .45 into Zermann, who howled with pain and rage. Wolf could handle the monstrosity, he was sure of it.

MacNeal zigzagged like a receiver on a football field, hopping over bodies, dodging fresh cracks as they opened in his path. Then Von Heïzinger started shooting at him from behind the framework, and he had to dodge bullets, too.

The quake continued to strengthen, bucking the ground up and down as he ran. Ahead, the stream of dark power continued to course down out of the cloud extruding from the portal.

There, underneath the framework, lay the body of Kutkha.

As MacNeal bolted toward it, Von Heïzinger's shots got closer. Firing the flash-gun as he ran, MacNeal hit Von Heïzinger in the chest, throwing him back and cutting off the barrage. Then he dove down into a slide that brought him to the base of the framework—and Kutkha.

It was time to test his theory and throw the god into the portal. Maybe the resulting backlash would shut off the heavenly power flow and stop the quake and tsunami.

Scrambling to his knees, MacNeal reached for Kutkha. He slid his hands under Kutkha's shoulders and tugged him back, raising him toward the framework.

Then suddenly, Kutkha's eyes shot open, and MacNeal dropped the body.

* * *

As the earthquake intensified, Tala broke the kiss with Taki. He'd really surprised her…but she couldn't say she regretted it. She hadn't been thinking about him that way, hadn't considered him romantically. But now that he'd kissed her, she realized she might have feelings for him after all. Or was it just the stress of the end-of-the-world conflict going on all around them, pushing them together?

Either way, she didn't have time to think about it. Things were literally falling to pieces, and Sergeant Brown was shouting her name over the cacophony.

She and Taki turned toward Brown's voice. He was standing on the far side of a crevice, hands cupped around his mouth to amplify his words. "You've got to get out of there! Come this way!"

Tala had missed a few things while under the influence of Von

Heïzinger's amulet. "What's going on here, Boomer?" She practically had to scream to make herself heard.

"That gateway!" Brown pointed at the framework. "It's setting off a tsunami that'll destroy the West Coast of North America!"

Tala looked toward the framework and saw MacNeal staring down at Kutkha. Above them, a seething cloud blasted the ground with dark bolts of energy.

"Now come on!" Brown gestured impatiently. "Hurry your asses up!"

"Ready?" Taki reached for her hand.

Tala looked back at MacNeal and Kutkha and the apocalypse in progress. The stakes were unbelievably high, the highest she'd ever faced. She wished there was something she could do, something that might help save the coast she loved and all those millions of people. It didn't seem possible at this late stage, though, with her being empty-handed and the ground falling out from under her.

Then she remembered that she wasn't empty-handed after all.

"Tala?" Taki tried to pull her toward Brown. "We need to leave."

Tala pulled her hand away from him. "Not yet, Taki. The major looks like he could use a little help."

"There's nothing you can do," insisted Taki. "You can't even get over there with those crevices in the way."

Tala smiled grimly. "Who said anything about getting over there?" Then she set her jaw and turned away from him.

* * *

MacNeal was stunned as Kutkha looked up at him. "I thought you were dead!"

Kutkha shook his head. "It takes more than a bullet to kill a god." As he boosted himself up on his shoulders, he winced. "Though I admit, that one *did* knock the wind out of me. Maybe the gateway weakened me a little."

MacNeal thought fast. Plan A was out the window; so much for tossing Kutkha's body into the mist. But maybe a live Kutkha was better than a dead one? "Can you shut this thing down?" MacNeal gestured at the framework. "Can you close the gateway?"

Kutkha sat up and glared. "I've spent a thousand years trying to open it! I wouldn't close it if I *could*."

"You don't understand." MacNeal grabbed his shoulder. "It's

destroying my homeland!"

"I am sorry." Kutkha frowned, looking genuinely sympathetic. "But my answer stands."

"Please!" MacNeal squeezed his shoulder. "We're talking about *millions* of people!"

"No," said Kutkha. "I won't do it."

MacNeal released him and sat back. "Damn it!" He rubbed his bearded chin, wracking his brain for some way to stop the Armageddon in progress.

Then, out of the chaos, he heard a woman's voice calling out to him. "MacNeal! Hey, MacNeal!"

Looking up, he saw Tala standing twenty yards away, separated from him by three wide fissures. Taki was behind her, watching nervously.

"I got something for ya!" Tala dug into her hip pockets. "Whatever you do, *don't* drop it!"

When her hands slid out of her pockets, they were both full of dynamite.

"You know what to do with *this* stuff!" Tala held the dynamite high—two bundles, each consisting of four or five sticks wrapped around the middle with brown tape. "If all else fails, blow the hell outta that thing!"

"Is that your answer to *everything*?" asked MacNeal. "Blow the hell out of it?"

"Pretty much, yeah!" answered Tala with a grin.

"Well, all else *has* failed!" said MacNeal. "So get it over here!" He jumped up and ran to the edge of the nearest crevice, getting as close as he could to her.

"Here it comes, MacNeal!" Tala hauled back her right arm, getting ready to throw. "Catch!"

She pitched the first dynamite bomb over the crevices with ease. When it flew within reach, MacNeal reached up and snagged it. His heart was pounding when the bomb first hit his hand; he half-expected it to blow on impact. But it didn't, and he shoved it into his right pants pocket.

The second one didn't explode on impact either. Again, she threw it right to him in a perfect arcing path over the steaming crevices. He stuffed it in his left pocket this time.

The lighter was another matter. Just as she chucked it, the ground heaved under her, fouling her throw. The lighter came in low, sinking toward the wall of the crevice…but MacNeal dropped to his stomach and whipped down an arm to nab it, just barely.

"Got it?" asked Tala. "I've got more if you need one!"

He held up the lighter as he crawled back away from the edge. "Got it."

"Then good luck!" said Tala.

"Thanks!" MacNeal got to his feet. "Now get the hell out of here! Get *all* our people out of here! That's an order!"

Without another word, he turned and ran, headed back to the framework with his very last hope in his pockets.

CHAPTER 4I

Kamchatka
20 April 1952
0103 Hours

When MacNeal got back to the portal, Kutkha was standing beside it, waiting for him. "What are you planning to do?"

"Destroy it, if I can." MacNeal pushed past him and pulled one of the bombs out of his pocket. "Now stay out of my way."

"No, don't!" Kutkha grabbed his arm. "My wife is still in there! It's my only chance to save her!"

In a smooth, swift motion, MacNeal swung up the flash-gun and jammed the barrel under Kutkha's chin. "I can send you *to* her, if you like. Problem solved."

There was a wild look in Kutkha's eyes. "I'm begging you! Don't destroy this gateway!"

MacNeal pushed the barrel deeper into the flesh under Kutkha's chin. "If I *can*, I *will*. End of discussion."

"No, listen! I might still be able to *reach* her. I just need more *time*!"

"All right." MacNeal withdrew the rifle. "You have as much time as it takes me to set and detonate the charges. Not a second more."

Kutkha's frantic look shifted, turning hateful. For a moment, MacNeal thought he might lash out.

But then Kutkha spun to face the portal instead. He paused, taking a deep breath…and then he plunged his arms into the roiling mist up to his elbows.

As Kutkha reached into the abyss, MacNeal hunkered down at the base of the gateway. He unwrapped the long fuse from around the dynamite bomb, then crammed the bomb between the toes of the claw at the bottom of the leg closest to him.

MacNeal crawled past Kutkha along the front of the framework, staying well clear of the bolts slashing down from the cloud. He trailed the fuse from the first bomb along with him; he needed to light both bombs at once.

When he'd crossed over to the other leg of the base, he reached for the second bomb. Just as he stuffed it into the clawed foot at the end of the leg, someone whacked him on the back of the head with something heavy.

Stunned by the blow, MacNeal dropped…but he had enough of his wits about him to roll away from the next strike. As he threw himself over on his back, he fully expected to see Kutkha staring down at him, desperate to stop him from destroying the portal.

Instead, he saw Von Heïzinger.

* * *

Hiruko watched from the rubble around Dr. Kondo's device as Von Heïzinger swung his weapon at the man he'd called "MacNeal." It was the giant tooth, the one with the map on it; he used the broad end as a bludgeon…but when the blow missed, he flipped it around and brandished it with the sharp point facing out.

Hiruko swallowed hard and wondered what to do next. He'd been lying low since Von Heïzinger had pistol-whipped him and thrown Nadia into the portal. It had taken a while for the dizziness to fade, and then everything had gone mad and he'd felt shell-shocked. But now, strangely, his mind seemed to be clearing. Things were at their worst—could they *get* any worse?—yet Hiruko somehow felt himself regaining his bearings.

Then there it was: a poem, appearing before his mind's eye in perfect lucidity.

The flower opens, closes, opens again,
Evoking the pulse of the cosmos in the flexing
Of its petals,
Inviting the gentle rain one silvery drop at a time,
As the sun god washes clean the green face,
As the wood god thrusts up poles to support the sky,
As the man god paints a masterpiece in dappled colors,
Expressed as the creaking of bones or the cracking
Of bamboo or the soft shivering of twinkling
Dew-flecked emerald boughs after the chickadee
Leaps from them, or the sigh of the ghost of a dream
Rising weightless in the last glint of sunlight
Before dusk, and all that once was
Shall be again, in ways you cannot imagine,
All that once was
Shall be again
As the flower opens,
Shall be again
Shall be again.

Hiruko felt breathless for a moment as the poem flowed through him. Something about it touched him more deeply than all his other poems put together. Something about it *inspired* him.

Suddenly, he was possessed by a vision. Closing his eyes, he saw himself standing before throngs of men as they cheered and saluted him. He saw himself sitting on a throne in royal robes, receiving dignitaries. He saw himself reflected in a mirror, glowing with the golden light that could only be the divine breath of god. And while he saw these things, he *felt* them too, felt the clarity and *reality* with every cell of his body.

Then, he opened his eyes, and the vision was gone. The reality vanished, leaving him back in the midst of the mayhem.

But he was no longer willing to remain idle in the face of it. Launching himself to his feet, he ran to the side of the Daimyō, who still lay wounded on the ground. Hoisting him up, he slung one of the Daimyō's arms over his shoulders and made ready to carry him away from the madness.

It was time he did his part. He'd been a follower all his life; maybe it was time for that to change.

* * *

"Die!" Von Heïzinger stabbed at MacNeal with the giant tooth. "Die as your precious Union is smashed to bits by the sea!"

MacNeal rolled away from the strike, then swung up his flash-gun…but Von Heïzinger kicked it out of his hands.

Baring his teeth, MacNeal sprang up from the ground and charged, plowing into Von Heïzinger's torso. The old man slashed with the tooth, slicing through MacNeal's uniform and into his back.

MacNeal grabbed both of Von Heïzinger's wrists and wrenched them upward, trying to shake the tooth free. Von Heïzinger's gaze locked with his as the two of them grappled for control.

"Here we are again, John." Von Heïzinger suddenly shifted his weight, but MacNeal countered and held on tight. "You and I fighting on the brink of Hell itself."

"And who always *wins*, Hermann?" MacNeal hissed out the words through clenched teeth.

"Individual battles mean *nothing* if you lose *everything* in the end!"

"I'll *tell* you who always wins." With one supreme effort, MacNeal hauled Von Heïzinger's arm down hard, forcing him to stab himself in the leg with the tooth. "*I* do!"

Clutching at the wound, Von Heïzinger stumbled back. "Not this time, John!"

"*Every* time!" MacNeal punched him in the face with so much force, it knocked his hat off and spun his head to the side. "You've never *won*, and you never *will*, you sick bastard!"

MacNeal threw a piledriver into Von Heïzinger's gut, then blasted his jaw with an uppercut. Von Heïzinger pulled the giant tooth from the wound in his leg and made a feeble swipe with it, but MacNeal easily dodged. Then he pumped one more punch into Von Heïzinger's face and followed it up by driving the heel of his hand into the gunshot wound in his chest.

Von Heïzinger wobbled, then toppled. The second he touched the ground, MacNeal whipped around and sprinted for the framework.

Crouching beside it, he grabbed the two fuses for the dynamite bombs. He pulled the lighter out of his shirt pocket, flipped it open, and thumbed the switch, sparking a flame.

Then he held the tips of the fuses in the flame. They caught instantly.

Dropping the fuses, MacNeal leaped up. Kutkha was still standing on the other side of the framework, up to his elbows in the misty portal.

"Time's up!" shouted MacNeal, but Kutkha ignored him. "You've got to get clear!"

When Kutkha still refused to answer, MacNeal ducked under the cloud and came up beside him. "I said you're done!" MacNeal grabbed Kutkha's arm and pulled.

Kutkha fought him. "No! I need more time! I've found something!"

"Then bring it through!" MacNeal wrenched Kutkha's arm out almost up to the wrist.

"Stop it!" Kutkha partly transformed, shifting his face from human to raven. He lunged, stabbing his beak at MacNeal's eyes.

But MacNeal was determined to get him out of there. The realization that he had about a minute left to do it gave him the burst of adrenaline he needed.

With a sudden surge of strength, MacNeal yanked Kutkha's arms free of the portal…and quickly saw the self-proclaimed god had been right. He *had* found something. Some*one*.

Someone small.

The baby cried as Kutkha cradled him in his arms. His head became human again, and he gazed in wonder, eyes moist with tears. "That birthmark. This is my son." A smile of pure joy spread over his features. "My *Ememkut*."

"Then get him out of here!" MacNeal slapped Kutkha hard on the back. "You've got *seconds* before the bombs go off!"

* * *

The unconscious Daimyō was dead weight on Hiruko's shoulder. He'd only taken a few steps when he had to stop and change positions.

As Hiruko bent down to heft the Daimyō across his back, he turned and caught one last look at the framework. His eyes flew wide in amazement—not because he saw Kutkha pulling a baby out of the portal, but because of what he saw next.

MacNeal slapped Kutkha on the back as he cradled the child in his arms. Then there were gunshots nearby, drawing the attention of both god and man. As they looked away for the briefest of instants, Hiruko saw something that made his heart race faster than ever, something neither Kutkha nor MacNeal seemed to notice.

A spiral streamer of golden light flashed out of the portal and dove into the baby's head. By the time Kutkha looked back at the child, the light was gone, fully absorbed.

Hiruko had seen the same thing not long ago, when Von Heïzinger had forced Nadia's astral form back into her body.

Could it be? Could Nadia have found a way back from the other side?

Hiruko allowed himself the smallest smile, and then he turned away to haul the Daimyō up onto his back, spanning both shoulders in a fireman's carry.

* * *

In the blink of an eye, Kutkha changed shape, shifting into his giant raven form, but keeping human arms to hold the child. His wings flapped, and he rose from the crumbling surface of the dais.

MacNeal was already running for his life by then, leaping crevice after crevice as he fled the bombs. Heart pounding, he hurtled across the dais, a solitary figure charging over the buckled earth. He wanted to get away, wanted to live to see what came next...to see the war end...to see the faces of the 42nd Marines when it did...to walk the Maine woods and eat lobster rolls and blueberry pie served by a smiling New England girl...to see his children come into the world, and his children's children...

And yet, as he ran, he thought it would be fine if he never got to do any of that, if only he died knowing that his beloved Union had been saved.

Behind him, the bombs exploded with a roar like that of a furious beast. MacNeal felt the heat of it lick the back of his neck as the shock wave raced toward him.

EPILOGUE

As the three inflatable rafts drew near to the *Pershing*, the surfaced submarine's crew lined up along the spine of the boat. Every one of them held a stiff salute, as did the welcoming party of uniformed men waiting on the fin below. It was a party of men and one woman, actually...a woman with short black hair and pink bangs.

Hoax.

As soon as he saw her, MacNeal's heart thundered with relief. When he'd left for the mainland, Hoax had been in dire straits, fighting for her life. He'd been out of touch ever since, at least until reaching the beach on the way back; he'd been able to radio Admiral Suerte there, and had heard of Hoax's recovery...but it was another thing entirely to *see* her looking healthy again.

Thank God.

"Looks like a hero's welcome, Major," Brown said as he paddled on the other side of the raft. "Maybe they'll pin another medal on you."

339

MacNeal raised his eyebrows and pulled his own paddle through the water. "You can have it, Boomer. I've got plenty."

"Ah, you keep it." Brown chuckled. "You can cover a bullet hole with it."

MacNeal wished he had a motor launch instead of a paddle raft. It was taking entirely too long to reach the *Pershing*. "I just want some damn sleep, Boomer." Exhaustion was dragging him down hard. The three-day slog from the volcano to the beach, on the heels of the grueling mission, had about done him in. It hadn't helped that a scorching heat wave had taken hold and never let up for the entire three-day hike.

"So what's the word, MacNeal?" asked Tala from the back of the raft. "Did we save the West Coast or what?"

"When I radioed in, Admiral Suerte said he would make a call." MacNeal dug the paddle through the sparkling sapphire water. "I guess we're about to find out."

"But you think we did, don't you?" asked Tala. "You blew up the portal and the earthquake stopped."

"Doesn't matter what I think," said MacNeal. "We'll know soon enough."

When they finally reached the fin of the *Pershing*, sailors ran out to drag the rafts out of the water, and to escort the Shōgunate prisoners aboard at gunpoint. There were five Shōgunate men divided between two rafts—three in one raft and two in the other, all wearing spare Union and Directorate uniforms. The men had been liberated from Kutkha's aerie by the 42nd and their Russian allies after the destruction of the portal. It had been the allies' last job together before the 42nd, the New Guard, and the Bogatyrs had gone their separate ways, each naturally a bit upset to be leaving empty-handed.

MacNeal stepped onto the metal decking, intending to salute Admiral Suerte…but Hoax dashed over and threw her arms around him first.

"You made it! Oh God, you made it!" She squeezed him—not too tight, perhaps because of the injury to her left side—then hopped up and kissed him on the cheek.

MacNeal couldn't help grinning. "How're you feeling, Hoax?"

Hoax ignored the question. "I had such a terrible dream about you! I thought you were doomed!"

"No such luck." He kissed her on the forehead, content that her lack of an answer was itself a good sign. If the girl he thought of like his daughter was back to ignoring her superior officer's requests, it was business as usual.

Just then, Admiral Suerte stepped forward. "Major MacNeal. Welcome aboard."

MacNeal let go of Hoax and snapped out a salute. "What's the good word, sir?"

"I've been in contact with HQ." The look on Suerte's face was grim. MacNeal had a sinking feeling in his stomach. "There was indeed a tsunami three days ago."

A pall fell over MacNeal and his people. It didn't seem possible.

"You mean we blew it? After all that?" The questions came from Paul Hamilton, one of the men who'd been captured and imprisoned by Wolf and Kutkha, then rescued by the 42nd and the Russians.

Suerte held a hand up. "Let me finish." He cleared his throat. "As I was saying, a tsunami did originate in Kamchatka. It threw us around pretty good, let me tell you. It caused considerable damage on many Pacific islands, including the Hawaiian Islands."

MacNeal clenched his jaw.

"But it did not result in any loss of life. Not in Hawaii." Suerte narrowed his eyes and nodded. "And not in the coastal regions of the Union."

The tension poured out of MacNeal all at once. He'd been expecting the worst—had prepared himself to accept it—but fate had handed him a far better result.

"I cannot attest to other regions of the Pacific rim," continued Suerte, "but the coasts of continental Canada, the United States, and Mexico are unharmed." With that, he stepped up to MacNeal and clapped a hand on his shoulder. "Congratulations, *amigo*. Congratulations to *all* of you." He looked around at the men and women of the 42nd arrayed behind MacNeal and Hoax. "Nice work."

All at once, the crew of the *Pershing* cheered and applauded. They took off their caps and waved them in the air. They whistled and whooped and roared.

And MacNeal joined them. He turned to face the men and women of the 42nd, the ones who'd come back alive, and he clapped for all of them, for the struggles they'd endured and the sacrifices they'd made.

He clapped for Brown, who nodded and grinned in reply. He clapped for Tala and Taki, who were standing too close to each other, trying to pretend that no one else would notice. He clapped for Hoax, who'd nearly died to get the information that had led to the Union's salvation. He clapped for Hamilton, who'd been lost and thought dead.

Then he imagined the other ones, too, right there among them… the ones who hadn't made it back at all. He saw their faces, big as life, smiling back at him in the golden light of the sunrise—Shankar and all the others they'd lost along the way. He clapped for them, too, and for the Russian comrades who'd also given their lives in service to the mission.

For that one glittering moment, they were all there together, celebrating the victory that had saved the people and places that were dear to them back home. The victory that had given pause to the bloodthirsty juggernauts of the Shōgunate and the Reich. The victory, perhaps, that would carry the heroes of the Union one step closer to the end of the Great War that for most of them was the only way of life they'd ever known.

Maybe, finally, the end was in sight.

* * *

"Hello? Kutkha?" Wolf peered into the shadowy cave, keeping one hand on the butt of his Colt .45…just in case. He hadn't seen Kutkha since the battle at the volcano; he wasn't sure how much things might have changed between them.

"Wolf?" Kutkha's tenor voice sailed out from the depths of the cave. "I thought you had already left."

"I couldn't leave without saying goodbye, could I?" Wolf smirked. "Nice place you have here."

"How did you find it?" asked Kutkha.

Wolf shrugged. "Dumb luck, I guess." In fact, he'd spent the last three days searching for Kutkha's new home. Since the aerie on *Kronotskaya Sopka* had been compromised, Kutkha hadn't gone back there. Wolf had scouted other volcanoes and mountains, and had finally hit pay dirt: the new aerie was located on the slope of *Klyuchevskaya Sopka*, the highest volcano in all Kamchatka.

Kutkha was silent for a moment. "Are you alone?"

"Of course I am." Wolf spread his arms. "So are you going to invite me in?"

"Come in," said Kutkha.

The Dark God's voice sounded a little funny, but that was to be expected. Of course he had to be more careful nowadays, given the circumstances. He wasn't just watching out for himself anymore, was he?

Now there was little Ememkut to worry about.

As Wolf entered the cave, he saw them in the shadows, back against the wall. Kutkha sat cross-legged on the dirt floor with the infant cradled in his arms, swaddled in a blanket of black down.

"He's beautiful, Kutkha." Wolf hunkered down in front of them. "A perfect child."

"Thank you." Kutkha smiled, and Ememkut smiled back. "For the first time in a thousand years, I am happy."

"I'm glad to hear it." Wolf nodded and reached out slowly to wiggle a finger over Ememkut. The baby grabbed it with his tiny hand and squeezed. "You deserve it, my friend."

"I do wish his mother were here, though. That has been hard to take." Kutkha lost track of the child and stared into space for a moment. "Miti was so close to freedom, Wolf. She was *right there*."

Wolf sighed. "I'm sorry things worked out the way they did."

Kutkha stared a moment more, then returned his gaze to the child. "At least I have Ememkut. I have a second chance with my son."

"It must be strange," said Wolf. "Having your grown son returned to you as a baby."

"Strange but wonderful," said Kutkha. "We have a clean slate, and all our lives to write a better future upon it."

"May I?" Wolf held out his hands.

Kutkha hesitated, then gently placed Ememkut in his grasp. "Just be careful with him, my friend."

Wolf grinned at the child as he rocked him in his arms. The chubby little face was adorable to behold.

Kutkha's warning to be careful had been unnecessary. Wolf could never be anything *but* careful with that child. For Ememkut was the fruit of all his labors in Kamchatka, the sole reason he'd worked with Kutkha to maneuver the warring factions to open the portal.

Ememkut had a *destiny*. He was more important than Kutkha or anyone else imagined. He would play a role in the war that no one but Wolf could foresee. And if Wolf had his way, he would turn the tide of that war in ways that no one but Wolf could *control*.

"What a cutie." Wolf handed Ememkut back to Kutkha. "I'll have to come see him again someday."

"You are always welcome with us," said Kutkha.

"Thanks." Wolf reached into his pocket and pulled out an object wrapped in a handkerchief. "In the meantime, here's a little something for him to remember me by."

Kutkha frowned. "What is it?"

"A pretty toy." Wolf unwrapped the handkerchief and exposed a gold ring with a flashing crimson gem: the *Orbis Christus*, extracted from the rubble of the dead portal. The *Orbis Christus*, which would begin to work its magic on the child so he would be ready when the time was right...and Wolf returned for him.

Wolf gave Kutkha the ring. Kutkha stared at it for a moment, then gently lowered it toward Ememkut. The child grabbed it instantly and stuck it in his mouth.

Wolf chuckled. "It figures."

"I think he likes it," said Kutkha.

"Good, good." The crimson gem glowed faintly as the child sucked on it. "Tell him his Uncle Wolf gave it to him."

* * *

Hiruko pulled the mop from the bucket, then slapped it down on the deck of the ship and sloshed it back and forth.

After all he'd been through in Kamchatka, this was what he'd come back to. During the battle of *Kronotskaya Sopka*, he had rescued the Daimyō and led his comrades to safety. With the Daimyō incapacitated and Itami not in his right mind, he had taken command of the battered remnants of the Shōgunate forces. He had spurred them to retreat through the wilderness, starting them on the path back to shore and the Shōgunate transport ships in the bay... at least until the heavenly power's effect had worn off and Itami had recovered his wits enough to assume command.

Hiruko had done all that, had truly risen to the occasion... and where had it gotten him? Had the leaders acknowledged his accomplishments and promoted him to a new position? Had he been given new duties commensurate with someone who had acted with honor under fire and demonstrated exceptional capabilities?

Not even close. As soon as the ship's *kyaputen*, Fujita, had finished debriefing Hiruko, he'd returned him to the ranks. Hiruko had gone right back to his old menial duties aboard ship, starting with mopping the deck.

It was as if none of it had happened at all. As if he'd never left the ship and set foot on Kamchatka. Nothing had changed for him here. He was as invisible as ever as he dragged his mop over the deck amidships.

Almost. As he slopped the grey mop over the grey deck plates, he heard voices approaching. Looking up, he saw the Daimyō coming toward him, walking side by side with giant Itami.

The Daimyō looked haggard; he was still recovering from his wounds but refused to stay in bed. His head was bandaged from when the Stosstruppen had slammed him to the rock floor of the dais in the volcano. Through the black silk robe he wore, sashed loosely at the waist of his fatigue pants, the white dressings over the gunshot wound in his left shoulder were visible.

As for Itami, he looked none the worse for wear. Soon after the portal had been destroyed, he'd started to bounce back. Now that he was far from every last trace of the heavenly energies, the headaches, nausea, and dizziness no longer afflicted him. He was back to his old, vigorous self…unfortunately for Hiruko.

At first, it seemed Itami took no notice of him as he passed. Hiruko ducked his head, eager to avoid undue attention, and kept mopping. Itami and the Daimyō kept walking, engrossed in conversation.

Then, just when Hiruko thought they were gone, and he was lifting the mop toward the bucket, he felt hot breath on the back of his neck. He froze, holding the mop out in front of him. He knew right away who it was; the feeling of irrational fear washing over him was a dead giveaway. The heavenly power had dimmed it back on Kamchatka, especially near the volcano. But now, far from that place, on the ship going home, it was back in force.

Itami was back in force. "You were right, little brother." His voice was a harsh whisper in Hiruko's left ear.

Hiruko swallowed hard. He had a lump in his throat, and it

wouldn't budge. "About what, sir?"

"When we first arrived in Kamchatka," said Itami, "I asked if you had every confidence in the impending glorious success of this enterprise."

"Yes, sir." Hiruko nodded. Even after everything he'd been through with Itami, he still found it hard not to run from the waves of fear he gave off. "I remember you said that."

"Yessss." Itami lowered his voice even more and hissed the word into Hiruko's ear. "That was your answer, little brother. *Yessss.*"

The mop felt heavy in Hiruko's hands. "I remember."

Itami's hand clenched on Hiruko's right shoulder. "You were *right*. You did have confidence." His claw-like nails hurt as they dug in deep and clenched. "Do you think you deserve a medal for that?"

Hiruko held his breath and shook his head.

Itami chuckled. "Right again." Suddenly, he switched ears. "But you *do* deserve *one* thing, little brother."

"W-what's that, s-sir?" Hiruko was afraid to ask.

"A *favor*," said Itami. "For helping me when I could not see. I *owe* you one."

Hiruko nodded, as mesmerized as he was terrified.

"*One* favor, my little brother," said Itami. "My little *guide*."

With that, he was suddenly gone.

The mop head fell to the deck, and Hiruko started breathing again. His heart pounded and his hands shook as he looked over his shoulder.

Itami had already moved on. His hulking sapphire body swayed as he led the Daimyō away. Hiruko wondered what they were saying, but their voices were lost on the wind.

He watched as they continued on toward the bow of the ship. The farther away Itami's fearful radiance got, the more Hiruko's head cleared…and the more he resented being toyed with by the horned behemoth. Without Hiruko's leadership, Itami might be *dead* now. Surely, Hiruko deserved better from him.

He hated being terrorized. He always had, but he hated it even more after everything that had happened in Kamchatka. He felt like a changed man since then; he resented being treated the same as before. Back in Kamchatka, he'd been forced to take a bigger role in things, and now he found that giving it up was not so easy. He wanted to continue with that bigger role.

Or, at least, he wanted to know what was going on. He felt like he *deserved* it.

That was why, when Itami and the Daimyō stopped at the railing between two armored gun turrets, Hiruko trudged over with his mop and bucket to eavesdrop. He swabbed the decking near the turrets, keeping quiet and looking down, hoping he was still invisible enough to listen in without alerting Itami and the Daimyō.

With a loud yawn, Itami leaned his forearms on the railing and stared out at the waves. "The heavenly power is lost to us. The Shōgun will not be pleased."

"Blame it on the Reich." The Daimyō winced and touched the dressing on his left shoulder. "The alliance with Von Heïzinger was a disaster."

"What if the Shōgun demands you commit *seppuku*?" asked Itami. "In reparation for your failure?"

"I will tell him to ask Von Heïzinger. *He* is the one who failed." Again, the Daimyō winced.

Hiruko moved closer to them, trying to hear every word over the wind rushing in from the sea…but not so close that he drew their attention.

"I think you will be all right," said Itami. "Operation Black Chrysanthemum is gaining steam—the guaranteed subjugation of the Union. The Shōgun will want all hands on deck."

"Then perhaps it is good our mission failed." The Daimyō lowered his voice; Hiruko could barely hear him. "Otherwise, he could have ordered us to kill ourselves when he liked, because he could just keep making more of us."

Desperate to hear more, Hiruko mopped around the corner of the nearest gun turret, then stopped and pressed himself flat against the armored housing. The lowered voices of the Daimyō and Itami came through clearly.

"You truly do not fear death, do you?" asked Itami. "Are you not worried about your soul? Are you not afraid that you might not have one?"

"Because I am but a copy of another man?" The Daimyō snorted. "You think that means I might not have a *soul*?"

Hiruko frowned in confusion. What were they talking about?

What did the Daimyō mean when he called himself "a copy of another man"?

"My concern is the opposite," continued the Daimyō. "I believe I might have *more* than one soul."

Itami laughed softly. "*Interesting*," he said quietly. "What makes you think that?"

"I am a copy of one man, yes? And I am living the life of *another* man, complete with the new memories, thoughts, and feelings that entails. I am an *amalgam* of the two, am I not?"

"Yes, I suppose you are," said Itami.

"And so are you. So are all the *han'ei*...all the copies," said the Daimyō. "Who's to say we don't *all* have more than one soul?"

"You really believe this, don't you?"

The Daimyō coughed. "Why do you think I named my katana *Dyuaru-Kontan*—'Dual Soul'?"

There was silence for a moment between the two.

"I wonder how many of the others feel the same," asked Itami. "The other *han'ei*."

"Most of them do not know," said the Daimyō.

"Of course," said Itami.

"Only the privileged few."

"Do you ever wonder what would happen if they all found out?" asked Itami. "If they knew of the greatness in their blood, would it compel them to make a power play? Or would they still be content serving the Shōgunate in other capacities? Mopping the deck or cleaning guns, for example?"

Hiruko's grip tightened around the handle of his mop.

"Greatness in the blood means nothing," said the Daimyō. "Look how many feckless sons there are, whose veins are full of the blood of great fathers." He paused. "Life is what you *make* of it."

"I suppose." Itami sighed. "But soon enough, we will all have the opportunity to prove our greatness. Operation Black Chrysanthemum cannot help but succeed."

"Black Chrysanthemum," said the Daimyō. He paused. "I wonder if we will find honor in a venture with such a name."

"Minamoto, my brother," said Itami, "I have no doubt that you could find honor in *any* venture."

The men stopped talking then. Hiruko heard their footsteps

moving away from the railing.

Before they could see him hiding behind the gun, he stepped to the edge of the main walkway and resumed mopping. The words he'd heard continued echoing through his head.

I am an amalgam of the two, am I not?

Yes, I suppose you are.

And so are you. So are all the han'ei…all the copies.

As the men walked past, heading aft, Hiruko dared to look up from his mop. The Daimyō met his gaze for a split second before turning away.

And in that split second, a chill raced through Hiruko. There had been a feeling when he'd made contact, something he'd never noticed before. Or maybe he'd noticed it on some level but hadn't understood it, hadn't known what to call it.

And now he did. *Recognition.*

His heart thrashed like a caged shark in his chest as he dragged the mop across the deck. The vision came back to him, the dream of himself as a leader of men, as someone royal.

If he and the Daimyō had something in common, if they were somehow copies cut from the same cloth, what had the original cloth *been*? Had Itami also been cut from that cloth?

And what did it all mean to Hiruko? To his destiny?

He was breathing too fast. He felt light-headed. He tried to dunk the mop in the bucket, and he ended up knocking it over instead. Filthy water ran over the deck plates, out of control. He tried to mop it up, but he couldn't get all of it. He couldn't put it back in the bucket, now that it had spilled.

In that moment, as often happened in his moments of greatest stress, another poem came to him, clear as a crystal shard spinning in his brain.

> *The ground beneath your feet has always been*
> *The skin of the bear.*
> *Each drop of rain,*
> *The tears of the bear.*
> *Each ray of sun,*
> *The gleam of the bear's teeth.*
> *You tear away a fistful of fur,*

See the scars underneath, the swollen proud flesh,
And you cry out to the darkness of Heaven,
Which now you realize is the blackness of his maw.
You howl along with the thunder,
Which now you realize is the boom of his roar.
You scream until your throat is raw
And spots dance before your eyes,
Because you want to leap clear.
This wild beast is no place to make your life.
But you cannot,
But you cannot,
For you have stared him in the eye you once thought was the moon,
And now you know in the sinking stone you once thought was your heart,
That this bear, the only world you have ever known,
Is the very creature you have been hunting
All your life.

THE END

ABOUT THE AUTHOR:

Robert T. Jeschonek writes hard-driving, twisted tales bursting with action and surprises. His characters include warlords, cannibals, serial killers, mad scientists, demented superheroes, and robotic messiahs. He has written for DC Comics, won the grand prize in the Strange New Worlds contest for his *Star Trek* fiction, and was nominated for the British Fantasy Award. According to Hugo and Nebula Award-winning writer Mike Resnick, Robert "sees the world like no one else sees it, and makes incredibly witty, incisive stories out of that skewed worldview." Join him on his thrill ride into madness at www.thefictioneer.com and www.tsetsepress.com. You can also find him on Twitter as @TheFictioneer.